MOST SECRET

It is winter 1941, and Nazi Germany has
a firm grasp over much of Europe. Almost
daily, Britain continues to endure the
destruction of the Blitz. To protect her
cities and vital airfields, men working in
great secrecy have dreamed up clever ways
to deceive the enemy. Countless innocent
lives depend on their success. Should the
enemy ever discover these deceptions, it
could prove catastrophic.

Finn Gunnersen and best friends Loki
Larson and Freya Haukelid have been
recruited into a clandestine organization
called Special Operations. Under orders of
the prime minister, Winston Churchill, this
most secret organization is tasked with
going forth and setting Europe ablaze, and
aiding fledgling Resistance movements in the
fight against Nazi oppression and tyranny.
If called upon, our heroes must also defend
Britain's secrets at all costs, even if it
means hunting down one of their own. Needless
to say, it is extremely hazardous work.

This story is inspired by real events.

D0270590

SPECIAL OPS

DEAD OR ALIVE

CRAIG SIMPSON

CORGI BOOKS

SPECIAL OPERATIONS: DEAD OR ALIVE
A CORGI BOOK 978 0 552 56046 7

First published in Great Britain by Corgi Books,
an imprint of Random House Children's Books,
in association with The Bodley Head,
A Random House Group Company

This edition published 2012

1 3 5 7 9 10 8 6 4 2

The Random House Group Limited supports The Forest Stewardship Council
(FSC®), the leading international forest certification organisation. Our books
carrying the FSC label are printed on FSC® certified paper. FSC is the only
forest certification scheme endorsed by the leading environmental organisations,
including Greenpeace. Our paper procurement policy can be found at
www.randomhouse.co.uk/environment

MIX
Paper from
responsible sources
FSC® C016897

Set in Bembo

Corgi Books are published by Random House Children's Books,
61–63 Uxbridge Road, London W5 5SA

www.**kidsatrandomhouse**.co.uk
www.**randomhouse**.co.uk

Addresses for companies within The Random House Group Limited can be
found at: www.randomhouse.co.uk/offices.htm

THE RANDOM HOUSE GROUP Limited Reg. No. 954009

A CIP catalogue record for this book is available from the British Library.

Printed and bound by CPI Group (UK) Ltd, Croydon, CR0 4YY

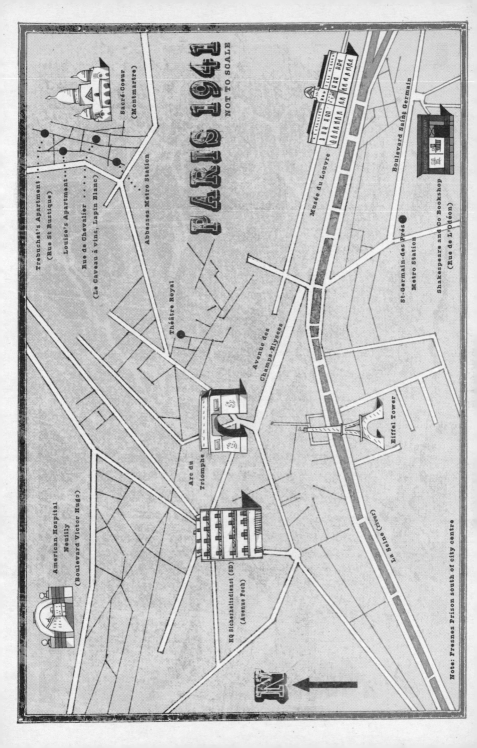

WESTLAND LYSANDER (SPECIAL DUTIES SQUADRON)
Photo courtesy of the Shuttleworth Collection and Darren Harbar
www.focalplaneimages.co.uk

I was there on that cold winter's night when the famous conjurer and escapologist, Madura the Magnificent, took to the dimly lit stage in Nazi-occupied Paris for the very last time. Understandably, he was extremely nervous. He knew that he had to give the greatest performance of his life. You see, there were those who wanted him dead. Madura's crime was simply that he knew too much.

With our enemies in hot pursuit, as agents with Special Operations we had to become magicians of sorts as well. Not to entertain or enthral a crowd, but in a desperate bid to escape and save lives.

Finn Gunnersen, December 1941

[For updated Personnel Files, see back of book]

Chapter One
The Ministry of Tricks

November 1941.

London was covered in dust. I'd never seen so much dust. Glowing embers drifted through the streets like a swarm of fireflies. The choking smell of charred timber hung in the air. It got right up my nose, making me cough and wheeze. Jabbing at the car's horn in frustration, our driver, Sergeant Walker, negotiated a way through the carnage as if taking part in a giant obstacle race. ARP wardens with armbands and tin hats waved frantically, yelling to him that the way ahead was blocked. Cursing under his breath, Walker crunched the gear lever into reverse.

Loki, Freya and I couldn't help gawping at the insane destruction. The sheer scale of it was mind-blowing. During the night, wave after wave of bombers, each one hundred strong, had unleashed tons of murder from their bellies. Parts of the city had been engulfed in a raging, swirling firestorm, while other areas had simply been pulverized into oblivion.

Windows had been blown in, and now and again we passed houses where entire walls had been ripped down, or had simply collapsed, exposing the insides. You could see wallpaper patterns, pictures still hanging crookedly on their hooks, chairs, beds and linen barely disturbed – it was really weird. Walker told us that stuff sometimes avoids the blast and looks untouched. 'Bodies too,' he added soberly. 'Recovered without a blemish on them. That's what happens in a firestorm. It sucks all the oxygen from the air. Basically, the poor sods suffocate.'

The thought made my blood run cold.

'Stop the car!' Freya shouted suddenly.

Alarmed, Walker slammed on the brakes and we screeched to a halt. Freya flung open the door and leaped out.

'What the devil?' Walker snapped his head round in consternation. 'Oi, come back, miss – we're late enough as it is.'

Freya shot across the road and knelt on the pavement in front of a small boy. Clutching a soot-stained teddy bear in one hand, a thumb firmly wedged in his mouth, he looked bewildered, as if he'd just woken up and found himself on another planet; a very hostile planet. Loki and I were out of the car in a flash too.

'Come back!' Walker shouted, slamming a fist on the steering wheel.

We ignored him.

'His name's Sam,' said Freya.

Sam was about three or four years old, his ill-fitting hand-me-down short trousers and tiny duffel coat filthy with the same reddish-grey brick dust that coated everything else. His blue eyes were piercing. Scrunching up his small round face, he opened his mouth as wide as it would go and yelled.

'There, there, don't worry.' Freya gave him a hug, and then used her handkerchief to wipe away his tears and the dribbles of snot from under his nose. 'Poor lamb. Must be lost. Where do you live, Sam? Where's your mum?'

Sam pointed. Twisting round, I looked back along the road and saw the mountain of rubble that had once been a row of shops. Fearing the worst, I swallowed hard. I didn't wish to alarm Sam, so I said calmly, 'Let's ask around. See if we can find someone who knows him.'

Our frantic enquiries met with blank faces and shakes of the head. Walker parked up further along the road and came marching back towards us, his purposeful stride practised on the military parade ground. 'Leave him! We must get to Whitehall. It's important. We've a long day ahead of us, and if it all goes pear-shaped, the brigadier will have my ruddy guts for garters. Somebody will no doubt take care of him.'

It came out sounding all wrong – way too blunt – and Freya turned on him. 'Not until I know he's in safe hands,' she demanded. Her fierce glare halted Walker in his tracks.

'I didn't mean it to sound . . . Sorry, miss, but, you know – orders and . . . Listen, we'll find a policeman, or—'

'Sam! Sam! Where are you?' The shrill woman's voice cut through the air like a javelin. '*There* you are, Sam. Thank the bleedin' Lord.'

A young woman dressed in navy blue overalls, her

curly blonde hair covered with a pale yellow and brown polka-dot silk scarf, was running towards us, elbows pumping, the steel-tipped heels of her stout shoes click-clacking a frantic rhythm on the pavement. Breathless, she scooped Sam up and cradled him in her arms. 'I thought I'd lost you,' she said, smothering his face with kisses while jigging him up and down and patting his back. She smiled at us over Sam's shoulder. 'Ta for looking after him. Silly sausage went wandering off. Told you not to, didn't I, Sam? I don't know – all I did was turn my back for a minute.' She jerked her head in the direction she'd come from. 'I was busy digging, see. Whole bleedin' street got taken out.'

'Find anyone alive?' Loki asked.

She nodded. 'Luckily most had taken to the shelters. But I was worried about my Uncle Jack. He lives at number twenty-three, see, and the daft old bugger always refuses to go underground. Reckons being in the shelter's like sitting in your own grave. He fought in the trenches in the last war – hated confined spaces ever since. Swore he'd never run from the enemy either. Stubborn, he is, and as tetchy as a mule with a splitting headache. Anyways, he was coming home from the King's Arms down Lanyard Street when the air-raid sirens started up their infernal whining. Said he just shook his fist at the sky and carried on walking. He was still a ways from home when his house was flattened. Saw it drop, he did. Bloody great big bomb – thousand-pounder, he reckons. Anyways, he's fine, and that's all that matters.' Sam's mother beamed with a cheerfulness that seemed completely at odds with the world around. 'We found Madge Warburton from number twenty-nine with nothing more than cuts and grazes too,' she continued brightly. 'Poor old dear was sitting on her outside lav when it fell. Blast blew the door right off its hinges. Gave her quite a fright, I can tell you. We found her still sitting there, knickers round her ankles, staring blankly into space and mumbling the Lord's Prayer over and over. Shock, I expect. We'll never hear the last of it!' She sighed heavily and looked expectantly at Sergeant Walker. 'What kind of world have our children been born into, eh, Sergeant? Explain it to me. I want to know. Why all the hate? Why can't we all live in peace?'

Punch-drunk from her tirade of impossible questions, a disconcerted Walker straightened his cap and briskly tapped his watch to bring our conversation to an end. 'Must be off. Nice meeting you. Come on, you three. No more dilly-dallying.'

Much to his relief, we said our goodbyes and were soon on our way again. The streets around Piccadilly were scenes of utter chaos as well, some blocked by rubble, others a jam of ambulances and fire tenders, their hoses snaking along gutters that had become swollen streams of muddy brown water. Men and women were frantically clearing busted masonry and wood, desperately searching for loved ones, friends, neighbours, total strangers, *anyone*.

Another hellish night had passed. And yet, as we drove through this vision of the underworld, I could see defiance and determination shining from weary, sweaty faces of Londoners who'd not had a decent night's sleep in weeks.

Sergeant Walker drove us up Shaftesbury Avenue, then down Charing Cross Road, past Nelson's Column, and finally into Whitehall. 'Here we are,' he announced, pulling up beside the kerb. 'Sit tight. Shan't be a tick.' He clambered out, and hurried in through a doorway hidden behind a shoulder-high stack of sandbags.

Loki stretched out his arms and yawned. 'This had all better be worth it,' he grumbled.

It had been an early start – up before dawn for the long drive from our HQ, Mulberry House, hidden away in the New Forest by the south coast. According to our commanding officer in Special Operations, Brigadier Devlin, he'd managed to pull a few strings. He wanted us to see something rather important, rather *hush hush*. Understandably, we were burning with curiosity.

Walker returned, accompanied by a gentleman in his late fifties dressed in a pinstripe suit, long black coat, fedora and leather gloves. Walker ran ahead of him in order to open the front passenger door. The smart man from Whitehall climbed in, pausing only briefly to acknowledge our presence with a faint nod and a brief touch of his hat's curled brim.

'This is Sir Hugo Foster,' Walker told us, jumping behind the steering wheel and slamming his door shut. 'Head of the Ministry of Tricks.'

'Really, Sergeant! I hate being referred to in that way,' Sir Hugo snapped gruffly.

Walker grinned. 'Well, technically, your lot are

just like us, sir. Officially, you don't exist either!'

'Quite so.' Sir Hugo turned in his seat and smiled at us grimly. The car filled with a faint whiff of stale tobacco and expensive cologne. His blotchy face was prematurely aged by the pressures of war: long hours behind a desk, endless meetings, and the responsibility that came with taking momentous decisions. He removed his hat and wearily ran his fingers through a receding mop of grey hair slicked back and glistening from an excessive dollop of Brylcreem. 'Must say, this little outing of ours is all very irregular. Winston twisted my arm over dinner at Number Ten. Wouldn't take no for an answer. Said that if your chaps saw it with their own eyes, they'd realize just how important it all is. Our work, I mean.'

'Very true, sir.' Walker glanced over his shoulder and pulled out into traffic.

Loki raised his eyebrows. Sir Hugo was on first-name terms with the prime minister, Winston Churchill. That surely made him a very important cog in the machinery of war, just like the shadowy X, the man in overall charge of Special Ops.

Crossing the Thames, we drove out of London, heading southeast through dense suburbs that gradually thinned, eventually fizzling out into countryside comprising endless fields, copses, villages and tiny hamlets. The road grew ever narrower and more twisting, and the hedgerows taller. I could figure out our general direction based on the time of day and position of the feeble winter sun. Loki whispered that we were probably heading for Kent. It was a guess – it was impossible to tell exactly which villages we were passing through as all road signs had been removed in order to confuse the enemy should they ever mount an invasion of Britain – but I suspected that he was right.

Resting her head on Loki's shoulder, Freya dozed off, and soon Loki's eyes were closed too. The pair were growing closer by the day. I don't think our superiors approved: emotion can cloud someone's judgement, and that can prove highly dangerous in our line of work. But the men in charge had said nothing, accepting that the three of us were a team whose bonds were forged from life-long friendships. We'd lived through many life-and-death moments together; situations that had strengthened our ties. While my friends slept, I remained awake, trying to figure out what all the mystery was about. Something was up, that was for sure. Telephones back at Mulberry hadn't stopped ringing for days, and Walker and the brigadier had been up burning the midnight oil poring over Top Secret intelligence reports delivered to Mulberry by a steady stream of motorcycle dispatch riders. Staring out of the window, deep in thought, I watched England pass us by in a blur.

'Any news regarding you-know-who?' Sir Hugo asked Walker. His question shattered a lengthy silence.

'No, sir. Not a dicky bird.' Pulling a face, Walker flexed his grip on the steering wheel and sniffed. 'Still, perhaps we shouldn't jump to conclusions. The situation may not be as desperate as we fear.' He leaned forward and peered out at a church spire to our left. 'I think we're nearly there, sir. I wasn't told its precise location, only to head this way and that you'd give me instructions for the final leg.'

Sir Hugo nodded and then, pointing towards a lay-by up ahead, told Walker to pull over. He did so, and the squeal of the brakes woke the others. 'Are we there?' Freya rubbed the sleep from her eyes.

'No, miss. Not quite,' said Sir Hugo. 'Be so kind as to put these on.' He passed three black velvet blindfolds into the back of the car. 'Tie them tight. Make sure you can't see a thing. That's an order. Have I made myself understood?'

'Yes, sir,' we replied as one.

Walker drove on, guided by Sir Hugo's directions. When we stopped again, voices at the window demanded to see our papers, passes and authorizations. Someone finally announced, 'Everything's in order, sir.' I heard the clack of heels and imagined a khaki-clad, pigeon-chested sentry snapping to attention and saluting.

A bumpy two-minute ride later, Walker stopped and killed the engine. 'Everyone out.'

We emerged into a breezy afternoon with a faint drizzle in the air. I buttoned my coat, turned up the collar and stretched the stiffness from my back.

'OK. You can take them off now.'

Yanking my blindfold from my head, I blinked wildly to adjust my eyes to the overpowering brightness. I turned round slowly and tried to take it all in. We were standing on the middle of a runway, surrounded by flat grass stretching almost as far as the eye could see. Beneath our feet lay rigid steel netting. I'd seen it before: Sommerfeld Tracking. It was used to construct temporary runways so aircraft could take off and land in all weathers where otherwise grass would quickly turn into mud. I'd heard that pilots of larger aircraft hated it because it sometimes damaged their tyres and under-carriage, and if they came in too heavily they might even tear the stuff up. In the distance stood a two-storey concrete building – probably the Watch Office, or what some were now calling the 'Control Tower'. A hundred yards to the left of it was a large blister hangar next to a couple of Nissen huts and a row of tents. Windsocks flapped at the tops of poles. At various locations close to the perimeter fence, aircraft – mostly Spitfires, I reckoned – lay idle.

Loki nudged me. 'I don't get it, Finn. Why have they brought us here?'

Freya couldn't stop yawning. She shoved her hands in her pockets and scuffed her shoe against the ground, looking bored.

'So,' said Walker cheerfully. 'What do you think?'

'About what?' Freya snapped irritably.

Walker could barely conceal the smirk on his face. 'OK. Tell me, where are we? What is this place?'

Loki replied sarcastically, 'An airfield. In the middle of nowhere. Can we go home now?'

'Splendid,' Sir Hugo remarked, appearing extremely pleased. 'Hoped you'd say that. Now look again. *Harder* this time.'

We did. 'Still looks like an airfield to me,' I said. 'Operational too, judging by the number of aircraft out at dispersal. How many squadrons are based here? Two? Three? Any chance of having a go in one of those Spits?'

Freya's patience ran out. 'I'm freezing out here. Getting wet too. For God's sake put us out of our misery.'

'Very well,' said Sir Hugo. 'Listen up and I'll explain. Despite winning the battle of the skies last summer, we're still losing hundreds of fighter aircraft and bombers, and precious, talented aircrew.' He paused and looked at me. 'Men like your father, Mr Gunnersen.'

I was about to snap back that Father was officially missing in action, and that I'd not given up all hope, when Sir Hugo went on:

'However, not all are lost during heroic dogfights or bombing raids over Germany's industrial heartland. The Luftwaffe has once again been concentrating on targeting our airfields. Bastards are clobbering our planes while they're still on the ground.' He paused to sneeze. Vigorously wiping his nose with a starched handkerchief, he continued, 'My department was established to dream up ways of limiting the damage. Naturally I recruited only the best minds – brainy men and women who could think the unthinkable. They began by devising various new forms of camouflage, and then tried working out the best ways to disperse aircraft around the airfield to minimize losses – that sort of thing. We had our successes. Unfortunately, they weren't enough. We had to come up with something else, something even better, *bigger*. And this is it.' He spread out his arms and turned through three hundred and sixty degrees. 'Ta-da! Impressive, don't you think?'

While Loki scratched his head in confusion, something clicked inside my brain. 'I get it. This isn't an airfield at all. It just looks like one. It's an illusion.'

'What on earth are you on about, Finn?' Loki clearly thought I was nuts.

'Top marks, Mr Gunnersen,' said Sir Hugo, rubbing his hands together gleefully. 'Go and take a closer look at those aircraft. Feel free to take one up if you like. If you can!'

'Race you, Loki,' I shouted, and set off at a sprint across the grass.

We arrived beside half a dozen Spitfires on the far side of the airfield. Hands on knees, drawing deep, rasping breaths, Loki looked as gobsmacked as I was. The aircraft were no more than plywood skeletons covered with painted canvas, like cheap toys, albeit full-size ones. Up close, they'd not fool anyone for a second. But from a distance – well, they'd had me convinced. 'Amazing!'

'Let me get this right,' Loki puffed. 'They're building decoy airfields to confuse the Luftwaffe?'

'Yes, so they waste their time bombing places like this rather than *real* airfields. It's a brilliant idea. Their reconnaissance planes fly over and photograph the area at high altitude, and then back at base they study the pictures and figure it's real. Sir Hugo's men must've realized they can't conceal an entire airfield from the enemy no matter how much camouflage netting they've got – it's simply too big. Building decoys is the next best thing.'

'Doesn't stop them from bombing our real airfields as well though, Finn.'

'Quite correct, Mr Larson.' Sir Hugo and the others caught us up. 'But it means that far fewer enemy raids are successful. We've built decoys like this in a number of places. But there's a humungous problem.'

Freya ran her fingers over one of the flimsy canvas wings and then poked a hole in it. 'And I think I know what that is, Sir Hugo. They'll only work as long as the enemy doesn't know that they're fake.'

'Exactly,' replied Walker.

'And you think there's been a leak?' I asked.

Sir Hugo shrugged and nodded simultaneously. 'Possibly. One of my team has disappeared, you see. Simply vanished. Unfortunately, he possesses detailed knowledge of all the locations. Most inconvenient!'

Walker added, 'It gets worse. This isn't the only deception the Ministry of Tricks has come up with.' He turned to Sir Hugo. 'With your permission, sir, I think it's time for our little demonstration.'

Sir Hugo agreed, and Walker removed a whistle from his pocket and blew hard on it. 'As this place is well away from prying eyes, Sir Hugo's chaps use it to test out many other ingenious inventions. We thought we'd show you just one of them. Prepare yourselves to be amazed.'

A man emerged from a building several hundred yards away and waved a red flag.

Walker waved back. 'Ah, good, looks like they're all set.'

'I suppose it's safe standing here, is it?' a slightly nervous Sir Hugo asked.

'Quite safe, sir,' Walker responded. 'I've been assured that we're well away from Project Starfish over here.'

An ear-splitting klaxon sounded. Three long blasts. Men went scurrying across the airfield's apron and descended into a bunker.

'What's Project Starfish?' I asked, just as several huge explosions smothered my words and shook the ground. Instinctively I threw myself down and covered my head with my hands. Loki and Freya did likewise, while Walker and Sir Hugo didn't budge. For what seemed like ages none of us moved a muscle. Then, realizing I was all right, I spat an annoying blade of wet grass out of my mouth and looked up. Huge fires! Five of them, flames leaping high into the sky beneath billowing columns of black, acrid smoke.

'What the hell . . . ?' Loki shouted, lifting himself up onto his knees.

'That, everyone, is Starfish,' Sir Hugo announced triumphantly. 'Impressive, eh?'

Scrambling to our feet, we gazed in awe. The fires were spread out, as if at the points of a star. At its centre I saw a concrete structure, and pipes radiating from it towards each blaze.

Walker explained, 'In London this morning you saw for yourselves that the Blitz is still in full swing. Of course, creating decoy airfields is one thing, but fake towns and cities – well, that would be impossible, wouldn't it . . . ? Or *would* it?' He winked at us.

'My team gave the matter considerable thought,' Sir Hugo continued, removing a large cigar from his coat pocket. He lit up and puffed vigorously. 'The key to it all was the simple observation that the Luftwaffe carry out the majority of their bombing raids at night.' He took the cigar out of his mouth and inspected the glowing tip. 'Each wave of bombers is preceded by a few special aircraft – called Pathfinders – that mark targets with incendiary bombs and flares. The success or failure of the raid depends on how accurately they pinpoint their targets.'

Walker expanded: 'The Luftwaffe developed a secret system they codenamed *Knickebein*, or Crooked Leg, which was based on two separate highly directional radio beams generated from different locations in Europe. The two beams crossed over at the precise position of their intended target. The Pathfinders carried receivers and flew along one beam until they picked up the second. "X" marks the spot, if you like. At that point they released their markers to show all the others where to drop their bombs. But we got lucky. We shot one of them down and were able to recover their equipment and figure it out. We found a way of jamming their system. More recently, however, their targeting has improved. We're pretty sure they've developed something new. We'd dearly love to find out what.'

'Thank you for the lesson, Sergeant,' Sir Hugo butted in. 'As I was saying. The trick we came up with was scarily simple. We decided to mark the targets ourselves . . . in the wrong places, of course. Starfish's role is to confuse the enemy. Basically, it comprises large reservoirs of fuel that we can set fire to in a controlled way. It can be turned on and off as and when we like. This one's just a prototype. The operational version is four times bigger. As you can see for yourselves, it creates an impressive show. Imagine it at night! You'd be able to see it for miles. We've built many close to our cities, but not too close – on farmland or wasteland, always in sparsely populated areas. When our radar picks up an incoming raid and we've worked out which city they're heading for, we'll ignite the appropriate Starfish. Enemy pilots will see the flames and assume they represent the markers dropped by their Pathfinders. If they're fooled, they'll drop their munitions somewhere they can't do much harm. Starfish should save many innocent lives.'

Freya brushed damp mud from her skirt. 'You said one of your team had disappeared, sir. Did he have information about the locations for Starfish as well? If he did, it could prove a disaster. Instead of Starfish working as a decoy, it would have the opposite effect.'

Loki frowned. 'How do you figure that out?'

'Freya's right,' I interrupted. 'Think about it. If you were the enemy and you knew the *exact* locations of Starfish, then they'd act as incredibly precise markers, even if they were miles from a city centre. Because if you knew where they were, you could simply make navigational adjustments and drop your bombs in the right place.'

'True, Mr Gunnersen. Hence the locations of Starfish are highly classified,' Sir Hugo responded. 'Each site is heavily restricted and guarded at all times. No unauthorized person is allowed anywhere near them. My man's disappearance has to be investigated urgently. We have to find out if our secrets are safe. Otherwise we'll have to start all over again.'

The fires suddenly stopped. In seconds the smoke had drifted away. We began strolling back towards the car. 'What can you tell us about this man who worked for you, sir?' I asked.

Sir Hugo exhaled a long stream of smoke and replied acidly, 'His name's Claude Chevalier.'

Freya beat me to my next question. 'Any idea where he might be?'

'Yes, miss. France. Paris, I expect.'

Loki stopped dead in his tracks. '*Paris?* How can you be so sure he's left the country?'

'Ah! This is rather awkward,' said Walker, lowering his eyes to the ground. 'A bit embarrassing. All our doing, I'm afraid. Claude's time with Sir Hugo's department was merely a temporary assignment. Claude's actually a member of Special Ops – with our French F-Section based over at Handelbury Manor. He's a man of many talents, is dear old Claude, as well as being somewhat unpredictable – your typical Frenchman, if you ask me. Anyway, once he'd finished working for Sir Hugo, he returned to active duty with us. A week ago we sent him back to France on a routine mission as a courier, only he failed to make his rendezvous. Not only that –

despite our best efforts to find him, he appears to have vanished off the face of the earth.'

Loki's shoulders slumped. 'And it's going to be our job to find out what's happened to him, I suppose.'

'Yes. We have to know whether he's got himself into a spot of bother, or whether he's decided the grass is greener on the other side.'

'Do you mean he might have become a double agent?'

'Yes, Finn, it's a possibility we have to consider. Claude knew a great deal, and information is power, or at the very least it's likely to ingratiate you with the enemy. The rewards for sharing such vital intelligence are unimaginable. Of course, it is also possible he's just had his fill of Special Ops work, or snapped under the pressure and decided to forge a new life somewhere with a new identity. He wouldn't be the first to cut loose. As you know, an agent's life isn't exactly an easy one. Some get superstitious and convince themselves that their luck's about to run out. Usually we spot the signs in time: their behaviour becomes erratic, you see. We sit them down and break the news gently to them – that their "career" is over – and then we cart them off to the Forgetting School. Maybe Claude didn't fancy the prospect.'

We'd heard about the so-called *Forgetting School*. Burned-out agents were sent to a remote house in the Scottish Highlands and held there twiddling their thumbs until it was decided they'd forgotten most of what they'd been taught, and that any secrets they knew were no longer of importance. For most it would mean sitting out the rest of the war in isolation – no visitors or outside communication; little different from an internment camp. Everyone in Special Ops dreaded the idea of being sent there.

'And . . . ?' Freya asked hesitantly. 'Supposing we do find him? Then what?'

Sir Hugo extinguished the stub of his cigar beneath his shoe, grinding it into the ground. 'A decision has been taken at the highest level. Claude Chevalier must either be forced to return to Britain or be silenced . . . *permanently.*'

Shocked, Freya swallowed hard. 'Y-y-you mean . . . we might have to . . . *assassinate* him?'

'Even if he's simply decided he's had enough of being an agent with Special Ops?' I added in astonishment.

'We can't run the risk.' Walker saw our horror and tried to play down the matter. 'In all probability Claude just needs your help and will be only too glad to return here.' He put on a smile.

Loki was shaking his head vehemently. 'This isn't what we joined up to do.' He looked to me for support. 'Is it, Finn? It's one thing taking on the Nazis, but going after one of our own . . . that's just plain wrong. You can count me out.'

On previous missions we'd had to take on the enemy and fight our way out of tricky situations, and that had sometimes meant killing them. Loki was right: this was different. I had a nagging question too. 'What makes you think he might have simply taken off? You said he was acting as a courier. What exactly was he carrying?'

'Money, Finn,' Walker replied. 'A whole suitcase full. Two million French francs plus some gold coins. Destined to fund the Resistance in Paris.'

Loki whistled. 'Two million francs. I reckon you've seen the last of Claude.'

Sir Hugo spun round and snapped angrily, 'No, Mr Larson. Dead or alive, I want his head delivered to me on a silver platter. *Understood?*'

Shaking their heads, Loki and Freya both backed away. 'No, we simply won't do it.'

The look of fury on Sir Hugo's face grew. He wasn't one to tolerate insubordination. 'Orders are orders!'

Chapter Two
Three Blind Mice

One week later.

Nick Carter understood a great deal about atmospheric pressure, prevailing winds and precipitation, but he knew absolutely nothing about the troubling incident involving Claude Chevalier and the suitcase bulging with cash. In fact, very few knew about it, and the fewer the better.

Before the war a much younger Carter had been a famous winger with Plymouth Argyle FC nicknamed the Devon Whippet: blindingly quick and with a fabulous left foot. Looking at him now, it was hard to imagine him hurtling down the touchline and flashing in a perfectly angled cross. He had put on weight since a broken leg forced him into early retirement from the game and left him with a pronounced limp. Unfit for active military service, Carter had to make do with a job at the Meteorological Office. Carter being Carter, he took it all extremely seriously. The high-pitched screech as he scraped his chalk across the blackboard set my teeth on edge. All arrows and wavy lines, the weather map he'd drawn for us looked as scary as it was complicated. Turning round, Carter's gaze fell on Loki, Freya and me. He said nothing, but I could sense the questions brewing in his mind: *Who on earth are they? What are they doing here?*

We were often greeted with puzzled expressions by those lacking the security clearance to be in the know about Special Operations. We'd grown used to all their frowns and stares. The fact that we were present, sitting in the same room, listening to their classified briefings, meant we had to be important, but most knew better than to enquire as to our role in this hellish war. Only a discreet handful of men and women, a very select few, knew of our existence and what we'd been trained to do. In fact, the reaction of men like Carter explained why we were there; why we were part of an organization designated Most Secret. The enemy would think the same as they did: surely they're too young to be taken seriously – hardly worth bothering about – hardly likely to be enemy spies. And so they'd be deceived too; *hopefully*. We were secret agents. Our purpose? To give Herr Hitler's men as much aggro as possible.

'Make it snappy, Mr Carter. We haven't got all night,' grumbled Brigadier Devlin, fidgeting in his seat and repeatedly glancing at his watch.

'First really bad storm of the winter, sir,' Carter began, stepping back to admire his handiwork. 'All flights should be grounded until further notice. We're predicting wind speeds of sixty miles per hour, gusts up to eighty. Only a complete idiot would attempt a dash across the Channel.' His gaze drifted pointedly in the direction of Captain Nils Jacobsen.

Nils was sitting in front of me, two rows from the

back. Ignoring Carter's remark, he continued scribbling notes on a pad resting on his left knee. I leaned forward to look over his shoulder and saw he'd begun calculating his aircraft's range based on a full load and stiff head-wind. A pilot with the clandestine Moon Squadron – set up to get agents in and out of enemy territory fast and with the minimum of fuss – it was Nils's job to fly the three of us into France. From his frequent mutterings I could tell he hardly relished the prospect.

Brigadier Devlin stood up from the front row of collapsible wooden chairs. He interrupted Carter with a loud, disdainful grunt, making no attempt to conceal his growing irritation. 'Yes, yes, all right, thank you, Mr Carter, we get the message. Unfortunately, circum-stances demand otherwise. What Captain Jacobsen requires from you is advice regarding the safest way to fly, and not your opinion as to his sanity.'

Carter flung down his chalk and pressed a finger against the blackboard. 'See these tightly packed isobars, sir? See the way the barometric pressure's falling through the floor? A deep depression is moving through the English Channel. The cloud base is so low it'll test the skills of even the most experienced pilot. You'll be flying through the worst of it blind, and odds on you'll fail to spot your landing site. To risk going in is foolhardy in the extreme. I implore you to wait at least another forty-eight hours. By then the worst of it should be heading into the Baltic. Forty-eight hours, sir. That's all. Surely . . .'

The brigadier shook his head. Carter threw up his

arms in despair. 'Then on your own heads be it. I shall be making an official complaint to the Air Ministry.'

The brigadier snorted. 'Do as you see fit.'

I thought he was going to add *for all the difference it'll make*, but he didn't.

'Then I've nothing more to add.' Carter began gathering up all his papers and stuffing them angrily into his bag. I had the feeling he'd assumed – quite wrongly, of course – that his warning would be heeded, that the war would be temporarily halted on his command, as if he were a referee in a Cup tie and had blown his whistle to abandon the match. The Devon Whippet had just learned an important lesson: war doesn't get postponed just because of a waterlogged pitch.

By now it was ten o'clock in the evening, and we were huddled inside a small briefing hut next to the tangled spirals of rusting barbed wire that comprised the perimeter fence to RAF Tangmere, situated a stone's throw from the Sussex coast. The air smelled earthy and dank, like mushroom compost, and I noticed the ceiling was dotted with splodges of creeping black mould. Lacking any form of heating, the place was freezing. Overcoats and tightly knotted scarves were the order of the day, worn over thick sweaters and two pairs of socks. We could hear the wind's bluster outside, and every couple of minutes an especially violent gust drove a mix of rain and hail hard against the windows as if someone had thrown a handful of dry semolina at it for a dare. It hammered down on the corrugated tin roof too, sounding like sacks of spuds being emptied onto our heads.

No doubt the deafening racket made Carter feel vindicated. Looking Nils in the eye, he advised sternly, 'Fly as low as you dare, Captain, and pray that your guardian angel will be looking out for you.' Carter wanted the last word.

The brigadier removed his favourite smouldering briar from his lips, and harrumphed. 'Right, Mr Carter, if you've quite finished . . .' He gestured towards the door with his cane. 'You're dismissed.'

The muscles in Carter's face twitched as he snapped shut the catches on his bag, mumbled something about a *ruddy waste of time* and limped towards the door. Grabbing hold of the handle, he hesitated, taking a moment to scrutinize Loki, Freya and me. The three of us were sitting in the back row and hadn't uttered a word since entering the hut. He opened his mouth as if about to speak, then changed his mind, and instead tutted while shaking his head. I could imagine his thoughts: utter foolishness, reckless, *insane*. Then his expression darkened: *lambs to the slaughter*.

Carter departed, slamming the hut door behind him. I leaned forward and tapped Nils on the shoulder. 'If the Devon Whippet's right, shouldn't we heed his advice? I mean, if we can't spot the landing lights, we'll have to turn round and come back. That's crazy.'

'True, Finn, but on the plus side, if the cloud base is as low as he says, then the enemy's coastal defences won't be able to see us either. Less anti-aircraft fire. Every cloud has its silver lining.' Nils's chirpy manner belied the danger that we faced.

'It grieves me to say it, but Carter's right,' the brigadier complained, flexing the stiffness from his shrapnel-filled leg. 'Damn and blast the man!'

Sergeant Walker rose from his chair and straightened his tunic. 'No point shooting the messenger, sir. Carter was only doing his job.' Walker was often the soothing voice of reason to counter the brigadier's brittle temper. He added helpfully, 'Perhaps you should ask Captain Jacobsen's opinion before coming to a final decision, sir.'

'Well?' Brigadier Devlin eyeballed Nils expectantly.

'Under normal circumstances, sir—' Nils began.

'But they're not normal, Captain,' the brigadier bellowed, thumping his stick angrily against the wooden floor. 'That's the bloody point. That's why we're all here. It's an unholy mess.'

Nils calmly waited for the brigadier to finish his rant before continuing: 'As I was about to say, sir, exceptional circumstances demand exceptional actions. I'm willing to give it a go.'

'Yes, well, good for you, Captain. Thank you. The likes of Carter have no idea. Finding out what's happened to Claude Chevalier has the very highest priority. The prime minister has demanded that the matter is resolved. Claude simply knows too much, and if . . . Well, it doesn't bear thinking about.' Biting hard on the stem of his briar, the brigadier gathered his thoughts. 'Right, I've made up my mind. I'm giving Operation Tally-ho the go-ahead. We can't wait for Mother Nature. Anyway, as you know, the wheels have already been set in motion. Yesterday evening the BBC broadcast a *Message Personnel* on our behalf to our friends in France, and they will be expecting us. We mustn't disappoint them – I'm sure they've gone to a great deal of trouble.'

Messages Personnels were a clever way of communicating with Resistance groups in Nazi-occupied France. Every evening, immediately after the news bulletin on the British Broadcasting Company's overseas French wireless programme, the announcer would repeat cryptic messages for the ears of *résistants* huddled beside their wireless sets in remote farmhouses, attics and parlours. To everyone else they sounded like utter nonsense, but to these brave men and women the words were like triggers, causing them to spring into action. Our message was for the attention of a man called Laurent Laval, a farmer located close to the town of Les Andelys, whose identifier, or codename, was 'Cabbages and Kings'. The message broadcast over the airwaves was short and to the point: *Cabbages and Kings . . . Three blind mice . . . Tomorrow night at two.*

Loki, Freya and I were the three blind mice.

Busy chewing a piece of gum he'd cadged from a Spitfire mechanic on our arrival at Tangmere, Loki cast his eyes to the heavens and muttered, 'At last!' He spoke for all three of us. We just wanted to get on with it. It was the hanging around that played havoc with our nerves. It felt worse than waiting your turn at the dentist's when you can hear the screams of the drill emerging from behind closed doors. For hours on end we'd rehearsed our cover stories, studied maps, read and memorized names and addresses, and digested the latest intelligence reports concerning the situation in and around Paris. We were more than ready for a mission none of us relished.

After meeting Sir Hugo we'd seriously considered refusing to follow orders, and to hell with the consequences. But then Freya said something that changed all our minds. If we did refuse to go in search of Claude Chevalier, she reckoned the brigadier would simply find someone else to carry out the mission – possibly someone who wouldn't give a damn who they were after; someone who wouldn't blink at assassinating one of our own. At least if we went, we could find out the truth and then act. If Claude *had* turned traitor, then he was effectively the enemy and a legitimate target . . . but if not, if he simply wanted out, then we could make a decision on the ground, maybe let him slip through our fingers. Maybe, in a weird way, we were Claude's lifeline.

'Time to perform your final checks,' Walker declared, stiffening to attention to indicate it was an order and not merely a polite request. 'Zero hour is midnight.'

We were going into enemy territory lightly equipped, with just two small suitcases between us. One contained a change of clothes and other items you'd expect to find in a traveller's possession: toiletries, several torches plus batteries, books, etc. – although some had been modified to conceal useful items such as money, ammunition, fuses, abrasive powders and corrosive creams. The other case housed our radio set for sending and receiving messages in Morse code. The clothes on our backs had a deliberately lived-in, seen-better-days look about them, just like those you'd observe on the streets of Paris after more than a year of Nazi occupation – like most stuff, new clothing was in short supply. Any English labels had been carefully removed and replaced by others, indicating either French or American manufacture. The latter was critical to our cover.

Being Norwegian, we'd been subjected to endless hours of mind-numbing French language practice – at the end of which only Freya was proficient enough to pass herself off as a Parisian. Loki and me were pretty rubbish, but could speak English fluently. That was the key. It was decided that the three of us would go in as Americans, brothers and sister, all members of the fictitious *Stevens* family hailing from Westport, Connecticut. I was Simon, Loki was Johnny, and Freya was Lorna Stevens. Because we'd been friends all our lives and knew each other inside out, we reckoned we could pull it off; we were so close that we often knew what the other was thinking or about to say.

There were other advantages too. The United States was yet to enter the war and so, for now at least, the German authorities had no beef with them; quite the opposite, in fact. Generally, waving American papers under the noses of German soldiers if you got stopped in the street meant they'd leave you alone, let you pass, not give you as hard a time as they did the locals. This comparative freedom would aid our movement about the city and was crucial to our mission. We were going hunting; rabbit-hunting, to be precise. Our target was

Claude Chevalier, codename *Lapin Blanc*, the White Rabbit.

At zero hour we said our goodbyes to Walker and the brigadier, swallowed our trepidation, and departed the safety of the briefing hut, our bellies sloshing with one final, comforting mug of piping-hot sweet tea. Outside, driving rain smacked into our faces, danced on our hats and pelted the glistening concrete as we hurried, dodging the puddles, across the airfield's apron to where our plane awaited. Lit by a single arc lamp, the Lysander struck me as woefully small, fragile, no match for the blustery tempest; her dragonfly-shaped wings rocked and flexed in the wind, making her look like an insect that could be swatted with a rolled-up newspaper.

Nils was already strapped in and running through his final checks as we scaled a narrow, slippery ladder attached to the outside of the fuselage and began clambering aboard. Leaning out of the cockpit window, he shouted, 'Contact!' and a bedraggled mechanic grabbed hold of a propeller blade and gave it an almighty yank. The Lizzie's engine spat and spluttered into life. The propellers spun to a blur, and as she warmed up, the smell of hot oil and burned fuel reached my nostrils. 'Hurry up,' Nils shouted over the engine's din. 'Let's get this over and done with.'

Inside, the aircraft proved hellishly cramped. The three of us squeezed in like tinned peas, settling down as best we could on bum-achingly uncomfortable wooden seats, Loki and Freya next to one another, me opposite.

I slid the canopy shut and twisted the handle. Belting up, Loki offered to rest Freya's heavy suitcase containing the radio set on his lap. I upended the other case and wedged it between my legs.

Nils waved a chart in the air over his shoulder to attract our attention. 'Not a night for dilly-dallying. I'm taking Carter's advice: as the crow flies and as low as we dare. We'll be fine as long as I'm able to locate the mouth of the river Seine. We'll follow it all the way to your rendezvous. Hang onto your hats because we're in for a bumpy ride.'

The chocks were dragged from beneath the wheels and the ground crew waved the all clear. As Nils opened the throttle, the plane's Bristol Mercury engine roared. Increasing power made the Lizzie rattle and shake, and everything vibrated.

Rolling forward, we taxied to the end of the runway and turned. Nils radioed for final clearance and, receiving the thumbs-up, we set off. Full throttle, maximum revs, engine howling, he held a steady line. As we accelerated, we felt every bump along the lumpy surface of the heavily used runway until, at eighty-five miles per hour, Nils pulled back the control column and we lifted off, climbing steeply into the night. No sooner had the wheels left the ground than I felt the plane lurch hard to port and sensed the wing dip. Freya reached out and grabbed Loki's hand, squeezing it tightly.

'It's fine, don't worry. Just the wind,' he said, swallowing hard and desperately trying to conceal the quiver in his voice.

Nils was determined to gain altitude quickly in case we stalled and he needed to recover control before we crashed back to earth. Loki and I knew how to fly too. Our fathers had taught us back in Norway before the war. They had gone into business together and dreamed of making their fortunes transporting freight and passengers. The war had put paid to such plans. It had changed everything. From reading up about her, I also knew enough about the Lizzie to understand that, like most aircraft, if the engine stalled, you pushed her nose down immediately and prayed the engine coughed back into life. Height was everything as it bought you precious seconds. Even if the engine did recover, hundreds of feet would be lost before it did so. Up and up we went, our angle of ascent so steep I was glad to be strapped in tightly.

Vigorously chewing his gum, Loki closed his eyes and pressed his head back. 'You know, I've been thinking about Claude. If someone gave me a large suitcase stuffed full of cash, I suppose I might be tempted to disappear too. I mean, two million francs – and that's not counting the gold coins stitched into the lining.' He whistled through his teeth. 'You could buy just about anything with that. What about you, Finn? What would *you* do?' He opened one eye and glanced across at me.

It had now been a fortnight since Claude Chevalier entered France. We'd been told that he was one of our F-Section's finest couriers, until now proving as reliable as the setting sun. It wasn't the first time he'd carried substantial sums of money either. On this occasion he was under orders to deliver the money to a Resistance leader codenamed *Trébuchet* at a safe house in Paris's colourful Montmartre district. Only, of course, he hadn't.

'That much money just makes life complicated, Loki, especially when it's not yours,' I replied, secretly imagining how wonderful it would be to be rich beyond my wildest dreams. 'Anyway, we mustn't jump to conclusions. Most likely he's been arrested and is languishing in prison somewhere, or has been interrogated and then shot. We stick to our plan. One step at a time. We find out what's happened to him and then figure out what to do. Personally, I just hope he's got into a spot of bother or decided to lie low, and that we can help him get back to England . . . Christ, it's freezing in here.'

'No, he's done a runner, Finn, I just know it.'

Trébuchet had sent a distraught, hurriedly coded message indicating that the White Rabbit had failed to make the rendezvous in Montmartre. Immediately all hell had broken loose, not least because we were pretty sure that German Intelligence knew of Claude; it was even believed that a hefty price had been placed on his head – dead or alive. But the enemy only knew him by his codename, and during our briefing we'd been told that Claude was devilishly good at changing his appearance and giving the authorities the slip. He'd always managed to stay one step ahead. Despite this, fearing that Claude and his fortune had been apprehended by German officers of the infamous Gestapo, Trébuchet made frantic enquiries among his numerous contacts in the police, the prisons, local French authorities, and even a few corrupt Nazi officials whose palms he'd greased in the past – all without success. No agent had been captured, no vast fortune seized. That was the official line Trébuchet met at every turn. There weren't even any ugly rumours floating about. The White Rabbit and the money had simply vanished. It was at that point our superiors started to suspect that Claude might have changed sides or made off alone.

Wiping condensation from the misted window with the sleeve of her coat, Freya peered out. Trails of rain tracked horizontally across the Perspex like cascading rivers. 'I can't see a thing. What a night!'

My thoughts remained focused on Claude. We'd been shown numerous photographs of him: a short, balding, slightly overweight Frenchman bearing an unnerving likeness to paintings I'd seen in history books of Napoleon Bonaparte. 'When I read Claude's file back at Mulberry, he didn't strike me as the treacherous sort,' I said, 'or a thief. Can't see him betraying his country.'

'Well, if you're right, Finn, and if Claude's still alive, then he's a man wanted by both sides,' said Loki.

'True.' Various scenarios played out in my imagination. 'Maybe . . . maybe . . . he did get apprehended, and whoever arrested him kept quiet about it in order to keep the cash. If that's the case, finding him won't be easy.'

'Hah, it'd be a wild goose chase, more like,' Freya muttered. 'Anyway, his personnel file struck me as rather thin. We hardly learned anything useful about him. I wouldn't be surprised if Claude Chevalier wasn't even his real name.' Flicking her fringe from her eyes, she went on, 'I'm with Loki on this one, although I'd bet my life's savings that Claude, or whoever he really is, has a damn good reason for his actions – more than just greed. Call it intuition if you like, but there's something distinctly fishy about him.'

'You haven't got any savings,' I replied, and promptly received a friendly kick in the shins. We laughed. 'Anyway, what good reason could he have?'

Freya pulled a face. 'Who knows? Maybe he *needs* the money for something. Something *très, très important*. His actions may be those of a desperate man.'

'Well, whatever the truth is, it's going to be like looking for a needle in a haystack,' Loki added. 'Paris is huge. What's worrying me is that our contact, Trébuchet, couldn't locate him, and *he* must know his way around the city. People who go around asking too many questions draw unwanted attention from the authorities. We're going to have to tread carefully.'

'If he's still alive, someone, somewhere will know something,' Freya reflected. 'We just need to get lucky.'

'Yeah, and pigs might fly!'

I reached inside my coat, removed a photograph and waved it in the air. 'We have one advantage over Trébuchet. We know what Claude looks like.'

The Lizzie suddenly flew into thick cloud and we were jolted by stiff turbulence; none of us spoke much while we rode it out. Nils reassured us all was fine but, sensing our nervousness, agreed with my suggestion of climbing in search of calmer air.

Our initial destination was a small town called Les Andelys to the northwest of Paris and a short distance southeast of Rouen. There the river Seine winds gracefully through a broad valley carved from chalk, a large spoon-shaped loop enclosing flat farmland given over to pasture and cabbage fields; farmland owned by our contact, Laurent Laval. Les Andelys was situated on the opposite bank, together with an isolated hill, on top of which perched the impressive stone ruins of Château Gaillard, a castle built centuries ago.

Having heard the message on the BBC, Laval's job was to organize our reception committee, marking out a landing strip on his fields using fellow *résistants* clutching lamps or torches. It was standard procedure, the lamp-holders positioned to form an L-shape. Nils would land along one axis, and use the other to turn and offload us. Then he'd take off again. The whole procedure could be completed inside two minutes if everything went smoothly. Our tiny Lysander was perfect for such manoeuvres, especially where landing space was limited. The Lizzie's saving grace was STOL – Short Take-Off and Landing. She could put down in a field and take off again, climbing to fifty feet, all in the length of a football pitch.

'What was that?' Freya fretted, pressing against the Perspex.

I'd seen the flash too. And then another. Above us the cloud seemed to light up.

'Lightning,' Nils shouted. 'By my reckoning we're still about five minutes from the French coast.'

The lightning chased us, surrounded us, circled us, getting brighter with each flash, forks interspersed with sheets of flickering light between layers of cloud. The wind came at us hard from all directions too, the Lizzie rocking violently as we lurched up and down as if on the world's craziest fairground dodgem ride, pockets of uneven air pressure causing us to be tossed about like a toy. Battling the controls, Nils increased engine speed in a bid to keep us level. On we went, punching our way through a never-ending wall of cloud. I'd been through horrendous storms before, flying with Father in his hog-nosed Junkers over Norway's mountains and fjords. He'd always assured me that we'd be fine, that our chances of being struck by lightning were a million to one, that by altering course or gaining altitude we'd avoid the worst of it. Now I felt less sure. Whereas Father's plane had three engines and a wingspan of almost a hundred feet, the canvas-covered airframe of the Lizzie felt far less solid, her single engine screaming, her mere fifty-foot wingspan all that was keeping us airborne. I could sense Freya's nerves getting the better of her as she hung onto the straps of her harness for dear life. Loki busily chewed his piece of gum as if it would be his last.

'It's no good,' Nils shouted. 'Visibility's zero, and all this electrical activity is playing havoc with my compass. I'm going to have to descend. We must get below this cloud. Sit tight. We'll be fine.' His voice sounded full of hope rather than conviction.

I felt the contents of my stomach rise as Nils adjusted the propellers to their coarse pitch, then pushed his control column forward and the plane's nose fell away. The angle of dive was brutal. Everything shook and rattled as if the strain would tear the plane apart.

As we emerged through the cloud base, rain hammered against the cockpit windows with such renewed ferocity I thought that the Perspex panes might crack. Nils struggled with the controls to bring us out of the dive as if wrestling an angry polar bear to the death. He was one man against the raging storm and inexorable pull of gravity, and had only his strength and the Lysander's one relatively puny engine to defeat the laws of physics. Gradually he gained the upper hand and the plane's nose began to lift. Levelling out at three hundred feet, he wiped his brow to clear the sweat that had seeped out from beneath his flying helmet.

'Guess that must be the Seine,' Loki announced.

I leaned across and pressed my nose against the window: although everything looked distorted and blurred, I was able to make out the winding satin sheen of a broad river below. As my eyes adjusted, I saw lights too – those of small villages and towns.

'By my reckoning we've passed Rouen,' Nils declared. 'Not far now. I'm going to keep the river to our right. Keep your eyes peeled for the loop and any signals from the ground. Let's hope they hear us coming.'

It was approaching two o'clock in the morning. All being well, Laval's team would be in position, eyes raised towards the heavens, ears straining to detect the drone of our engine; once they'd spotted us, they'd point their torches upwards and flash them until we landed. Other members of our reception committee would be armed and ordered to take up defensive positions in case any German patrols came sniffing.

The large patch of land enclosed by the sweeping loop of the river was flat and, most importantly of all, virtually uninhabited apart from Laval's farm. Trees close to the riverbank also meant that anyone in Les Andelys on the opposite side would have difficulty observing the goings-on. Even if they did, they'd have to cross the river in order to investigate. That would buy us precious time.

'Tight bend ahead,' Loki shouted. 'Bet this is it.'

'Torchlight to starboard,' Nils informed us. He sounded mighty relieved. 'Three long flashes followed by two short. They're signalling that it's safe to land. Right on cue. Hang on, I'm going to turn and go straight in.'

Freya screamed, 'Look out!'

A sheer wall of stone loomed in front of us.

Chapter Three
France

Nils slammed his control column hard back and as far to the right as it would go. The Lysander's nose lifted sharply as we rolled through ninety degrees. It all happened in the time it took me to gasp in fright. I braced myself for an impact I expected to send us into a dizzying tailspin: we'd surely drop out of the sky like a dead wasp, possibly splashing down into the river. Instead, we continued climbing and rolling all in one movement, finishing upside down. Our hats fell off, and Freya's suitcase flew off Loki's lap and crashed against the cockpit's canopy. Luckily, through sheer fear, I'd tensed up and gripped the other case tightly between my knees. Nils completed the roll and levelled out. His language was unrepeatable. 'Are you three OK?'

'Think so,' I replied, helping Loki to retrieve the case containing the radio set that had bashed the side of my head and come to rest on my shoulder. 'I guess that was the castle.'

Frantically looking left and right, Nils agreed, 'Must've been. I'm going to land from the opposite direction as I don't fancy risking that again. Say a prayer and wish me luck.'

Completing several tight turns, Nils lined the plane up towards the flashing lights and began our final approach.

Loki looked across at me, puffed out his cheeks and shook his head. Even in the dark I reckoned I could tell that the blood had drained from his face. Freya simply shut her eyes.

It seemed to take for ever. I wondered what Laval would be thinking as he watched us coming in to land from the wrong direction. Loki breathed heavily and muttered under his breath. My mouth suddenly felt bone-dry. Freya was on the verge of freaking out. Our near miss had unravelled our nerves.

The textbook method for landing the Lizzie was to glide her down, throttle back – suicide in these windy conditions. Instead, Nils had to use an engine-assisted approach, keeping the pitch of the propellers in their coarse setting for maximum control. It also meant we came in fast; very, very fast. He gave us a running commentary: 'Winding back tail-actuating gear. Brake pressure OK. Airspeed one hundred and twenty. Almost there . . . almost there . . . Fifty feet . . . forty . . . twenty . . .'

The main undercarriage briefly touched down, but Nils deliberately didn't throttle back in case he decided to abort at the last moment. It meant we rose a good thirty feet back into the air before dropping again, this time striking the earth quite hard. We passed one torch beam, then another, and another. We bounced along like a pebble skimming across a pond. I'd counted six torches when a gust of wind pushed us sideways and lifted the starboard wing. An awful realization struck me – we might overrun the landing strip. And we were heading in the *wrong* direction. Coming down again with a thud that jarred my spine, Nils throttled back. This time we lifted just a few feet before he cried out, 'Oh, no . . . Hedge! *Brace!*'

A loud crack and a ripping noise accompanied a savage, jolting deceleration, so savage that it threw us forward — only our harnesses saved us. Smacking onto the ground, the Lizzie skidded, rocked, and then violently pitched forward, her propellers ploughing into the ground and splintering into pieces on impact. With a terrifyingly loud scraping noise and the unmistakable sound of metal twisting under immense force, we crunched and juddered to a stop. I felt dazed and confused as noise and mayhem were replaced by silence, interrupted only by the wind and rain, a faint hissing, and the ticking of hot metal. Feeling oddly light-headed and fuzzy, I drew breath and reached down to undo my harness.

Freya unfastened hers and shot forward. 'Something's wrong. Nils isn't moving. Nils? *Nils?*'

Shaking Nils by the shoulder only made his limp head rock to and fro. He was still breathing but out cold.

'Smell that? Fuel vapour! She might go up in flames at any moment. We've got to get out!' Loki yelled.

The cockpit was so cramped that you couldn't swing a dormouse, let alone a cat, but I managed to reach past Nils and use my fingertips to shut down the stalled engine properly by pulling the carburettor cut-out control on the left-hand side of the instrument panel; then I turned off the main ignition switches and fuel cock.

'Come on, Finn – no time to waste, we've got to get out,' said Freya, frantically tugging at the handle to release the sliding canopy. 'We'll have to pull Nils out too.'

Our hurried exit from the plane was met by a cluster of torches shining into our faces through heavy, slanting rain. The beams were blinding and disorientating. There were voices too, chattering in French, sounding confused. A figure reached out and grabbed Freya's hand, helping her down the ladder. Loki followed, and I passed the two cases out to him. Then I swung out, grabbed hold of one of the struts supporting the wing, and clambered round to Nils's part of the cockpit. The Lizzie's wings were attached to the top of the fuselage and supported by angled struts beneath; that was partly what made her look like a giant dragonfly. Nils's canopy wouldn't budge, no matter how hard I tried. I hammered a fist against the Perspex and shouted, but Nils didn't respond. He remained slumped forward. Drastic action was needed. Unbuttoning my coat, I reached into a large inside pocket and removed my revolver.

'What the hell are you doing?' Loki shouted. 'She's about to explode.'

'It won't open. Got to release the catch on the inside somehow.' Holding the gun by the barrel, I hammered the grip against the Perspex again and again. The canopy failed to crack or shatter. In desperation, I turned the gun round and took aim.

I felt someone tugging hard at me. 'No! Leave it,

Finn. Don't shoot or you'll go up with her. The blast from your gun will ignite the fuel.'

'But we've got to save Nils, Loki. We've got to.'

'Wait!' Loki climbed up the other side and began bashing the canopy with his fists. The catch finally released. I returned my gun to my pocket, and we slid the canopy back and leaned in. 'Nils? Can you hear me? Are you OK? Damn it. He's still out cold.'

Together we managed to haul him out. Laval's men emerged through the darkness to help us, reaching up to take the bulk of Nils's weight and carrying him a safe distance away before lowering him gently to the ground. I jumped down. Freya grabbed a torch from one of Laval's men, sank to her knees next to Nils and set about checking him over.

An extremely large figure splashed through muddy puddles towards us. The beam of someone's torch briefly lit his face – a face I could only describe as sinister. An old hunting rifle was slung over his broad shoulders. Rain dripped from his massive beard and from a matted mop of thick black hair. '*En voilà du propre!*' he bellowed. He *was* right. It was all one hell of a mess.

'*Monsieur Laval?*' I called out.

'*Oui.*' He raised his torch and shone it at each of us in turn. '*Trois souriceaux aveugles?*'

'Yes – I mean, *oui*, Monsieur Laval, three blind mice.'

Dropping to my knees, I saw that Loki was hurriedly loosening the collar of Nils's flying jacket while Freya was taking his pulse. Nils appeared to be coming round.

'He's in a bad way. He's bleeding from his mouth . . .

He needs a doctor – *fast.*' The horror caused Loki to choke on his words.

Laval barged me out of the way. Crouching down, he prised open Nils's eyelids and shone his torch into each eye in turn. Nils's pupils reacted by getting smaller, and Laval murmured, '*Bon!*' He turned his head towards Freya. '*Pouls?*'

'About one hundred and ten per minute. Oh, erm, *cent dix.*'

'*Bon!*' Laval gazed at Nils for a second, and then prodded him in the stomach with his finger. Nils let out an agonized groan and tried to curl up, clutching his belly. Laval clicked his tongue against the back of his teeth and cursed. '*Merde!*'

'*Docteur? Hôpital?*' Freya shouted at him.

Laval blew a huge sigh. '*Oui.*' He stood up. '*Jacques,*' he called out. A man came running, and Laval spoke quickly to him. The man nodded, turned and ran off.

Loki was fuming. 'Laval, you should have warned us. You know the rules. You're to advise us of any obstacles near the landing strip or have them removed before we arrive.'

The huge French farmer stared at him in disbelief.

'We flew in from the wrong direction,' I said, trying to remain calm. 'It's not his fault.'

'Yes it is!'

Laval shook his head. He said nothing, but I could tell he was riled by Loki's accusation.

In her best French, Freya began explaining to Laval what had happened. He listened for a few seconds and then roared, '*Taisez-vous!*' and when Freya ignored him, he switched to English, bellowing, 'Shut up! I'm trying to think.'

He shifted his torch beam towards the Lizzie, and we saw the full extent of the damage: her nose was resting on the ground and the tailfin pointed upwards at an angle of thirty degrees. The rear undercarriage was missing. We all stared at her, anticipating a hideous explosion, a blinding, ferocious fireball, a beacon of flame that would betray our arrival and bring the enemy running. But she didn't explode, didn't give us away. I wiped sweat from my brow and took stock of our surroundings. The field had been given over to growing cabbages – the muddy ground was strewn with what looked like small footballs.

'We must move what's left of your aircraft before daybreak,' Laval announced. 'Otherwise our little game will be up. The enemy will see it from the road.'

Semi-conscious, Nils whimpered like a fox that had received a mauling from a pack of hounds. He reached out and grabbed the sleeve of my coat tightly. 'I'm sorry, Finn. Bad idea . . . Should've stuck to the rules . . . Should've landed from the east . . . It's my fault . . . Don't blame them.'

'Don't worry, Nils. We'll get you to a doctor. Try not to talk. Save your strength.' I glanced up and saw a look of fearful desperation on Loki's face. Nils was a good friend. He'd helped us a great deal since our arrival in England; he'd also flown Spitfires alongside my father in the Battle of Britain. There was a strong bond between us, and I was damned if I was going to let him end his days in some soggy French field, or get captured by the Krauts and see out the rest of the war in a prisoner-of-war camp. 'We've got to get him to your farmhouse, Monsieur Laval.'

'Yes, but you'll have to carry him. I've sent Jacques to fetch a doctor from town – a doctor who knows better than to ask awkward questions.'

Several more of Laval's fellow *résistants* arrived, clutching rifles. He spoke to them quietly, and they hung on his every word. I barely understood any of his instructions, although I did hear him say something about *cheval de trait*, which I think had something to do with horses. Freya translated: 'One of Monsieur Laval's men will take us to his farm. Laval's going to fetch his draught-horses and harnesses and will drag the Lysander to the barn.'

Peering around, Laval asked his comrades, '*Où est Le Môme?*'

A woman pointed her gun into the darkness. Laval shoved two fingers in his mouth and whistled loudly in that direction. Moments later a boy dressed from head to toe in dark clothes, his face blackened with burned cork, came charging at full lick across the field. He skidded to a stop. '*Oui, mon oncle.*'

Laval spoke gruffly to his nephew and, when the boy's attention drifted towards us, gave him a sharp cuff across the back of the head as a reminder to concentrate. Once Laval had spoken, the boy tore his cap off and held out a clammy hand to greet us. His English was perfect.

'Pleased to meet you. My uncle's asked me to take you to his house. Please, come this way. Quickly. We can't be sure when the next German patrol will come across the river. George and Eric will help carry your friend.' He gestured towards two shapes to my left. 'Probably best to bring him piggy-back and take it in turns. By the way, my name is Ross, although most call me *Le Môme*. It means the "The Kid".'

Chapter Four
The Kid

Laval's farmhouse nestled amid a small cluster of semi-derelict buildings on the edge of woodland. Torrents of rainwater cascaded off roof tiles and spurted from bust guttering as we entered a yard awash with stinking cow dung that had formed slurry several inches thick. The Kid thumped the farmhouse door open and hollered out to Madame Laval. A large, buxom woman appeared wearing a stained apron and clutching a bread knife. 'Ross? *Dieu merci!*' Startled, and slightly off-balance, she stepped back to give us room to lug Nils through the doorway.

I was immediately struck by a wall of warmth radiating from the kitchen range, and there was a sweet, smoky tinge to the air from the burning of damp logs. Madame Laval hurriedly swept some dishes and cutlery off a large wooden table. Loki and one of Laval's men carefully lowered Nils onto it. Teeth clenched, Nils clutched his stomach. His distress proved contagious: just seeing him like that made me jittery and unable to think straight. Freya grabbed a cloth, moistened it, and began mopping Nils's brow while offering soothing words. Turning to Ross, she asked anxiously, 'How long until that doctor gets here?'

Unsure, The Kid shrugged.

Keen not to hang around, George and Eric shook our hands, wished us luck and departed into the night.

Overcome by events, I slumped down onto a chair and buried my head in my hands. The bump caused by the heavy suitcase radio now throbbed incessantly and added to my misery. Loki paced the room. The Kid's gaze followed him. 'You're not English, are you?'

'No, we're American,' Loki replied. 'I'm Johnny Stevens. That's my brother, Simon,' he added, gesturing in my direction, 'and that's our sister, Lorna. Best not to ask any more questions. What you don't know can't harm you.'

It was really weird being introduced as Simon, as if it wasn't really me, but someone by the name of Simon standing behind me. But the lies flowed naturally from Loki's lips, and neither Freya nor I reacted in any way that might cause doubt. There was just one tiny flaw – not in what Loki said, but how he said it.

'You don't *sound* American,' The Kid countered. He was clearly suspicious of us. 'I'm thirteen, and you're not much older than me!' A quizzical crease formed on his brow.

'We don't all sound like those cowboys you see in the movies, you know,' Loki parried irritably, giving him a stern *Shut up* stare.

'We're from the East Coast, a town in Connecticut. The accent is more subtle there,' I interrupted, hoping it would satisfy the boy's curiosity. 'What about you, Ross? Your English is perfect.'

'That's because I *am* English. Well, half English. My

dad fought over here in the last war, and after the Armistice decided to stay, get married and settle down. But he sent me to school in England for a few years – a rat-hole near Canterbury.' He turned his attention to our two suitcases. 'Does one of those contain your wireless set?'

'Yes,' Freya replied while continuing to mop Nils's brow.

'Can I take a look?' The Kid ventured across the room to where the two suitcases stood behind the door.

'Leave it!' Loki snapped, the threat in his voice enough to halt Ross's advance.

'Later, maybe,' I said steadily, trying to calm everyone down. 'Lorna, perhaps you should send a message to HQ letting them know our situation. They'll be worried when Nils doesn't return on schedule.'

'What? Oh, let's wait and see what the doctor says first, Simon,' Freya replied. It took a second or two for her to realize I was talking to her. 'And let's pray that the radio wasn't damaged during the crash.'

The elderly Dr Renault was not best pleased to be dragged from his bed in the early hours, asked to trudge through the foulest of nights to visit a patient whose discovery could land him in prison or maybe place him before a firing squad. Nevertheless, he removed his jacket and rolled up his sleeves, draped his stethoscope about his neck, and began examining Nils.

Madame Laval boiled some water on her range for making *ersatz* coffee – brewed from chicory and acorns, it made a passable alternative to the real thing – and offered us bowls of thick vegetable soup from a large pot on the range. While we nervously awaited the doctor's pronouncement, Loki wanted to learn more about the local set-up. Ushering The Kid into the next room, we gathered around the hot embers of a dying fire to dry out, and set about questioning him. If the lanky thirteen-year-old was to be believed, Laval's group comprised about a dozen local men and women, effectively a closed network. Apart from welcoming new arrivals like us, they'd not undertaken any serious forms of resistance. This lack of direct action seemed to annoy The Kid immensely.

'What's the point,' he argued, 'of carrying guns and having endless secret meetings if all anyone ever does is talk? *Yak, yak, yak.* That's all they do. Sit around on their arses, talking and drinking until dawn. My uncle's the worst. Everyone looks up to him. God knows why, although it's probably because his dad was a bloody hero in the last war. People round here are always saying, *Tel père, tel fils* – like father, like son.'

'Things take time to organize, Ross,' Freya offered by way of consolation. 'Patience is needed.'

'Ha! All he needs to do is say the word.' He slumped down onto a threadbare chair, picked at a loose seam and curled his lips in disgust. 'If words alone could win this war, we'd have thrashed the Krauts months ago. That's what Luc says.'

'What about your father? Is he working for Laval?' I asked.

The Kid shook his head. 'When the Krauts came, Dad wanted to leave for England. He figured an Englishman over here would be in for a rough time. So we packed our bags and headed for Dunkirk, hoping to hitch a ride with either the British Expeditionary Force or French soldiers being evacuated across the Channel. God, it was a nightmare. Utter chaos. Nobody knew what was the hell was happening, and shells were exploding all round us. We got separated. Dad made it aboard a boat. Yours truly got stuck behind, and so I came to stay with Uncle Laurent.'

'And your mother?' asked Freya.

'Died giving birth to me. There were complications.'

An awkward silence filled the room.

'Who's Luc?' Loki piped up to change the subject while bending towards the embers to warm his hands.

'My best friend. He's like me − can't bear to sit by and do nothing either. So we don't.'

'Meaning . . . ?'

The Kid glanced towards the door and lowered his voice. 'We do loads of stuff together. Got the Krauts running in circles chasing shadows. Only last week we broke into a supply depot and nicked a load of food. Nearly got caught, but we were too fast for them. Luc's as quick as lightning and not frightened of anything. The Krauts around here are fat and lazy − mainly old geezers too unfit to fight at the Front. So we take advantage. When they first arrived, we kept moving the road signs, turning them round, swapping them over, changing the village names and altering the distances.

That confused them. Nowadays, we go out at night on *patrol*, letting down the tyres of any Kraut vehicles we stumble across, smashing the windscreens and peeing into the petrol tanks. Only yesterday Luc dusted a whole load of German uniforms on their way back from the laundry with itching powder.' A thought struck him and his eyes widened. 'Say, did you bring any carborundum powder with you?'

Startled, I flashed Loki a frown and got one in return. How did The Kid know about carborundum? The powder was a grey crystalline substance that acted as a powerful abrasive. Boffins working behind the scenes in Special Ops had developed it for us to use in the field. We'd tried it out in training. You mixed it with lubricating oil and applied it to wheel bearings. Its effect was to make the bearing seize up, the vehicle eventually grinding to a halt. 'Maybe,' I said, still frowning. In fact we did have some in our suitcase – disguised as a tin of talc – but I didn't want to encourage him. 'How come you know about that stuff, Ross?'

Ross leaned forward in his chair and spat onto the embers of the fire. He stared at his boiling spit as it bubbled and frothed into steam. 'Luc and me were going to use it to disrupt the German supply train that runs from Paris to the coast every Thursday night. We've planned the raid: how to get in and out of the goods yard at Rouen undetected, how to avoid the guards when applying the powder. The last agent who came through here had some. He showed us and explained how best to use it. Even left me a small tin of it as a present. But I don't think I've got quite enough for a *whole* train.'

'Did he now? When was this?' I asked.

'Some while back.' He looked up at us to judge our reaction and saw that Loki wasn't impressed by his plan. 'I know what you're thinking. You're just like my uncle . . . They're not childish pranks, you know. What we do really hacks the Krauts off.' He grinned with satisfaction. 'And that makes me happy.' Flashing a glance at Loki, he added, 'I mustn't say any more about it. Our plan's secret. What you don't know can't hurt you.'

Though riled, Loki let the remark pass.

'And your uncle approves?' Freya sounded doubtful.

Ross whispered conspiratorially, 'No.'

Loki tore into him. 'You and this Luc are foolish idiots. If the Germans catch you, they'll make you talk. You'll end up spilling everything, including all about your uncle's network. There are lives at stake.'

'No, we wouldn't. *Jamais! Never!*' he countered angrily. He looked mortally wounded at the very suggestion.

'Can't blame them though,' I said, instantly winning Ross's approval. 'We were just the same back—' Freya's scowl cut me short. Hell, I'd nearly let something slip. I was about to say *back home in Norway*, blowing our cover. Fortunately Ross wasn't really listening. He'd begun to worry that he'd already said too much.

'For God's sake don't go telling Uncle what we've been up to or else he'll give me a thrashing to remember. Luc will get into a shedload of trouble too.

His dad's the bloody Mayor. His old man's supposedly still in charge of this god-forsaken dump, but he does exactly what the Krauts tell him. Doesn't want to rock the boat. At least, that's what he keeps telling everyone. He's always saying, *Tout ce que tu voudras, mais laisse-moi tranquille!*'

Freya laughed sarcastically and translated: 'Anything for a quiet life? If only . . .'

'Of course, Luc's dad has his own way of resisting – mainly through insisting on doing things the French way whenever possible. The French are famous for their red tape. It slows things down; frustrates the Krauts no end. His dad's like an annoying fur ball caught in the throat of a vicious tomcat. Marvellous!'

Madame Laval appeared in the doorway and spoke to Ross. From the look on her face and slight tremble to her lips I guessed the news wasn't good.

'Sounds bad,' Ross said. 'Your pilot needs to be taken to hospital. He must have an operation. Monsieur Renault's worried that he might be bleeding inside.'

Freya drew breath and stiffened with determination to confront our situation head-on. 'Right! Where's the nearest hospital?'

'Well, there's one in Rouen and another in Beauvais. They're closest. But you can't take him to either of those.'

'Why not?'

'Too dangerous. Crawling with Krauts. Everyone knows that! Ever since they stumbled across a group of doctors hiding Jews from the SS, they check every patient going in and out. As you can imagine, any doctor or nurse found helping the enemy will be in big trouble, so few are willing to take the risk. And I don't suppose your pilot's got a set of French identity papers on him, has he?'

Ross was right. Nils's already perilous predicament now seemed ten times worse. 'There must be a way,' I said, tearing at my hair. 'There must be. What about Paris? There are dozens of hospitals there. One of them will surely take him in without papers, especially if we get him out of his flying uniform and dress him in borrowed civvies.'

We heard Monsieur Laval return, and moved back into the kitchen. Peeling off his sodden jacket and stamping his boots to shake off the mud, Laval nodded to Dr Renault and then approached the kitchen table. Leaning forward, he peered closely at Nils, studying him as if he was a fancy sculpture on display at the Louvre. Renault filled him in on the diagnosis; as he did so, now and again, Laval's eyes turned towards us. His stare was intense, questioning. I reckoned he was wondering why three such young people had been delivered into his care – I had little doubt we weren't quite what he expected.

Madame Laval handed her husband a towel for drying his hair. Beneath a thin veneer of calm she clearly wished that her husband wasn't leader of the local partisan group, that we hadn't arrived on her doorstep, and that we'd all go away pretty sharpish.

Casting his towel aside, Laval finally broke his silence.

'The doctor has made your pilot as comfortable as he can. I'm sorry, but I'm afraid there is nothing more we can do for him. We must just hope that his injuries aren't too serious. Maybe you can ask your superiors to send another plane to pick him up.'

'No!' I shouted. 'We have to get him to a hospital.'

'Impossible,' he snapped back.

Ross saw my look of utter horror and quickly suggested, 'Uncle, what about the American Hospital in Paris, in Neuilly? They'd treat him, wouldn't they? After all, our visitors are American too. They'd be able to persuade them to take their pilot.' He turned to us. 'It's a very famous hospital. One of the best in France. Your pilot will be well cared for there, and by all accounts the Germans leave the place pretty much alone.'

'Yes, they'd probably take him,' Laval replied, 'but how on earth do we get him there?'

'Surely there's an ambulance somewhere in town,' Loki said. 'And if you don't trust the driver, we'll steal it and drive it ourselves.'

Laval snorted. '*Imbécile*. There are no ambulances. There are no cars. The Germans confiscated them all. Even if they hadn't, there's hardly any petrol to go round. The situation's terrible. All we're left with is our horses and carts. There are checkpoints on every road into Paris to contend with too. And to go anywhere you need permission from the Germans: special papers, permits, loads of documents. We have none of these things. *None*.' He began pacing the room angrily.

The situation had clearly deteriorated since our last mission into France.

'Ross, are there really no cars or trucks?' Freya asked.

'No. Hardly any for miles. The Red Cross did run a voluntary ambulance service for a while after the invasion, but not any more. Within days of the Germans arriving in Paris, they'd commandeered all the decent vehicles. Most others are banned from the city's streets. The only ones you'll see now have either WH licence plates – they're reserved for the Germans – or SP ones, which are for a few French men and women who've found favour with the enemy for some reason or other. Untrustworthy types. Although . . .'

'Although what?' Freya was quick to encourage what looked like an idea brewing in Ross's head.

'Well, there is one. Not a car exactly. Mother Thérèse has a sort of truck. She lives at the convent a couple of miles from here.'

'What do you mean a *sort* of truck?' I asked.

'To tell you the truth, it's a bit of a monster, really. Very noisy. And it's rather slow. Actually, I'm lying. It's *really, really* slow. But it works. Because it runs on gazogène rather than petrol the Krauts don't mind them using it. It has plenty of room in the back too . . . to hide your friend.'

'And she'd let us borrow it?' asked Loki, somewhat doubtful.

The glint in Ross's eye told me that he would find a way of persuading her. I wondered what on earth gazogène was: he tried to explain but failed miserably;

all I could fathom was that it was some sort of petrol substitute and involved wood. I suspected he'd got confused – how could a vehicle run on wood? Nils drifted off into a deep sleep. Whatever the doctor had given him was powerful medicine.

Laval showed the doctor out, Madame Laval pressing a bottle of red wine into his hand in gratitude. Dr Renault said he would return first thing in the morning to check on his patient if a runner came and asked for him. I could tell from his manner that he'd rather no one did. No sooner had the door closed than Laval's expression darkened. 'I want to know why you've come. Why have they sent you? You don't look much older than *Le Môme* here. This is all madness. What are the crazy British doing sending us children?'

'We can't say. It's safer all round if you know nothing of our mission,' Freya replied. 'But you should be in no doubt that it's important.'

'It's good that you think we're too young to be involved in such work,' Loki added. 'That's precisely why we're here.'

Laval shook his head slowly.

'Our intention was to take the train into Paris,' I explained. 'We have business there, starting in Montmartre. We have all the necessary travel papers. But after what's happened to our pilot, we'll have to revise our plans. We won't abandon him.'

Laval sank wearily onto a chair and stared blankly towards the range, his brow etched with worry. Our arrival had landed him with problems he could well do without: a wounded British airman lying on his kitchen table and a bust-up British aircraft languishing in his barn.

Freya picked up her suitcase. 'Time for me to check the radio's OK and contact our HQ. Maybe they *can* send another aircraft. I'll transmit from the barn. We should have a look at our Lysander too. See what state she's in. Ross, lead the way.'

'She's virtually a write-off,' I said, shining a torch at the Lizzie and seeing the shattered stubs that were once propellers. 'One thing's for sure — she won't get us home, not unless someone's got a new set of props ferreted away somewhere.'

There was some good news — the radio was working fine. Having received the reply from HQ, though, we almost wished it wasn't. Flustered, Freya tore off her headphones. 'No chance of another aircraft for at least a week. *A week!*'

'What do they want us to do?'

'Press on with our mission. That has top priority.'

'And Nils?'

'Do what we can for him. But we're not to jeopardize or delay locating the White Rabbit. Although they didn't say it exactly, the message came through pretty loud and clear — Nils is expendable!'

'No way.' I paced the barn, gingerly rubbing the throbbing bump on my head.

A bemused Ross asked, '*White rabbit?*'

'Never you mind,' Loki snapped.

Lost in our thoughts, we didn't speak again for what felt like ages. Then Ross piped up with, 'You said earlier that you were heading for Montmartre.'

'What if we are?' Loki glared at him.

'Well, with only a slight detour you'd pass the American Hospital on the way.'

'What are you suggesting?'

'I'm sure I could persuade Mother Thérèse to either lend you her truck or maybe even drive you into Paris. In fact, it would be best if she did. She's a formidable woman. She might come in handy if you get stopped.'

'What's our excuse for driving into the city? We need a cover story,' I said. 'It's no good claiming we're on some sort of mercy dash: they'd suspect a rat as soon as we failed to produce identity papers for Nils.'

Ross pointed to a pile of sacks and boxes on the far side of the barn. 'There's your cover story, Simon. Cabbages! Oh, and some carrots, turnips and whatever else Uncle has harvested recently.'

I crossed the barn, redirected the beam of my torch, and inspected what turned out to be quite a store of vegetables. 'You mean, we could make out that we're making a delivery of essential foodstuffs to the hospital kitchens . . . ? Might work, I suppose.'

Loki put a dampener on Ross's brainwave. 'I reckon that at the first checkpoint we come across they'll confiscate it all, and in the process find Nils concealed in the midst of it. Daft idea, Ross. Madness. Monsieur Laval was right – it's impossible without having the right papers.'

Ross screwed up his face. 'Just because they call me The Kid doesn't mean I'm stupid. I've thought of that. What if you have written orders from the local German Kommandant, stating that *he's* authorized a "donation" of surplus food as a gesture of goodwill, and that his orders are to be strictly obeyed – under no circumstances should the truck be interfered with?'

Loki sneered. 'Dream on, Ross.'

'No, wait . . .' I said, realizing the boy wasn't joking. 'You know how to lay your hands on this rather special document, don't you, Ross?'

'Yes. I'm not saying it'll be easy, but there is a way, if I can persuade Luc to help us. After all, it's his dad who's got the key to the back door of the town hall – the building the Krauts are using as their local HQ. We'll break in and write the letter on the Kommandant's official notepaper. We can make sure we include all the official stamps too. Knowing Luc, he'll be up for it.' He shot Loki a glance. 'But . . .'

'But what? What's the catch?'

'It'll cost you.'

'I should've guessed. How much?'

'Shall we say a tin of carborundum powder? That last agent who passed through said it was standard issue now. So I reckon you must have some in that other suitcase of yours.' Ross spat into the palm of his right hand and held it out. 'Well, do we have a deal?'

After receiving the nod from Loki and Freya, I reached out, grasped his hand tightly and shook it. 'Yes, it's a deal. In fact, if we succeed in getting Nils to safety,

I'll order the RAF to drop ten tons of the stuff with your name on it, Ross.'

He laughed. 'No, just one tin will do. For now! Right, well, we'd better get a move on. There's a lot to be done before dawn.'

'I'll stay here and look after Nils,' said Freya. 'If he wakes up, I'm sure he'd appreciate seeing a friendly face.'

Chapter Five
Faking It

We had our first glimpse of the enemy at the stone bridge across the Seine – two sentries, smoking and chatting as they walked slowly back and forth across the span, rifles slung over their shoulders, the rain cascading off their heavy greatcoats. Somehow, we had to get past them. The three of us slunk into the deep cover of nearby undergrowth and I gestured to Ross, asking whether it was possible to circle round them and cross the river elsewhere. He shook his head.

'Do we take them out?' asked Loki, reaching for his revolver.

Ross lunged forward and grabbed his arm. 'No, Johnny, there's an easier way. All we need to do is distract them – draw them away from the bridge long enough for us to dash across unseen.'

'And how do you propose we do that?'

'With this, Johnny.' Delving deep into his coat pocket, Ross removed first a catapult and then a fistful of smooth stones. Selecting one, he placed it in the catapult's leather pouch, raised his weapon, stretched it to full tension, and aimed towards woodland on the other side of the road. Letting go, he dispatched the pebble into the dark. It seemed to fizz through the night. Two seconds later we all heard it: a quick succession of loud, dull, hollow thuds as the pebble ricocheted off trees like a marble in a game of bagatelle. The sentries heard it too. Halting abruptly, they cut their idle chatter and peered into the darkness. 'One or two more should do it,' Ross declared, hastily reloading.

The second hollow knock of pebble against tree had the sentries reaching for their rifles and striding purposefully towards our end of the bridge.

'Now for one in the water, just beneath the bridge,' Ross whispered, seeking out an irregular, lumpy-looking stone from his pocket. 'The bigger the splash, the better.' Again he stretched the catapult as far as it would go, took careful aim, and fired.

It did the trick. The splash drew the soldiers down a steep, slippery bank towards the water's edge, leaving the bridge momentarily unguarded.

'It's now or never. Stay close and don't stop, no matter what.' Ross sprang to his feet and began running, his arms pumping and stride lengthening as he gathered pace. Loki and I were right on his heels. The bridge seemed much wider once we were on it, and I felt sure the noise of six pounding shoes would give us away. Gasping for breath, we made it across undetected, and on the other side threw ourselves into some bushes.

'Let me have a look at that catapult,' I said while catching my breath.

Proudly Ross pressed it into my hand. 'My dad made it for me. Best catapult for miles. I was even offered fifty francs for it once.'

The solid Y-shaped piece of wood was furnished with

lengths of what appeared to be bicycle tyre inner tubes that had been twisted together to form an astonishingly powerful elastic. The pouch, I suspected, had once been the leather tongue of a shoe. 'Neat,' I said, handing it back. 'Is it accurate?'

'Uh-huh – I can hit an *écureuil* in the treetops at fifty yards,' Ross claimed triumphantly.

'What on earth's an *écureuil*?' asked Loki.

'A squirrel, stupid.' Ross laughed. 'People round here mostly hunt birds, though. Kill them by the thousands.'

'Why would they do that?'

'Dunno. It's a French thing. All the kids do it. Well, most. Actually, I don't. Don't see the point. Everyone thinks I'm rubbish with a catapult but they don't know that I miss deliberately. I aim for something else, like a tree or a particular branch. I hit the target eight or nine times out of ten. Luc got a German officer once, just as he was getting out of his staff car. Knocked his cap off. Luc laughed so hard he nearly forgot to run away.'

'Good fortune's going to desert you two one day,' I said.

Ignoring me, Ross stood up and pointed. 'It's not far to Luc's house.'

The Mayor's residence – a large detached villa – was situated on the main road on the western edge of town. Even in the gloom I could detect a faded splendour. Just beyond the eight-foot-high wrought-iron gate whose hinges squeaked horribly when we opened it, Ross signalled for us to remain hidden while he crept along the drive, stooping midway to gather a handful of fine gravel. This he threw in small amounts at one of the upstairs windows until, after what seemed like for ever, it slid open and a bleary-eyed head poked out.

Ross and Luc exchanged various gestures in what amounted to a silent argument, until Luc finally nodded and vanished back inside.

'Ross's plan is crazy,' Loki muttered, hunching his shoulders against the wind. 'How did we ever let him talk us into it, Finn?'

'Out of desperation. No one came up with anything better.'

I glanced at my watch – four in the morning – and suddenly felt incredibly tired. Shivering, and unable to stop myself yawning, I sat down next to the gate, cursed the gale and incessant rain, and waited patiently for Ross and Luc to return.

After five minutes Luc emerged from the house, and the two of them scurried towards us. Shorter and thicker-set than Ross, Luc nevertheless possessed a spark that left me in no doubt that the two of them were as mad as each other. After endless '*Bonsoir*'s and much hand-shaking, the four of us set off into town.

'You didn't wake them, I hope,' Ross said to Luc once we were well away from his friend's house.

Luc turned and, walking backwards, replied, '*Non!* Of course not.' He grinned. His English was good but coloured by a thick accent. 'Not even a blast from a Howitzer could wake them. They get very drunk last evening . . . again! Drank *mon père*'s best Napoléon brandy. He makes them pay for it. Ten times more expensive than usual.' He laughed. 'If this war lasts long enough, Father will be rich.'

'Who got drunk? Don't tell me – you've had to billet soldiers at home.'

'*Oui*, Simon,' Luc responded cheerfully. 'Two members of the SS. They're very polite, you know.'

'Polite!' Loki gaped in disbelief.

'*Oui*. They give Mother gifts. Always apologizing for the inconvenience. Father doesn't like them staying, of course, but there are advantages. We don't get trouble from Gestapo. Our house never gets raided. And, because Father has no choice, people can't accuse him of being a collaborator. It'll work out well . . . as long as we're careful.' We reached a junction and Luc pointed. 'It's this way to the square.'

Ross and Luc moved with all the stealth of cats on the prowl, the slightest noise causing them to freeze on the spot or dip into a doorway. Rather than talking, they signalled to one another using hand gestures that had clearly been practised; curiously, many were the same as those we'd been taught during training.

The square was deserted apart from a parked army truck and a few empty market stalls, the rain spilling from their striped awnings and pitter-pattering noisily onto glistening wet cobbles beneath. Shops, mostly with their shutters down, lay in darkness. There were just two feeble streetlamps located at diagonally opposite corners. I reckoned the absence of German sentries standing outside the front door to the grand municipal building beneath the inevitable pair of swastikas was good news too. 'This is going to be easier than I thought,' I whispered.

'*Non!*' Luc grabbed hold of a piece of my jacket and pointed to a narrow basement window, barely visible from our vantage point. 'Look hard. You can just see a little light. There's a guard's office. Usually only two or three soldiers. They're supposed to patrol every hour but I expect they're asleep. We must be careful. Not make a sound or it'll be like you Americans say – *curtains for us.*' Letting go of me, he added, 'Follow me and stay close. We go in through the back door. *Quietly.*' Delving into his pocket, he produced a key. 'I must return this to Father's coat pocket by the time he wakes up or else he'll have me sweeping the streets until I'm as old, fat and ugly as he is.'

One by one we shot across the square, diving into the black of an unlit alley. Luc hurried on ahead and frantically waved for us to join him in a large yard behind the town hall.

'I'll stay here and keep watch,' offered Loki.

Pressing up against the rear door, Luc slipped the key into the lock, turned it, and then gently prised the door open an inch. He listened out. Once he was certain that the hallway was clear, he gave us the thumbs-up and beckoned Ross and me inside. We followed him up the back staircase two steps at a time. Reaching the second floor, he pointed to one of half a dozen partially glazed doors. 'That's Herr Oberst's office – the colonel. I'm sorry but I don't have the key for it.'

I pushed him to one side and drew a fountain pen out of my pocket.

'That's no use,' Ross whispered. 'Let me break in?'

'No!' Unscrewing the pen, I tipped out into my hand the selection of lock picks hidden inside. Each slender steel rod had a differently shaped hook on the end. I tried them in the lock until I felt one connect with the mechanism. Ignoring Ross and Luc's growing impatience, I concentrated hard, trying to sense the position of the hook inside the workings. I knew what I was doing. We'd been taught back at Mulberry by one of the best: Nathan O'Connor, a professional house-breaker with more convictions than I'd had birthdays. He'd agreed to be our instructor in return for a few days away from his cell at Wormwood Scrubs. I recalled his soft Irish brogue, the timbre of his patient voice: he was forever telling us that locks needed to be picked gently; that it was no good trying to rush. Rushing got you nowhere.

With a barely audible click the lock yielded. 'Hey presto,' I whispered as the handle turned and the door opened with ease. I screwed my pen back together while the others shot inside.

'*Magnifique!* You must teach us how to do that,' said Ross, removing a small torch from his pocket. 'Let's get down to business.'

'You've been in here before, haven't you, Luc?' I observed as he ran to and fro grabbing forms out of filing cabinets and gathering up a set of official stamps. 'You seem to know where everything is kept.'

Luc glanced up. 'We help others. That is all I can say.' Licking a finger, he continued thumbing through a pile of papers.

'This is the first time we've broken in at night, though,' Ross added. 'Usually we nip in and out during the day while Herr Oberst is inspecting his men or out in the countryside giving us locals grief. We pretend we've come to see Luc's dad. Here – this is his official notepaper.' He handed me a pristine sheet. 'You must type the official order onto this, and then I'll forge Herr Oberst's signature. I've got it down to an almost perfect likeness.'

'OK. What do I write?'

'Up to you. Basically you need to authorize Mother Thérèse of the Order of St Anne's to be allowed to drive to the American Hospital in Neuilly – and make it clear that her truck must not be delayed or obstructed in any way. *Compris?*'

'Yes.'

'Good. You *can* write in German, can't you?'

'*Naturellement*,' I replied.

'*Bon!* While you do that, Luc and I will prepare the standard travel permits and documents covering the food we're transporting. With your personal order from Herr Oberst, it ought to prevent any but the most inquisitive SS officer from searching the truck. Right – heads down. You use that typewriter over there, and we'll use this one.'

Quietly we set about our tasks, listening out for any sounds outside in the corridor and wincing each time we pressed a key on the typewriter – the clacks seemed deafening but probably couldn't be heard from more than a few feet beyond the office door. Nevertheless the prospect of imminent discovery made me sweat.

After a few minutes I looked up and saw Luc and Ross hard at work together, checking each other's efforts by feeble torchlight and virtually inaudible whispers, and going about their business with a purpose that wouldn't have looked out of place in Special Ops. I decided to keep Herr Oberst's personal order short – just a few simple lines.

A cough – I froze. Boots clomping up the stairs – I shot a glance towards the door and saw a flash of torchlight in the stairwell. Luc and Ross heard it too, extinguished their torches and slunk down beneath their desk. The footsteps grew louder, the torchlight brighter. A door handle further along the hall rattled as the guard tested it to make sure it was locked. Panic-stricken, I realized there wasn't time to lock our door from the inside now. Another door handle rattled – closer. Luc dropped his torch and it clattered against the tiled floor. Had the guard heard? Luc cursed under his breath. Had the guard heard that too? Discovery was surely just seconds away. *Do something, Finn.* I was about to reach for my revolver when I had second thoughts. Struck by an idea, I leapfrogged over the desk and took two strides to gain momentum before diving, sliding bum first across the highly polished floor tiles. Reaching the door, I spun round, planted my feet, and pressed my back firmly against it.

My breaths came quick, and I fought to slow them to a shallow, silent, calm in and out, in and out. Footsteps grew louder and then shuffled to a stop. The guard was standing right outside the office, just inches behind me. I could hear him breathing heavily, as if he was old and unfit, two flights of stairs enough to exhaust him. Quietly I reached into my pocket, drew my revolver and undid the safety catch. From my other pocket I removed the silencer and began attaching it to the end of the barrel. I needed a Plan B. A very drastic Plan B. A torch shone through the glazed panel and lit the room, moving to and fro like a searchlight. Would the guard notice that one of the filing cabinets was open? That there was a piece of paper wedged in the typewriter? That a jumble of documents and official stamps lay strewn across the desk? The Germans were usually fastidiously tidy – everything filed away, their desks cleared, pens and stamps neatly arranged. I also realized with considerable alarm that the top of my head was just an inch beneath the glass. If he angled the beam down, he'd spot me. And surely my feet stuck out too far. I drew my knees up to my chin and tried to make myself as small as possible. The door handle lay next to my right ear. It turned noisily. Pressing my back hard against the door, I willed myself to be as immovable as a mountain.

I felt pressure. The door moved a fraction. Was it enough? Enough for the guard to be suspicious? I gripped my revolver so firmly my hand throbbed, and clenched my teeth hard enough to make my jaw ache.

If he shoved the door any more, I decided I'd roll away to one side, let him tumble in and shoot at point-blank range. The handle turned once more. I prepared to make my move, dreading the moment. Then . . . then the torchlight faded. The guard moved away. I dared not move a muscle – not until I was sure he was on the stairs, heading for the next floor.

Emerging from behind his desk, Luc looked shaken.

'At least he won't be back for a while,' I whispered. My observation seemed to reassure him. 'Let's finish up. We're nearly there.'

Luc applied the final inky stamp of eagles and swastikas and passed my letter to Ross for signing.

'*Done!*' Ross announced, blowing on the ink to hasten its drying. 'Now, may I suggest we get the hell out of here?'

'Sounds good to me,' I replied.

Outside, I gave Loki the nod to indicate our success. A sense of euphoria gripped Ross and Luc, and they could hardly contain themselves. 'We got away with it. Right under their noses.' Ross beamed. 'And Simon was ready to shoot that guard.'

'Well, I'm glad I didn't have to,' I said. 'That would have just complicated things.'

Luc led the way across the square, and then stopped and shook our hands firmly. 'I must get home . . . before Father wakes up. He always rises at dawn. Good luck, my friends, and I hope you all make it safely to Neuilly.' He started to head off, but stopped and turned after just a few steps. Forming a fist, he punched the air. '*Vive la*

France!' His words disturbed the night, and somewhere in the distance a dog barked.

'Right,' said Ross, gathering his wits. 'By the time we get to the convent the nuns will probably be up for morning prayers. They always rise ludicrously early. By the way, let me do the talking. Mother Thérèse can be a bit difficult.'

'Difficult?'

'Never mind, Simon. I don't have time to explain.'

Chapter Six
The Order of St Anne's

Yanking the bell pull, Ross whistled softly under his breath a tune that sounded like the hymn *All Things Bright and Beautiful*. For the first time since we'd met he struck me as nervous. It was five o'clock in the morning and my head was spinning with fatigue. Leaning heavily up against the wall, Loki looked pretty shattered too.

'Listen, Ross, are you sure we can trust them?' I asked. 'I know they're nuns, but . . .'

'Well, it's rumoured they've assisted others. That much I've heard. And I've had – how shall I put it? – *dealings* with Mother Thérèse in the past. She's originally from Dublin, you know, as is Sister Maude. Anyway, I don't think we have much choice.'

The convent was well outside town, tucked away at the end of an arrow-straight avenue lined with tall poplars. Ross had led us there without even the use of his torch; such confidence made me suspect he'd made the journey in the dark before. Impressive old medieval stone buildings formed a courtyard, one side bearing ornate ecclesiastical windows suggestive of a chapel. Ross tried the bell again. '*Allez, réveillez-vous!*' he called out. '*Réveillez-vous!*' He hammered a fist on the ten-foot-high door of solid oak planks braced with heavy ironwork.

His persistence was eventually rewarded with the clunks of hefty bolts being slid across on the inside and the jangle of keys. The door swung open, and a nun clutching a candle squinted at us. The light bathed her round, perfectly smooth face. I figured she was in her early twenties, and probably quite pretty if it hadn't been for her unflattering black habit. Her steadfast calm was replaced with a sudden look of alarm the moment she recognized Ross. '*Le Môme? Qu'est-ce que tu peux bien faire ici?*' She backed away and made to slam the door in our faces. Waving us away, she hissed, '*Allez-vous en! Allez-vous en!*'

Ross advanced and wedged one foot inside to form a doorstop. '*Non!* Summon Mother Thérèse at once, Sister Maude.' He pointed at Loki and me. 'These are my friends, Simon and Johnny Stevens. They're American. They've just *arrived*, if you know what I mean. Their friend's hurt and they desperately need your help.'

Again the nun tried to shut the door. 'How dare you show your face here.'

'Ouch! *S'il vous plaît?*' Ross held firm. 'Pleeease! You know I wouldn't dare come unless it was really, really important.'

Sister Maude dithered for a moment before finally relenting. She glanced up to the heavens. 'Holy Mother of Jesus, may the Lord forgive me!' Heaving a sigh, she stepped aside. 'Even though every fibre of my being tells me that this is a bad idea . . . you'd better come in . . . Well, don't just stand there.'

Grateful for her change of heart, we filed in.

'Mother Thérèse is in the chapel. After early prayers she likes an hour of solitary contemplation. She will not be best pleased at being disturbed. Especially not by . . .' She tutted and handed Ross the candle. 'Wait here, and don't touch *anything*. And I mean *anything*. Keep your grubby thieving little hands to yourself, Ross Munro. *Compris?* I'll go and find out whether she is willing to see you.' She spun round and headed off into an unlit passageway. She seemed to float across the flagstone floor, the candle in Ross's shaky hand casting an eerie, other-worldly flickering light about her.

'Is she for real?' Loki joked. 'She didn't seem very pleased to see you, Ross.'

Ross laughed nervously. 'No. I expected that.'

'Why?'

He hesitated before confessing, 'A couple of months ago they caught me nicking the lead flashing from the chapel roof.'

'What on earth for?' I asked.

Ross delved into his pocket, removed something and dropped it into my hand. 'Luc and me had this idea, you see. We wanted to melt it down to make bullets. As you know, you need lead for that. Lots of lead. So far we've only managed to make about a dozen.'

The bullet was large, slightly misshapen and surprisingly heavy. I laughed so loud my voice echoed. 'What – and you were going to create your own arsenal?'

Ross grew deadly serious. '*Non!* They are very special bullets. Big ones. Each will have a name etched into it –

names of those we know are collaborating with the Germans; names of those who've informed on others.'

'And what exactly are you going to do with these bullets?'

Ross's reply was venomous. 'Send them as a warning, Simon. Let them know that *we* know who *they* are.'

'Bloody hell,' Loki responded. 'That would make them think twice.'

From Ross's bitterness I suspected that, among the *they*, there was someone particular that he was thinking of. 'Sounds to me like it's personal, Ross. I'm right, aren't I? Some sort of personal vendetta?'

He nodded. 'My sister . . .'

Wafting along briskly, Sister Maude returned, calling out and interrupting Ross. 'Follow me. You're in luck. Mother Thérèse will see you in her office.' She clapped her hands loudly, as if trying to scare off a flock of pigeons. '*Vite! Vite!*'

Although we'd been granted an audience, I had the distinct impression that our presence was an unwanted intrusion — an impression that gained weight the moment we entered Mother Thérèse's office and saw the stern look on her face. Sister Maude ushered us in and stood behind us.

'I thought I said you were never to come near this place again, Ross Munro,' Mother Thérèse thundered, her voice unnaturally deep. She was a vast woman too, dominating the small, sparsely furnished room. Apart from a desk and chair there was only a wooden cross and a picture of Jesus nailed to the whitewashed walls.

'Yes. I'm sorry,' said Ross meekly. 'But it's important. *C'est une question de vie ou de mort!*'

'A matter of life and death, you say,' she responded cautiously. She peered at Ross intently, as if trying to reach into his mind, to separate truths from lies. She leaned back in her chair, folded her arms and sniffed. 'Very well, I'm listening. You have five minutes to explain yourself.'

Ross left nothing out in his description of events so far that evening, and Mother Thérèse listened to his rambling explanation with the patience of a saint. When we handed over our newly forged papers authorizing the delivery of vegetables, she scrutinized them at length, holding them to within inches of her face and angling them against the candlelight. Ross concluded with, 'So, you see, we need to borrow your truck. It's the only way. Better still if you would be willing to drive it to the American Hospital for us.'

Mother Thérèse leaned forward in her chair and studied Loki and me in turn. 'So you've just arrived, you say? Let me see your identity papers.'

Loki and I handed them over.

'From Connecticut. That's on the west coast, isn't it?'

'No, east,' I replied instantly, reckoning she knew full well it was on the eastern seaboard of America – that she was simply testing us.

'Why are you here?'

'We can't tell you anything. You must surely realize that?' Loki responded firmly.

'I see. And is your pilot really as seriously injured as *Le Môme* here makes out?'

'The doctor believes so,' I replied. 'Says he needs an urgent operation.'

Mother Thérèse exchanged glances with Sister Maude. 'You do realize what will happen to us all if we get caught?'

'Yes,' I said. 'We understand we're asking a great deal of you. It might be far safer for you not to come with us. Let us simply borrow your truck. If we get caught, you can tell the Germans that we stole it.'

'Yes, that would be safer for us, but far more dangerous for you, I think. The Germans wouldn't be convinced by a truck driven by people of your age, and I very much doubt your forged orders would see you through. They're a suspicious lot, especially at the check-points close to Paris. No, you'd need us to accompany you.'

'Then you'll help us?' asked Loki.

Rising majestically from her chair, Mother Thérèse placed her hands on her ample hips, contemplated a moment, sighed, and then threw her shoulders back. 'Very well. We will help you get your pilot to Neuilly. Sister Maude, fetch Sisters Agnès and Lavinia. Tell them to meet us in the coach house in five minutes. Time to fire up *Belzébuth*!'

'At once, Mother Thérèse.'

'And then come back here to collect *Le Môme* and his new partners in crime.'

While Sister Maude ran her errand, Mother Thérèse paced the room. 'We'll aim to be at Monsieur Laval's farm by seven o'clock, Paris by lunch time, and home in time for evening prayers.' She stopped and looked Loki and me up and down. 'Just the two of you, is it?'

'No. There's a third. A girl, Lorna,' Ross replied.

Mother Thérèse tutted irritably. 'Too many of us. We'll need a cover story.'

'Say we're just hitching a ride,' I suggested. 'You sit up front and we'll ride in the back.'

She nodded. 'Yes, that would be best. But . . . why are you heading into Paris? If we're stopped, the Germans will demand to know.'

I'd already thought about this and had an idea. 'We'll say we've got to meet someone at the American embassy in Paris about making travel arrangements for returning to the States.'

'What's the embassy's address?' she asked.

'Number two Avenue Gabriel, not far from the Place de la Concorde.'

'Good. And who is it that you'll meet there?'

'Mr Charles Thorpe, Chargé d'Affaires,' I responded instantly.

'Is there such a man, or have you just made that name up?'

'Oh, he exists,' I said.

'And what if the Germans test out your story? Supposing they make us wait while they put in a telephone call to the embassy? Will your version hold water?'

'Yes. Don't worry. Charles Thorpe can be relied upon.'

In our briefing back at Mulberry, the brigadier

instructed us that should we get ourselves into any nasty scrapes, provided our cover identities withstood scrutiny we could seek assistance from Charles Thorpe. He had been alerted to our imminent arrival in Paris. Charles Thorpe was more than just a Chargé d'Affaires; as well as the head of the diplomatic mission he was also a member of a recently formed organization known as the Office of Strategic Services, or OSS, an American intelligence service not entirely dissimilar to Special Ops. He would help us if he could.

'Very well, then – I think we have everything covered.' Mother Thérèse came towards Ross, towering over him; he visibly shrank into her shadow. She reached out and grabbed him by the collar, twisted it in her fist and lifted him onto his toes. Nose to nose, she thundered, 'Trouble, young man, runs through your veins and follows you around like an evil smell. I've heard about what you get up to with that friend of yours, Luc, the Mayor's son. I'd hoped the thrashing I gave you after our last little encounter had knocked some sense into you, but I fear there's no taming the Devil's number-one disciple. After today's little adventure I don't want to see your face within a mile of here. Understood? Or else you'll learn that you don't actually have to be dead to discover the fires of Hell.'

'*Oui, Mother Thérèse.*' Ross looked genuinely terrified.

'Earlier you mentioned you had a sister, Ross,' I said as we hurried along a labyrinth of dark passageways behind a scurrying Sister Maude.

He nodded. 'Sophie. She's older than me. She got left behind too. Like me she wanted to do something to fight back. A man from our village said he knew of a way of getting information about what the enemy was doing over to the British. Sophie agreed to help. Her job was to cycle about and note where the enemy was, what defences they were building – stuff like that. She wrote coded reports and left them at pre-agreed drop-off points.'

'We call them dead letterboxes,' Loki said.

Ross nodded. 'Yes, but someone informed on them, and one night the Gestapo came for her. She was living with a friend on the other side of town. They surrounded the house, broke down the door and took her.'

'And you think you know who spilled the beans to the enemy – hence the bullets with names on them?' I said.

'Yes. A neighbour next door to our old house. Ages ago, my dad got into a dispute with him over a piece of land, a tiny corner of a field, barely big enough to build a shed on. It's crazy how some arguments get out of hand. I mean, it's hardly worth a life, is it?'

'Is she still alive?' Loki asked hesitantly.

'Yes, for now. She's in Fresnes prison, awaiting trial. It's a few miles to the south of the centre of Paris. A vile place. It's huge, it stinks, and it's full of all sorts – from those who've simply spoken out against the Germans, to what Uncle Laurent refers to as "intellectuals possessing the wrong point of view", common criminals, murderers, arsonists, and members of the Resistance like Sophie. I go and visit her when I can.' He stopped and, wavering unsteadily, peered down at his boots. 'Of course, they'll execute her. *Eventually.* Uncle Laurent said that I had to prepare myself for it. Be ready to deal with that horrible day when it comes . . . That I couldn't do anything about it so I shouldn't dwell on it . . . That it was all beyond my control.' His words came out awkwardly, broken. He lifted his head and looked at me. Even in the gloom I saw his eyes glistening. 'Spies and Resistance people are always shot, aren't they? I mean, that's what the Krauts are always telling us.'

'You never know,' Loki offered. 'Maybe because she's young they'll let her off with a prison sentence instead. It sometimes happens. Don't give up hope.'

Ross wiped his sleeve across his face. 'Perhaps. Her lawyer's trying to get her trial delayed. He says the longer it gets put off, the better . . . It's all he can do. And some trial it'll turn out to be. More a tribunal really. There'll be Sophie on one side and the prosecutor on the other, both being heard by a panel of senior German officials. No jury, no fairness. The outcome is a foregone conclusion . . . Maybe we can win this war before . . . Or maybe—'

'Keep up,' Sister Maude called out shrilly. She clapped loudly again too. 'No time for idle chatter.'

We had to run to catch up. I knew just how Ross felt, and desperately wanted to tell him so – make him realize he wasn't alone. My mother and sister were in prison too, in Norway. Unlike Ross, however, I had an additional burden to carry: their predicament was largely my fault. I'd had some secret documents the Nazis wanted, and they knew I had them so they came after me. Arresting Mother and Anna was their way of applying pressure. But Loki and I had escaped to Britain. Like Ross, every day I fought the feeling of utter helplessness, the sheer frustration tying me up in knots inside. I knew only too well that trying to console him was as pointless as trying to swim the Atlantic Ocean with one arm tied behind your back. We had more in common than he could ever imagine.

Sister Maude reached the end of a passageway, threw open a door and dashed out into the driving rain. '*Vite!*' she shouted, gesturing for us to follow her without delay. Crossing a courtyard, we arrived at the coach house. Its two heavy wooden doors were wedged open and oil lamps glowed within.

'This is Sister Lavinia,' Sister Maude announced, 'and that's Sister Agnès.'

Cradling a heavy armful of chopped wood, an industrious Lavinia smiled at me as she trotted past. Sister Agnès's head appeared from beneath the raised bonnet of the truck. Both looked about eighteen. With hands covered in grease, Sister Agnès waved a spanner in the air to acknowledge our arrival. Neither, I quickly realized, spoke much English.

'And that's Belzébuth,' Sister Maude declared, gesturing towards the truck.

'Do you mean Beelzebub?' Loki asked. 'That's another name for the devil, isn't it?'

'Yes, Johnny. You wait till you hear it running,' Ross replied. 'Then you'll understand. It gets unbelievably hot, billows black smoke, clatters like it's about to explode, and farts from the exhaust like the devil after he's eaten a large bowl of my aunt's bean stew.'

Clucking about like a mother hen, Sister Maude got us organized. 'Sister Lavinia would appreciate your help. We'll need a lot of wood to get to Paris and back. It must be loaded onto the truck. There's a special place for it next to the burner.'

As we moved back and forth, lugging armfuls of kindling and depositing them in a neat stack by a six-foot-tall metal cylinder erected behind the truck's cabin, I began wondering what on earth we were doing. I paused with Loki to examine the contraption.

The elderly truck had seen better days. Two tyres were bald, and the rest of it appeared to be held together with rust. There were strange pipes running from the tall metal cylinder towards the front of the vehicle. Welded to the front bumper was another, smaller cylinder that had been mounted horizontally; the pipes entered one end, exited the other, and then disappeared beneath the bonnet through a makeshift hole in the bodywork. There were modifications under the bonnet too. The back of the truck was empty apart from a few folded tarpaulins, which I realized we'd need to haul over the metal framework to create a covered place for trans-porting the food and for hiding Nils.

'So, how does this thing work?' Leaning over the engine, Loki tried to figure it out. 'I mean, I know you say it uses wood. Do you use it to heat water and create steam? Only that surely wouldn't work with this type of engine.'

'*Non*,' Sister Maude replied. 'It's not a steam engine. We burn the wood in here.' She pointed to the big cylinder behind the truck's cabin. 'With very little air. That's the secret. The wood only partially combusts, and gives off gases like methane. These gases — what we call *gazogène* — then pass through that filter at the front, and then it is ready to be used by the engine.'

'And it really works?'

'Sort of,' Ross replied, passing us with the last of the fuel. 'I've seen her do twenty miles per hour ... *downhill*, of course. Uphill she'll do maybe ten, at a push.'

'And how far is it to Neuilly?' I asked.

My unwelcome question remained unanswered.

Sister Agnès lit the fire in the tall cylinder, closed the access hatch, stood back and waited.

As Mother Thérèse entered the coach house, I saw her slip something into a pocket in the folds of her habit. In the lamplight I got only the briefest glimpse, but I was pretty certain it was a pistol she was intent on concealing. I recalled what Ross had said — that there were rumours the nuns had helped others — and began to wonder whether such assistance had extended beyond merely offering sanctuary.

The coach house began to fill with smoke leaking out of the contraption.

'Belzébuth will be ready to go in ten minutes,' Sister

Maude announced triumphantly. Then she coughed violently.

'*Excellent!*' Mother Thérèse seized hold of Ross roughly. He flinched. 'I want you and your friends to run on ahead to your uncle's farm and warn him of our arrival. Make sure your airman's prepared for the journey and that all the food is ready for loading. The earlier we set off for Neuilly, the better. We're going to have to use crates or sacks to make some kind of space for the airman to hide in. And give me those papers you've forged. I'll need them when crossing the river.'

Back at Monsieur Laval's farm, our return was greeted by a fretful Freya. 'You've been gone ages. Nils doesn't look good at all. The doctor left some pills just in case, and I've given Nils as many as I dare. They should make him sleep.'

Nils had been moved into the room adjoining the kitchen, and a new fire lit in the hearth to keep him warm. He lay there on a sofa covered with blankets; his breathing sounded shallow and quick.

'How are you?' I asked, crouching beside him.

He spoke to me in slurred Norwegian. 'Finn, you're back. Not too good, I'm afraid. Guts hurt like hell. But don't worry – I'm sure I'll pull through.' He winced and, turning his head away from me, groaned.

'Listen, we're taking you to the American Hospital in Paris. Ross says it's one of the best in France. Everything's arranged. We're just awaiting our transport. You've never seen the like, Nils. A truck powered by gazogène.'

Nils reached out, felt for my arm and pulled me closer. 'Finn, listen to me — you mustn't risk compromising your safety for me. You must get on with your mission. That's the way it works. You have to let Monsieur Laval turn me over to the enemy.'

'*What?* Are you *mad*? No way!' I tore myself free and stood up.

'I'm in RAF uniform, Finn. I'm an airman. They'd put me in one of their hospitals, treat me, and then, when I'm better, they'd move me to a POW camp. I'd be all right, Finn. Really.'

'No more talking, Nils. Try and rest,' said Freya soothingly. Then, ushering Loki and me out of Nils's hearing, she whispered, 'I've been thinking it over. He's got a point, you know. The Germans *would* treat him reasonably well because he's in uniform. Laval could simply put the Lysander back where we crash-landed and alert the Germans that a plane came down during the night. Nils's chances might be better that way. He might not survive the journey into Paris. What do you think?'

Loki pulled a face. 'I . . . I . . . I don't know, Freya. Perhaps. But we've risked a lot already just organizing things. In doing so we've placed other lives at risk too.' He looked to me. 'What do you reckon, Finn?'

I shook my head. 'Over my dead body. Nils is our friend. We can't abandon him to the Germans. Not unless it's a last resort. And think about it — the Germans would be suspicious of a Lysander flying in such bad weather. They'd realize it was some sort of Special Op, and that would mean they'd interrogate Nils – maybe withhold treatment until he talks. We know all about their hideous methods. No, to hand him over is the worst possible idea. If Nils talked, everything would be compromised: Laval, us, our mission even. Don't worry, it'll all be fine. We'll get him to Neuilly with Mother Thérèse's assistance. And when he's better, he can get back to England via one of the escape routes.'

Freya slumped down onto a chair and covered her face with her hands. 'This is turning into a nightmare.' She looked up at us both questioningly. 'What are we doing here, anyway? It's all madness. Searching for someone who calls himself the White Rabbit. I mean, it's . . . it's ridiculous.'

Freya's outburst took Loki and me by surprise. She was normally so cool, calm and level-headed – but she hadn't finished. Waving her hands in the air, she added bitterly, 'Even men like Trébuchet can't find him. And he's a leader with the Paris Resistance, with local knowledge and contacts. For God's sake, what chance have we got?'

'A lot's at stake, Freya,' I said. 'Remember what Sir Hugo and Walker showed us – Project Starfish and the fake airfield. Who knows what other secrets might be at risk? At the very least we need to find out the truth about Claude.'

Drawing up her knees and wrapping her arms about them, she cursed the world. 'That stupid Sir Hugo Foster and his crazy Ministry of Tricks. Why doesn't he simply build new decoys in new locations, Finn? Or . . .

or . . . dream up some other incredible illusions to outwit the Luftwaffe? That would make the problem go away. Then it wouldn't matter what happened to Claude, and we wouldn't need to be here.' She looked up at us. 'We wouldn't need to hunt him down and, and . . . and we wouldn't have to decide whether to kill him or not.'

Loki put his arms around her and gave her a hug. 'I know, Freya. We all feel the same. I'm asking myself what on earth we're doing here too; why we ever agreed to this mission. We've all been through a lot in the last year or so — we've seen enough of this war to last a lifetime. Until now, it's all been for a cause we believe in: the fight for freedom from Nazi tyranny. But this time . . .' He looked across as if waiting for me to say something.

'What we're all feeling is only natural. Look on the bright side: we may never find him,' I said.

'Huh!' Freya scowled.

'Remember our plan,' I added. 'We might be Claude's best chance. Let's take it one step at a time like we agreed.'

There was a cough at the door. We all turned and saw Ross. 'Sorry to interrupt. We need to get the food supplies ready.' Jabbing a thumb over his shoulder, he added, 'I'd appreciate a hand. I've explained to Uncle what's happening. He's not best pleased. Those vegetables will need paying for, or else he claims he'll starve this winter.'

'Damn your uncle,' Loki snapped.

Ross had this slightly guilty, knowing look about

him. I wondered just how long he'd been loitering in the doorway, or eavesdropping from the parlour. I was sure he'd been listening in on our conversation. Nils and I had spoken in Norwegian. Freya, Loki and I had switched to using our real names. In an unguarded moment we'd slipped up. Ross now knew far more about us than was safe.

Chapter Seven
A Close Shave

'You're all going to wind up in Fresnes prison just like *Le Môme*'s sister,' Monsieur Laval informed us as soon as we set foot inside the barn. He threw another sack of carrots onto an accumulating pile next to the barn door. 'It's madness.' He paused to glare at us. 'If I could stop you, I would.'

'We'll make sure you get paid for all this,' Loki said, grabbing hold of some potatoes. 'We'll instruct London. They'll pay you over the odds. You'll make a good profit.'

'It's not about making a profit,' Laval bellowed. 'It's about having enough to eat. Last winter many starved. Do you have any idea what it's like over here? The Germans steal most of our food, and if we dare complain, it means trouble comes knocking at our door.'

'We're grateful for all your help,' I said, trying to fashion myself into some sort of peacemaker. 'We know the risks you're taking. Ross is very courageous too. You should be proud of him.'

Snorting disdainfully, Laval glowered at his nephew. '*Le Môme* is a wild child. There's no taming him. He takes after his father — reckless, without a thought for the consequences. The way he carries on he'll be the death of us all.'

Ross shrugged and tried to look innocent, as if butter wouldn't melt in his mouth. Loki and I laughed at him, and he laughed too. Monsieur Laval didn't see the funny side.

We set about sorting out crates and sacks until we reckoned we had enough to fill the truck and create a space to hide Nils. Then it was a question of waiting for Mother Thérèse and her truck.

Laval turned his attention to our Lysander. 'A beautiful little aircraft. She's probably beyond repair . . . although . . .'

'You know about such things?' Loki asked.

'Uncle Laurent hasn't always been a farmer,' Ross interrupted. 'He trained as an engineer. His brother's one too. Uncle Paul runs the garage in town. He did the conversion of Mother Thérèse's truck last year. He's a genius. He can fix anything.'

'But not this, I fear,' said the big Frenchman, stroking his beard thoughtfully. 'Such a shame. Of course, it's too dangerous to keep her here. I'll have to get rid of her. Break her up into smaller pieces. What I can't burn I'll bury in my fields or dump in the river.'

A strange racket outside distracted us from the Lizzie. Peering out of the barn door, we saw the first hint of approaching dawn on the horizon and the familiar shape of Beelzebub hissing, clattering and bouncing her way slowly off the lane and onto the track leading up to the farm. Smoke leaked out of the large cylinder and left a trail behind the beast. With a loud bang she came to an abrupt, shuddering stop about fifty feet from the farmhouse. Mother Thérèse leaned out of the window and called out, 'Sorry we took so long. More wood, Sister Agnès, more wood!'

Loki leaned on my shoulder, groaned, and whispered into my ear, 'This all suddenly seems an incredibly bad idea, Finn. That heap will never make it all the way to Paris.'

Ross had hearing as sharp as a bat. 'Yes she will. She's made the trip before.'

Within the hour all the crates and sacks of food had been loaded, and we'd created a cavity large enough for Nils to lie in. A few spare blankets offered a little comfort. Loki and I helped him aboard. He proved quite a dead weight. No sooner had we got him in position than he started drifting in and out of consciousness.

'I hope I didn't go too heavy on those pills the doctor left us,' said Freya. 'He might fall asleep and never wake up.'

We placed our suitcases in the cavity too, and then concealed it with a number of sacks. With Beelzebub refuelled, we were ready for the off and said our goodbyes.

Laval shook our hands. Warily he said, 'Supposing your plan goes horribly wrong . . . the Germans will want to know where you got your food from.'

'Don't worry. We won't mention your farm. We'll say we stole it,' Freya replied.

'*Merci.*'

As Loki began lowering the tarpaulin to cover the back of the truck, Ross leaped on board. 'Hey, what do you think you're doing?' Loki tried to grab him.

'Hitching a ride. Thought I'd go and visit my sister. Any objections?'

Loki looked at Freya and me, but we just shrugged and so he let go of Ross.

'Thanks. And I've been thinking ... I can show you around Montmartre if you like. I lived there for a while.'

'Listen, Ross,' I said. 'We're really grateful for all the help you've given us. Without you, none of this would be possible. But once Nils is safely in hospital we have our mission to carry out, and that's something we three have to do alone.'

'Why?'

'Well, that's just how it has to be. Sorry.'

Ross slumped down and sulked. At least, I thought he was sulking. He was unusually quiet and distant. He was either sulking or *scheming*.

For the next hour Beelzebub clunked, banged and hissed away from Les Andelys, our route following the twists and turns of the river. Every ten minutes or so Freya called out to Nils to see if he was awake. Despite the noise and discomfort he slept soundly; his breaths were shallow and barely audible unless we crouched down and pressed our heads into a small gap between two sacks of carrots.

Eventually Sister Lavinia honked the horn as if celebrating that we'd made it that far without breaking down, before turning onto the main road signposted for Paris. Peering out of the back of the truck, I was struck by the absence of other traffic. There were few motorized vehicles on the road. Occasionally cyclists waved as they overtook us, and a couple of horse-drawn carts travelling in the opposite direction even more slowly than us waved and shouted '*Bonjour!*' to the nuns sitting up front. In the rare instance we heard the approach of an engine, we presumed it was military and were quickly proven right. On each occasion Sister Lavinia slowed to a crawl and hugged the roadside ditches as motorcycles and trucks crammed with Wehrmacht soldiers trundled past at speed, their grim faces barely giving us a second glance.

Despite the bumpy ride and incessant racket, tiredness won out, and soon I was dozing off, only to be awoken twenty minutes later by singing from the cab. The voices of Sisters Agnès and Lavinia were strangely beautiful and comforting. I had no idea what it was they were singing about, but it quickly sent me into a deep sleep.

'Wake up!'

I felt myself being shaken. I opened an eye and saw Freya's face. She held a finger to her lips. 'There's a checkpoint up ahead. Mother Thérèse has told us to sit tight. She said she'll deal with them, but we should be ready with our identity papers. I've told Nils not to make a sound. I just hope he heard me. He didn't reply.'

I yawned and lifted myself up onto my elbows. 'Well, I guess we're about to find out how good a job we did with those false documents.'

'Better be prepared for trouble, just in case, though,' said Loki. He'd been peeking out of a crack in the tarpaulin. 'There are three of them. One's standing well back from the road to give the other two cover.'

'What's he carrying?'

'MP40 sub-machine gun. He looks a little twitchy, as if he's expecting trouble. The others have their rifles slung over their shoulders, though, so they'll present less of a problem.'

'So we go for the one with the machine gun first. Agreed?' I said.

Freya nodded and, gently moving Loki to one side, glanced out. 'Yes, I can get him from here.'

Ross looked shocked.

'Lorna is the best marksman among us by far,' I explained. 'In fact, she's the best our organization has ever recruited. She was taught by her father.'

Freya's father was Heimar Haukelid, the great Norwegian hunter and outdoorsman. From an early age he'd taken her out hunting elk in our homeland's vast wilderness and taught her how to shoot.

Ross removed his catapult from his pocket.

'Put that away,' Loki barked.

Ross slid it back and looked down at his feet in embarrassment.

Loki stuffed his silenced revolver into the back of his belt and did up his coat. 'We're almost there. Act normal. We're just delivering food. Nothing more.'

The brakes squealed, and Beelzebub juddered to a stop. I heard Mother Thérèse's booming voice, and the

German sentry attempting to speak French with an appalling accent.

'What are they saying?' Freya whispered, straining to hear.

'Mother Thérèse is explaining about the food,' Ross replied. 'And she's sticking to the story you agreed earlier. She's telling him that there are three Americans in the back hitching a ride.'

'You heard all that? I must be going deaf,' Loki whispered.

Ross scrambled on top of a pile of sacks. '*Vite!* He's going to check us out. Pray your pilot doesn't make a sound.'

'Stay calm,' I said.

I needn't have worried. Ross reached into an inside coat pocket and took out a pack of playing cards; he shook them out, and speedily dealt out four hands of five cards each. 'Poker. You all know how to play, I assume?'

'Yes.' Loki grabbed one of the hands.

The barrel of a rifle slid underneath the tarpaulin and lifted it. Next a soldier's face appeared. He was barely old enough to be shaving, and had acne so fierce that just looking at him made you want to scratch your own chin. I watched him do a quick head count. He seemed confused. Panic fizzed inside me like a mild electric shock. *Oh hell*, I thought, realizing Mother Thérèse didn't know that Ross had sneaked aboard at the last moment, and that meant the number of passengers didn't tally: when things didn't add up, that's when the enemy's suspicions were raised. With a sweep of his arm, the soldier hauled back the tarpaulin, took two steps backwards and held his rifle at the ready. '*Raus! Raus!*' He gestured for us all to climb out.

Standing in a persistent drizzle while our papers were scrutinized, Freya leaped in with an explanation of Ross's presence: 'He's a farmer's son. Going to help unload at the other end. Isn't that right, Mother Thérèse?'

Mother Thérèse hid her astonishment well. At the sight of Ross, a look of surprise and fury passed over her face before she regained her composure and confirmed Freya's story. For their part, Sisters Agnès and Lavinia stood there quietly, meekly, their faces pictures of innocence.

Ross's identity papers received a thorough inspection. Ordered to turn out his pockets, he reluctantly proceeded to produce his catapult, a selection of stones and marbles, a screwdriver, flick-knife, several empty bullet cartridge cases, a box of matches, a snot-filled handkerchief, his crudely cast oversized lead bullet and, strangest of all, three eggcups. He put all the items down on the top of the side-car of the motorcycle, which the Germans had parked at the side of the road. The soldier looked on with amusement, as if as a boy he too had once filled his pockets with all sorts of really useful rubbish.

Mother Thérèse proffered her identity papers, along with those of Sisters Lavinia and Agnès, together with the various documents we'd forged in the early hours.

Their mission to deliver food to the American Hospital appeared to be accepted without question. Just as I was beginning to think everything would turn out well, the second soldier, who'd been examining our American papers, called the third soldier over – the one carrying the sub-machine gun. A discussion ensued, and I observed that for some reason they were comparing Loki's and my details.

Loki caught my eye and mouthed, *Any ideas?*

I shrugged, but was fearful that in the mad rush to get our false documents ready, HQ had made a fatal error. I recalled checking mine over very carefully: everything had seemed in order. But I knew that even the tiniest mistake could land us in hot water. False documents could save your life or get you killed – it all depended. No cover story was ever completely watertight. If you delved deep and thoroughly checked up on all the details, eventually the truth would emerge. I'd heard stories of agents who'd managed to pass through dozens of checkpoints and random searches without a single hint of trouble but who, through sheer bad luck, had made a fatal blunder, one so small and innocent as to seem trivial. One man had been stopped by the French police for riding a bicycle at night without lamps – he was detained and his identity thoroughly checked out, at which point things unravelled: the police realized the personnel number on the identity papers didn't really exist. My heart began thumping a warning inside my chest.

Loki slowly loosened a few buttons of his coat. Freya

edged towards the side of the truck. I glanced about, taking in our surroundings, trying to figure the best direction in which to run should we be forced to make a break for it. I noted the absence of traffic in both directions. We were alone on this dull and dreary wet winter's morning. The road was straight for almost as far as the eye could see, and bordered on both sides by farmland. Woods offering decent cover lay some distance away. Mother Thérèse, hands on hips, grew impatient and took to complaining about all the delays. Her sharp tongue did nothing to endear us to the soldiers – normally someone venting their spleen like that would suffer dearly for their impertinence; I think Mother Thérèse's religious dress offered her protection.

One of the soldiers beckoned me closer. 'Simon Stevens?' He eyed me suspiciously.

'Yes,' I replied, trying to appear casual, unflustered.

'He is your brother, yes?' he asked in broken English, nodding towards Loki.

'Yes, he's my brother. Why?' I didn't like the soldier's sceptical tone, and when he pulled a face indicating that he was plagued with doubt, I knew something was seriously wrong. Was it simply that Loki and I didn't look like brothers? He was large and as strong as an elk, and I was much smaller. Was that it? No, I decided, there was more to it.

'Then tell me this,' snarled the soldier at me. 'How is it that your dates of birth are five months apart? How can that be possible?'

'I . . . I . . . well . . . erm,' I stuttered. Alarm bells were ringing loud in my head. *Shit, shit, shit.* How could we have overlooked such a mistake?

'Different mothers,' Freya said calmly.

The soldier snapped his head round and glared at her. '*Was?*'

'Our father got divorced and remarried. Simon is our stepbrother – *mon frère utérin.*'

The soldier didn't understand.

'*Mein Stiefbruder, Dummkopf,*' Freya snapped irritably.

The penny dropped. The soldier nodded. Reluctantly he handed my papers back.

'Pure genius, Freya,' I whispered as I stuffed my papers safely into my pocket.

But as we rejoiced at the prospect of getting on our way again, a faint noise came from inside the truck. Nils was waking up. If he groaned any louder, it would herald disaster for all of us. Sisters Agnès and Lavinia must've heard him too: they both spontaneously began humming, and then broke into song in an attempt to drown out his voice. It was well-meaning but nevertheless a huge mistake. One of the soldiers stared at them incredulously. Then he grew suspicious. The young nuns stopped singing abruptly and fidgeted self-consciously, their cheeks glowing red with embarrassment, both clearly regretting their sudden outburst. A weird silence took over, the air thick with tension. Nobody moved. Nobody spoke.

Ross remained on my left, next to the Germans' motorcycle and side-car. The contents of his pockets were spread out on it. He casually began gathering them back up. 'Time for a little distraction, Simon,' he whispered to me. I glanced at him and he winked. He called one of the soldiers over. 'Hey! *Komm!* Want to see a trick?'

I risked a furtive glance towards the back of the truck and willed Nils to remain silent. If he was still groggy from all the pills Freya had fed him, he might not even realize where he was, or that remaining still and silent was a matter of life and death for all of us. The spotty young soldier wandered across to the back of the truck and peered inside. Mother Thérèse stopped fiddling with the large crucifix dangling on a chain about her neck and reached down into the folds of her habit. Loki surreptitiously slid one hand behind his back, ready to draw his revolver. Freya readied herself too. The soldier continued to gaze into the truck. *For God's sake, don't make a sound, Nils.* I stiffened in readiness and flashed glances at the others. They too were like coiled springs, ready for action.

The soldier whose attention Ross had attracted suddenly laughed out loud. '*Bravo! Friedrich, Gerd – komm, seht euch das mal an!*' He waved his comrades over.

Having placed the three eggcups upside down, Ross was sliding them about wildly on the top of the side-car. He stopped and the soldier pointed to one. Ross lifted it up – nothing. He then lifted a second to reveal a marble. The soldier scratched his head. '*Nochmal! Nochmal!*'

As Ross obligingly repeated the trick, switching the positions of the eggcups at lightning speed, the other two soldiers were quickly distracted too. The first soldier guessed again as to which cup hid the marble, and again got it wrong. The other soldiers insisted on having a go. Every time they guessed wrong, no matter how hard they concentrated, but each time it only made them more insistent on having another try. *Clever*, I thought. *Very clever. Simple too*. The soldiers' job standing out in the foul wind and rain for hours on end was a miserable one. Seeing a magic trick was a welcome alternative to the endless boredom. Within minutes, who we were and what we were doing there seemed to have been forgotten. And Ross had drawn them well away from the back of our truck . . . and, thank God, Nils hadn't made another sound.

'Where did you learn how to do that?' asked Loki as we rattled on towards Paris.

'Dad taught me.' Ross gathered up the poker hands he'd dealt when we'd been stopped, gave the pack of cards a quick shuffle, and then fanned them out. 'Choose a card, any card,' he said to Loki with supreme confidence. 'Memorize it and then put it back. Don't let me see it.'

Loki obliged, choosing the six of clubs which, shielding it with a cupped hand, he showed Freya and me. He returned it, and Ross set about shuffling the pack vigorously, even cutting it several times using just one hand. Then he stopped and turned over the top card – the six of clubs. 'That was it, wasn't it?' he said, grinning.

'How on earth . . . ?' Loki demanded in astonishment.

'Ah, it's a secret. We magicians have to swear never to reveal how it's done, under pain of death! Dad taught me loads of tricks.' He stared at the cards longingly. 'Madura the Magnificent, the best magician in Paris — maybe the whole of France.'

'Your father was a magician? A real one, I mean?' I asked.

'Yes, Simon. Or should I say, Finn . . . I overheard you talking earlier, and it wasn't in English, either. Or French. What was it? Danish?'

'Norwegian,' Loki confessed. 'Best stick to our cover names.'

Ross nodded. 'Not far wrong then, was I? Don't worry — your secret's safe. Yes, my dad used to thrill packed audiences every evening at various clubs in and around Montmartre. But people were always demanding more and more spectacular tricks. Dad's hero was the famous Harry Houdini, the greatest escapologist who ever lived. Dad even met him once. One day he decided he'd try out some of Houdini's famous tricks, like being bound in chains and immersed in a huge tank of water. Dad had to escape before he ran out of breath. And then . . .' He hesitated. 'And then one night it all went horribly wrong.'

All ears, Freya moved closer to us and asked, 'What went wrong?'

'He couldn't get free. You see, all the padlocks holding the chains were real, and Dad held a master key in his mouth. Once immersed in the water, the top of the tank was sealed and covered in a cloth. Dad had to drop the key into his hands, which were always bound to his chest, just beneath his chin. Then it took just seconds to undo the padlocks. One night he had really bad stomach cramps, and accidentally dropped the key. In the dark tank he couldn't find it . . . He nearly drowned . . . They had to break the glass with sledge-hammers to save him . . . And after that he refused to perform in public ever again. That's when we moved to a village not far from Les Andelys. Dad got a job as a waiter in a nearby hotel.'

A distressed whimper emerged from under the pile of sacks and crates. Freya called out to Nils. Receiving no reply, we hurriedly shifted enough of the food for Freya to be able to crawl in under the crates. 'Nils. *Nils!* . . . Hand me a torch, Loki.'

Loki reached under and handed her his torch. An anxious few moments' wait resulted in Freya hurriedly backing out on all fours. 'He looks really awful. White as a sheet. Burning up too.' Scrambling up over the sacks, she hammered on the rear of the cab. 'Go faster!' she shouted. 'As fast as you can!'

Chapter Eight
The American Hospital

Reaching the outskirts of Paris we negotiated three further checkpoints without trouble. The entrance to the American Hospital on the fashionable Boulevard Victor Hugo in Neuilly was impressive; passing through a stone and brick archway, the drive led to a ramp and ended in a turning place outside the main doors. The hospital was the biggest I'd ever seen: six storeys high and comprising a central block with matching wings. Beelzebub shuddered to a halt. We heard the opening and slamming of doors as the nuns piled out of the cab. Freya lifted the tarpaulin and jumped down. Loki, Ross and I began shifting the food. A nurse wearing an ankle-length white dress apron, white shoes and white hat came running out of the hospital. She took one look at our mode of transport and bellowed something in French while gesticulating wildly with both hands. I roughly translated it to mean we couldn't park there.

Mother Thérèse strode forward and took control of the situation. 'Summon Dr Alexander,' she demanded. 'We've got an injured RAF pilot in the back. He needs to be seen to at once. *At once*, do you hear me?'

The nurse's expression instantly changed from one of

annoyance to one filled with purpose and deference to the nun's imposing figure. She nodded, spun on her heels, and hurried back inside.

'Hey, Finn,' whispered Loki. 'Are you thinking what I'm thinking?'

'Probably. Mother Thérèse knows the doctor's name.'

'Exactly.'

'Maybe—'

'Don't just stand about like flagpoles,' Mother Thérèse barked. 'Start unloading.'

Moments after we'd begun hauling sacks and crates off the back of the truck, two orderlies carrying a stretcher emerged from the hospital at a jog, accompanied by the nurse and a middle-aged doctor. He exchanged glances with Mother Thérèse but said nothing, instead hurrying round to where Ross was busily emptying stuff out while Loki and I had begun trying to lift Nils to his feet.

'Wait!' the doctor shouted. 'Don't move him.' He jumped aboard, knelt, and began examining Nils. 'How long has he been like this?'

'We crash-landed this morning. About two o'clock,' I said.

The doctor glanced at his watch. 'Ten hours. And has he been unconscious all that time?'

'No. Comes and goes. One moment he's awake, the next he's asleep. Another doctor gave him some pills.'

'What pills?'

'I'll show you,' said Loki. He leaped out and ran over to Freya. She removed a small bottle of pills from her pocket and handed it to him. 'These,' said Loki, passing it over.

Dr Alexander inspected the bottle. 'I see.'

'Will he live?' I asked, unsure I wanted to hear the reply.

'Early days. He's in shock. No bones broken as far as I can tell, but he almost certainly has internal injuries.' He called out to the orderlies to come and transfer Nils to the stretcher. 'Take him straight to theatre,' he instructed, before turning his attention to the nurse. 'Nurse Stanley, get scrubbed up. We're going to operate immediately. And check on our blood supplies. I've a feeling this man's going to need at least five units.'

We all pursued Dr Alexander as he hurried along behind the stretcher towards the hospital entrance. He looked over his shoulder and called out, 'No. There's nothing you can do for now, so make yourselves useful. Take the food round to the courtyard.' He pointed. 'And tell Chef it's all unofficial. He'll know where to hide it. Mother Thérèse, a word in your ear, if you please.' He eyeballed Loki, Freya and me. 'And I'll talk to you later. So don't go wandering off anywhere.'

As Nils, Dr Alexander and Mother Thérèse vanished inside, I felt a wave of relief sweep over me. We'd made it. Now it was up to the surgeon's skill. We'd done all we could for now. I sensed someone at my shoulder and turned. Sister Lavinia smiled at me and grasped my arm gently. '*Une prière* . . . erm . . . Time to say a prayer.' She squeezed my arm and smiled again.

Her eyes shone with . . . well, the only word that

sprang to mind was *kindness*. 'Y–y–yes,' I stuttered. 'And thank you, Sister Lavinia. Without your help Nils wouldn't have made it this far. We owe you all a great deal. And we owe Ross much too. It was all his idea.'

Hands in pockets and scuffing his feet at the ground, Ross had wandered a little way away from the rest of us and seemed lost in thought. '*Le Môme*'s not as bad as Mother Thérèse thinks,' I added. 'Did you know his sister's in Fresnes prison?'

Sister Lavinia struggled to understand me and so I tried again in my rubbish French. Against the odds, I think she actually figured out what I saying because she nodded. Having searched for the right words, she replied slowly, 'It must be hard . . . but it is hard for many . . . That is war . . . it brings out the worst.'

'True. But it brings out the best in some too,' I said. She blushed and looked away.

Off in search of the courtyard, Loki had disappeared down the side of the hospital. He returned at speed with a look of alarm. 'There's a German car parked round there with two soldiers.'

'Doing what?' Freya asked.

'Didn't hang around to find out.'

'Wait here,' I said. I ran to take a look for myself, fearing that we'd driven straight into trouble. The sight that greeted me as I peeked through a bush was, to say the least, unexpected; in fact it was downright bizarre.

One soldier was sitting lazily on the bonnet, a lit cigarette stuck to his upper lip. He was talking to a completely bald, chubby fellow in white aprons. A wad of money changed hands, the soldier placing it in his tunic pocket. The other soldier was leaning into the back of the car and swearing loudly. Then I heard a hideous, piercing squeal. Bent double, the soldier emerged with a piglet gripped beneath one armpit, a second held by the scruff of the neck. Then four more piglets tumbled out of the car and scattered across the yard. The other soldier leaped off the bonnet and, together with the bald man in the apron, began trying to round them up, arms outstretched, calling to them, trying to intercept them as they sped frenetically to and fro.

Somehow they managed to shepherd the piglets into an outbuilding. The man in the apron shut the door and, laughing, pretended to wipe sweat from his brow. He shook hands with the two soldiers and they clambered into their car. I waited for them to drive past before cautiously approaching the man, who was still chuckling to himself. '*Monsieur?*' I called out.

Surprised to see me, and quite possibly fearful of what I might just have witnessed, he stopped laughing immediately. Flexing his enormous fists, he stormed towards me. He was the sort of thick-set, heavy-boned bloke you didn't want to mess with; the sort who could probably lift twice his own considerable bodyweight. He growled something at me, and was about to seize hold of me when the others arrived and Sister Agnès explained that we came bearing gifts for his kitchen.

Overjoyed at the bounty of food Beelzebub yielded,

Chef instructed us to carry everything to his storeroom, located next to the shed containing the piglets. We could hear their grunts and squeals, and it made Chef anxious – not least because their discovery by the Germans would land him in a whole heap of trouble. Keeping pigs was strictly prohibited, punishable by a lengthy prison sentence. And yet it was Germans who'd delivered them. Confused, I broached the subject with Chef, Freya doing a decent job as translator.

'But they weren't really Germans,' Chef replied with a wry grin. 'They were Frenchmen dressed up as Germans.' He chuckled again. 'It's the only way.'

In a covered corner of the courtyard several cauldrons were set over open fires. From one, Chef offered us small bowls of boiled vegetables. The others, I quickly realized, were used for sterilizing hospital instruments and bed linen. Having eaten, we sat down and shivered, waiting for news about Nils.

'Ross, you must still have a way to go,' Freya said. 'To visit your sister, I mean. You said Fresnes was to the south of the city.'

Ross nodded.

'Go on if you want to. We'd understand. If you leave it too late you'll have to find somewhere to stay the night. And then there's the curfew to worry about. Don't want you getting arrested.'

He thought for a moment. 'I'd like to stay to find out about your pilot. Then I'll go.'

Freya had placed our suitcases beside her and I could see she was toying with the idea of killing time by making a transmission to HQ, to let them know that we'd made it into Paris, that Nils had reached the hospital. 'Bad idea,' I remarked, and she understood what I was referring to. 'In case the Germans have detector vans nearby. Send one later, when we get to Montmartre.'

Sisters Agnès and Lavinia found some shelter from the wind and, side by side on their knees, offered up prayers.

At four o'clock, with the light fading, Mother Thérèse reappeared. 'We must be heading home,' she said wearily. 'Dr Alexander wishes to see you in his office. Go inside, turn immediately left, and it's the third office on the right.'

'How is our pilot?' Freya asked.

'Not out of the woods yet. Dr Alexander will speak to you about him.' She turned her attention to me. 'This morning you mentioned a Charles Thorpe from the American embassy. Dr Alexander is well acquainted with him and has telephoned to ask him to join your meeting. He's just arrived.'

'Why on earth would he ask Charles Thorpe to come here?' Loki asked.

Mother Thérèse looked to the heavens and muttered something. 'Open your eyes,' she replied. 'See what's around you. This hospital has the finest facilities and best doctors and surgeons, all paid for by donations and money from America. Dr Alexander has spent years making this into one of the best hospitals in France. The Germans would dearly love to have this place. They dream of taking it over. Never a week goes by without them trying to use its facilities. Dr Alexander has to keep them out at all costs. To do that he needs friends in high places – like Charles Thorpe – and he has to tread extremely carefully. Your pilot being here is dangerous. *Your* turning up on his doorstep is very dangerous too. I expect he's looking to Charles Thorpe for guidance on how to handle the situation.'

'But surely it wouldn't be that disastrous if they treated the odd sick German officer,' Freya observed, gazing at the myriad windows. 'This place is vast. It wouldn't be hard to keep them separated from Nils.'

Mother Thérèse stared hard at Freya, as if she wanted to explain something but couldn't; as if an oath of secrecy had been sworn, an oath before God.

'I get it,' I said. 'Our pilot isn't the only *secret* patient, is he?'

Almost bursting to talk, Mother Thérèse shook her head.

'There are others – British airmen, and wounded or sick French soldiers who never made it to England during the evacuation at Dunkirk, aren't there?'

Mother Thérèse nodded.

'And when they're better, Dr Alexander helps them escape, doesn't he? Possibly with the assistance of Charles Thorpe.'

Her cheeks now ruby red, Mother Thérèse nodded again.

'So this is much more than just a hospital, isn't it?'

'Yes,' Mother Thérèse blurted, unable to hold her

tongue any longer. 'You will find that the hospital is always full. *Always*. There is never a spare bed for a German soldier. That way they can be kept away. As you can imagine, making sure it's full every day of the year is no easy task. Dr Alexander is a brave, wonderful, self-less man, and his staff are utterly loyal to him. But he knows he's walking a very dangerous tightrope. One slip-up could be unimaginably costly. The Germans make frequent visits and checks, looking for the slightest excuse to accuse him of something that would permit them to order the handover of the hospital to the German Reich.'

'And you know all this because you've made this trip before, haven't you?' said Freya.

'Yes. Listen, I don't know why you've come to France, but I expect Charles Thorpe will insist on knowing if he's going to be willing to trust you.'

'Don't worry about Charles Thorpe,' Loki replied confidently. 'He knows he can trust us.'

Mother Thérèse frowned before continuing, 'Well, even if that's true, I expect he'll impress upon you that the situation here in France is changing . . . *rapidly*. The Germans don't really want you Americans here. And every time your President Roosevelt is seen to be aiding the Allies in some way, he is making the situation worse. Very soon, I fear carrying American papers will mean trouble for you. My advice is to go home as soon as you're able. Don't stay in France a moment longer than necessary.'

'We don't intend to,' Freya said determinedly.

We all shook hands. 'Thank you for all your help,' I said. 'We really do understand the risks you've taken.'

'Yes, well, I'm not one to turn away the needy from my door, even if one of them goes by the name of *Le Môme*!' She stared back towards the grand entrance to the hospital grounds, the high wall and ornate arch, and sighed. 'Out there a dark shadow has been cast over the earth. They used to call Paris the City of Lights, you know. But now she lies in darkness.'

'One day the light will return,' I replied. 'To all the dark places.'

Mother Thérèse barely managed a smile. 'Wise words for one so young. And despite your age, I have the sense that your mission is important.'

I nodded. 'We believe so. Many lives are at stake.'

Before heading towards a fired-up and waiting Beelzebub, Mother Thérèse gave Freya a hug. 'May God be with you – may He look over you, and keep you all safe.'

'Amen,' muttered Sisters Agnès and Lavinia.

Chapter Nine
Charles Thorpe

When we entered his office, Dr Alexander was sitting behind his desk. He was in his late forties, his dark hair greying at the temples and receding up his forehead. He struck me as someone who exuded an air of authority, and yet he looked nervous: his dark eyes darted at each of us in turn. He rose to his feet and motioned for us to sit down in front of him. He then introduced us to Charles Thorpe.

Thorpe occupied a chair in the far corner of the office, behind the door. Dressed extremely smartly in a dark charcoal suit, he did not get up or say a word of greeting. He didn't smile or scowl. He sat motionless, legs crossed, damp raincoat draped over his lap, trilby perched at a slant on his head.

'Now, I expect you'd like the latest news about your pilot,' Dr Alexander began, relaxing back down into his leather chair. 'Well, there was a lot of internal bleeding and he'd ruptured his spleen. We had to remove it. It's early days, but I'm confident he'll pull through. From what Mother Thérèse told me about your crash, it sounds like he had a lucky escape. It's remarkable you weren't hurt either.'

'You mean he's going to be OK? Really OK?' I asked. Inside I was jumping for joy.

'I believe so.'

'Can we see him?'

'Later perhaps. He's still coming round from the anaesthetic. Tomorrow maybe.'

I stood up, leaned across and insisted on shaking Dr Alexander's hand. Loki and Freya did likewise.

'Of course, he'll take time to recover fully. He needs total rest. I want to keep him here for a while.'

'And then?' Loki asked.

Dr Alexander shot a glance towards Charles Thorpe. We all turned to look at him too.

'Certain arrangements might be made, I suppose,' Thorpe replied cryptically, having taken a moment to look down and casually flick specks of dandruff from his jacket's lapel. 'It will take time, of course. Always does, I'm afraid.'

Thorpe struck me as cool and unflappable, and he spoke slowly and deliberately as if every word was measured for its meaning and impact before it left his lips. I guessed his manner arose from his experience of living and working under the Nazi occupation, where you needed to be on your guard twenty-four hours a day.

'Will you be able to get him home? To England, I mean?'

'First things first. He needs to be as fit as a fiddle for such an arduous journey, and we'll have to generate false papers. Then we'll have to determine the safest route – possibly to Spain in the first instance. Then perhaps on to Lisbon, where he may be able to get a boat . . .

Anyway, let's see how things go. We must be careful; take things one day at a time.' Removing a gold case from his pocket, Thorpe clicked it open, took out a cigarette and lit up using an equally expensive-looking gold lighter. Snapping shut the lighter's cover to smother the flame, he drew on the cigarette deeply, exhaled long and hard, and announced coldly, 'We need to have a serious little chat.' His eyes narrowed. 'If you're really who you say you are – all members of the Stevens family from Connecticut – then my name's Charlie Chaplin. Let me see your papers.'

We handed them over. He studied each in turn but said nothing.

'You were informed of our arrival, weren't you?' Freya asked.

He nodded, handing our papers back. 'No details. Never any details. Just a short note in the diplomatic bag from Washington. Coded, of course. Saying that I was to assist you should the need arise.' A pained and resigned expression passed across his face. 'And here I am.'

Dr Alexander rose from his chair again. 'I'll leave you to talk. Got my rounds to do. Like I said, if you wish to visit your friend, come back tomorrow . . . or the day after. He's not going anywhere for now.'

No sooner had the door clicked shut than Charles Thorpe got up and leaned his back lazily against it. 'Why are you here?'

'You should know better than to ask that question,' Loki replied.

'It's just that things are a bit sensitive at present,'

Thorpe continued, taking another drag from his cigarette. 'We don't want people running around drawing attention to themselves or causing a nuisance. The German authorities aren't as sympathetic as they used to be. So, if you're planning some sort of sabotage raid or assassination of a high-ranking Nazi official, I've been instructed to warn you off, to make it crystal clear that we do not want such things to occur. At least, not on the streets of Paris, not at the moment. Have I made myself understood?'

'Yes,' Freya replied. 'You don't need to worry. We aren't here to do anything like that.'

Raising just one eyebrow, Charles Thorpe seemed surprised.

'We're looking for someone,' I added. 'That's all.'

'I see.' His thin lips twisted as if he didn't believe us. 'Well, anyway, I've said my piece, delivered my warning, job done.' He gestured towards our suitcases – he clearly knew that one contained our wireless set – and added, 'Pass it on to your superiors when you have the chance.'

'We were told you were OSS,' I ventured. 'The Office of Strategic Services. It sounds similar to our set-up.'

'Never heard of it,' he replied bluntly. 'Then again, I would say that, wouldn't I? Who is it you're looking for? I might be able to help. An American citizen?'

'One of ours. Not an American. A Frenchman.'

'Tricky, that – this country's full of them,' Thorpe replied dryly, allowing himself a smile at his own joke.

'That's the problem,' Freya muttered under her breath.

'Disappeared,' Loki added. 'Gone AWOL. With a suitcase of cash.'

The smirk on Thorpe's face grew. 'Oh dear, how unfortunate. And distressing for your superiors too, I expect.'

I didn't like his manner. I wondered if relations between our two organizations were strained, with old transatlantic rivalries rearing their ugly heads, each relishing the opportunity to have a dig at the other's expense.

Thorpe glanced at his watch and sighed. 'Well, whoever it is, sounds like they've decided to seize the opportunity to make a fast buck. The way things are going, I can't say I blame them.'

'Meaning?' I recalled Mother Thérèse had made hints along similar lines.

'Meaning that the Germans have realized America can't sit on the fence for ever. And they figure that if we do join in, it's likely to be against them – and that sure is making them nervous. Are you positive I can't help you find this runaway of yours? I mean, if you told me more, I'm sure I could assist you . . .'

Realizing that we weren't going to reveal anything more, he held up his hands as if in surrender and changed tack. 'OK, I know when to back off. Listen, maybe there is a way I can help you, though. In case you run into trouble.' He removed a street map of Paris from his pocket and spread it out on Dr Alexander's desk. 'I didn't know how familiar you were with the city or how good a briefing you received before you arrived, and so, after I received the telephone call from Dr Alexander, I took the liberty of bringing this with me.'

We gathered round.

'I've marked all the places that have been issued certificates by our embassy – this means they are American property and protected under international law. As long as your false identity papers withstand scrutiny, in an emergency you can treat them as safe houses. As well as our embassy, there's the American Library on the Rue de Téhéran, and the Hôtel Bristol in the Rue du Faubourg Saint-Honoré. If you do take refuge in one, call me and I'll come and rescue you.'

Loki caught my eye and pulled a face. It was the way Charles Thorpe had said *come and rescue you*; as if we were hopeless idiots, way out of our depth; as if it was inevitable that we'd need rescuing at some point. If only he knew who we really were, and what the three of us had been through, I thought, he might not be so quick to dismiss us as bungling amateurs.

'Anyway, I must be off. You can keep that map. My car's outside. Can I give you a lift anywhere?'

'No thank you,' Freya replied quickly.

'Very well. Then I'll say cheerio for now.' He touched the brim of his hat and turned to leave. 'You know where I am if you need me, but I'd rather you didn't. *Au revoir.*'

Freya shivered the moment Thorpe vanished down the corridor. 'God, he gives me the creeps. Slippery as a snake.'

★　★　★

As we were unable to visit Nils at his bedside until at least the following day, we decided there was only one thing to do – proceed with our mission. First stop was an apartment in Montmartre rented by Trébuchet. Like Thorpe, he'd been warned of our arrival and we'd been told we should greet him using the code phrase, *Cette année le noël tombe un dimanche* – This year Christmas falls on a Sunday – to which Trébuchet would reply, *Non, mardi* – No, Tuesday. Such coded introductions were bread and butter to agents in the field. Although we knew little about Trébuchet, we'd been told he often carried a distinctive cane made of ebony and topped with a solid silver grip.

As Thorpe's map was more detailed than the silk versions hidden in the lining of our clothes, we decided to use it to figure out how to get from the hospital to Trébuchet's apartment. Making for the hospital entrance, Loki scrutinized it and clicked his tongue against the back of his teeth in irritation. 'Ross said coming here was just a short detour. We're *miles* from Montmartre. We can't walk it. We'll have to take the Métro. Agreed?'

Reluctantly Freya and I nodded. Using public transport meant having to enter stations with limited entrances and exits, and they were always patrolled by soldiers. Our papers would almost certainly be scrutinized at least once. And we'd have to ride in train carriages from which escape would be virtually impossible. The slightest suspicion could result in our luggage being searched, and that would signal disaster.

As soon as the suitcase containing our wireless set was opened, that would be it – arrest, interrogation, imprisonment, and execution as enemy spies would follow as surely as night follows day. But for agents in the field that was simply how it had to be. The risks came with the territory. We needed our wireless set and so we had to carry it with us. Walking the streets with it wasn't much safer either.

Outside the hospital entrance we buttoned up our coats and put on our hats. 'Will it ever stop raining?' Loki cursed, lifting his jacket collar.

It was dark now too. Gone five o'clock, I realized, peering at my watch. The curfew didn't begin until eleven, so we had plenty of time to reach Trébuchet's apartment.

'Come on,' said Loki, wearily picking up one of the suitcases and handing it to me.

'Where's Ross?' said Freya. 'He said he was going to wait to find out about Nils.'

'I'm still here.' Ross emerged from the shadows. Shivering from the cold, he rubbed his hands together and then blew into them. 'Is your pilot going to be all right?'

'Think so. We owe you one, Ross,' I replied.

'I'll help you on the Métro,' he offered. 'You don't know Paris, do you? I saw you peering at that map. I know the city like the back of my hand. Whereabouts in Montmartre are you heading? What's the address?'

'As Simon told you this morning, this is as far as you go, Ross,' Loki responded. 'Anyway, I thought you were going to visit your sister in Fresnes. That's in the opposite direction, isn't it?'

Undeterred, Ross replied, 'Yes, but it's much too far away for me to get to before the curfew. So I'm going to have to stay the night at the house of someone I know. And guess what?'

'What?'

'She lives in Montmartre! So, whether you like it or not, we're all going in the same direction. I might as well help you. Come on.' He marched off towards the archway.

'He's beginning to irritate me,' Loki muttered. 'He's like an annoying lump of chewing gum stuck to your shoe.'

'We should probably be grateful,' Freya responded, and then she laughed at the face Loki was pulling.

A different thought occurred to me. I had a sneaking suspicion that, right from the start, when Ross first leaped onto Mother Thérèse's truck that morning, he'd had the whole day planned out: he'd had no intention of going to Fresnes, and knew he'd find a way of tagging along. Ross, I figured, wanted to be in on the action, part of our mission, even though he didn't have a clue why we were here.

Chapter Ten
Montmartre

The Métro was crowded. It was rush hour. Ross queued and bought our tickets, and then we descended several long flights of steps before patiently waiting for our train on the underground platform. Soldiers milled about and manned the turnstiles, but thankfully they hardly stopped anyone. We all got through without a hitch. When our train arrived, hundreds of people spilled out of the sausage-like string of carriages; we fought through a mass of bodies to squeeze aboard. The doors closed. With a jolt the train departed.

It quickly gathered speed. No one spoke as we rocked to and fro, packed in like sardines. The warm, moist air reeked of stale body odour, foul breath, damp clothes, soot and cigarette smoke, a hideous cocktail that made you want to pinch your nose. The floor was wet and slippery. It was hard to keep your footing as the carriage rattled and swayed. What struck me most, however, was the faces. I never knew there were so many shades of grey. Every face was different, and yet somehow they looked the same – all drawn and hungry, wearied by a lack of decent food and the endless restrictions to their freedom. They looked sad, resigned, *defeated* by the Nazi menace.

Lights in the carriage kept flickering on and off,

plunging us into moments of complete darkness. While most passengers gazed blankly straight ahead or down at their feet, I noticed a man opposite had fixed his icy stare on Loki. He was clad in a black leather raincoat, and his manner instantly led me to think he was a member of the Gestapo. They were always suspicious of everyone, and were renowned for picking on people at random, giving them a tough time, just in case they knew something useful.

The train pulled in to the next station, and passengers shoved and cursed as they carved a path to the nearest carriage door. Cool air rushed in. People spilled out and others pressed aboard, crammed uncomfortably shoulder to shoulder. A young woman near to me stood on an old man's foot. She said, '*Pardon!*' but only received a nasty scowl in return. The man in the leather coat remained unnervingly focused on Loki.

After several more stations Ross announced that the next stop – Abbesses – was where we should get off.

I'd never felt so relieved to step out of a train, and paused to take deep breaths as others lugging bags and briefcases pushed past me. Praying that the man in the dark leather raincoat had remained on the train, I waited in case he brushed past me too. And he did. That sounded the alarm bells in my head. He'd got off at the same stop, and was following the others as they headed towards the steps up to the exit. I pursued him at a safe distance. Freya glanced round to see where I'd got to. I caught her eye and signalled. She understood. She turned her head away and whispered to Loki.

As the throng started up the steps, I dropped back a little further so that I'd have time to assess the situation and react should my worst fears be confirmed. In the end I found myself pushing and shoving to keep the others in sight, rising onto my toes to catch glimpses of their heads. We all moved up towards the exit like a tidal wave, six abreast, hats bobbing and shoulders rubbing. Why had the oaf picked on Loki? Did my best friend just *look* suspicious? Was that it? My heart began racing. With every step I grew more certain that the man was indeed Gestapo. I'd seen enough of those thugs to spot one a mile off. And, worryingly, they rarely operated alone. Did he have henchmen waiting? Was there a car full of them outside? Would he bide his time? Wait until Loki was outside before apprehending him? The swirling questions felt as if they were burning a hole in my head. I reached down into my pocket and grasped the handle of my revolver. At least Loki knew he was being targeted. At least Freya had passed on my warning. He'd be ready. *I'd* be ready.

Reaching street level, everyone emerged onto the wet, glistening pavement. Travellers set off briskly in all directions. Loki, Freya and Ross advanced about a dozen steps and then paused. Freya turned, and I saw her eyes flitting to and fro in search of me. The man in the leather raincoat was twenty feet behind them and striding purposefully in their direction. He raised a hand, signalled to someone in a car parked nearby, and then quickened his step, dashing forward like someone in a sudden hurry to catch a departing bus. At the same time he dipped a hand into a pocket and drew something out. A Luger pistol. Swallowing hard, I realized that this was it, the moment I'd dreaded.

I barged my way past an old woman who, unable to regain her balance, cursed and spat at me as she toppled over like a skittle. Keeping my revolver hidden until the last possible moment, I drew breath and was about to yell out the alarm when the Gestapo thug reached out and grabbed the collar of an unsuspecting man in his early twenties standing just feet behind Loki. Yanking him to one side, the Gestapo officer flung the man up against a wall, kicked his legs apart, and pressed a Luger into his ribs. The man's expression – I shall never forget it: that look of utter horror. Everyone in the street froze and gawped. Tyres squealed as a car drew up at the kerb. A door was flung open and the prisoner, shouting and screaming, was bundled inside. Car doors slammed. The car careered off. Ashen-faced, Loki puffed out his cheeks and looked to the heavens.

'Guide us to the Sacré-Coeur. We can make our own way from there,' I said calmly to Ross once we'd recovered our wits. I felt all churned up inside. The near miss was a horrible reminder of the risks we were taking by just being here.

'Who do you think he was?' Ross ventured, peering after the car as it screeched round a distant corner and disappeared. He couldn't stop trembling. He'd not seen me signal or heard Freya's warning to Loki, so when the thug pounced it had come as a complete shock. 'Maybe he was a member of the Resistance. Someone like us. A comrade in arms.'

'God knows. I reckon he'd been followed all the way. The Gestapo had probably planned his arrest,' Loki replied.

'We should have done something. Helped him escape,' Ross added. 'That's the problem with people here. Everyone just stands by and watches. Nobody does anything. Nobody fights back.'

'Yeah, right – and bring a whole division of the Wehrmacht or SS down on us,' Loki snapped back. 'They'd have this place sealed off in minutes. They'd round people up, maybe shoot one or two in the street just to let everyone know they were serious, and they'd not give up until they had us under arrest.'

'They wouldn't—'

'Oh yes they would, Ross,' I said, recalling the horrors we'd witnessed on our last mission in Holland. I'd experienced just what that young man was going through. I'd been arrested and interrogated. Luckily I'd escaped, but not before the enemy had begun the painful process of extracting information. 'Remind me one day to show you my feet, Ross.'

'*What?*' He looked at me incredulously. 'Why?'

'You'll be able to count that I have fewer nails than toes.'

He frowned.

'You see, Ross, I've experienced the hospitality of the enemy at first hand. They can be quite persuasive. Best to steer well clear. Not take too many unnecessary risks.

Or at least, you need to choose your moments carefully. And it's not just about saving our own skins. If we get caught, others will be in danger – like our local contact, your uncle, Mother Thérèse and Dr Alexander. Understand?'

My comment had the desired effect. Ross gulped and said no more about it.

The vast, domed basilica of the Sacré-Coeur was a famous landmark and I knew it was situated high up above the city, but my heart sank when we'd made it as far as the Rue Tardieu and saw that the cable railway, or *funiculaire*, as it was called, was shut; it left us with no option but to climb the steep hill through terraced gardens. Ross pointed towards the silhouette of the church and cheerfully declared, 'See that dome? That's the second highest point in Paris.'

'Feels like it,' I replied, switching the heavy suitcase from one hand to the other, my sides hurting. 'I suppose the highest is the Eiffel Tower.'

'Yes.'

'Thank God we're not going there, then,' Freya muttered, and we all laughed.

Just before reaching the uppermost garden terrace, Loki stopped and placed the suitcase he was carrying on top of an ornate stone balustrade, opened it and rummaged around inside. Removing a tin of talc, he offered it to Ross. 'A deal's a deal. One tin of carborundum powder. Payment in full.'

Ross took it and dropped it into his jacket pocket.

'This is it, then, I suppose,' he said awkwardly. He sounded decidedly downhearted.

'Afraid so. You and Luc have been fantastic. Quite a team. Keep up the good work,' I said. Seeing that our gratitude made no impression on him, I added, 'When we get back, we'll make sure we tell our superiors all about you – how you helped us, and quite possibly saved our pilot's life.'

A look of horror came over his face. 'No! . . . Please say nothing. Nothing at all.'

'Why ever not?' Freya asked.

'It . . . it . . . it's . . . Well . . . I mean . . . I want . . .' He searched frantically for the right words. 'Please, just don't.'

'All right, if that's what you want.' I held out my hand and he shook it.

'Here, take these as well,' said Loki, forcing several packets of cigarettes into his clutches. 'Give them to your sister when you get to Fresnes prison. Maybe she can bribe the guards to make her life a little easier. And we'll all say a prayer for her.'

'Thanks,' he said, moving away from us. 'Good luck . . . and . . . goodbye.'

'You too. Be safe, Ross. And thanks once again.'

He slipped away and vanished into the night.

Crossing the Rue du Cardinal Dubois, we ascended the last flights of steps leading to the Sacré-Coeur and then headed left down the Rue Azaïs. Trébuchet's apartment was a stone's throw further on, located on the fourth floor of a large building on the Rue Saint-Rustique.

Despite the wind and spitting rain, the area buzzed. Music and laughter emerged from cafés and restaurants, and Parisians clutching umbrellas hurried along the pavements, some splashing through puddles, others dodging them. A long queue stood outside a cinema. For now the streets belonged to them. When the curfew came, that would all change: like flicking a light switch, the city's streets would empty. Clubs, dance-halls, theatres and restaurants would close, apart from a select few staying open to entertain the Germans. Such venues were *nur für Deutsche*, as the signs outside stated – for Germans only.

'There it is,' said Loki, lifting his eyes towards the tall grey-brown façade of the building on the Rue Saint-Rustique. We spent a few minutes checking that it wasn't being watched from the street, and then, while Loki and Freya waited, I made for the rear to suss out possible escape routes, should we need one in a hurry. At the back lay an alleyway filled with bins and rubbish. There was also a door to the apartment block that looked as if it hadn't been used in years. I noted the absence of streetlamps. Pitch-black darkness was good for covering a getaway, but I figured we'd have to tread carefully to avoid tripping over the rubbish. Clattering bins would make enough noise to wake the whole neighbourhood.

Parallel to the back of the apartment block ran a wall the length of the alley. It was way too high to climb unless the bins were used as a step-up. Possible in an emergency – but it was hard to tell what lay on the other side. A better bet would be to use one of the narrow walkways between the buildings – the one

I'd ventured down was barely two feet wide – and at least we knew what was at the end of it. Satisfied I'd figured out all the options, I returned to the street and briefed the others. We decided it was safe to venture inside and locate Trébuchet's apartment.

'Looks a real dump,' Freya muttered as we pulled open the main door.

She was right. You couldn't help but baulk at the foul smell in the lobby. Someone, probably drunk out of their skull, had pissed beneath the staircase, and the plaster on the walls was coming away in places to reveal the stonework behind. To our left were the mailboxes for each apartment. Loki took a moment to inspect the one for Apartment 412, Trébuchet's place, and saw that not only was it empty but that someone had forced it open, breaking the hinges of the lockable metal flap. Others were bust too. Noise filtered down the stairwell from upper floors: a couple arguing, shouting at the tops of their voices; a baby wailing inconsolably.

Slowly we climbed, floor by floor, trying not to make a sound. It was always best if neighbours did not hear the arrival of visitors to safe houses; that way they could not inform the authorities of comings and goings if questioned.

As we approached the second floor, a door slammed. We froze, and Freya raised a finger to her lips and craned her neck to see if she could catch a glimpse of the goings-on. Voices, angry chatter, definitely a man's voice, then a different one, then a woman's – all in a language I didn't recognize. Freya retreated a few steps and pressed herself against the handrail. We waited. Eventually it fell quiet. We crept on up.

The whole fabric of the building reeked with neglect. I reckoned it was probably home to foreign workers and those close to destitution. And that made me nervous. It was the kind of place the police and German authorities would raid frequently; the kind of place where information changed hands for money or threats, where people sold out their fellow man for a few French francs. *Trébuchet,* I thought, *why couldn't you have chosen somewhere a little nicer, a little more upmarket . . . a little bit* safe*r?*

Reaching the landing on the fourth floor, Loki raised a fist and tapped lightly on Trébuchet's front door. No reply. He knocked again, a little louder. Still no reply. 'I suppose it was asking too much for him to be here to welcome us.' He stepped aside. 'Finn, would you like to do the honours?'

I removed my pen and set about picking the lock.

'Home sweet home,' Loki announced once I'd opened the door.

Inside, we checked out all the rooms. The apartment was simply furnished and immaculately tidy; all the heavy velvet drapes were drawn. The place was freezing, and exposed pipes clunked and rattled when I turned on a tap for a drink of water. There were pictures and photographs hung on the walls: all scenes of Parisian streets and landmarks. There was nothing personal about them. It gave you no inkling as to who lived there. Likewise, rifling through cupboards and drawers, we found most empty, others containing ordinary stuff; but no paperwork, no post, nothing bearing a name, nothing hidden. 'Our Monsieur Trébuchet's certainly a very careful man,' I observed. 'Any food in the house?'

Freya emerged from the kitchenette and grimaced. 'Does anyone like tinned potatoes? It's all there is.'

Loki fell onto a sofa and rested his feet on a low table. 'No! I guess we just wait for Trébuchet to show up. We know he's expecting us.'

Freya slumped down next to him and rested her head on his shoulder. 'Suppose so. We should work out our plan of action. Trébuchet may be able to assist us in moving about the city, but that's about it. He's already exhausted all his contacts.'

'Well, we have the addresses of Claude's associates and places he used to live,' I said, recalling how we'd spent hours memorizing the list. 'Our first question to Trébuchet has to be which ones he's already checked out. The rest we visit in turn. Find out what we can. Maybe we'll get a lead.'

Freya studied her watch. 'God, I feel exhausted. Do you realize we haven't slept properly since we left Mulberry. Whether Trébuchet turns up this evening or not, there's nothing we can do until morning, so I suggest we all get some rest. Make a fresh start tomorrow. We need clear heads.'

'Gets my vote,' said Loki, closing his eyes and yawning so wide his jaw cracked. 'We'll take it in turns to keep watch. You can take the first shift, Finn.'

'Thanks,' I grumbled. 'What about radioing HQ to update them?'

Loki's yawn was catching, but Freya managed to stifle hers. 'I'll do it first thing tomorrow.' Nestling into Loki's shoulder, she closed her eyes.

While they drifted off to sleep on the sofa, I killed the lights, dragged a chair over to the window and placed my revolver on a table next to it. Sitting down, I moved the left-hand curtain a couple of inches to glimpse outside. For hours I gazed across at the building opposite and traced the silhouette of the rooftops. Clouds raced across the night sky, a crescent moon showing its face now and again. Hooray! It had finally stopped raining. Reaching up, I unlatched the window and pushed it open a fraction. Cool, deliciously fresh air rushed in, and I drank in lungful after lungful to keep me awake and alert. I could hear voices on the street below. Laughter too. And footsteps. *So this is Paris*, I thought, *famous for romance, art and culture. A city the Germans relished conquering; a jewel among their spoils of war.*

Sitting, watching, listening, I had to fight waves of fatigue intent on drowning me. I tried pinching myself, getting up and stretching, walking to and fro. Raised voices could be heard from other apartments too: couples bickering, drunken shouting. It was a hellish place. The others slept through it all, Loki snoring his head off, Freya tossing and turning, her sleep light, her dreams troubled.

Returning to my view of the city, I noticed that the streets were suddenly busier. In the distance I heard the blast of a siren; someone shouted out a warning of the imminent start of the curfew. The booming voice repeated the same sentence over and over, loudest when a police car sped down the street, a pair of loudspeakers mounted on the roof barking out the order to be off the streets or else risk arrest. It was a quarter to eleven. The curfew affected not just Parisians but low-ranking German soldiers and any German women in the city. Non-commissioned German officers were permitted to stay out until midnight. German officers, however, like the Paris police, were allowed to roam the city all night if they wished. Now people were hurrying. I peeled back the curtain a little more. Heels click-clacked noisily on the pavements below. People shouted their goodbyes and waved to one another. Slowly the numbers dwindled. Eventually a distant church bell rang out the hour. The street was utterly deserted now. No – wait . . . I could hear frantic footsteps. A straggler ran past on the opposite side of the road. A door crashed shut. Now there was silence; an eerie, unnatural quiet. The transformation was unsettling.

Realizing that Trébuchet was unlikely to risk breaking the curfew, I figured he wasn't going to turn up that night. I could relax a little; just a little. I thought about all that had happened that day: leaving Tangmere in the early hours, crashing in Monsieur Laval's cabbage field, hitching a ride with the nuns to the American Hospital; now we'd made it here, to Trébuchet's safe house. And Nils was safe too. He was going to be all right.

As my eyelids grew heavy, pounding boots on the staircase outside the apartment had me out of my chair in a flash. Snatching up my revolver from the table, I hurried to the door and pressed my ear against it. Had Trébuchet made it here at the last minute? I waited for a knock or the sound of keys jangling. Instead, a shout came from the stairwell. A muffled cry. A scuffle on our landing. A man groaning as if in pain. More sounds of a struggle, a clatter, something smashing. Then more footsteps; lighter and less hurried this time. Nothing.

I waited a moment and then opened the apartment door a fraction. The dimly lit hallway was empty. A pottery jardinière containing a small plant that had been standing on the opposite side of the landing now lay broken into a thousand shards, the soil spilled everywhere. I shut the door and quickly bolted it, then sat back down and rubbed my cheeks. I was feeling on edge, ragged. I desperately wanted to close my eyes for a minute, just to rest them, to calm my nerves, to count to ten to slow my pulse. I knew I daren't – I couldn't risk dozing off. I took several deep breaths instead.

The bloodcurdling scream came from outside. Startled, I jumped to my feet and yanked the curtain right back. I pushed the window fully open, leaned out and looked down. A man's body lay on the pavement below. He was twisted and still . . . lifeless . . . dead. Beside him rested a walking cane, ebony coloured, with a silver grip. *Trébuchet!*

'Wake up! Wake up! We've got to get the hell out of here,' I shouted, shaking Loki and Freya from their dreams. 'Now!'

Chapter Eleven
Trébuchet and Louise

Grabbing our small suitcases, we hammered down the stairs. I led the others towards the back exit. Locating the door, I punched it open and spilled out into the night. I couldn't see a thing. Stopping abruptly, I blinked wildly to adjust my eyes. Freya was right behind me and, equally blind in the darkness, bumped into me so heavily she sent me careering into a pile of refuse. Fortunately it softened my fall and I sprang back up. 'Come on, we need to put as much distance between us and this place as possible. As soon as the body's discovered the whole area will be crawling with police and soldiers. Where's Loki?'

Barely awake, Loki stubbed his toe on the door frame and let out a stifled cry of pain as he stumbled, sprawling to the ground and ending up flat on his face. His suitcase containing our spare clothes flew out of his grasp, bursting open on hitting the ground. The contents spewed out. While I dragged him to his feet, Freya crouched down and began gathering everything up, frantically stuffing things back into the case as best she could.

Without warning, a pile of rubbish beside Freya erupted like a volcano. Springing out from amongst flying cardboard and bags of stinking refuse, a figure pounced on her. Manhandling her to her feet, he grappled her in front of him, placing one arm tightly about her neck, his other hand holding a pistol, which he pressed hard against her head.

I snatched my revolver from my pocket and aimed it at them.

'*Laisse tomber le pistolet!*' he growled. '*Laisse-le tomber et haut les mains! Haut les mains!*'

He was telling me to put down my gun and raise my hands. I refused.

His agitation doubled. '*Laisse-le tomber!*' He cocked his pistol and pressed it harder against Freya's temple.

'Do as he says, Finn,' Freya shouted. 'He means business.'

Slowly I lowered my weapon, bent down and placed it on the ground. I stood up again and raised my hands above my head.

It was hard to tell in the dark, but I reckoned the man was in his mid-thirties, and well dressed in a suit and tie and fashionable overcoat, all of which had seen better days and were soaked through. The rain cascaded from the brim of his hat. Like us, he was extremely nervous, twitchy and, most of all, fearful. He took a few steps back, dragging Freya with him so roughly that when she momentarily lost her footing she dangled in the air like a puppet. Now that he had total control of the situation, the questions flew from his lips thick and fast. My brain went into overload as I tried to translate them.

'Who are you? Who sent you? How many more of you are there? How did you get this address?'

He kept flashing glances over my shoulder towards

the end of the alley and the street beyond. When neither Loki nor I offered answers, he tightened his grip on Freya, choking her, and repeated his questions. Loki was all for reaching for his own gun, wedged in the back of his belt, or for rushing the oaf should he be distracted for even a split second. Barely ten feet separated them; just three strides. Risky, I thought. Our assailant looked way too trigger-happy for my liking. I caught Loki's eye and shook my head just enough for him to realize I knew what he was thinking.

Freya tried to struggle free, but the man's grip was like a noose; the more she wriggled, the tighter he held her.

Then, in desperation, she had a brainwave. Barely able to speak, she croaked, '*Cette année le noël tombe un dimanche . . . Cette année le noël tombe un dimanche.*'

The man relaxed his grip on her. Coughing and spluttering, she staggered away from him.

'*Non, mardi . . .*' he replied. Before he could continue, something fizzed through the air and struck him hard on the back of the head. As he fell to his knees, his gun slipped out of his hand. A large, smooth, round pebble ricocheted off him, struck an overflowing metal bin with a loud clunk, and eventually came to rest by my left foot. I spotted a figure emerging from the shadows.

'Got the bastard!' Ross called out. 'Told you I was good.'

Loki ran to check that Freya was all right, while I retrieved the guns. 'Ross, what the hell are you doing here?'

Ignoring me, Ross ran and stood over the figure he'd just felled with his catapult. 'Well, aren't you going to shoot him? He nearly strangled Lorna.'

'No, we're not going to shoot him because he's on our side. He's Trébuchet, our contact.'

Ross looked understandably confused. 'B-b-but he was trying to kill you.'

I pushed him aside.

The man remained dazed. Still on his knees, he blinked repeatedly while rubbing his head. I offered him a hand and pulled him to his feet. 'So you're Trébuchet,' I said. 'Nice to meet you. We're the three blind mice. Actually I thought you were dead. I saw the body in the street. There was a cane lying next to it, so I assumed it was you.'

Still wincing and unsteady from the blow, Trébuchet nodded. '*Oui*, an easy mistake, I suppose. The cane was indeed mine. I'd not been expecting trouble this evening, but I had the distinct feeling I was being followed here. So, once I got inside the building, I waited in the stairwell rather than coming straight up to the apartment. It didn't take long for my suspicions to be proved right. He spotted me lurking and we ended up confronting each other on the stairs. We fought all the way up to the roof. He drew a knife and we struggled. I struck him with my cane. He lost his footing and fell.'

'Who was he?' Loki asked.

'His name's Fabien Cassou,' said Trébuchet sharply. 'Good riddance, I say. The three Cassou brothers are well known around here for all the wrong reasons.

They're ignorant thugs and fully paid-up members of the *Front Jeune*.'

'What's the *Front Jeune*?' asked Freya, still rubbing her throat and trying to catch her breath.

'The Youth Front,' Trébuchet hissed. 'Basically, a bunch of fascist guttersnipes, the lowest forms of life walking the streets of Paris. The Germans encourage them. They entertain themselves in the evenings by harassing the Jews, vandalizing their homes and shops, chucking bricks through windows – the usual stuff. No one can stop them. They seem to be immune from prosecution. It's even rumoured they carry special permits issued by the Germans – permits that stop them from being detained if the police catch them. A kind of *keep out of jail* pass.'

Ross nodded. 'Luc and me have been after one for ages so we can forge copies for ourselves.'

'Why *are* you here, Ross?' I said, repeating my earlier question.

Before he could answer, we heard a commotion in the Rue Saint-Rustique. 'Best we scarper – *vite!*' said Trébuchet. 'Do you have somewhere else to stay? Somewhere safe?'

'Well,' Freya began, 'we know of several places under American control. We'd be safe at any one of them. But they're all some distance from here. Can't we come with you?'

Trébuchet shook his head. '*Non.* Where I'm going wouldn't be safe for so many of us.'

'It's all right, you can come with me,' said Ross. 'It's

not far. Just in the next street. And I know the alleyways like the back of my hand so we can avoid the main road.' He picked up one of our suitcases. 'Come on. It's this way.'

Trébuchet hurriedly removed his wallet from the inside pocket of his jacket, took out a small card and handed it to me. 'Meet me at this address, tomorrow at midday. Be on time. Then we'll talk.'

He turned and fled.

'So, where exactly are you taking us?' Loki whispered as we filed down a foot-wide narrow gap between two buildings.

'My sister's place.'

'Sophie lives here? I thought you said she was arrested in your village,' I replied.

'Not Sophie. *Louise*. My other sister.'

'How many sisters have you got, Ross? You never mentioned her.'

'Just the two. Louise is the eldest. She's twenty. But we don't talk about her. Back at Uncle Laurent's farm it's forbidden to speak her name. As far as Uncle Laurent is concerned, Lou doesn't exist.'

'Why?' asked Freya.

'She's disgraced my family name. At least, that's what Uncle Laurent says. He reckons flitting off to Paris to become an exotic cabaret dancer is no job for a decent young woman. Personally I don't see the problem. She makes good money. Her apartment's pretty flashy too. You wait till you see it. Uncle Laurent came here a month ago and tried to persuade her to come home to Les Andelys to help out on the farm. She refused. They must've had a real barney because when he came back he was spitting furious and said that I wasn't to visit her any more and he'd not tolerate her name being uttered under his roof.'

'A big falling out then. And here you are, doing exactly the opposite of what your uncle tells you.'

Ross stopped and turned round. 'I'll make up my own mind, thank you very much. Uncle Laurent doesn't own me. He can't tell me what to do. She's *my* sister.'

'Good for you, Ross,' I said. 'Family feuds are stupid. Live and let live, I say.'

'Exactly. Lou's a free spirit. You'll like her.'

Ross led us to the end of the narrow gap and then checked that the street ahead was clear. He pointed to a window opposite. 'That's her place. I can see light behind the curtains so she must be in.'

'Hi, Lou – guess what? I've come to visit my favourite sister. And I've brought some friends with me. They're American.'

The barefoot young woman who'd opened the door paled in shock. She was dressed in a thick, flamingo-pink, fluffy bathrobe and had a white towel wrapped about her head; her look of shock soon turned to one of alarm. 'Ross, what on earth are you doing here? And it's after curfew!'

'Yeah, I meant to arrive earlier but we got held up.' He threw his arms around her and hugged her tightly.

'It's good to see you, Lou. Uncle Laurent told me I wasn't to come here, but he's an idiot.'

Louise regained her composure. 'You can't stay here, Ross. It simply isn't convenient.'

'Too late now. With the curfew, we can't go anywhere else. By the way, this is Simon, that's Johnny, and she's Lorna. They're from a place called Connecticut, *apparently*.' Ross winked at us. Loki scowled back.

With great reluctance, Louise stepped aside and let us in. Loki grabbed my jacket and whispered angrily into my ear, 'I know she's his sister but there's no need for The Kid to make it so obvious, Finn. Loose tongues cost lives. Right from the start she's going to be wary of us. I could wring his neck.'

'We'll have a word with him,' I said. 'As soon as he's alone. Impress upon him that this isn't a game.'

'Yeah, well, if he does it again, I won't be held responsible for my actions!'

The apartment was large and comfortably furnished. Ross made for the living room and jumped onto a sumptuous, plump-cushioned sofa. 'So, how are you, Lou?'

She peered at us uncertainly and then tried to smile, but I could sense her discomfort. 'Oh, OK.' I saw her cast an eye at a clock on the dresser. 'Listen, Ross, I have to go out.'

'Out? Where to at this hour?'

'Work,' she said.

'Oh.' Ross frowned. 'At one of the cabaret clubs for German officers?'

'Yes, something like that. I'm sorry, Ross, I don't like

it either, but a girl's got to make a living. Life is tough here. Really hard!'

Ross shrugged and then grinned. 'OK. Just don't go showing those bastards too much leg.'

Louise didn't laugh. Instead she seemed to flinch at his remark. While she disappeared into a bedroom to get dressed, I located the bathroom as I was desperate for a pee. It was hot inside and full of steam. A small cupboard was jam-packed with make-up, tins and tubes neatly stacked; much of it looked the theatrical sort, and I tried to imagine it plastered on Louise's face, exaggerating her big hazel eyes and delicate bone structure. Above the bath, parallel cords were suspended for drying clothes. Everything draped over them looked expensive; not least the half-dozen pairs of silk stockings. Probably got them on the black market, I supposed, or from some leering German officer hoping for a good time. They were like gold dust and highly prized. During our briefing we'd been told that French women – like their English counterparts – could only dream of such luxuries: they often dyed their legs brown with tea to simulate stockings.

I pulled the chain and returned to the living room, where Loki was stuffing his face with a massive sandwich. In the hallway I bumped into Ross coming out of Louise's bedroom. His cheeks were burning and, although he smiled at me, he had a guilty look. I wondered what they'd been talking about in private and was about to ask when Loki pointed a finger in Ross's direction and declared, 'Had a word and we've reached an *understanding*. Isn't that right, Ross?'

Ross nodded sheepishly. 'Sorry. It won't happen again.'

'Delicious,' Loki added, licking his fingers with his mouth full. 'Didn't realize I was so ravenous. Help yourself – the cupboard's full. And I mean *full*!'

He wasn't kidding. Hands on hips, Freya was examining the stash suspiciously. 'Where did she get all this?' She showed me a jar of honey. 'Just a rumour that a shop has this stuff would lead to a mob gathering outside. And she's got two jars. *Two!* And look, *real coffee*!'

Ross began constructing his own open sandwich in the shape of the Arc de Triomphe, using ham and cheese. 'Lou's always been clever. She knows how to survive. Just has to wink at someone and they seem to want to shower her with gifts.'

Minutes later Louise emerged from her bedroom transformed: hair pinned up, glowing cheeks dusted with powder, bright red lipstick on her lips; floral dress, silk stockings and high heels completed the ensemble. I nearly choked on my sandwich.

Ross wolf-whistled and laughed. '*Ooh, la la!* You look a million dollars, sis.' He turned to me. 'Isn't that what you Americans say?'

'Uh-huh.' In truth I was a bit taken aback. She was indeed extremely pretty.

Quickly pulling on a fashionable blue overcoat and swinging a fur wrap over her shoulders, Louise kept one eye firmly on the clock. It was eleven-thirty. She paced the room, agitated, impatient, and chewed the tips of her painted nails. 'You can sleep in my room, Ross. The rest of you will have to make yourselves as comfortable as you can in here. And don't make too much noise. The neighbours don't like it. They're trouble enough as it is.'

There was a brisk knock on the door. Although she'd been expecting it, it nevertheless made her jump.

'Don't wait up,' she said, making a beeline for the door to the hall, then closing it behind her. I heard the front door open, she greeted someone, and then the door slammed shut.

Loki sidled up to the window and peeked round the curtain, watching her depart. Whatever he observed, he kept it to himself, but I saw him swallow hard.

Ross eventually turned in. Loki waited for a while and then checked he was asleep before whispering to Freya and me, 'Tomorrow we find somewhere else. It's too dangerous staying here.'

We were all thinking along the same lines. 'Yes, look at this place. All that food. All those expensive clothes,' Freya chipped in. 'Somehow, I don't think being an exotic dancer would pay for all this.'

'She's *fraternizing* with the enemy,' Loki whispered sternly. 'I saw them when they left. I think the uniform was Luftwaffe, but it was hard to tell. They got into a car with WH plates. Do you think Ross knows?'

'Doubt it,' I responded.

'After Ross's little slip-up when we arrived, do you think she suspects anything about us?' said Freya. 'In her position she'd go crazy if she knew we had anything to do with the Resistance, let alone that we're agents with Special Ops.' Then she stopped to think for a moment.

'At least she wouldn't say anything – that would land Ross in it too.'

'True. I saw Ross coming out her room earlier. He looked pretty guilty – as if he'd been talking to her about us.'

'I'll have a go interrogating him in the morning,' Loki said with relish. 'Find out what he said to her.'

'Maybe she's working for the Resistance too,' I said. 'You know – fraternizing with the Germans in the hope they'll let stuff slip in an unguarded moment.'

'Possibly,' Loki replied. 'Either way, I don't feel safe here. I figure Trébuchet's apartment will be a better base for us once the authorities have made their enquiries about Fabien Cassou. We should move in there, as originally planned.'

'Agreed. We don't have many other options. We'll discuss it with Trébuchet tomorrow.' I suddenly remembered the card he'd given me. I dug it out. It was for a café-bar called *Le Caveau à Vins* – the Wine Cellar. Turning it over, I saw printed directions to it in the form of a simple map. 'Ha, now there's a coincidence.'

'What?' Loki snatched it from me.

'It's next to a restaurant called *Le Lapin Blanc*. The White Rabbit!'

'Perhaps Claude knew the place and thought of it when deciding what codename he wanted to use. Maybe it's some sort of private joke.'

'Wait a minute,' I said, a thought flashing into my head. I grabbed hold of the card and studied it again. The address printed on it was abbreviated to *Rue du Ch,*

Montmartre. 'Let me have a look at that map Charles Thorpe gave us.'

Loki removed it from his coat and handed it to me. Hurriedly I unfolded it and traced a finger across the city until I spotted the unmistakable Sacré-Coeur and the streets of Montmartre. I matched the map on the back of the card to our larger street map. My suspicions proved right. 'Freya, remember what you said when we were in the Lizzie? You reckoned that Claude Chevalier might not even be his real name.'

'Uh-huh.'

'Guess what, I think you're spot on. The restaurant called the White Rabbit is located in the Rue du Chevalier!'

'Oh, great!' Freya threw up her hands in frustration. 'We don't even know his real name. That's all we need. This mission will go down in history as the biggest farce ever. Tomorrow I'm going to send the brigadier a message and I shan't mince my words. They can't expect us to do the impossible. They simply can't . . . I mean . . . it's crackers.'

I said nothing. Freya was right, of course, but I think we all knew a simple truth: Claude, or whoever he really was, had to be found, and that needed manpower on the ground. And we were here. The brigadier wouldn't give up so easily. He'd expect us to try. And I saw the faintest glimmer of hope too. In trying to be clever in his choice of codename and false identity, Claude might have given us a lead.

Chapter Twelve

The White Rabbit

Freya gently shook me awake and handed me a mug of coffee – *real* coffee. The aroma was wonderfully bitter and chocolaty, almost intoxicating. 'Louise hasn't returned, and when I woke up, Ross was gone too,' she said.

I blinked my sleep away. 'What's the time?'

'Just after nine. Loki and I thought it best not to disturb you. I've been to the top of the building and found an area of flat roof that's not overlooked. It's accessible via a small hatch and ladder. We're going up there to transmit an update to HQ.'

I sipped my coffee and nodded.

Finding myself alone in Louise's apartment, I decided to use my time productively by having a good nose around. During training we'd learned that every opportunity had to be seized. If Louise was fraternizing with the enemy, then she couldn't be trusted. But who was her companion? A regular soldier? A member of the SS or Gestapo? Had he left clues in the apartment? In her bedside drawer I found a framed photograph lying face down. I presumed it was the man she was seeing: he was in full military dress – a *Staffelkapitän*, or squadron leader, in the Luftwaffe – and looked to be in his mid thirties. *Liebe Wolfgang, 12th June 1941* was scrawled across it in blue ink. An airman; I figured it could have been worse. I replaced it and shut the drawer.

A writing desk in the main living room was locked, the key nowhere to be seen. It took me under thirty seconds to pick the simple mechanism. Inside lay the usual things: love letters neatly tied with red ribbon, old theatre and cinema tickets, Louise's birth certificate, a scatter of old photos, coins, and numerous dog-eared old programmes from the Folies-Bergère, Lido and Moulin Rouge cabaret clubs. I lifted out some of the photos for a closer look. They were mostly family snaps, some posed in a studio, others taken outside on the streets of Paris, in front of Notre Dame, one overlooking the Seine. Glancing up, I scanned the shelves and sideboard in the room. It hadn't struck me before, but there weren't any photographs on display. Paintings, yes, but no photographs. And those in the drawer were old, taken when Louise was about ten or twelve, I reckoned. The slightly younger girl present in most of the photographs was, I supposed, Sophie, a plain Jane in comparison, and rarely pictured smiling. A small boy, always to the front of the photograph and pulling hideous faces, was unmistakably Ross. I laughed. Oddly, their father was absent from all the pictures – though he might have been behind the camera.

Hearing someone at the front door, I quickly put the pictures back and closed the drawer.

Ross came in clutching a bag containing freshly baked bread. He saw me, glanced around and asked, 'Where are the others? The door was left on the catch.'

I pointed to the ceiling and replied, 'Sending a message. From the roof. You should have told us you were going out, Ross. Stop us worrying about you.'

'Sorry,' he said, putting the bag down. 'There's always a long queue. Even bread's hard to come by, and it's not like it used to be. There's a shortage of flour. Rumour is that they bulk it out with sawdust. By the way, in case you need it, Lou always leaves a spare key above the door . . . So, are you going to visit your pilot today?'

'Yes, I expect so. Probably this afternoon, after we've met up with Trébuchet. Are you going to Fresnes prison to visit Sophie?'

He nodded. 'Can I come to your meeting with Trébuchet first?'

'Best if you don't. So, tell me, why were you in the alleyway last night? I never did get an answer from you.'

'Oh. Remember I said to you that Luc and me wanted to fight back. I reckoned that's what you're here for too, so I hoped I might tag along and make myself useful.'

He responded without a second's hesitation, and it struck me as being well-rehearsed. As if fearing his face might give something away, he slipped into the kitchen, picked up the kettle and began filling it at the sink. I followed him.

'What did you say to Louise last night? I saw you coming out of her room. You had that guilty look.'

'Nothing.'

'I'm not sure I believe you, Ross.'

'I said nothing. Nothing. *All right?*' he snapped angrily.

'All right, keep your hair on.' Studying him carefully, I went on, 'It's just that, well, you do know that your sister's fraternizing with the enemy, don't you?'

He pressed his eyes shut for a moment but kept his cool. Turning off the tap, he put the kettle on the stove and leaned heavily against it. 'Yes.'

'And?'

'His name's Wolfgang Müller. He's a bomber pilot. A squadron leader, I think. She doesn't know that I know, of course. She thinks it's her little secret.'

'And you don't mind? She's *still* your favourite sister?'

Ross shrugged like he didn't care, or didn't want to think about it. I thought it odd, so I tested him a step further. 'She's not mixed up in anything we should know about, is she?'

His face snapped round and he glared at me. 'No! Anyway, mind your own business.'

'Listen to me, Ross. This isn't a game. You mustn't say anything about us – including how we got here. You mustn't utter a word to Louise about the American Hospital either. Understand? *Understand?* Promise me, Ross. It's important.'

'I'm not stupid,' he spat back at me angrily.

Returning to the apartment, Loki and Freya overheard Ross's raised voice. 'Everything all right?' asked Freya.

'Yes,' I replied. While Ross had his back turned, I mouthed to the others that he'd not said anything about us to Louise. 'What did HQ have to say?'

Freya put down the suitcase containing our radio set and heaved a sigh. 'We're to try and find out anything we can. They will review all their records in case Claude let something slip along the way as to his real identity. Don't hold your breath, though. I reckon he's covered his tracks perfectly.'

'This Claude you keep talking about . . .' Ross enquired cagily. 'He's the same man as that "White Rabbit" person you mentioned before, isn't he?'

'Yes. It's a long story, Ross. The less you know the better,' said Loki.

Ross looked at Freya. 'When I overheard you talking about him at the farm, you said that when you do find him you'll have to decide whether to kill him or not. Why? What's he done?'

'We're not sure. Partly, that's why we're here. To find out.'

'And then kill him?'

'Maybe,' I replied. 'It all depends.'

'Oh.' Ross thought for a moment before announcing, 'I've got to go out again now. I may be some time.'

Quite a gale blew up the Rue du Chevalier, picking up fallen leaves and swirling them about our heads. On our way to the Le Caveau à Vins we passed the entrance to the *Lapin Blanc*. Hanging on the wall outside was a large painted sign of a white rabbit dancing about madly, clutching a bottle of wine in one hand and a stick in the other. It had a crazy *Alice in Wonderland* look about it.

Now I understood why the card for the Caveau à

Vins had directions drawn on the back: only a small sign and an arrow pointing down a flight of steps indicated the existence of the place. Blink and you'd miss it. It was ten minutes to midday when we descended, shoved open the door and ventured inside.

Half the tables and chairs were occupied by locals who, *en masse*, ceased talking, glanced round at us and then, observing we weren't uniformed Nazis, quickly returned to their idle chatter. An overworked and flustered waitress clutching a tray sped past and pointed to a free table. Unable to spot Trébuchet in the room, we sat down and waited.

The subterranean café-bar was lit by rows of feeble flickering wall lights bearing small, crimson, tasselled shades. It gave the place a secretive feel. The ceilings were vaulted, held up by a series of ancient-looking brick pillars. Wisps of cigarette smoke seemed to hang in the air like vapour trails, creating quite a fug. Adding to the gloom, all the walls were plastered in old theatre, cinema and cabaret posters, arranged haphazardly, many overlapping, in places several layers thick. Most were faded, some yellowed by time, the few newer ones strikingly gaudy in comparison.

'This is cosy,' said Freya, settling onto her chair. 'Great atmosphere. You can almost smell the history.'

'Or is it damp?' Loki muttered. 'This place looks like it's been here since Roman times.'

The overstretched and harried waitress returned. Holding a small pad and a pencil, she flicked hair from her eyes and asked impatiently, '*Oui?*'

Freya ordered three *ersatz* coffees.

Midday came and went. We sipped our vile, bitter drinks and Loki drummed his fingers on the table impatiently. 'Where has he got to, Finn? Do you think he ran into more trouble last night?'

'Let's hope not.'

Luckily everyone else ignored us. Awkward conversation was the last thing we wanted. Sitting closest to the wall, I found my gaze wandering over the crazy mishmash of posters. I was still peering at them when Trébuchet breezed in and hurriedly sat down at our table.

'*Pardon*, I was held up.' Whipping off his hat, he looked up and waved to the waitress. '*Bière, s'il vous plaît.*' He held out a hand for us to shake. 'We didn't really have a chance to introduce ourselves properly last night. Trébuchet at your service.'

'I'm Simon Stevens, that's my brother Johnny, and she's our sister Lorna. How's your head?'

Pulling a face, he reached up and gingerly touched the bump. 'I'll live.'

'Do you know why that thug Fabien Cassou came after you?' Freya asked.

Trébuchet leaned back in his chair and shook his head. 'Not for sure. Two possibilities spring to mind. The Cassou brothers are little more than petty criminals with a liking for violence. Joining the *Front Jeune* gave them the opportunity to branch out, victimizing people round here, especially the Jews – beating them, stealing their money and possessions, all with the Nazis looking the other way. A while back, some of my men got involved in a brawl with Fabien and a few others. So maybe it was a revenge attack. On the other hand, I've been asking a lot of questions about Claude, including my contacts in the police and local German command. It can't have gone unnoticed. If your superiors are right and Claude has switched sides, then the German authorities may have decided it's best if I'm silenced or, at the very least, warned off. For a few francs, those bastards in the *Front Jeune* would be only too happy to do their dirty work for them. Still, I'm just guessing.'

'So it might be best if you lie low for now. Until things calm down.'

'In an ideal world, perhaps. But time is something we don't have much of. Your superiors want the matter sorted without delay.' Leaning forward and hunching over the table conspiratorially, he folded his arms and added, 'So tell me, just how *exactly* do you plan to find Claude? I've looked everywhere. No one's heard or seen anything. No sign of the money, either.' Extracting a packet of cigarettes, he offered them to us and, when we all declined, sparked one up for himself, vigorously waving the lit match in the air to extinguish it before snapping it in half between his finger and thumb. 'What does London think you can do that I can't?'

He sounded defensive, as if he feared that our presence was a reflection of his failure.

'To be honest, we don't know where to start,' said Freya. 'We have a list of names and addresses – Claude's supposed contacts and acquaintances. I wouldn't be surprised if they were all made up. I expect you've already tried most of them.'

The waitress delivered Trébuchet's beer. He extracted his cigarette from between his dry, cracked lips, lifted his head and blew smoke towards the ceiling. 'Try me.'

Freya recalled three names and addresses, all in central Paris. Trébuchet laughed. 'The first two people are dead, and that third address doesn't even exist.' Freya recalled four more and Trébuchet's response was equally curt. 'No. They don't exist either. Our Monsieur Chevalier has been – how do you say? – ah, *oui* . . . pulling the wool over our eyes.' He sat back and laughed again. 'He's running circles round all of us.'

'Well, there is one thing I am pretty certain of,' I declared.

Trébuchet wolfed down half his beer in a series of gulps and smacked his lips. 'Go on.'

'Claude Chevalier isn't his real name.'

Stubbing out his cigarette, Trébuchet nodded. 'I believe you are right. So you figured it out as well. The Lapin Blanc and the Rue du Chevalier. I've come across other agents who've chosen false identities and their codenames in similar ways. When making my enquiries I've focused on the description of Claude your superiors gave me. But it's made no difference.'

'He's a master of disguise, apparently,' said Freya.

Trébuchet threw up his arms in surrender. 'Then what hope do we have?'

'There is just one possibility,' I ventured. 'That his choice of codename and *nom de guerre* weren't entirely random. Maybe he knows this area pretty well. Possibly even lived here for a while before the war.'

Trébuchet agreed with me. 'You may be right. But I don't see how that helps us. If we don't have his real name and if he's using a disguise, then . . . well, finding him will be impossible. We might have had a slim chance if we possessed a recent photograph. Someone might remember his face from the past.'

'Exactly!' I said triumphantly. Opening my coat, I took out a photograph of Claude we'd been given during our briefing back at Mulberry and handed it to him.

He stared at it for a few seconds. 'When was this taken?'

'Just a few months ago.'

'Can I keep it?'

'Yes, we have more copies,' I replied.

He placed it carefully in his coat pocket. 'Thank you. At last, something that might just give us a lead. You don't know how many times in the last fortnight I've wished I had such a photograph. Of course, usually pictures of fellow agents would be the last thing you'd want to carry around with you, but on this occasion it may prove crucial. After all, a picture's worth a thousand words. It may lead us to a name . . . his *real* name.'

'Let's hope so. By the way, is it all right to use your apartment? The place we went to last night may not be safe,' I said.

'*Oui*. I don't think Fabien Cassou knew I have an apartment in the Rue Saint-Rustique. He was just following me. In fact, other than you and your superiors, the only person who knows about that place is Claude, or the White Rabbit, or whoever he really is. The police won't waste much time questioning people there about Fabien's death either, of that we can be sure. That's how it is these days. Unless it's a German, the authorities don't seem to care who gets beaten up or murdered.

'One word of caution, though – don't transmit your Morse messages from the apartment. The Germans have detector vans out most days and nights. I don't want them catching you there while on air. Choose another building or transmit from the roof. And keep your messages as short as you can. If your wireless set can be worked using battery power, then use that rather than mains electricity whenever possible. The Germans narrow their searches by cutting power to individual buildings, one at a time. If they flip a switch and at the same time it cuts your transmission, they know they've found the right place.'

'Thanks for the warning,' said Freya.

'There's a hidden space at the back of the broom cupboard where you can hide your radio set too: look for a false panel on the left-hand side.' Trébuchet reached into his pocket and handed over a set of keys. 'There were four of you last night. Where's that boy who's an expert with the catapult? I had a lump the size of Mont Blanc when I woke up this morning. I'd like to be properly introduced to him so I can wring his neck.'

'He's just someone we stumbled into on our travels –

we don't seem to be able to get rid of him,' Loki replied. 'Keeps turning up like a bad penny.'

'That's unfair,' I said. 'He has helped us. More than once.'

'True,' Loki admitted reluctantly. 'But I can't help feeling that one day he'll land us all in big trouble. He's got a big mouth.'

'How much do you know about Claude?' Freya asked Trébuchet. 'Do you think he's been captured or turned traitor?'

'Or decided to run away and take the money with him. New identity. New life,' I added.

'Anything is possible,' Trébuchet replied, and then looked thoughtful. 'I see it like this. At some time or other we have all had to take a momentous decision – whether to resist the Nazis or not. Our work carries great risk, day in, day out. Like all of us, Claude took that decision. But think about this . . . to then decide to disobey orders, to appear to vanish with a large sum of money, to destroy all the trust built up with your superiors, to become the hunted by both sides – well, that I think is an even harder decision. If that is what Claude has done, then I can only think that it must be the act of a desperate man.' Trébuchet glanced at his watch and then downed the rest of his beer. 'I have to go. I suggest we meet here again in a week from now at the same time – midday. If you need to contact me before then, do it through London. I'm in communication with them almost daily. By the way, you do know, don't you, that they've instructed others to look for Claude too.'

That was news to us. 'No. Who?'

Trébuchet got up and shrugged in a typically French manner. 'God knows. By the way, try to avoid any contact on the street with members of the *Front Jeune*. They are often dressed in dark clothes – almost a sort of paramilitary uniform – and occasionally travel by car: petrol and permits are provided by their contacts in the SS and Gestapo. There aren't many of them, but I fear the death of Fabien may lead to reprisals. Remember, one week from now, same time, same place. Good hunting.'

After Trébuchet had left we waited a couple of minutes and then readied ourselves to leave as well. Freya's thoughts turned to visiting Nils that afternoon. 'I hope he's is awake and feeling OK. Can't wait to see him.'

The waitress zigzagged between the tables towards us, clutching the bill. While Freya counted out the cash plus tip, the waitress said, 'I hear you speak English. You American?'

'Yes,' I lied.

Her eyes lit up. '*Bon!* From New York?'

'Connecticut. It's not far from New York. A couple of hours, that's all.'

The waitress leaned on the back of Loki's chair and added dreamily, 'Ah! The glittering lights of Broadway. I've always wanted to go there. I wanted to be an actress, you know. A star!' She sighed heavily as her dream evaporated. 'So, you live in Paris?'

'Just visiting. We're looking for someone.'

'Oh. When Germans come, many people leave city.

Some come back. Others stay away. Many people look for missing family.'

'This is him,' said Loki, removing his copy of Claude's photograph from his pocket. 'Recognize him? We think he may have lived around here before the Germans invaded.'

The waitress gave it a cursory glance. '*Non!* But I only work here for six months. Please, wait a moment.'

Taking the photograph, she wove her way between the tables to the far side of the room and stopped next to three old men playing dominoes. I watched her show them the photo, point towards us and talk animatedly. First one man shook his head, then another, but the third removed his wire spectacles and peered at the picture closely. Then he lifted his watery gaze and began scanning the walls. He pointed at something and the waitress turned to look.

Flushed with excitement, she hurried back to our table. 'Monsieur Cabot has lived in Montmartre all his life. He recognizes your friend. Why you not tell me he a famous man?'

'Famous?'

'*Mais oui! Un célébrité très importante.* Come, see – I show you.'

She led us to the opposite end of the room. Like everywhere else, every inch of the wall had been pasted over with old, yellowing posters. 'Here! This one.'

Annoyingly, we could only see one tiny section of the poster in question. The rest was covered up. All I could read was a large M.

'*Attendez un moment.*' Reaching out, the waitress began lifting the edge of the uppermost poster with a fingernail. Then, gripping the corner, she gently applied a constant pressure and it peeled away in her hand, revealing, as if by magic, the one she wanted us to see. '*Voilà!*'

Loki's mouth flapped open in astonishment.

'Is this some sort of sick joke?' said Freya. 'It's impossible. *Impossible.*'

Stunned, I read the poster out loud: '*Avec le plus grand plaisir, le Théâtre Palais Royal présente Madura le Magnifique, le meilleur magicien de Paris . . . With great pleasure the Royal Palace Theatre presents Madura the Magnificent, the best magician in Paris . . .* He's the man in our photograph? . . . Are you sure? . . . Bloody hell!'

Chapter Thirteen
Pieces of the Jigsaw

'What do you mean *it all makes sense*, Finn?' Loki grabbed hold of me and stopped me dead in the middle of the street. 'Explain it to Freya and me one more time.'

'All right. Think back to Sir Hugo Foster and his Ministry of Tricks. Someone like Madura would be worth his weight in gold to Sir Hugo. An expert in illusion and deception – just what Sir Hugo was after.'

'Yes, we get that bit, Finn. The bit we don't get is that he's Ross's father. That's a miraculous coincidence – us turning up here in France, and the first person we bump into is the son of the very man we're after. The chances of that happening must be a million to one.'

I shook my head. 'No. Much, much better than that. Think about it. During our briefing we were told that he's visited France before, that he's supposedly one of F-Section's most reliable couriers. Remember?'

'Yes, Finn. But . . .'

'Now, put yourself in his position. He has family close to Paris, in and around Les Andelys – family including Laurent Laval, a leader of the local Resistance. I bet you he arrived like we did, by Lysander. Right smack in the middle of Laval's farm!'

'That would make sense,' Freya interrupted. 'He'd know he could trust his welcoming committee. And it would be a chance to see his family and catch up on the latest news.'

'Exactly! Freya, we'll check it out by asking HQ to confirm how "Claude" enters and leaves France,' I said, adding, 'But I know I'm right. I can feel it in my bones.'

Loki scratched his head. 'Let's find a bench. I need to sit down. I've got brain ache trying to figure all this out.'

Locating a seat in a small, windswept park, well away from eavesdroppers, the three of us huddled together against the cold. Freya continued, 'It explains Ross's behaviour as well. All his crazy antics with his friend Luc – asking us for carborundum powder, his willingness to take risks, his burning desire to fight back. I can see it now as clear as day. He's desperately trying to emulate his father.'

'And each time his father passes through, he teaches Ross some of our Special Ops tricks of the trade,' I added. 'Remember, Loki, how Luc and Ross used hand signals on our way into Les Andelys – exactly the signals that we'd been taught. And the way they went about forging those documents. I thought they were just like us lot. No agent would waste precious time teaching any old kid that kind of stuff, but if it was his son – well, that'd be different. Probably wanted to impress him.'

'But there's still one thing I don't understand, Finn. And I reckon it bashes a pretty massive hole in our theory.'

'What's that, Loki?'

'Why didn't the brigadier or Sir Hugo tell us that Claude Chevalier was a false name, his *nom de guerre*?

They must know he's Madura the Magnificent. After all, why else assign him to the Ministry of Tricks?'

Freya took a sharp in-breath. 'Hell. They must also know his real surname is Munro. Why didn't they tell us that either? It simply doesn't make sense.'

I felt I was sinking like the *Titanic*. Loki had just steered a massive iceberg into our path of reasoning. I let out a groan of frustration. 'There's only one thing for it. We'll transmit a message to HQ explaining what we've deduced. It'll be interesting to see what the brigadier has to say.'

Freya shot up from the bench and turned to face Loki and me. 'Hang on a minute. What if Sir Hugo and the brigadier *don't* know he's Madura the Magnificent?'

'Go on . . .' I said hesitantly.

'Look, we have no reason to doubt the brigadier. He'd not mislead us like that, surely. And sending us here without such obvious intelligence would be pointless. No, they don't know. The more I think about it, the more certain I am.'

'But why would Claude — Madura, or whatever we ought to call him — lie to our superiors?'

'Because there has to be more to this, Finn.'

'The money?' Loki offered.

'Could be. Maybe he gambles. Owes people a lot of money,' I suggested. 'Perhaps when he ran off to Britain, he was escaping more than just the invading Nazis.'

Freya rapidly thought it through. 'So he decided to adopt a false identity so no one would ever be able to find him. The evacuation of Dunkirk was the perfect cover: hundreds of thousands of people trying to escape amid a continuous barrage from approaching German troops. Utter chaos, the perfect smokescreen. Arriving in England, all he'd have to say was that he lost his identity papers in all the confusion.'

'And having joined Special Ops and been entrusted as a courier carrying millions of francs, maybe he saw the chance to pay everyone off, to clear his debts and wipe the slate clean,' Loki added.

We all felt briefly euphoric. We'd fashioned a version of the truth that fitted all the facts. A shadow was cast over us, however, when we realized that even if it was true, it didn't solve a fundamental problem – we still didn't have a clue where Ross's father was.

'At least the brigadier ought to be impressed that we've found out who Claude really is.'

'No, Loki!' Freya blurted. 'We're not going to tell HQ anything. Not yet. Remember what Trébuchet said? They're sending more search teams.'

'Yeah. So?'

'If they locate him before we do, they may well shoot first and ask questions later. We stick to our plan. We find him and ascertain the truth as to whether he's a double agent or not. We're one step ahead. Let's keep it that way.'

Loki peered up at the grey, brooding sky, and whistled. 'So *that's* why he's been so keen to hang onto our coat tails.'

'What do you mean?' Shivering, Freya grabbed hold of her hat to stop the wind from whipping it off her head.

'Ross overheard us at the farm talking about Claude and the White Rabbit — saying that when we found him, we might have to shoot him. He pretended he didn't know who we were talking about, but he's lying. I'm sure of it. He knows we were referring to his father. He's sticking to us like glue to make sure he can either stop us, or at the very least warn him. The clever little sod. He had me fooled.'

I rose to my feet and slapped the palm of my hand against my forehead. 'How could we be so blind? You're a genius, Loki. Of course. Ross! He holds the key. I'll bet you a million francs he *knows* where his father is. And I'll bet you another million francs he knows what his father's up to, as well.'

Loki got up and rubbed his hands together feverishly. 'Then I think it's about time we cut through all the bullshit and had a quiet little chat with Ross. And if we need to do some serious arm-twisting — you can leave that to me.'

Chapter Fourteen
'Tally Ho!' The Hunt Begins

As there was still no sign of Ross in Louise's apartment, we decided to visit Nils as originally planned. We also agreed that, despite the risks, we'd confide in Nils about our mission and seek his advice about what to do with Claude when we finally caught up with him. Nils was one of the few people we could trust to keep his mouth shut.

A different nurse was on duty at the front desk of the American Hospital; she eyed us suspiciously when we asked to see the man who'd arrived and undergone surgery the previous day. We weren't sure what name Nils was registered under. Recalling what Mother Thérèse had told us about the hospital, we figured they'd be extremely careful to make sure all their patients had either French or American sounding names in case the Germans carried out a routine search. She pretended not to understand, and so we asked to speak to Dr Alexander.

'Ah, yes, follow me,' the doctor said when he emerged from his office; he smiled, nodding an *It's OK, we can trust them* to the nurse at the desk. 'We've given him the name Frank Carlisle, from Minneapolis, and I'm happy to inform you that Frank is doing swell.' With his white coat flapping behind him, he trotted quickly up a staircase and led us along a corridor. 'Not too long now. Don't want to tire him.' He stopped outside a door. 'Thought it best to keep him separate from the other patients for the time being. Nurse Céline overheard him mumbling in his sleep. Not in English or French.'

'Norwegian,' I said.

'Ah. Just as well then. Here we are. Twenty minutes. No more. All right? I'll be in my office if you need me.'

Freya ran and gave Nils a hug. 'We were so worried about you. You looked terrible yesterday. There was a moment in the truck when I didn't think you'd make it.'

Nils was sitting up in bed, his head resting on plumped-up pillows. He looked drowsy and a little pale but pleased to see our familiar faces. 'You three took one hell of a risk. And I'm grateful. But, like I told you, you should've handed me over to the Germans. It could all have turned out so horribly differently. If you'd been caught bringing me here, your mission would have been over before it had even begun.'

'Freya and I half thought about it,' said Loki apologetically. 'You've got Finn to thank. What was it you said, Finn? Over your dead body, wasn't it?'

Nils grinned at me. 'Sounds just like you, Finn. Thanks. They're treating me like a king in here too. I'm amazed anyone would ever want to get better.'

We explained to Nils that we'd met Charles Thorpe from the American embassy, that he was OSS, and that he'd assist Dr Alexander in planning some sort of escape back to England when Nils was well again.

'He paid me a visit this morning.'

'Who? Charles Thorpe? That was quick.'

'To be honest, I got the distinct feeling he was on a fishing expedition. Kept going on about how appalled he was that the British were sending over kids to do a man's job – said you'd mentioned to him that you were looking for someone. He droned on and on, saying that such matters ought to be left to the professionals, that if he knew more, he'd find whoever it was in half the time and with the minimum of fuss.'

'What did you say?'

'Just that I'm a pilot and know absolutely nothing about your mission, Finn. I said I'd never met you before you turned up at the airfield the other night. I followed standard procedure. Tell nobody anything. Deny everything. I hope I did the right thing.'

'Absolutely,' I said. 'We've radioed HQ, so they know you're here. I guess you just need to sit tight. From what we've heard, so long as Dr Alexander manages to keep the Germans out, you should be as safe here as anywhere in occupied France.'

Nils grew embarrassed. 'Sorry I made such a hash of everything. I should never have agreed to fly in such atrocious weather. I took an unnecessary risk. I could've got us all killed.'

Freya sat down on the edge of the bed. 'I think the brigadier would've insisted you fly us in, anyway. We've heard from our contact that he's instructed others to join the search. I guess finding our target really is as important as the brigadier said. Listen, Nils, can we ask your advice about something?'

'Sure, Freya, fire away.'

Nils knew we were after a man in possession of secrets, but he had no idea that he was a member of Special Operations or that we might have to *eliminate* him. Freya filled him in. 'We won't kill one of our own, Nils – not unless we have proof he's double crossed us and changed sides. And even then only if . . .' She glanced round at Loki and me before adding, 'We realize that it may mean disobeying direct orders – orders that have come from Mr Churchill himself. But we won't do it. What do you think? Are we right? I mean, this is war, and we know that in war sometimes awful things have to be done for the greater good and all that, but . . .'

Nils reached out and took her hand. He considered his reply carefully. 'I understand your predicament. The way I see it is this. You locate this man Claude, or Madura, or whoever he is, if you can, and determine the truth. If he is a traitor, then you should carry out your orders. If he isn't a traitor, however, and simply has his own problems to sort out, then I think it is your duty to try and persuade him to return with you to Britain. If he refuses, then maybe you can leave it at that. You inform the brigadier that you've done what you can. Let him slip through your net if need be – if that's what it takes.'

'What, and let the other agents deal with him?' I asked.

Nils shrugged. 'There is only so much you can do, Finn. You can only act according to your own conscience. You can't do so for others. They must make their own choices.' He could see Freya looked unhappy. 'Listen, I bet this Claude isn't a fool. He knows the score.' He smiled. 'Do what you feel is right. Be guided by the voice of reason inside you. I know it has served you well until now.'

'What will happen to us if we disobey orders?' I asked. 'Will they send us to the Forgetting School? Will that be it? Will our time in Special Ops be over?'

'It's a possibility,' Nils replied solemnly. 'X and the brigadier might decide that you can no longer be relied upon to carry out orders. They may figure it's too dangerous to employ you again in another mission. On the other hand, they must appreciate that you are here, in the thick of it, while they're far removed from all the action. Agents have to make difficult decisions in the field, respond to changing situations, be flexible and adapt to survive. Of course, if you find out that Claude's still on our side, maybe HQ will be satisfied and leave it at that, provided his loyalty can be proven.'

'Thanks for the advice. Anything we can get for you?' Loki asked.

'No. In fact, it may be best if you don't visit me again. I have to get well and then try to head home. You have your job to do. Every time our paths cross, it may simply add to the risk for all of us. Best if we say "Cheerio" and look forward to being reunited back at Mulberry someday soon.'

None of us liked the idea but we knew he was right. We talked a while longer and then said our goodbyes. Leaving the hospital, we headed for the Métro. Next stop Louise's apartment again to see if Ross had returned.

Leaning into the strong, gusting wind, cyclists battled their way along the hilly streets of Montmartre, occasionally ringing their bells to warn absent-minded pedestrians thinking about dashing out in front of them. Outside an ironmonger two men in overalls busily unloaded crates from the back of a horse-drawn cart. Parisians of all shapes and sizes walked the pavements. Long queues snaked from the doorways of butchers' and bakers'. A middle-aged woman pushed a pram against the slope of the hill, her shoulders hunched against both the biting gale and misery of her frugal existence under the Nazi jackboot. Without a uniform in sight, the area almost looked normal, like a Parisian street ought to on a bitter winter's afternoon.

We were a hundred yards from Louise's apartment block when a car screeched round a nearby corner, accelerated hard and zoomed past us. With so few vehicles about, it was a noise that instantly struck fear into us. The car swerved, mounted the pavement on the other side of the street and came to an abrupt halt. Doors swung open and three young men leaped out, two brandishing hefty sticks. They were all dressed in dark clothes and wore armbands. Shouting obscenities, they began smashing the plate-glass windows of a shop, their actions frantic, vicious, manic. They were barely twenty yards in front of us. We dipped into a doorway and watched as people scattered, and frightened cyclists did U-turns and pedalled hard in the opposite direction.

'What the hell is going on?' Loki whispered. 'A robbery? What do we do now? We have to go past them to get to Louise's.'

'We wait,' I replied. 'I reckon they'll scarper. Just as soon as they've finished what they came here for.'

Having destroyed the windows, two of the men hurriedly filled their pockets with items that had been on display and then barged their way into the shop. It was a *bijoutier*, a jeweller's. Like Loki, I suspected a robbery was underway until I saw the name of the owners painted above the shop sign: R. & R. WEITZMANN. They were Jews. I feared the worst. 'Hell, I reckon this is about to turn very nasty. We should double back.'

Before we could make a break for it, an elderly couple emerged from the shop. It looked like they'd both been given an almighty shove through the door because the woman stumbled and fell heavily. She cowered there on the ground.

Amid yells of '*À bas les Juïfs! À bas les Juïfs*' – down with the Jews! – one of the men began beating them with his stick. The second took delight in kicking them both. The third began daubing something on the wall beside the shop door in bright yellow paint. It was a grotesque gallows, with a stick-like figure on the end of a hangman's noose. And on the chest of the figure he painted the Star of David. Beneath, he scrawled in thick paint, *Pour Fabien!*

'Jesus, it's a revenge attack for their fallen comrade,'

Loki hissed. 'They must be *Front Jeune*. The bastards! Finn, we should do something.'

'And get arrested? No way. This isn't our fight.'

There was a fourth man who had remained behind the steering wheel of the car. Leaving the engine running, he jumped out clutching a length of rope. He threw it expertly over a tall lamppost, and we saw that the rope had a noose on the end of it.

Loki grabbed my arm and glared at me. 'Then what *is* our fight? They're going to murder them, Finn. In broad daylight. We can't let it happen.'

'He's right,' said Freya. 'You have to stop them. But no guns in case the Paris police or Germans arrive. Hand me your revolvers for safekeeping. I'll cover you. Only if they get the better of you will I intervene.'

Unarmed, we purposefully strode towards the unfolding nightmare. Taking deep, fortifying breaths, Loki flexed his shoulders and cracked his knuckles. 'Time to make Killer proud of us, Finn. Time to put all those hours of practice to good use.'

Back at Mulberry, Kip 'Killer' Keenan had been our instructor in unarmed combat. Having worked in the Far East, Killer knew a thing or two – he was an expert in jujitsu, and had made us practise bone-breaking moves until we were exhausted and ached from head to toe. But this was for real. Four against two. Poor odds – but then Loki was worth two of them any day. He was as strong as an elk.

'You take the one slinging that rope over the lamppost, Finn. I'll handle the two dishing out the hiding to that poor woman. The fourth can't do much damage with a paintbrush.'

We moved swiftly but calmly. We didn't shout or yell. It wasn't a case of bundling in with fists flying. Killer had taught us that it was all about using minimum force to disable the opponent. He'd shown us how even the biggest oaf could be reduced to a whimpering, gibbering wreck by targeting vulnerable points. We were almost upon them when, out of the corner of my eye, I spotted another car turn into the street − a metallic-grey German staff car. About to warn Loki, I realized it was too late. He'd quickened his stride and reached one of the thugs dishing out the kicking to the old woman. In a single swift movement, with one hand he grabbed the youth's chin from behind and, placing his other hand against the back of his head, executed a perfect head-throw.

My target was attempting to force the noose over the head of the old man − who, I realized, had wet himself. His terror redoubled my determination. I seized the youth's left wrist and twisted it, effectively locking his elbow joint. His arm now acted as a pivot as I spun him round and slammed him against the lamppost. Someone seized me from behind and tried to yank me away. He placed his arm about my throat and yelled something nasty. Big mistake. I lifted my right foot and slammed it down, scraping his shin and bringing my heel down with maximum force onto the arch of his foot. I heard a crack, and he yelped in agony. Then I slammed an elbow into his ribs − not once but three times in quick succession. His grip slackened, and then he was gone as Loki hauled him off me.

'*Halt!*'

The youth I'd flung against the lamppost spun round and tried to land a punch to my face but I ducked just in time.

'*Halt!*'

He launched his fist again, and I blocked it with my forearm.

'*Halt!*'

Forming a tight fist, I sank it into his chest, driving the air from his lungs.

A single loud gunshot rang out. Everyone froze.

A German officer stood with his Luger pointing into the air. From his uniform I knew instantly that he was an airman. Beside him his driver brandished an MP40 sub-machine gun. My gaze returned to the officer. I recognized him from the photograph in Louise's apartment – Wolfgang Müller.

Müller took in the scene before him – the destruction of the shop, the broken glass by his feet, the daubed painting, the noose dangling from the lamppost, the weeping woman curled up on the ground, the elderly man shaking like a leaf, four youths dressed all in black . . . and Loki and me. He ordered us to place our hands on our heads and to line up, facing the wall. As we did so, the youths scowled at us in a manner that left us in no doubt they'd deal with us later. I reckoned they were barely older than us.

Gently Müller helped the old woman to her feet. She

was covered in cuts and bruises. The old man took her in his arms and they stood there together, weeping.

Hearing a familiar voice, I risked turning my head and saw Louise climbing out of the back of the German's car. She was still wearing her floral dress. Our eyes met. When she recognized me, a shadow of horror crossed her face. I willed her to say something, anything to help us out of the mess.

'*Papiere*,' Müller barked.

While his driver steadied his sub-machine gun at us, Müller ordered the police to be summoned *immediately*. A neighbouring shopkeeper nodded and disappeared inside his shop to make the call. Awaiting their arrival, Müller moved down the line, inspecting everyone's identity papers. He took his time, studying each closely and at length. Freya kept her distance. I could see her watching via a reflection in an adjacent shop window. Eventually Müller reached me and snatched my papers out of my hand.

'*Ah! Amerikanisch.*'

Louise stepped forward and whispered something in his ear. She did so hesitantly – so much so that I figured she wasn't sure it was a wise thing to do. Müller acknowledged her with the faintest of nods. Then he eyeballed Loki and me. 'So, I understand you are acquainted with Fräulein Munro here,' he said in English clipped with a heavy German accent. 'Tell me what happened.'

I explained and he listened. The youths from the *Front Jeune* cursed my every word, only shutting their mouths when Müller bellowed at them coarsely and his driver released the safety catch on his weapon. When I'd finished, he handed back my papers.

The Paris police arrived in force: two cars and a Black Maria – a windowless prison van – squealed to a stop behind Müller's staff car. The police piled out onto the pavement and hurried towards us. All except one were in uniform. The odd one out, a pot-bellied middle-aged chap with a bloated face, creased raincoat, stubble-framed chin and greying moustache, flung down his smouldering cigarette in the leaf-filled gutter and hitched up the sagging waistband of his trousers. He announced in French that he was Commissaire Touvier and informed everyone that he was now in charge.

'Very well, Commissaire. Arrest these four men for criminal damage, theft and attempted murder,' Müller barked in almost perfect French. 'Now! And get someone to clear up this mess. And get rid of that rope.'

Scratching his stubbly chin, Commissaire Touvier studied the line of *Front Jeune* recruits and the noose dangling from the lamppost. His gaze then shifted to the damaged shop front and, tutting loudly, he nodded to his men. They seized hold of their prisoners and began dragging them towards the back of the Black Maria.

'*Attendez!*' one of the youths pleaded, repeatedly insisting that he had something to show them.

Touvier raised a hand and ordered his men to stop.

The youth eagerly reached into a pocket and took out a permit, handing it to the commissaire. The police inspector studied it for a moment and then looked to the heavens and swore aloud. He approached Müller and thrust the permit into his hand.

'They have permission,' he said sharply, with more than a hint of contempt. I managed to follow the gist of their conversation. Touvier added, 'From your colleagues in the SS. If I arrest them, I shall get into a great deal of trouble. With this permit they will be back on the streets within two hours. Please, what else can I do? I have to let them go.' He glanced at the pitiful old couple who owned the jewellery shop. 'After all, it's a lot of unnecessary fuss over a pair of decrepit old Jews, isn't it? I expect they'll be rounded up in the next week or two anyway, just like the others. Maybe we can pretend this never happened, Herr Squadron Leader. It would be simpler all round.'

Müller was so outraged that he looked as if he was going to punch the commissaire in the face. But I read the French policeman differently: he was only saying what he thought the German wanted to hear, and he seemed mighty surprised at the airman's reaction. Yelling angrily, Müller demanded to know whether all the youths possessed such permits. They did, and they hurriedly fumbled in various pockets to produce them. Their initial trepidation had now been replaced by an almost arrogant confidence that they were untouchable. They fed off one another's expectant grins, clearly assuming that they were about to be released. And they were staring at Loki and me with all the hunger of a starving pack of wolves, as if we were already dead men.

Müller gathered up their permits, straightened them in his hand, and then tore them to shreds.

'*Non!*' one of the young men yelled, trying to rush forward. Touvier's men restrained him.

Looking the police inspector in the eye, Müller said dryly, 'What permits, Commissaire? I see no permits.'

Touvier beamed like a Cheshire cat given a double helping of cream. He rubbed his hands together gleefully. For once he had the upper hand. Without the permits he'd be free to bring charges; free to place the youths before a magistrate; free to watch them being carted off to prison. '*Bon!*' With delight he signalled for his prisoners to be bundled into the van. They went kicking and screaming. 'What about the other two?'

'Witnesses. Tried to help. That's all,' Müller replied dismissively.

'I'll need statements.'

'Yes, yes, I'll get them to write it all down, Commissaire. I will also write down what I saw – just in case the magistrate has any doubts. I'll have my driver drop them all off at the police station later today.'

'Thank you,' I said as we watched the police cars and the Black Maria turn off into a neighbouring street. My gratitude was aimed towards both Müller and Louise in equal measure.

'Staffelkapitän Wolfgang Müller at your service,' the airman replied, clacking his heels together and offering a slight, well-practised bow. 'You took quite a risk intervening like that. There were four of them and just two of you. They were armed as well. You're either brave or stupid, or both.'

'What else could we do? Watch them murder that innocent old couple?' Loki spat.

Wolfgang shook his head. 'No. I suppose not.'

We introduced ourselves properly to him and waved Freya over. With typical German formality he bent forward and kissed the back of her hand. Freya said nothing, but I knew what she was thinking: *I've got several revolvers in my pockets and I'd like to use one of them.*

'We should go inside,' said Louise, conscious of the stares we were getting from her neighbours.

'Yes. Good idea. I need the statements from these two.' Wolfgang turned to his driver and ordered him to wait outside.

'So you want us to write everything down, just like we saw it?' I asked. I was sitting with the blank sheet of paper on the table in front of me, a sharpened pencil in my hand.

Wolfgang sank into the deep cushions on the sofa and, blowing the steam from the top of his cup of coffee, replied, 'Yes. Write your name and address, your identity number and today's date at the top of the page. Summarize what you saw and then sign it at the bottom.'

Loki was sitting opposite me, pen poised. He caught my eye and pulled a face. *Which address?* he mouthed at me.

It was a good point. The last thing I wanted was for the authorities to know about Trébuchet's flat as we were intending to use it. Also, Louise wouldn't thank us for giving her address. 'Staffelkapitän Müller, sir, is it all right if we give the American embassy as our address? They know us there, and we're in contact with them about making arrangements for heading home. It might be better than giving our current address,' I lied.

Wolfgang nodded and, when he looked away, Loki gave me the thumbs-up.

Loki read what I'd written and checked it against his version for consistency. Meanwhile I decided to find out a little more about Staffelkapitän Wolfgang Müller. 'What kind of aircraft do you fly, sir?'

'Various, Simon. Mainly Dornier seventeens. Occasionally Heinkel one-elevens.' He dug out a photograph of himself alongside his flight crew standing next to a large Dornier bomber. 'We've been through quite a lot together, I can tell you.'

'I bet.' I studied it closely. The young faces. The smiles. It was weird. Their flying gear looked different from that worn by the RAF, of course, but somehow the picture was familiar – very similar to many I'd seen of British aircrews. 'Thanks.' I handed it to Loki. 'Johnny and I want to be pilots too.'

Wolfgang smiled approvingly.

'The Dornier's nicknamed the *Fliegender Bleistift*, the Flying Pencil, isn't it? It's so sleek I can understand why,' Loki observed.

'Yes, she's fast. Some might say beautiful, even. Not very well armoured though. But she has quite a sting in her tail.'

'Do you mean her bomb load?' I asked.

'Yes.'

'Do you ever think about the people on the ground? When you drop your bombs?'

I thought Freya's question unwise but Wolfgang reacted as if he got asked it every day of his life.

'Yes, sometimes,' he reflected. 'But high up, engines droning, flak exploding all around us, to be honest there isn't much time to think about it. It is only later, back at base, that you have time to dwell on it. We are proud to be pilots in the Luftwaffe, but, like any decent person, we question the need to bomb British cities. I mean, industrial and military installations are fair targets, but destroying densely populated civilian areas leaves a bad taste in our mouths . . . I would rather avoid them, but orders are orders. I can only imagine the hell the poor people of Britain are experiencing. Mind you, our cities are getting bombed too. All in all, pretty insane. But we are mere *Untergebene*.'

Freya translated. 'You mean underlings or servants.'

'*Ja. Danke.* You speak German?'

'A little.'

I wondered whether his view would be hardened if he saw the Blitz for himself; if he was made to stand on a street corner as the air-raid sirens wailed, bombers thundering overhead, and was forced to remain there while everything about him was flattened, broken, turned into fire and dust. What if he had to dig through the rubble with his bare hands to drag out the charred remains of loved ones? Of course, I said nothing. In fact, far from hating our enemy, I was warming to Wolfgang.

Loki had a question. 'I know you tore up their permits, but won't they be let off when they appear in front of the magistrate? All they need to do is ask for the SS or Gestapo to intervene on their behalf.'

'Possibly. But that's why I shall submit my report too as evidence. I think it highly unlikely that the SS would bother to counter my statement. Those youths aren't worth their time and trouble. No, I expect them to spend a long time behind bars at Fresnes prison.'

Having gathered up our statements and read them through, Wolfgang rose from the sofa and declared that he needed to get going.

Louise had said little since we'd arrived back, and merely grimaced with a mix of relief and disappoint-ment. Her manner, the way she looked at him, however, left me in no doubt – she *was* in love with him. And there was something else. Every time he looked up at her and smiled, his eyes then fell upon her midriff, as if attracted there by a powerful magnet. Having dropped his cap back on his head, he kissed her goodbye and, placing a hand on her stomach, gently patted it. Freya noticed it too. Was it possible? Was Louise pregnant?

She showed Wolfgang to the door. When she returned from the hall, she stood in the middle of the living room with her hands on her hips. Her manner had changed. She'd turned inquisitor. 'Who are you? Why are you here?'

'We're the Stevens family from Connecticut,' Loki replied bluntly. 'We bumped into Ross the other day.

It's a long story. He's been a great help.'

'I saw the way you dealt with those youths earlier. Just two against four of that lot would normally be suicide, but you knew what you were doing. They didn't stand a chance.'

'True.' Loki caught my eye and grinned.

'You haven't dragged Ross into any kind of serious trouble, have you?'

Freya laughed ironically. 'Ross is pretty good at getting himself into trouble. He doesn't need our help.'

Louise studied us uncertainly, trying to figure us out, as if we were a really tricky cryptic crossword puzzle.

'Ross told us that your father was a famous magician,' said Loki, hurriedly changing the subject. 'Madura the Magnificent. Great name. He even showed us a card trick his father had taught him. Impressive.'

Louise's twisted expression softened. 'Ross idolizes his dad. But, unlike me, Ross didn't have to work as his assistant. Dad could be – how shall I put it? – *demanding*. Everything on stage had to be just perfect, night in, night out. Quite a strain.'

'You were on stage too?'

'Yes. I was the one always disappearing from cupboards or being sawn in half. I'm double-jointed, you see. I can make myself really, really small.' She made her way over to the writing desk and took out some of the programmes I'd seen when having a snoop. She found the one she was looking for, opened it and held it out. 'That's me next to Dad.'

Loki and I gawped at the photograph of an exotically dressed Louise posing seductively next to a man in top hat and tails.

'At first, I was quite relieved when Dad decided he wanted to try and recreate Harry Houdini's most famous escapes. It meant I just had to stand and look gorgeous while he did all the work.'

'But it went horribly wrong, didn't it? That's what Ross told us.'

She nodded. 'Yes, Dad thought the Water Torture Cell escape would be the pinnacle of his career. It was madness. Being trussed up and immersed in a tank of water, so many things could go wrong. And it *did* go wrong. A glittering career over in a flash. One mistake that nearly got him killed. Afterwards, I made him swear never to take to the stage again; never to perform another trick in public.' Returning the programme to the drawer, she slid it shut and then asked, 'Please don't say anything to Ross about Wolfgang and me.'

'He already knows,' I said, and Louise stiffened with a jolt.

'But I don't think he knows you're pregnant with Wolfgang's child. It is Wolfgang's, isn't it?' Freya added.

The colour drained from Louise's face, and she reached out and grabbed the arm of a chair to steady herself. 'B-b-but how . . . ?'

'It was the way he looked at you,' said Freya. 'Seems to me like you've got yourself into quite a mess.'

Louise crumbled before us. She sank down onto the sofa, bent forward over her knees and wept. 'It wasn't meant to happen,' she wailed. 'Everything's gone so horribly, horribly wrong. What am I going to do?'

Freya sat down beside her and offered Louise her handkerchief. 'Ross told us your uncle Laval visited you recently to try and persuade you to go back to his farm. He said the two of you fell out big time. Your uncle knows, doesn't he?'

Louise nodded. 'He blew his top. Said I had to get rid of the baby. Said if I didn't, the family would disown me.'

'Will you get rid of it?'

'No! How could I do such a thing? Wolfgang's asked me to marry him after the war is over.'

'Have you said yes?' I asked.

Lowering her hankie, she gazed up at me, her large hazel eyes bloodshot and glistening wet. She looked like a cornered mouse. 'No . . . not yet. Maybe . . . oh, I don't know.'

Freya had a knack of reading people, of sensing the truth behind their faces and their words; her intuition rarely let her down. 'Meeting Wolfgang in the first place wasn't accidental, was it? You deliberately set out to attract him in the hope of learning something useful, didn't you? I'm right, aren't I? You're working for the Resistance.'

Louise baulked at hearing the word *Resistance*. Her instinct was to vehemently deny it, and she blurted out, 'No!' but she could see we didn't believe her. 'No,' she repeated less convincingly, and then added, 'Not the Resistance *exactly*.'

Freya pressed her further. 'Only, having got to know him, you found yourself falling in love with him, didn't you? And that wasn't part of the plan, was it?'

'No.'

'What did you mean when you said "not the Resistance *exactly*"?' Loki asked.

Louise hesitated. 'Ross told me all about you – that you flew here from England, and that you're after someone called the White Rabbit. That you're going to kill him. Is it true?'

Loki shook his head angrily. 'I knew it. I knew The Kid couldn't keep that big mouth of his shut. Just wait until I catch up with him.'

Freya told Loki to calm down. 'Listen, Louise,' she began. 'We can't tell you anything except to say that many lives are at stake. Our mission is important. Extremely important. That's all we can say other than you can trust us.'

The alarm bells clanged in my head as it dawned on me that Louise almost certainly knew that her father and the White Rabbit were one and the same – and that therefore our reason for being in Paris was to locate and eliminate him. We had to tread extremely carefully. On the other hand, it also occurred to me that she might know his whereabouts. If only we could get her to talk. I had an idea. I took Loki and Freya to one side and whispered, 'I think it's time we came clean. We owe Louise that much. After all, she intervened earlier in the street to help us out. By telling Wolfgang that she knew us, she almost certainly prevented our arrest. And in doing so she risked making life difficult for herself.'

Horrified, Loki interrupted, 'No, Finn, it's too risky.'

'But don't you see? She already knows why we're here. If we deny it, God knows what she'll do. We should explain that our intention isn't to eliminate Claude, rather to persuade him to return to Britain.'

'And what makes you think she'll believe us? If I were in her position, I wouldn't trust us further than I could throw us.'

'True. I've thought about that. Despite what she thinks our mission is, she still helped us earlier. She could have left us to hang out to dry, but she didn't. Ask yourself why . . .'

Loki turned to Louise. 'Why did you come to our rescue outside earlier?'

'I supposed that if you were caught and interrogated there was a lot of information the Gestapo could extract from you – information that might place others' lives in jeopardy. It was a split-second decision. I just hope I don't live to regret it. And anyway, I saw you take on those thugs of the Youth Front. There aren't many who are willing to do that.'

'Most of what Ross told you is true, Louise,' I confessed. 'But he's wrong about one thing. We don't *want* to kill the White Rabbit. The problem we face is that he went missing with a lot of money and a head full of secrets. Our superiors don't know why he vanished, but they are concerned that he may have turned traitor. Our mission is to find him and take him back to Britain.'

I wasn't telling the whole truth, of course. What I neatly avoided saying was that if he refused to return to Britain or if he'd turned traitor, then we might well *have* to eliminate him.

'Do you know where he is?' asked Freya.

Louise shook her head. 'No. I haven't seen him in months.'

Was she telling us the truth? I found it hard to tell. 'Is there *anything* you can tell us? For example, when did you last see him?'

Louise was growing increasingly apprehensive. Our ploy of openness seemed to be backfiring. Freya broke an uneasy silence, saying, 'You know we're part of the same organization as your father, don't you? Presumably Ross told you that too.'

Louise nodded.

Freya continued, 'There's something Ross doesn't know. In fact, neither did we until recently. We're not the only ones after your father.'

Louise's face filled with alarm. 'Who else?'

'We don't know,' said Loki. 'But believe me – it really would be best if we reached him first!'

'It's possible that the others will shoot first and ask questions later,' I added for good measure.

Anxiously twisting her handkerchief about her hands, Louise swallowed hard. I could see that her brain was in turmoil.

'Why Wolfgang? Why did you target him?' Freya asked. Suddenly changing the subject was a technique we'd been taught back at Mulberry. It often catches people off guard, especially those under stress. It worked. Louise began to open up.

'About nine months ago Dad came to see me. He said he was working against the Nazi occupation and asked if I was willing to help. He said it was really important, and so I agreed. He pointed Wolfgang out to me at a café and asked me to try to get close to him. Wolfgang is the leader of an elite bomber squadron called the *Kampfgruppe* 100. It was formed to test new systems for their Pathfinders. Dad wanted me to extract anything I could about the Luftwaffe's latest targeting methods.'

'And have you?' I asked.

Louise nodded. 'The Germans know the British have worked out how to jam the radio beams of their old system—'

'What – the one they codenamed Crooked Leg, or *Knickebein*?' Loki interrupted.

'That's right.'

'Go on,' I said encouragingly. 'What you've found out may be of great interest to our superiors.'

'Well, they've invented a new system. Wolfgang mentioned it a few times, but only in passing and in vague terms, kind of boastfully. I think he was trying to impress me. I tried piecing it together like a jigsaw, but there were still too many missing bits to make sense of it all. Of course, no way would Wolfgang elaborate as the system's a closely guarded secret. And anyway, if I showed too much interest it would arouse his suspicions. So, when I stay over at his apartment I use the opportunity to sneak a look at some of his papers. My German's not bad and I've found out that their new system's codenamed *X-Verfahren*. I'm no expert, but I think it's much more sophisticated than the old one. Now they're using four radio beams instead of two, and there's some sort of clockwork timer linked to the Pathfinder's bomb-release mechanism. I think it's enabled them to be far more precise in marking their targets.'

'Have you passed this on to your father?'

Louise didn't respond. Her thoughts drifted back towards her predicament and tears welled up again.

'Are you sure you don't know where your father is?' Loki asked – more forcefully than Freya had.

Louise shook her head slightly and then buried her face in her handkerchief.

'Falling for Wolfgang has certainly complicated things,' Freya muttered.

'Well, if it's any consolation, Wolfgang struck me as a pretty decent man,' I said. 'For a Nazi, that is.'

Louise blurted emotionally, 'He's no Nazi. He's so kind. He hates this war. He wants it to be over. He wants to go home to Heidelberg and take me with him. He's not like the others. He's not like the SS or the Gestapo. He's not like them at all. He hates Adolf Hitler. He thinks trying to take over the world is the vision of a lunatic, a complete madman. And he says you only have to look at what's happening to all the Jews to see that pure evil walks this earth. He even said to me that if he ever got the chance to meet Herr Hitler face to face he was equally likely to shoot him as shake his hand.'

'Fine words, but he's still wearing the uniform of the Third Reich,' Loki responded sharply. 'You should never forget that. Wearing that uniform means that he's part of it, whether he likes it or not. Whether *you* like it or not. He blindly does what he's told. We've witnessed the effects of the Blitz – the blasted streets, the firestorms, the countless deaths. Has he no conscience?'

Louise was quick to defend him. 'No conscience? Hah! The world is full of hypocrites. The British are doing the same. And I don't see very many Frenchmen acting to stop the Jews being rounded up. Everyone knows about the camps in the east. Everyone knows it's a one-way ticket to forced labour, maybe far worse. They just stand in the street and gawp as men and women are dragged from their beds and loaded onto trucks and trains like cattle. I've even heard one or two shout *Bon débarras!* – good riddance – and I'm sure others think it. And what about the Allies? Why haven't they done something? No, Johnny Stevens, we all have blood on our conscience. But what you did earlier today for the Weitzmanns was very brave. I just wish more had the courage to stand up to our *real* enemies, whatever colour uniform they're wearing.'

'Given your predicament, I wouldn't be surprised if part of you is praying the Germans win this war. Otherwise life could turn out really badly for you and your child.'

'Neighbours already shun me in the street, Lorna,' Louise hissed. 'They spit at me and call me filthy names for fraternizing. You can almost smell the hate. But I can hardly shout from the rooftops that I'm resisting the occupation, can I? Anyway, who are they to judge? Have they risked so much to find out information that might help the Allies win this war? Even if I *were* just fraternizing, would it make me any worse than those who steal food? And there are many out there who do steal; men and women who pretend to be *respectable*. My conscience is clear. I'm not an informer. I've not betrayed a fellow Frenchman. All I did was fall in love.'

'If liberation does ever come, Parisians will want revenge, big time,' I said. 'You should be prepared for it. They may not believe that you were doing work for us. You should make plans to start a new life somewhere else.'

Louise nodded weakly.

Although I had the distinct feeling we'd outstayed our welcome, we hung around at Louise's apartment, waiting for Ross to return from Fresnes prison. He didn't show up.

Freya glanced at the mantel clock for the umpteenth time. 'It's getting late. Tell me, Louise, how long does it take to get back from Fresnes prison?'

Louise pulled a face. '*Fresnes prison?*'

'Yes. Ross was going to visit your sister today.'

Louise frowned. 'They don't allow many visitors into that place, and certainly not for spies and members of the Resistance. Sophie's in solitary confinement. No privileges whatsoever: no books, no letters, no visitors. I don't know where Ross went today, but it wasn't to Fresnes prison.'

Chapter Fifteen
Dangerous Liaisons

For a week we trawled the streets, shops and cafés of Montmartre, asking after Madura – whether anyone recognized our photograph, whether anyone knew him, had seen him, or could tell us where he might be. We covered miles up and down the steep hills, and our feet grew sore and our legs ached abominably. We drank so much disgusting *ersatz* coffee and fizzy Coca-Cola that we often emerged from cafés feeling light-headed and sick. And we had to tread extremely carefully. Cafés were notorious places for informers to loiter, and a good many were frequented by off-duty soldiers too. We kept our eyes peeled for members of the *Front Jeune*.

Many locals had heard of the great magician, quite a few had seen one of his shows before the war, one or two claimed to have witnessed the night it all went wrong on stage for him. But, frustratingly, there'd been no recent sightings. One woman declared with absolute certainty that he was dead; another insisted that she'd heard he'd gone to America to start a new life.

Trébuchet had been doing the rounds as well: several customers informed us that a man had shown them an identical picture just the day before.

We were getting absolutely nowhere.

Our endless failure filled us with growing frustration.

Each day was becoming more of a grind, an exhausting waste of time. Loki said he felt like climbing to the top of the dome of the Sacré-Coeur with a loudhailer and barking out to the whole of Paris, *Oi, Madura, we give up. You win. You can come out of hiding now.*

As planned, we moved into Trébuchet's apartment. With the weather turning exceptionally cold, we slept with our clothes on, sometimes our overcoats too. Not that we slept much. Cold, real cold, has strange properties: it's somehow able to penetrate deep inside you, making your bones throb as if you have toothache in your whole body. The apartment block had a central heating system fuelled by a large furnace and boiler in the basement, but the pipes remained cold to the touch; you needed coal or wood to make it function. But there was no coal or wood; none whatsoever. Most nights I lay awake, exhaling misty breaths into the darkness, any hope of drifting towards sleep rudely disturbed by sudden bouts of shouting and cursing that reverberated in the stairwell at all hours, and the sudden slamming of doors, and the *thump, thump, thump* of heavy footsteps on our landing.

But the evenings were the worst. There was nothing to do. We couldn't risk going out, and all we had to amuse ourselves was our own company. It felt like we were imprisoned. Outside, empty, silent streets lay in darkness. Just occasionally we'd hear the pitter-patter of someone hurrying past, running flat out; someone daring to risk arrest. Once I thought I heard a distant gunshot echo. Was it someone resisting? I wondered who they were and whether they'd got away.

Our nerves were balanced on a knife edge. Frequent power cuts had us reaching for our weapons. They came without warning, the lights suddenly going off. Each time we feared it wasn't the whole of Paris being plunged into darkness but just our building, the Gestapo cleverly trying to tease out the location of Resistance fighters operating their wireless sets. Freya only had one spare battery, so she kept our messages short and only transmitted from the rooftop. Hard frosts made it extremely slippery, and she had to take care scrambling up through the hatchway and edging her way behind parapets and around chimney stacks. Dropping our suitcase radio or having a heavy fall would alert others that more than just prowling cats were out on the tiles.

HQ confirmed that 'Claude' had previously arrived and departed France via Cabbages and Kings – Laval's farm – and so at least that part of our reasoning had proved correct. As we'd agreed, we said nothing about knowing Claude's real identity. Apart from the brigadier's growing impatience at our lack of progress, we learned nothing new, and HQ refused to provide us with information about the 'other' groups that had been sent to expand the search. Their reluctance was understandable: it was best if groups acted alone just in case one or more got apprehended by the enemy. It was standard procedure in Special Ops.

As the temperature plummeted further, we awoke to a dusting of snow. Although it reminded us of Norway, our homeland, it did little to cheer us up.

There was also no news about Ross. Every afternoon we checked with Louise in case he'd called in on her. Loki began to wonder if he'd simply returned to his uncle's farm at Les Andelys.

Louise didn't appreciate our brief daily visits, but always relented and let us in. We asked to borrow food from her – we always said *borrow*, although she knew none of it would ever be returned. Our pleas for supplies weren't out of greed. It was simply that Paris was running out of food. The situation was grim: few doubted that a long hard would winter would kill thousands from malnutrition and starvation. It had happened the previous winter too. Everywhere we went, Parisians grumbled about it, saying that this year it might be ten times worse. HQ had supplied us with fake ration books and we had plenty of money, but neither was of any use if the shops had nothing to sell. And often they hadn't. We queued alongside other Parisians for what little there was on offer and it was barely enough to survive on. Louise's cupboard, however, was always full. It was our one source of amusement – little did Wolfgang realize that, indirectly, he was feeding his enemy.

After a week it was time to meet up again with Trébuchet. The waitress at the Wine Cellar smiled warmly at us. 'Any luck finding your friend?'

Feeling dejected, we shook our heads and reluctantly ordered three Coca-Colas while we waited for Trébuchet to turn up for our planned rendezvous.

'Never mind. Keep looking,' she said cheerily before breezing off to another table.

Trébuchet arrived just after midday. He threw himself down onto a spare chair at our table. '*Bonjour.*' He sat back and clasped his hands behind his head. He positively beamed at us.

'What are you so happy about?' said Loki from behind his raised glass of fizz.

Trébuchet shot forward and lowered his voice. 'Mystery solved, my little three blind mice. I, Trébuchet, have achieved the impossible. I know who we're looking for.' He sat back again. 'Well, aren't you going to congratulate me?'

'No,' said Freya.

Trébuchet was surprised. 'Really? Why not?'

'Because we already know who he is. *Monsieur Madura le Bloody Magnifique,*' Loki muttered. 'Also known as Monsieur Munro.'

Trébuchet was initially flabbergasted, then confused, and finally a little angry. 'Why didn't London inform me?'

'Because we haven't told them,' Freya responded.

Trébuchet's face went blank. '*Je ne comprends pas. Pourquoi?* Erm . . . why not?'

'Because we want to get to Monsieur Munro before the others do,' Freya replied. She went on to explain our reservations about our mission.

Trébuchet listened intently, assimilated it all, and then raked his fingers through his curly black hair. 'I wish you had told me all this from the start. I'm afraid I'm the bearer of bad news.'

'What bad news?' I asked.

'I've just sent a message to London. I've told them who Claude really is.'

'Oh hell.' Loki slammed a fist onto the table, making all our glasses jump.

'It gets worse,' Trébuchet continued. 'London's reply was short and to the point. My work in this matter is done. The others will be informed, and they are to be instructed to terminate Claude with extreme prejudice – together with anyone found assisting him and who therefore may also know his secrets.'

I felt my stomach sink into my boots. 'Jesus! You were right, Freya – they're going to shoot first and ask questions later. They have to be stopped.' To Trébuchet I added, 'Do you know who they are? Can we get London to call them off?'

'No. I have no idea who they've sent. You can try to get London to reconsider, but . . .' He paused to fire up a cigarette. 'But what if you're wrong? What if he *has* turned traitor? He must be stopped. Surely you understand that.'

'Yes,' Freya replied. 'Of course. But he's one of us, an agent with Special Ops. He must at least be given a chance to explain himself.'

Trébuchet shrugged. 'In an ideal world, perhaps. Sentiment is a luxury that runs out quickly during wartime.'

'It's not about sentiment,' Freya snapped. 'It's about doing what's right. What if it was you or me being hunted like an innocent fox?'

'Listen, I will help you if I can. I will keep my ears and eyes open and ask my people to do the same. If we find out anything, I'll come to the apartment and inform you. I can do no more than that. I have other work to do. Keeping a network going is virtually a full-time job.'

If we'd been feeling downhearted on going to meet Trébuchet, then we returned to our safe house under a cloud of depression. None of us dared utter what we each knew the other was thinking – we were going to fail. All our efforts had been for nothing.

Opening our apartment door, I noticed that someone had slipped an envelope underneath it while we were out. I picked it up and tore it open. 'What the devil . . .?'

Inside was a playing card: the six of clubs.

'Ross!' I announced, showing the others. 'Looks like he left a calling card. Remember, Loki – it was the card you chose when he did that magic trick.'

'Yeah, I remember, Finn. But there's no message. What's he playing at?'

Freya's face darkened. 'He might just be telling us that he knows where we are, that he's watching us; that if we get too close to his father, then—'

Loki snatched the card from my hand. 'The little tyke. Sounds just like him. Remember those bullets he and his pal Luc wanted to make, Finn, to send to others as a warning? This is just the same. A warning. Wait until I get my hands on him.'

'I'm not so sure, Loki,' I said, beckoning him to hand the card back. 'For all his faults, Ross isn't stupid. I think he's trying to tell us something. He's resourceful and ingenious, and from what we've seen, his father's taught him well.' I examined the card closely, staring long and hard at the pattern on the back. 'The card's not marked on the back or front. Maybe . . . just maybe . . .' I held it up to the light and then examined the edge. 'Yes. This is no ordinary card. This is one of ours – one of Special Ops'. We were shown them during training.'

Boffins working behind the scenes in Special Operations had come up with literally thousands of ways of concealing and disguising stuff. Playing cards were a typical example. Our experts had perfected a way of making cards from several incredibly thin layers that could be peeled apart. Unless you knew, they looked completely normal. Miniature maps and coded instructions were frequently printed on the hidden insides. I flicked at a corner of the card and, slowly, the two layers began to separate. 'Aha! Thought so. He's written something inside . . . *Meet at the Eiffel Tower. Tomorrow. Ten o'clock. Come unarmed and don't be late.*'

Chapter Sixteen
Vertigo

'Bleeding heck, it's only when you get up close and personal that you realize how big it is,' Loki said, gulping.

We craned our necks and gazed up at the magnificent metal framework of the Eiffel Tower. The way the four main pillars rose up in a curve towards the top somehow made it look as if the structure was so impossibly tall that it pierced the sky.

Next to the entrance to lifts and stairs awaiting eager sightseers, signs informed us that you could venture to the first level, at a trifling one hundred and eighty-seven feet, the more adventurous to the second level, at a heady three hundred and seventy-six feet; anyone wanting a real thrill could go all the way to the top. Level three, just over nine hundred feet. Loki shivered at the thought. He hated heights.

Standing beneath the tower, we took in our surroundings while waiting for Ross to arrive. He'd chosen well, I reckoned. It was an open area, and busy too, despite the bitter chill. There were soldiers milling about, some armed and on patrol, others off duty and strolling arm in arm with their Parisian girlfriends, taking in the sights, posing for photographs, laughing in a happy, carefree way. I couldn't blame them. For the first time since we'd arrived, I actually thought Paris looked beautiful. The clear blue sky, winter sunshine and crisp air made everything seem unnaturally bright and vivid.

Out of nowhere a boy of about nine or ten, hollow-cheeked and as skinny as a rake, ran up to us. He removed his cap to reveal a scramble of unwashed hair, and held it out as if begging.

'*Allez-vous en!*' Loki snapped, pushing him away. '*Allez-vous en!*'

'*Trois souriceaux?*' he asked in a squeaky, high-pitched voice. '*Trois souriceaux aveugles?*'

'*Oui?*' Freya replied.

We stared at the lad in astonishment. He'd asked if we were the three blind mice. Then I spun on my heels and looked about. *Clever, Ross*, I thought. *Staying out of view until you're absolutely sure it's safe.*

The boy gave us a toothless grin. '*Bon!*' He looked up and pointed to the top of the Eiffel Tower. '*Le sommet.* The very top. *Le Môme* there. *Le sommet.*' Still grinning, he turned and ran off, shouting at the top of his voice, '*Au sommet* − the very, very top.'

Loki shook his head. 'I'm not going up there, Finn. No way. Not in a million years. I simply won't, do you hear me? We can wait for Ross to come down. He'll have to eventually.' Agitated and breaking out in a cold sweat, he paced about, cursing. 'No . . . no . . . I can't . . . no way . . . You go . . . I'll stay here . . . Yes, that'd be best . . . You go and I'll stay.'

Freya took his arm. 'Come on. We do this together. You'll thank me afterwards.'

Loki tore himself free. 'No!'

'You've faced your demons before,' I said, recalling that he'd climbed onto roofs, even parachuted from the belly of an aircraft. 'Just imagine you're flying. You never have a problem flying.'

'That's different, Finn. I mean, just look at it – all the open girders and struts. I'll get vertigo. I just know I will.'

'We'll look after you.' I helped Freya ease him towards the entrance. 'Anyway, it's best if we stick together. We can't be sure what Ross is up to. Maybe he isn't alone up there. If it helps, close your eyes once we're inside.'

Several lift journeys were necessary in order to reach the large viewing gallery at the top, and when the lift doors opened, Loki had to be coaxed out like a frightened rabbit from its hutch. Visibly shaking, he stepped forward with all the apprehension of someone crossing a minefield. 'I can feel it moving, Finn. It's swaying. It's not safe.'

'It's not moving, you daft oaf. It's you who's swaying.' I peered around, trying to locate Ross. Few others had braved the top floor. I spotted just two couples. Both were gazing out over the rooftops of Paris, admiring the stunning panorama. 'No sign of him. Let's try round the other side.'

Ross was standing there alone, his back to the view, both hands deep in his coat pockets. He saw us, but didn't wave or call out.

'We've been trying to get hold of you all week,' Freya said. 'Where the hell have you been?'

'None of your business. What's the matter with him?'

'He hates heights,' I replied. Quaking in his boots, Loki had grabbed hold of a rail with both hands; he was a pale shade of green.

'They say you can see over forty miles from up here.' Ross leaned out and peered down. 'So, Lou said you urgently wanted to talk to me. Well?'

'We need to speak to your father, Ross. It's vitally important. And urgent,' I explained.

'I don't know where he is. Sorry. Guess you've had a wasted journey.'

'Stop messing about, Ross. I'm not in the mood,' Loki snapped. 'Jesus, it feels like the whole world's whirling around me.' He pressed his eyes shut. 'Just tell us.'

'What, so you can kill him?' Ross spat. 'Never!'

Freya stepped closer to Ross.

'Stand back. I'm armed. I warn you.'

'Don't be silly, Ross. There are others up here. Make a scene and we'll all get arrested.'

'Stand back, Lorna.'

Freya took another step forward.

Ross removed his hands from his pockets. In his right hand he clutched a grenade. In a flash he grabbed hold of the pin. 'One more step and we all die.'

'For Christ's sake, what are you doing?' I said. 'Are you mad? Put that away.'

'Why do you want to kill my dad?'

'We don't,' Loki hissed.

'Liar.'

'He's telling you the truth, Ross.'

'No he isn't. I overheard you talking. Remember? *Find the White Rabbit and kill him.* That's what you said . . . But it's not going to happen. I'm going to see to that – I'm going to stop you.'

Freya backed off.

'Why do you want to kill him?' Ross was growing impatient, his grip on the pin tightening.

'How much do you know about your father's work?' Freya asked.

'Answer my question,' he snarled.

'All right! Your father works for the same organization as us, Ross,' I said. 'But you already know that, don't you? You know about Special Operations because your father's taught you stuff each time he's been to your uncle's farm. But the last time he came he was carrying a suitcase full of money. And I mean a *lot* of money, Ross. Millions of francs. Money destined to fund the Resistance here in Paris. Only your father didn't deliver it. He vanished into thin air, taking the money with him. Quite appropriate, given he's a magician. At first our superiors thought he'd been arrested. But he hasn't, has he?'

'It's only money,' Ross replied. 'That's no reason to kill him. It makes you lot as bad as the Nazis.'

'It's not the money, Ross, it's what your father knows. His head is full of secrets – things that mustn't fall into the hands of the Germans. Many lives are at stake. Our superiors reckon he might be a traitor, a double agent.'

'Never! He'd never betray his country.'

'Then why?' Freya asked. 'Why did he take the money and run?'

'Can't tell you. It's a secret.'

'But you must if you don't want him to be hunted down.'

'I can't. Anyway, if you die here, today, now, he'll be safe.'

A couple approached. Ross hid the grenade inside his coat, keeping his finger firmly wrapped around the pin. The couple peered out at the view for a few moments, smiled at us all, and then moved on arm in arm, oblivious to our precarious situation.

'You're wrong, Ross,' said Loki. 'We're not the only ones after your father.'

'Liar. You're just saying that.'

Freya shook her head. 'No, Ross, he's telling you the truth. In fact, that's why finding you was so urgent. We don't know who they are or how many of them there are. HQ won't tell us. But they have orders to shoot and ask questions later. And we've just met with our contact, Trébuchet – the man you felled with your catapult. He found out your father's real identity as well. He's informed HQ, and that means all the others will be told. So killing us won't solve anything. In fact, we're possibly your father's only hope.'

Ross grew agitated. 'Lies. All lies. You're trying to trick me. I know your methods. My dad warned me. He said never trust anyone.'

'We very nearly refused to come on this mission, Ross,' I said. 'You see, we don't believe in killing one of our own just because he or she knows too much. It's one thing if they've joined the enemy, but quite another if they have other reasons for going AWOL. So our plan was to find your father and discover why he disappeared. If, like you say, he's not a traitor, then all we were going to do was try to persuade him to return with us to Britain. If he refused, end of story as far as we were concerned.'

Confusion engulfed Ross. 'All lies,' he repeated over and over. 'All lies.'

'It's God's honest truth,' Freya pleaded. 'But if we're going to help you and your father, we need to know what the hell is going on.'

'I can't. You don't understand. I can't tell you anything. I can't risk . . .'

Ross had worked himself up into quite a lather. I could see that he was torn between wanting to tell us everything, and biting his lip because he'd sworn not to tell a soul what he knew. Or was there even more to it? Worryingly, I reckoned he really *was* willing to kill us all here and now. But why? Why be willing to go that far . . . unless . . . An idea began taking shape in my head, an explanation of what was really going on.

'I'm getting tired of all this,' Loki snapped. 'Somehow, I don't think you're going to blow yourself up. Not today, or anytime soon. So put that grenade away and cut the crap.' He straightened up, let go of the railing and, desperately trying to ignore the fact that he was nine hundred feet above the ground, advanced slowly towards Ross. Hand outstretched, he said, 'Come on – game over, Ross. Give it to me.'

'No!' Alarmed, Ross pulled the pin out of the grenade.

Loki was all for lunging and engaging in a deadly struggle with Ross, but I stepped between them. 'Back off, Loki. It's way too dangerous. He's willing to let go and kill us all.'

All that stood between us and a messy, bloody end was Ross keeping a firm hold of the grenade and his thumb wrapped around the lever. Until he put the pin back in, our lives lay in his hands.

'It's a bluff, Finn. That's all. Why would anyone be so daft as to blow themselves up?'

'To stop us at all costs ... To make the ultimate sacrifice ...' I turned and glared at Ross. '*To make amends.*'

'Amends for what, for God's sake? You're not making any sense, Finn.'

'Ross's father's no traitor. And this mess doesn't have anything to do with the money either, does it, Ross?'

He shook his head.

Loki groaned. 'Then what is it about?'

I turned to Freya. 'You were right. Remember what you said in the Lizzie during our flight over here? Your sixth sense was telling you that Claude's drastic actions were probably triggered by something *très, très important.*' She nodded. 'Well,' I continued, 'I reckon this is all about Ross's sister, Sophie. Ross's father's going to try to rescue her from Fresnes prison. That's why he's gone AWOL.' I eyeballed Ross. 'I'm right, aren't I, Ross?'

Reluctantly he nodded.

'And Ross is willing to die for the cause out of guilt. I reckon it's his fault that she's there in the first place.'

'What, Finn?' Loki screwed up his face in confusion. 'At the convent he told us it was a neighbour who sold her out; over a land dispute or something.'

'Yes, but I think there's more to it than that. I reckon he blabbed in front of his friends, bragged about what his sister was doing to resist the Nazis, hoping to impress people. Well, Ross? Was that how your neighbour found out what Sophie was up to? Did he overhear you? Was it *your* fault?'

Ross started to tremble. Tears welled up in his eyes and trickled down his cheeks. Slowly he began to nod.

'Didn't I say he was a right little blabbermouth,' Loki hissed angrily. 'Loose tongues cost lives, Ross. This war isn't a game.'

'I know!' he cried. 'I was stupid. I wasn't thinking. We have to save her,' he added, all choked up. 'It *was* my fault. And I'm going to make it up to her. You'll see. Dad and me, we're going to get her out of there. We're going to set her free. And you're not going to stop us. No one else is, either. If I have to die to save her, then so be it. I'll die willingly.'

'Jesus!' Loki shook his head in disbelief.

'That's just great, Ross.' I clapped my hands slowly. 'Bravo! I bet your father would be really proud of you blowing yourself up at the top of the Eiffel Tower. Then he'll be left to rescue Sophie all by himself. That's just plain crazy.'

'Listen,' said Freya calmly. 'I have a suggestion to

make. If the others agree, I propose that we join forces. We'll help you and your father rescue Sophie. Surely having the help of three fully trained agents from Special Operations must improve the odds of you succeeding.'

'What's the catch?'

'No catch. Other than we have the chance to ask your father to return to Britain with us.'

'I'm in,' I said. 'I was beginning to think we'd come all this way for nothing. Rescuing a condemned Resistance fighter is a good enough mission for me. Loki?'

He shrugged. 'Count me in.'

'Do we have a deal, Ross?' Freya held out a hand.

'How can I be sure I can trust you?'

'You can't. It's a risk you'll just have to take.'

He considered our offer. 'I'll discuss it with my dad. If he agrees, then we'll talk again. Meet me at ten o'clock tomorrow in the Rue de l'Odéon, outside a bookshop called Shakespeare and Company. You can't miss it. If I'm not there by eleven, you can assume my dad has said no. I'm going to leave now. And you must wait for the next lift. Do not try and follow me or else the deal's off.'

'How do we know you'll keep your word, Ross?' said Loki. 'Why should we risk letting you out of our sight?'

'You don't. You'll just have to trust me.'

'OK. Any chance of you putting that pin back in now?'

Chapter Seventeen
The Man with No Legs

That evening, back at Trébuchet's apartment, we came to a decision. We were going to have one more go at getting HQ to see things our way. Time to lay what we knew on the table and hope that the brigadier would let us handle things. Freya set about enciphering our message, which we kept short:

THREE BLIND MICE — STOP — KNOW TRUE IDENTITY OF WHITE RABBIT — STOP — NOT TRAITOR — STOP — REPEAT NOT TRAITOR — STOP — WHITE RABBIT PLANNING PRISON RESCUE OF DAUGHTER — STOP — MICE WILL ASSIST — STOP — CALL OFF ASSASSINS — STOP — REPEAT CALL OFF ASSASSINS — STOP — END

Up on the flat roof of the apartment block, Freya's frozen fingers tapped out our message on her radio's Morse key. The open suitcase rested between us, the long aerial draped up and over a chimney stack for the best reception. We huddled there against the penetrating frost and waited for a reply. 'Fingers crossed,' whispered Loki, blowing hot breath into clasped hands.

An hour later, with all three of us numbed stiff by the cold, Freya's eyes suddenly widened, and we knew that the rapid stream of dahs and dits comprising HQ's reply were emerging through her headphones. Listening intently, she hurriedly wrote down their response. It took her a further five minutes to decode it:

MESSAGE UNDERSTOOD — STOP — ABORT TALLY HO — STOP — REPEAT ABORT TALLY HO — STOP — MISSION BEING HANDLED BY OTHERS — STOP — RETURN TO CABBAGES AND KINGS — STOP — AWAIT PICK UP — STOP — WILL SEND LYSANDER NEXT FULL MOON — STOP — END

'No,' I cursed under my breath. 'Freya, send the second half of our message again and add that we insist they let us handle the matter our way.'

'All right, Finn. Give me a minute to code it.'

Freya furiously tapped out our revised version, sending our instructions out over the airwaves. Ever since joining Special Operations she'd shown herself to be a natural wireless operator, or *pianist*, as they were often called because of their deft touch on the Morse key. Keeping her arm steady, her astonishingly rapid dahs and dits arose from small, almost imperceptible movements of her wrist. When she'd finished, she reached out and flicked the switch from transmit to receive. 'I hope that got through. And they'd better hurry up with a reply. The battery's almost flat. And that's the spare. We'll need to get a replacement, or find a way of charging it, or risk using the mains supply.'

'If we bump into Trébuchet again, we'll ask him. Someone in his network's bound to have a supply of spares,' I suggested.

HQ's response flew back to us within five minutes.

REQUEST DENIED — STOP — RETURN CABBAGES AND
KINGS IMMEDIATELY — STOP — DO NOT ASSIST WHITE
RABBIT — STOP — WARNING EXTREME DANGER — STOP
— ANYONE ASSISTING WHITE RABBIT WILL BE
TARGETED AND ELIMINATED — STOP — ORDERS COME
FROM HIGHEST LEVEL — STOP — CANNOT OVERRIDE —
STOP — LEAVE PARIS — STOP — THAT'S AN ORDER
— STOP — END

'Shit!' Loki clenched his fist and looked like he
wanted to punch someone, anyone. 'Why won't they
listen to us?'

Freya began packing her headphones and aerial into
the small storage box inside the suitcase. 'I think important men in Whitehall have made up their minds,
Loki. The easiest way to make sure is to eliminate
everyone involved. They're only seeing the bigger
picture. It's not the brigadier's fault.'

'All I can say is that I hope Ross turns up tomorrow.
We're his dad's only hope.'

Loki punched me in the shoulder – in a friendly way.
'For a moment there I thought you were going to
suggest that we do as the brigadier says, Finn – follow
orders and head back to Les Andelys.'

'Don't be daft.'

'So we're agreed then,' Freya declared. 'We disobey
orders, and to hell with the consequences we'll face on
our return.'

Loki and I nodded.

'If they end up sending us to the Forgetting School, then so be it. I could do with a rest, anyway,' said Loki sarcastically. 'But we've got a fellow agent to rescue first. Who knows, it may all turn out OK. Just pray we don't go home empty-handed.'

Like the Eiffel Tower, the Rue de l'Odéon lay south of the Seine, and we figured it would take ages to walk from Montmartre. We took the Métro instead, getting off at Saint-Germain-des-Prés, two stops before the one called Odéon, which was located just yards from our rendezvous. This was deliberate. We wanted to get a feel for our surroundings in case anything went wrong and we had to make a run for it.

We trudged down the Boulevard Saint-Germain and eventually turned right into the Rue de l'Odéon. The bookshop, Shakespeare and Company, was somewhat shabby, its dusty windows protecting an impressive display of books. Ross was waiting.

'We wondered if you'd be here,' I called out. 'Well, what did your dad say?'

'He wants to talk. I'm going to take you to him. You must follow me at a safe distance. Keep at least twenty yards behind me. When it's time, I'll pick my nose. That's the signal that it's OK for you to rejoin me.' He turned and set off, back the way we'd come, crossing the Boulevard Saint-Germain and heading towards the river. Reaching the Seine, he turned left and strode purposefully alongside it. We followed.

'How far do we have to walk?' Loki cursed. 'This is ridiculous. What if he's messing us about?'

'I expect he's just following his father's orders,' I replied. 'I reckon we're being watched. His father's probably checking that we're not being followed, that we're not part of some elaborate trap. When he judges it's safe, I'm sure he'll reveal himself.'

The roads and pavements bordering the river were busy. I found myself eyeing everyone as they approached and passed us, even looking over my shoulder a few times. Suddenly Ross stopped, turned and gazed out across the river. He raised a hand and picked his nose.

As we hurried to catch up, we studied everyone and everything within our field of vision. There were no parked cars. Two German soldiers were crossing a nearby bridge, separating as they strolled to pass on either side of an elderly woman pushing a wheelchair. Some youths ran amok. Laughing and shouting, they charged past us. A man carrying a briefcase headed our way. Was this him? No. Too tall.

Ross leaned on a wall overlooking the river. He pointed. 'That's the Louvre over there. You know — the art museum. It's pretty famous.'

'Is he there? Are we going to meet him at the museum?'

'No.'

The reply came from behind us. We spun round to see an old man in a wheelchair. He was wearing a thick scarf wrapped about his neck, and a heavy green and blue tartan blanket was draped neatly across his knees.

He appeared to have lost both legs from the knee down. A grey hat was pulled down over his ears, making it hard to see much of his face.

'My name's Alan Munro. I understand you've offered to help us. Is that correct?'

'You're Madura, alias the White Rabbit, alias Claude Chevalier?' I asked in disbelief.

'Indeed, and many other names besides. I must warn you, I am armed. As is my lovely daughter, Louise. But I believe you are all already acquainted.'

'So you *did* know where your father was all along,' said Loki.

The elderly-looking woman pushing the wheelchair wore a silk scarf, sunglasses and stooped arthritically over the handles. She smiled and muttered, 'Yes, but only a fool would risk trusting you with that information. I couldn't take the chance.'

'B–b–but what happened to your legs?' I asked, staring at the place where Alan Munro's shins and feet ought to be.

'Oh, don't worry. I still have them. You just can't see them. It's a simple illusion. They're tucked beneath me, resting in a shallow hidden compartment. I find travelling this way means I'm not stopped and questioned by the Germans too often. For some reason they leave us cripples alone. Come, let us stroll and talk. Johnny, you look like a big strong chap – perhaps you'd do the honours and push me along in this contraption.'

Ross's father looked nothing like his photograph – at least thirty years older – and Louise's make-up did more than just hide her beauty. Somehow she'd turned the smooth rosy cheeks of youth into pale, wrinkled, grey skin; skin that had a thin, almost translucent look. She had also mastered the mannerisms of the older generation. Loki seized the wheelchair and we began our walk.

'Ross managed to convince us that you'd not turned traitor,' I began. 'But we'd like to hear it from your own lips.'

'He is correct. I have merely taken a break from official duties in order to sort out some urgent personal matters. I believe you know that my other daughter's currently in Fresnes prison.'

'Sophie. Yes – and that you intend to rescue her. But why didn't you come clean to our superiors? Why not simply tell them? Surely they'd have understood.'

'Couldn't take the risk. F-Section doesn't like people dashing about doing their own thing. Take my word for it – they'd never have sanctioned a rescue attempt.'

'How can you be so sure?' asked Freya.

'Simple, my dear. At a rough estimate, I reckon at least fifteen Special Operations F-Section agents have been caught and ended up at Fresnes prison at one time or another over the last year or so. To that you must probably add several dozen local partisans who worked alongside them. Most have either been moved on to camps in the east or been condemned and executed. Despite knowing their predicament, the exact number of rescue attempts authorized by HQ is zero. Do you understand? *Zero!*'

'Maybe no one's ever suggested a decent plan?' said Loki.

'No, it's not that,' Munro replied. 'They train us well, and as long as we remain at liberty to do our clandestine work under the enemy's nose, we are valuable assets. The moment we're caught, however, we become liabilities. But what do they know?' He tutted sourly. 'Men safely hidden behind closed doors, smoking their cigars and quaffing their brandies late into the night, planning, scheming, treating us like pawns in their stupid, dangerous war games. I'd like to see those idiots in Whitehall try living it for real. They'd not last a week.'

'But we all know the score when we sign up,' I said. 'We accept the dangers involved.'

He looked up at me and smiled. 'I understand you're codenamed the three *blind* mice. How very appropriate!'

'So,' said Loki, giving the wheelchair an extra hard shove, 'what's this plan of yours? Being a magician, I suppose you're simply going to wave your magic wand and make Sophie vanish from her cell in a blinding flash and puff of smoke . . . and then make her miraculously reappear again on the outside.'

Alan Munro shook with laughter. 'Very good, young man. Yes, that would indeed be a fine trick. Alas, that is beyond even Madura the Magnificent.'

'Fresnes prison is a fortress, under the strict control of the SS,' said Louise.

Freya halted abruptly. 'Then I don't understand. How are you going to rescue your sister?'

'Like all good illusions, the secret lies in keeping it simple,' Munro replied. 'I want to show you something. It'll help me explain what we're up against. We've a long walk ahead of us. We need to cross the Seine and head for the Arc de Triomphe. And I warn you now – once we get there you'll need to be on your guard. Where we're going is potentially extremely hazardous. We must have our wits about us. But if you're going to help us, then you need to see it for yourselves.'

Chapter Eighteen
The Avenue of Evil

While we headed for the Arc de Triomphe, Munro began filling us in — it was more like one of the brigadier's briefings back at Mulberry.

'Following her arrest, the Gestapo quickly moved Sophie to Fresnes prison, France's largest *maison de correction*. It's huge. To get in, you have to pass through iron gates that lead to an inner courtyard. From there you gain access to the main hall. All new arrivals pass through it. There they are stripped and searched. Apparently, one side contains tall wooden cupboards, each just big enough to house a single person. Prisoners are often locked in them for hours on arrival before being "processed".

'Fresnes has three blocks, two entirely for male prisoners, a third being mixed. These are accessed from the main hall via an underground passage. Each block is effectively a series of five floors or galleries, one set on top of the other, each gallery comprising a row of cells. The cells measure barely twelve feet by eight, and although some have windows, these are merely tiny panes of frosted glass and are hermetically sealed. Sophie is being held in cell number two-one-seven. Prisoners rarely leave their cells, except the few selected to push the food trolleys about. Being a member of the

Resistance, Sophie has been given especially harsh treatment. Signs on her cell door remind the warders that she's not permitted to receive visitors, books or parcels, or take showers, or receive any special favours.'

'It could be worse,' interrupted Louise. 'Some prisoners are designated *ständig gefesselt*, which means they are permanently chained up. Barbaric!'

Munro continued, 'The female warders are nicknamed *les souris*, the mice, which is a kind term for women who are better described as vermin – the worst sort, willing servants of their masters in the SS.'

'Wish we'd chosen another codename now,' I said.

'Quite,' said Munro.

Freya had a question. 'This is all very interesting, but it sounds like you can't rescue her from inside the prison.'

'True, we can't go in there all guns blazing. Can't bribe the mice either. What I've said is merely to reassure you that we've done our homework. That we *know* it's impossible to take the place by force. We have to be far more subtle.'

'Despite the difficulties, we've been able to establish contact with Sophie,' said Louise.

'How?'

Munro elaborated. 'Each cell has a small air vent that communicates with cells above and below. Prisoners have learned that they can talk and exchange small items by this route. The woman in the cell above Sophie, a petty thief called Madame Fournier, made contact with her. Acquiring that information alone took much effort and cost me a great deal of money. Anyway, Madame Fournier is permitted parcels and the occasional visitor, and so through such intermediaries we have learned more concerning Sophie's present plight.'

'Which is?' I asked.

'Sophie has been informed that her final tribunal hearing will take place this Friday. It goes without saying that she'll be found guilty of all charges. The evidence and testimony against her is damning. Naturally, she'll be condemned to die. That is the only penalty for such crimes. In all probability her sentence will be carried out that same day.'

'The day after tomorrow! So we haven't much time, then,' I said.

'No. I'm afraid not.'

'Ross, didn't you tell me about Sophie's lawyer – that he was trying to delay things?'

'Yes, Simon – but he's not even allowed to speak to her. He's appointed by the Germans to represent her, but the Germans ignore him. It's a farce.'

Alan Munro added, 'As I'm sure you'll appreciate, the SS only delayed proceedings while they thought she might still have useful information to divulge. I suppose they've now concluded that she has nothing more to offer.'

'But they've interrogated her half a dozen times already,' Ross snarled. 'From what we've heard, the first time it was all very pleasant, simply an informal chat. The second time they tried loosening her tongue by placing a red-hot branding iron against her naked back.

The third time they tore out her toenails. After that we don't know what they did to her. She wouldn't say to Madame Fournier.' He looked at me. 'It must've been horrific. You know what she's been through, Simon. You said you've been tortured.'

'Yes, I know exactly what she's been through. At least, some of it. I was lucky. I escaped before it got really nasty.'

Alan Munro looked up at us from his wheelchair. 'You've been on other operations?'

'Yes,' said Loki. 'Several.'

He seemed impressed.

'So how are we going to do this?' asked Loki. 'All I've heard so far points to us being doomed to failure.'

'Ah, we're almost there,' Alan Munro announced brightly.

Ahead of us stood the towering stone arch of the Arc de Triomphe. We approached it from the direction of the Champs-Élysées. Munro raised a hand and pointed out the various streets radiating outwards like the spokes of a bicycle wheel. 'We're going that way,' he declared, gesturing towards a broad avenue lined by impressive eighteenth-century villas set well back from the road. 'We are about to wander along a most delightful avenue – possibly one of the finest in Paris. Ladies and gentlemen, welcome to the Avenue Foch. I prefer to call it the *Avenue of Evil* for reasons I'm about to show you. You will take due note of the increased activity of the enemy here. Please be on your guard and keep your voices down. I trust your papers are in order – it is highly probable that we shall be stopped for inspection. I shall be pointing things out to you, and I do not wish to see you stare or gawp at them in a manner likely to attract unwanted attention.'

'We *are* fully trained,' Loki responded.

'Forgive me, I keep forgetting,' Munro replied. 'You all strike me as too young for this kind of work.'

'Yeah, and you look way too old,' Loki added. 'But looks can be very deceptive, can't they?'

As we strolled down the Avenue Foch, Munro indicated to us the various buildings that had been taken over by the German security services, including the *Abwehr*, which was roughly the equivalent of the British military intelligence organization, and the offices of the infamous Gestapo. About midway, two soldiers stopped us and demanded to know our reason for being there. Calmly, Munro explained that he lived nearby. We dug out our identity papers, waited patiently while they were examined, and then quietly blew a collective sigh of relief under our breaths as they waved us on.

'Number eighty-four is of most interest to us,' said Munro. 'It is the headquarters of the SD, the *Sicherheitsdienst*. Run by a chap called Major Kleb.'

The SD, the Nazi's secret police, comprised thousands of detectives, agents and informers. It was effectively a branch of the Gestapo. I glanced at the building as we approached. It was ornate, five storeys high, the tall windows of the second, third and fourth floors set behind neat little balconies.

'This is where they brought Sophie for questioning,

and where her tribunal will take place on Friday. They hold prisoners in cells located on the fifth floor. We believe her tribunal will be held in a room on the third floor, next to Kleb's office.'

Freya asked, 'Are you planning to raid it?'

'No. Too well guarded. When prisoners are summoned from Fresnes, they are brought here by Black Maria, or *panier à salade*, as some Frenchmen like to call it. Why on earth a prison van reminds them of a salad shaker escapes me. Anyway, the point I'm trying to make is that they arrive outside and offload prisoners in the street. Once inside, any attempted rescue is practically impossible.'

Loki slowed down. 'So what you're saying is that we only have a slim window of opportunity: basically while she's in this salad-shaker thingy.'

'Precisely, young man. And given that it's likely to be her last journey, we will have only the one chance. Screw it up and she's dead!'

Slowly turning on my heels, I took in our surroundings. I stopped, knelt down and pretended to re-tie my shoe laces, all the while examining the possibilities. I caught up with the others. 'This street is too busy with Germans, and many are in civvies – which might make it tricky spotting who's friend and who's foe during an operation. We'll have to strike before the van gets here.'

'Splendid, Simon. Couldn't agree more. Now, we've seen what we need to. How about a spot of lunch? My place is just round the corner. I can explain to you how we're going to do this over a nice cup of tea. Don't know about you, but I'm gasping.'

Munro's third-floor apartment was small, dingy and smelled of damp and mothballs. We reached it via a tiny lift that clunked and clattered as if it was about to collapse. Inside, the furnishings were cheap, the sofa threadbare and the cushions faded. The contrast to Louise's flat was striking. Even Trébuchet's place suddenly seemed cosy by comparison. Alan Munro spun the wheelchair expertly through the doorway with half an inch to spare either side, and then extracted himself from the contraption. For several minutes he hobbled about the room, rubbing life and circulation back into his legs. Louise boiled a large pan of water and then brewed a huge pot of tea using tea leaves that had already seen the pot twice before. The result was a foul, brackish-tasting pale brown liquid.

'Being members of Special Operations, you will have undergone training in evasion, disguise and deception,' Munro began, settling down on a rickety wooden stool. 'Such skills are similar to those we magicians have to perfect. Magic is really nothing more than that. Mostly, it is about making the audience believe that what they're seeing is normal, ordinary. And so we lull them into a false sense of security and allay their suspicions. That is the essence of misdirection. What they see is what we want them to see. But beneath that layer we deceive.'

'Go on,' I said. 'We're all ears.'

'The warders at Fresnes will have been informed by

Major Kleb's office that Mademoiselle Munro, located in cell number two-one-seven, must be transported to the SD's offices on the Avenue Foch this Friday. So they will be expecting a *panier à salade* to arrive to pick her up. The Germans are creatures of habit and punctuality. I've been observing their routine. Prison vans arrive every morning at precisely eight o'clock. Not ten past, or ten to, but exactly on the hour. At great expense I have twisted some arms, called in some favours, and acquired a *panier à salade* from some acquaintances in the French police.'

'You've got a prison van?'

'Yes, Simon. And what's more, I have obtained the use of numerous German uniforms and four motorcycles belonging to the Wehrmacht. All are fuelled up and ready to go. You see, there are always four bikes escorting the van. So we must use four as well. Any fewer might raise suspicion. At precisely eight o'clock on Friday morning my van and its escort will arrive at the gates of Fresnes prison to collect Sophie. From there she will be driven somewhere safe.'

'What about having the right paperwork? Won't they check?'

'Indeed they will. Ross has kindly created forgeries of the necessary papers.'

Ross grinned. 'I went back to Les Andelys this week. Luc and me got all the necessary official stamps from the town hall. Dad also managed to *acquire* an example of Major Kleb's signature and I've been practising it until my hand nearly dropped off. Still, although I do say so myself, I've cracked it. A perfect likeness.'

'Your plan seems simple enough,' I said. 'But won't the *real* prison van turn up at the same time?'

Munro shook his head. 'They will be delayed. The fools always take the same route, you see. On Friday morning they'll unexpectedly encounter road works. Just to make sure, an explosive tyreburster will be placed beneath one of their wheels. I estimate that they'll be held up for at least half an hour while they organize a replacement van.'

'Who's helping you?' Loki asked.

'That's a good question, Johnny. Wishing to remain under the radar of our superiors, I naturally could not call upon Trébuchet and his network. So I made contact with another group I've had dealings with in the past. Unfortunately they're all unscrupulous black marketeers, led by a young chap – Marcel Vallette. Bit of a communist. Not ideal. Still, beggars can't be choosers, and at least we all have one thing in common – we hate the Nazis. Marcel's pretty keen on direct action too. Keen to get his hands dirty. His assistance, however, has come at quite a price. One million francs!'

'I don't suppose there's much of the money left, is there?'

'No, Simon. Not much at all. Marcel drives a hard bargain. The prison van wasn't exactly cheap, either. Then there were the motorcycles and uniforms. Still, I've got the gold coins ferreted away safely for a rainy day.'

Louise and Ross knocked up some lunch comprising stale bread, soft, stinking Camembert cheese and slices of pickled onion. Even though I was hungry, when I saw Ross stamp on a cockroach that had the misfortune to scurry from beneath a cupboard, I suddenly lost my appetite. 'I'm surprised you haven't shared some of the food Wolfgang gave you, Louise,' I remarked. 'This stuff's barely fit to eat.'

'Dad won't have any of it in the house in case the Germans come. They carry out frequent random raids around here. He doesn't want his cupboards to be full of food that could lead to awkward questions.' She then made her excuses. 'Must be off. Got to meet someone this afternoon. Ross, come back with me to my place?'

Alan Munro saw his son and daughter to the door.

'OK, back to business. How can we help in this scheme of yours?' Loki asked.

Munro settled down on the tatty sofa. 'Hmmm, I've been giving that a great deal of thought. Can you two lads both ride motorcycles?'

We nodded.

'Splendid. To be honest, I'd feel much happier if I had people I can really trust accompanying Sophie during her escape. And who better than fellow agents with Special Ops? I'd like you to be part of the van's escort. I want to be sure Marcel keeps his word.'

'Why? Where will you be during all the action?'

'The Theatre Royal. I'll be getting ready to perform my side of the bargain.'

I didn't like the sound of that. 'What bargain?'

'Forgive me, but I had to wait until Lou left before explaining everything,' Alan Munro responded uneasily.

'It's best she doesn't know. She'd blow a fuse if she did. You see, once Sophie has been rescued, she will be taken to a secret safe house run by Marcel's group. I don't know where it is. She will be held there until I have carried out my side of the agreement. Only then will they reunite her with me.'

'Sounds odd,' I said.

'Sadly, trust is thinly spread these days, Simon. That's why Sophie will temporarily be held hostage, as Marcel's bargaining chip. His group has been trying to plan something big for ages, but needed a suitable opportunity to strike the enemy hard. One has now arisen. The Germans are holding a special cabaret show at one of their *nur für Deutsche* theatres this Friday night. The Theatre Royal. They're bringing in the best talent from all Paris: musicians, singers, dancers—'

'And magicians,' I interrupted. 'He wangled it for you to go on stage one more time.'

Munro stiffened and puffed out his chest proudly. 'Yes. When the Germans organizing the show learned from Marcel that I, Madura the Magnificent, might be available for a one-off performance, they leaped at the chance and insisted that I appear. I shall be the star of the show. And some show it'll be. High-ranking Nazi officials and invited guests will cram into the theatre. Undoubtedly the audience will include the likes of Major Kleb of the SD. Maybe even one or two senior officers from Berlin. Rarely have so many been in one place at the same time since the Nazis marched into our great city. Marcel was right when he told me that it was simply too good an opportunity to miss.'

'And just what exactly is going to happen?'

Munro moved to the shabby window and gazed out. 'I shall perform a version of Harry Houdini's greatest ever spectacle, the infamous Chinese Water Torture Cell escape. I'll be bound in chains and immersed in a huge glass tank of water. I will either escape or drown. The audience will be on the edge of their seats. They will gasp in amazement. They will fear that I'm doomed. But I *shall* escape – just in the nick of time too, just before midnight.'

'Midnight?'

'Yes. The tank of water is raised several feet above the level of the stage by placing it on a strengthened box. The box will be crammed with plastic explosives set to detonate as church bells strike twelve o'clock. Naturally, I have to escape and leave the theatre by then, or else I will be blown up too.'

'Sounds pretty dangerous to me. A lot could go wrong. What if the show runs late? What if . . . ?' Freya was shaking her head.

'Last time you attempted that trick, Louise said you nearly drowned for real. And that you swore never to go on stage again,' I said.

Munro nodded. 'Yes, that's true. I made a mistake. If she knew I was going to try again, Lou would do almost anything to stop me. It was she who made me promise never to perform again after last time. That's why I haven't told her. That's why I can't ask her to assist me on stage. This time, I shall have to do it alone.'

'Maybe I could help you,' said Freya. 'Let me be your assistant. I can try to make sure it all goes like clockwork.'

Munro's eyes lit up. 'Yes . . . yes . . . That would be fantastic, young lady. Thank you.'

'I suppose you also know about Louise's little *problem*,' Freya added. 'That she's pregnant.'

Alan Munro turned away from the window. 'Yes. I blame myself. I asked her to spy on Wolfgang Müller for me. I never predicted she'd fall for him. It complicates matters for her, of course. A casualty of war, you might say. Still, these things happen. Who are we to judge in matters of the heart?'

Loki was still worried about the dangers associated with the trick. 'Couldn't you just try a different illusion?' he suggested. 'One less hazardous?'

Alan Munro shook his head violently. 'No. Out of the question. That piece of equipment is the only one I possess that is large enough to conceal sufficient explosives.'

Loki plainly didn't like the idea of Freya being on stage next to a ticking bomb, but he held his tongue, instead saying, 'If Freya's going to be there, then so will I. Simon too. We'll help you. We can be your stagehands. Once we've rescued Sophie we'll come to the theatre.'

I could see a potential problem with this. 'If we know where Marcel takes Sophie, he might insist on holding us until after the show as well. Just to make sure we don't let Alan know where she's being kept.'

'We'll make it clear to Marcel that we need to go to

the theatre. If it's a problem, then he'll just have to make sure we don't know Sophie's final destination. It'll be fine.'

Munro was delighted, and readily accepted Loki's offer. 'I'll make sure they know to expect you. When you get there, come to the back entrance and ask for Henri Moreau. He's the stage manager. I've known Henri for years and he can be trusted. He knows about the plan and will attempt to get the performers and backstage staff out of the theatre before the bomb goes off.'

'That's settled then. But did Ross explain to you *our* side of the bargain?' said Freya. 'In return for our assistance, we want the opportunity to persuade you to return with us to Britain.'

Alan Munro waved his hands dismissively. 'Yes, yes. But you needn't worry. I am happy to do so, and will gladly face the music in front of Sir Hugo, the head of Special Operations, and whoever else wants to give me a dressing down. But only on one condition: I must be sure Sophie's safe. That is all I care about.'

'Define *safe*?' I said cautiously.

'At the very least that she's made it out of Paris, well out of harm's way.'

'What are your plans for getting her out of the city?'

'I haven't thought that through yet,' he confessed. 'Figured we'd lie low here until all the fuss dies down and then make our way out as best we can.'

'And did Ross tell you that there are others from Special Ops looking for you?' Freya asked.

'Indeed. Never realized I was so popular. They really needn't have gone to so much trouble. Don't suppose you know who they've sent?'

'No. HQ won't tell us. Standard procedure, as you well know. Teams always operate in isolation in case one gets compromised. What's worrying is that they've been ordered to eliminate you – to shoot first and ask questions later. Worse, they now know who you really are.'

Alan Munro scratched his chin thoughtfully. 'Yes, I must admit I hadn't considered that happening. I'd banked on my false identity seeing me through all this. Their knowing complicates things somewhat. Still,' he added fatalistically, 'can't do much about it. Just have to pray they're not as good as you at finding me.'

'Amen to that,' Loki muttered. 'By helping you we're in the firing line too.'

'Indeed.' He smiled warmly. 'I'm sorry you've all been dragged into this mess. But if we succeed I'll be eternally grateful. Now, let me give you the address where the prison van is being concealed. It's a bit tricky to locate, but when you get there, tap out Marcel's initials, MV, in Morse on the door. As it'll be an early start on Friday morning, I suggest you two lads go there tomorrow afternoon. I shall inform Marcel so he'll be expecting you. It'll also give him time to brief you on the route and for you to make sure your uniforms fit all right. Attention to detail is everything. Lorna, it would be best if you come here tomorrow and stay the night with Ross and me. We need to run through my act so you'll know what to do. Early on Friday morning we'll head to the theatre. I have to check all my equipment to make sure it's working perfectly. And we'll also have to fix you up with something suitable to wear. The theatre has a decent costume department, so I'm sure you can pick out something that takes your fancy.'

'And once we know Sophie's safe, we'll come and join you,' Loki added.

'Yes. That would be perfect,' said Munro. Then he frowned. 'Did you bring much in the way of equipment with you?'

'No, we travelled light.'

'I see. Then before you go, let me give you a few items.' Shifting a table, he drew back a rug. Kneeling down, he set about lifting a loose floorboard. Reaching deep into the cavity, he continued, 'Having considered our operation from every angle, I think one or two in particular might come in useful – just in case.' He held up two pairs of wire-cutters. 'Take these. Now, don't forget that this mission with Marcel's lot is an unusual alliance. Normally I wouldn't trust him and his team further than I could throw them. So remember to keep your wits about you at all times. Ah, yes, here we are.' Having reached into the cavity again, he withdrew several small tube-like objects the size of shotgun cartridges. 'Tape these flash charges to your shins to conceal them. They're my own invention. I'll explain how they work . . .'

Chapter Nineteen
A Cat Among the Pigeons

We returned to Trébuchet's apartment. Even before I inserted the key into the lock I knew something was wrong. Someone had paid us a visit. I knew this because every time we'd left the place I'd tugged a single hair from my scalp, moistened it with spit and stuck it across the gap between the door and the frame. The hair was gone. It meant that someone had opened the door. Close inspection of the lock suggested it had been clumsily picked – there were scratch marks. Gently turning the handle, we realized the door was still unlocked.

Drawing their revolvers, Loki and Freya covered me. I took a short run-up, barged the door open with my shoulder, and immediately dropped to the floor, pointing my gun straight ahead.

Charles Thorpe looked up from the sofa and smiled. 'Ah, there you are.'

A quick search of the apartment indicated that Thorpe was alone.

'What are you doing here?' I asked.

'The obvious question, I suppose. So predictable,' Thorpe replied sarcastically. 'Swell place. I see you've got a pot of honey in the kitchen cupboard. Helped myself to a spoonful. Hope you don't mind. That stuff's almost impossible to get hold of in Paris these days.'

'Answer the question.' Loki aimed his revolver at Thorpe's chest.

'OK, I'll come clean.' Thorpe nonchalantly raised a hand and flicked some dandruff off the collar of his rain-coat. 'Heck, I can barely bring myself to admit it but . . . I've come begging. Good old Uncle Sam needs your help . . . the OSS needs your help . . . *I* need your help.'

'Go on,' said Freya. 'We're listening.'

'When we last met, you said you were here to look for someone. Don't suppose you've found him, have you?'

'What business is it of yours?' Freya snapped.

Thorpe idly walked his fingers along the arm of the sofa. 'Well, I was just hoping that you had and that you were willing to tell me where he is — so that my boys could go and pick him up and we could have a nice, quiet little chat, just me and him.'

'No chance,' Loki snarled.

Thorpe rose to his feet and adjusted the angle of his hat. He glared at Loki. 'This ain't a game, son. This is where it all starts to get serious. And I'm figuring that right here, right now, you three mice are swimming way out of your depth. Now, I don't want you three to drown. Get my drift?'

'Piss off. You've got ten seconds to leave,' said Loki.

Thorpe was unmoved. 'You do realize that your pilot's wellbeing and his chances of making it back to England depend entirely on my co-operation. I could always just leave him to rot in that hospital. Or I could drop a hint or two to the authorities.'

'You wouldn't dare,' Loki hissed.

'How did you know we were here?' Freya interrupted. 'We weren't followed. I'm sure of it.'

Thorpe didn't answer.

'Oh hell,' I muttered. 'Our superiors have asked your lot in the OSS to help locate Alan Munro, haven't they? They gave you this address.'

'Your brigadier did indeed ask me to drop by and pass on some friendly advice. Said you'd got your priorities in a bit of a muddle, and that I might be able to straighten things out. So, guys, let's thrash this out here and now. Just tell me where he is.'

Silence.

'All right,' said Freya. 'You win.'

'What?' Loki snapped his head round. 'Be quiet, Freya.'

'No, Loki. Put the gun down. This has gone far enough.' She turned her attention to Thorpe. 'We don't know exactly where Alan Munro is, but it doesn't matter. You see, we are due to meet him next Sunday morning. We might be able to persuade him to come with us to the embassy or one of those other protected places you marked on that map you gave us. It's up to you.'

'Where's the rendezvous?'

'Top of the Eiffel Tower. We've checked it out,' I responded quickly, thinking that if we had been followed by Thorpe's men, then he'd know we'd been there. I hoped it might add credibility to Freya's suggestion. But would Thorpe buy into our little deception?

He considered our proposal. 'Sunday, you say. No possibility of making it sooner?'

'Sorry, but we've no way of contacting him. He's in control.'

'Then Sunday it'll have to be. At the Eiffel Tower. What time will he be there?'

'Ten o'clock sharp. We're to meet him on the third level viewing gallery,' I replied. 'That's the very top.'

Thorpe scrutinized our faces for a moment and then nodded. 'See, that wasn't so hard, was it? Thank you. I'll be off now.' He brushed past me and made for the door, then stopped and turned. 'Oh, one other thing, I don't suppose you've heard any rumours on the grapevine, have you? About a raid of some sort?'

'No.'

'Pity.'

'Good thinking, Freya,' I said as soon as Thorpe had departed. 'That's bought us some time and should keep him and his colleagues off our backs until we're well away from here.'

Loki moved across to the window and glanced furtively up and down the street. 'Don't be too sure about that. Thorpe accepted what we were saying far too readily for my liking. I bet he'll have us followed everywhere from now on.'

'Then we sit tight here until tomorrow afternoon. And we don't leave here by either the front or back doors as they're bound to have them covered.'

Loki threw me a horrified look. 'You don't mean . . . that we go across the roof!'

'Only way to make sure we're not followed, Loki. Don't worry, it'll be fine.'

Chapter Twenty
Marcel and the Men from Marseille

'See? There at the corner of the street. He's been standing there for an hour. There's another one lurking in that doorway opposite.'

Freya had been studying the goings-on in the Rue Saint-Rustique from our apartment window all morning. It seemed Charles Thorpe did indeed want to keep us under surveillance until the supposed meeting with Claude at the Eiffel Tower. 'We'll head across the roof to the block on the corner. There are attic windows we can use to gain access.'

Loki was far from convinced. 'Can't we try the back way like before? Surely that's safer.'

Freya shook her head. 'Bet it's being watched too. They're not stupid. Come on, we'd better get going. We'll leave our suitcases here. The spare battery's flat so there's no point risking carrying it with us. Anyway, it'll only slow us down. Best if we travel light. It's still freezing out there, so that roof's going to be slippery too. We'd better give ourselves plenty of time.'

Hard frosts and a light dusting of snow meant that a tricky rooftop escape was going to be doubly difficult. Although Loki had willingly ventured up there before to help Freya when she'd used the radio set, he'd remained on a flat section of roof close to a chimney

253

stack and had deliberately avoided looking down. He knew this foray was going to test his nerve to breaking point.

Quietly we slipped out of the apartment. I locked the door and planted a moistened hair across the gap, pressing it firmly for about twenty seconds to make sure it stuck in position. For once the stairwell seemed quiet and empty. Hugging the walls, we made our way to the top floor and the access hatch to the roof. Climbing onto my shoulders, Loki pushed the hatch open and lifted himself up. Outside, he checked that we couldn't be seen from windows of the buildings opposite and then reached back down inside to pull Freya up from my shoulders. I grabbed a rickety old chair we'd placed close by and climbed onto it. The others took hold of my outstretched arms and hauled me out too.

The roof of our block was flat, and we made light work of scurrying across it from one chimney stack to another. At the far side we reached a low parapet.

'This is madness. We can't jump that.' Loki drew back from the sheer hundred-foot drop that filled the two-foot gap between the buildings. 'And there's only a narrow flat ridge over there. Then the roof's steeply pitched. We've no chance.'

Ignoring him, Freya declared, 'I'll go first. Then you jump, Loki. Finn will go last.'

Taking a short run-up, Freya leaped and landed lightly on the other side. Crouching, she turned and beckoned for Loki to follow.

'I'm not happy about this, Finn. Not happy at all.'

'Shut up and get on with it,' I told him. 'You don't have a choice.'

Loki readied himself, taking several fortifying deep breaths and glancing to the heavens in prayer. Then he ran, planted a foot on the parapet, and jumped, letting out an anguished cry of terror as he bridged the gap. Under his weight the ageing low brick parapet crumbled and two loosened bricks fell away. Moments after he landed, so did the bricks in the alleyway below. They made quite a racket as they smashed to smithereens. I risked looking down. Luckily the alley was empty. It was my turn. Unsettled by Loki's near miss, I jumped with my heart in my mouth, but landed safely, with a feeling of euphoria, momentarily invincible; one jump down and, by my reckoning, just two more to go.

'This is the last one,' Freya said encouragingly to Loki. 'I know it looks a long way to jump, but you can do it. I know you can.'

It had taken us half an hour to edge slowly and care-fully along the rooftops, each footstep on the precariously slippery narrow ledges undertaken with extreme care, our hands numbed with cold from resting them against the sloping roof tiles that glistened with ice and frost. The last building offered us our way back down to the street – a shabby attic window in a rotten wooden frame that would be easy to force open. The hardest part was reaching it. This time there was no possibility of a decent run-up. There was a drop of about six feet too, which meant we'd all land heavily.

Loki rubbed life into his cold cheeks and cursed. 'That ledge looks pretty icy. Maybe too icy. Can't we retrace our steps and get inside *this* building? Then we won't have to jump.'

'Afraid not. Can't risk Thorpe's men spotting us. Remember, there's one loitering on the corner. In order to avoid him, we need to reach the next street, and to do that we must get inside the building on the corner. There's no other way.'

Freya counted to five, and before Loki could protest further she flung herself across the gap, falling and landing awkwardly but safely. 'See? Wasn't so bad.'

Loki rolled his shoulders to loosen his muscles. 'Well, it's been nice knowing you,' he said, and then he took the plunge, flinging himself forward.

Landing flat on both feet, he let his knees absorb his weight. It looked the perfect jump. He straightened up. 'Ta-da! Easy!' But he'd spoken too soon: his left foot suddenly slid backwards, and he flung both hands against the sloping tiled roof to steady himself. Then his right foot slid back. Finally his whole body began to slide. Freya reached out to grab him, but the handful of jacket sleeve was soon torn from her grasp. All I could do was watch as Loki slithered down like an eel. Letting out a stifled cry as he fell, he managed to catch the edge of the narrow ledge with his fingers in a last-ditch attempt to save himself. Dangling precariously, he swung his legs from side to side and then began pedalling them to try and get some purchase against the wall.

'Oh Jesus, I'm losing my grip. I can't hang on. I'm going to fall.'

Freya dropped to her knees and grabbed one of Loki's wrists. 'I've got you – but I don't know how long I can hold you. Pull yourself up!'

'I can't. Oh shit! I'm . . . I'm . . . I'm slipping.'

Shuffling three feet to my right, I hastily prepared to jump. 'I'm coming. Hang on.'

Loki's hand lost its grip on the ledge and, flailing desperately in the air, he tried to regain his hold. I had only seconds to get over and lend Freya a hand. Surely there was no way she could manage to pull Loki up by herself. He was far too heavy – much, much bigger than she was. Bending my knees, I threw my body forward and plunged, as if in freefall, across the gap, dropping down onto the ledge. I landed heavily, falling forward and smacking my head against the sloping roof. Briefly dazed, I spun round and saw something astonishing. Squatting, Freya had her back towards the sloping roof, her feet planted as firmly on the ridge as she could manage. For once being small was to her advantage. Leaning slightly forward, she had hold of both Loki's wrists and was desperately trying to pull him up. I'd never seen such a look on her face. It was as if she was possessed. Slowly she began lifting him, all by herself. The muscles in her neck and face rippled and her cheeks ballooned as the strain took its toll. But she kept on heaving with all her might. By the time I reached down to lend a hand, Loki's boots had managed to find some purchase on the wall, and in moments he was out of danger. Scrambling frantically, he made it back onto the ridge. Freya slumped back against the sloping roof, her gasps for breath sending clouds of mist into the air.

I just stared at her. 'How did you . . . ? I mean, I couldn't have done that. Not by myself.'

Her teeth still gritted, Freya lifted her head and glared at me. Her eyes were on fire. 'What? Because I'm a girl?'

I shook my head. 'No. It's just that . . . I didn't know you were that strong. That *anyone* was that strong.'

Loki grabbed hold of Freya and hugged her tightly. 'Can we get off this damn roof, please? I've had enough of these crazy antics to last a lifetime.'

Having given Thorpe's fellow OSS operatives the slip, we parted company, Freya heading for Alan Munro's place. Loki and I made for the address at which Marcel would be waiting. It was getting dark when we reached the southern suburbs of Paris.

The gloomy back streets, crammed with workshops, garages and cheap housing, were like a maze, and it took us ages to locate the doorway on which three parallel deep scratches had been carved into the wooden frame. As Alan Munro had instructed, we tapped out the letters MV in Morse: two slow taps, three quick ones, then one final slow one.

'*Pssst!*'

Looking up, we saw a face at an upstairs window. The man leaned out and gestured wildly with his left hand.

'I think he wants us to go round the back, Finn.'

Behind the building was a garage workshop. Marcel was waiting for us in a dimly lit doorway.

'I don't like last-minute changes of plan,' he snapped irritably as he led us inside. 'Still, it's Alan Munro's show.'

That was as warm a welcome as we were going to get.

The grim windowless prison van took up much of the space inside the garage. Four motorcycles leaned against a wall, and we had to squeeze past carefully. There was an oily, greasy smell in the air, edged with a tinge of petrol fumes. At the rear of the garage was a workshop. Half a dozen men were sitting round a table, playing cards, smoking and drinking beer; they barely gave us a glance. There were no '*Bonsoirs*', no smiles, no nods of acknowledgement, no getting up and shaking our hands. They just carried on joking, drinking and smoking.

Marcel was in his early twenties, tall and sharp-featured. His face had a permanently sour expression. He pointed to a box. 'Uniforms are in there. Find one that fits you. Boots are over there in the corner. Limited range of sizes. Sorry! Weapons are in the next room.' He turned and looked us up and down. 'Don't suppose you're familiar with the MP40, are you? I guess I'll have to show you.'

'That won't be necessary,' Loki replied.

'Good. Come though and I'll show you the route we'll be taking.'

We studied the map on which Marcel had high-lighted the route to Fresnes prison. The first thing that struck me was that the return route ended up some distance from our present location. 'So we're not coming back here, then?'

'No. Too risky. A friend has said we can use his warehouse.'

'And that's where you're going to hold Sophie until after the show at the theatre,' I added, placing a finger on the spot.

'Correct.'

'After we've rescued Sophie we have to go to the theatre to help Alan Munro. So if you don't want us to know where she's being kept until after the show then I think you'll need to move her from that warehouse,' Loki said.

Marcel nodded. 'I've already thought about that. Don't worry, everything's arranged. Now, I was told you know how to ride motorcycles. You can follow the *panier à salade*. Roger and Xavier will lead the way up front. I will drive the van, with my brother, Pierre, alongside me. So all you have to do is follow us and keep up. Do nothing and say nothing. Let us handle everything. *Understand?*'

'Yes.'

'Good. Alan said you were Americans. How did you get caught up in all this?'

'Long story. We'll tell you all about it after the war.'

The faintest of smiles formed on Marcel's lips and then evaporated. 'Help yourselves to a beer if you want. And don't mind the others. They're not exactly a talkative bunch. Couple of the big fellows are from

Marseille. They're a rough lot down south. Do most of their talking with their fists.'

'Can they be trusted?' I asked.

'Can *you*?' Marcel responded acidly.

The others continued to ignore us completely as we selected our uniforms and checked over the motorcycles to make sure we were familiar with the controls. Neither of us were exactly experts at riding such machines, although we'd come across them before during our last mission in France. Finally we got round to selecting our sub-machine guns.

Loki screwed his face up in disgust. 'Jesus, these are filthy. They've not been cleaned for ages. I reckon they've been stashed somewhere. Buried possibly. Pull the trigger and this one's likely to explode in your face.' He hunted about for some brushes and cloths. 'Come on, Finn, let's strip them down and clean them up properly. We've got nothing better to do, and I've got a feeling it's going to be a long night.' He threw a glance towards the door: we could just see Marcel's men at the table, laughing, chatting, smoking and drinking. 'Bloody amateurs!'

During training at Mulberry we'd got to know many different sorts of weapons, both British and foreign. Stripping down a German sub-machine gun was child's play. In fact, German engineering was far superior to British in many ways. In minutes we had the MP40s in pieces. Marcel wasn't best pleased.

'*Merde!*' With a look of horror, he slapped his palm against his forehead and the cigarette wedged in his mouth fell to the floor. 'What the hell are you doing?'

'Making sure you lot don't blow your own hands off. You need to treat your weapons with respect,' Loki replied. 'Here – I'll show you how to clean one properly.'

At seven-thirty on Friday morning one of Marcel's men hauled open the garage doors. The sun was yet to rise, and a thick frost lay on the ground. In full German uniform, and with gleaming MP40s slung over our shoulders, we mounted our motorcycles. Marcel started up the *panier à salade*. The engine sounded rough. A plume of blue-grey smoke coughed from the exhaust. We kick-started our bikes and gunned the throttles. Up front, Xavier, a burly chap from Nantes, pulled down his goggles, raised a hand and then let it fall. We were off, emerging into the city's back streets. Loki and I slithered, swerved and weaved as we grew accustomed to our machines, but thankfully, by the time we reached the main road we'd mastered them and rode confidently.

As usual there were relatively few other vehicles about. The combined roar of our engines startled many walking the pavements and upset quite a few horses hitched up to carts and wagons. Cyclists pulled over to let us pass, and they watched us overtake with hostility written all over their faces. Some swore and shook their fists after us.

On we went, maintaining a pretty constant speed of about forty miles per hour. Xavier and Roger carved our path, giving all the right hand signals, and, like any proper German convoy, ignored all the stop signs. At precisely eight o'clock we swung round a corner and saw the grim reality of Fresnes prison.

The gates swung open and we drove through to the inner courtyard and stopped, although we all kept our engines running just in case we couldn't get them started again. My heart began to thump. If our plan was going to go wrong, it could happen now. Marcel calmly climbed out of the *panier à salade* and walked towards the entrance clutching the forged papers bearing the fake signature of Major Kleb, head of the SD. Fingers crossed Ross had done his job well.

Marcel's younger brother, Pierre, followed about three paces behind him, gripping his weapon nervously. Marcel disappeared inside. Pierre remained outside the entrance. All we could do now was wait and pray to God that Marcel's other team, including the thugs from Marseille, had succeeded in delaying the arrival of the *real* prison van. If not, we'd soon be in big trouble and would have to shoot our way out. I didn't fancy our chances. The prison was heavily guarded.

The minutes ticked by: still no sign of Marcel, or Sophie, or the real prison van. Pierre remained outside the entrance and grew twitchier by the second. He began pacing to and fro. Eventually he took out a cigarette from his tunic pocket and fired up. Still he paced, back and forth, taking drag after drag. I glanced across and caught Loki's eye. He just pulled a face and shrugged. He was right: there was nothing we could do about his suspicious behaviour.

After ten nerve-racking minutes Pierre spotted a commotion inside, threw down his cigarette butt, and hurried to open the rear door to the prison van. Marcel emerged from the main entrance dragging Sophie. Two prison guards followed. The sight brought a lump to my throat. She looked so tiny, so feeble. Her hair was a matted, filthy mess, her pale blouse and dark skirt stained and torn. I realized these must be the same clothes she'd been arrested in months ago – they were totally un-suitable for the cold winter weather. Worst of all she could barely walk. Her feet were bound in rags with brownish stains – dried blood. All she could manage was a miserable, agonizing shuffle. Her hands were bound in front of her. I expected her to resist, to scream, to shout and kick, but she didn't. There was a hollow look in her eyes, as if her soul had already departed, as if she'd accepted that horrors awaited her at every new dawn.

Marcel manhandled her across to the back of the van. Pierre unlocked an inner door to a steel mesh cage, and together they threw her inside. Doors slammed shut and keys turned in the locks. The two prison guards saluted Marcel and then ambled back to the main entrance. Pierre and Marcel clambered into the front of the *panier à salade*. As they were about to pull away, one of the prison guards rushed out and stood in front of the van, holding up his left hand, palm facing forward. '*Halt! Halt!*'

My heart skipped a beat. My mouth turned dry. I flashed my eyes about, counting the number and location of sentries. Just in case, I eased my MP40 round. I kept it strapped over my shoulder but readied myself to grab it at a second's notice. Marcel leaned out of the cab and shouted, '*Was ist los?*'

'*Haben Sie nicht etwas vergessen?*' the sentry snapped, shaking his head. He reached out and handed Marcel back the forged papers. He'd left them inside.

Marcel took them. '*Ja. Danke. Entschuldigung.*'

'Idiot,' Loki muttered under his breath. 'Stupid mistakes cost lives.'

Then we were on our way, turning round in the courtyard and heading out of the front gates. In seconds we were thundering along the city streets, and after twenty minutes our small convoy turned off into a deserted industrial area. Leading the way, Xavier and Roger swerved sharply right and bumped down a narrow cobbled road between two warehouses. Beyond lay a third warehouse, neatly hidden away – perfect for clandestine operations. We drove straight in. As we stopped, more of Marcel's men appeared out of nowhere and closed the warehouse doors behind us.

I killed my motorcycle's engine and lifted my goggles.

'Like clockwork,' Loki called across to me. 'How easy was that?'

Alan Munro was right. It was all about making it seem perfectly normal, perfectly routine. The staff at Fresnes prison saw only what they expected to see. They were blind to the deception.

Marcel's men busily set about congratulating themselves, slapping one another's backs and laughing as they relived every moment. Loki and I waited impatiently for Pierre to unlock the back of the van and the inner cage. Inside, cowering and impossibly scared, lay the tiny figure of Sophie. 'It's all right, Sophie,' Loki said calmly. 'You're safe. We've rescued you. We're working with your father and Ross. It was their plan to get you out.'

Large round eyes blinked back at us in disbelief. 'Where are they? Are they here? I can't see them.'

'All in good time. You'll soon be reunited.' I removed my uniform tunic and threw it to the ground. 'It really is OK. We're British agents. You can trust us.' I held out a hand. 'I'll help you out of there. Don't be afraid. Come here and I'll untie you. I expect you could do with something to eat and drink.'

She didn't move. I supposed it was all too much for her. I guessed that during her questioning her interrogators had tried every trick in the book – one minute snarling, threatening and extremely brutal, the next kind, full of deception and trickery. Was this yet another ruse to lull her into a false sense of security? I couldn't blame her for wondering. I backed away a few steps and wished Freya had been here. She'd have known what to say.

'Gather up all the guns, Xavier, and place them in that crate over there,' Marcel barked. 'The van and bikes can remain here. We may find a use for them again.'

I reached out, beckoning to Sophie, quietly repeating that it was safe, that she was free.

'Free' – a word that trips off the tongue so easily; a word that must've been an implausible dream to her during all those interminably long days and nights in cell number two-one-seven. The next second I sensed someone behind me and instinctively glanced round. It was the pair from Marseille. Wearing sick grins, they seized hold of Loki and me and gave us both an almighty shove. Tumbling forward, we landed inside the cage in a heap next to Sophie. The cage door slammed shut and one of them hurriedly locked it.

'What the hell do you think you're doing?' Loki shouted. He scrambled to the mesh door and shook it violently. 'We've got to get to the theatre.'

Marcel's face appeared. 'Change of plan, gentlemen.' He grinned wickedly. 'I heard you say you were British agents. Just like Alan Munro, eh? I suspected as much. Maybe I should turn you in.' He called out to the others, 'How much do you think Major Kleb of the SD would pay us for these two?'

'Thousands of francs,' came a reply.

'And how much for that runaway sewer rat?'

'Thousands more.'

Marcel nodded. 'I think my friends are correct. Forty thousand francs in all, I imagine. Not bad for a morning's work.'

'You bastard,' Loki hissed. He rattled the cage again. 'You won't get away with it. As soon as our superiors find out you betrayed us, they'll come after you. They'll hunt down every last one of you to the ends of the earth.'

Marcel was unperturbed. 'Under normal circumstances, perhaps they would. However, the truth is

they'll never know it was us. You're forgetting something, I think. Alan Munro came to us because he
couldn't risk working with anyone else. He wanted to
keep the matter totally secret, especially from your Top
Brass. So apart from us, only he knows the truth. And,
well, let's say that won't pose us a problem for much
longer.'

'What do you mean?' I spat angrily.

'In our line of work, the only way to stay alive is
to cover our tracks. Sadly, that requires sacrifices along
the way.'

'If you hand us in to the Germans we'll tell them that
your group was responsible for the bomb at the theatre,'
I shouted.

'They'd never believe you. And you have no proof.
Now, please excuse me, but I have important matters to
attend to. I believe those in the business usually say,
Whatever happens, the show must go on!'

I slumped down in the wire cage and cursed.

While we languished helplessly in the back of the
panier à salade, Marcel and his men changed back into
their civilian clothes. Then they sat around waiting for
hours, talking, smoking and laughing. We tried calling
out to them, tried reasoning with them, but all to no
avail. It was dark outside before they got ready to leave.

Pierre changed into an odd-looking uniform, a bit
like a bellboy you see in posh hotels, all gold braiding
and shiny buttons.

'You two stay here and keep an eye on them,' Marcel
instructed the men from Marseille as he threw on his

heavy overcoat and hastily buttoned it up. 'We'll be back as soon as it's safe.'

Taking Pierre to one side, Marcel spoke to him at length. I tried desperately to keep up with their French, but struggled. Marcel appeared to be going over a set of complicated instructions, repeating them again and again. Pierre responded by waving his arms wildly in a typically French manner. Their conversation ended with Marcel gripping Pierre's shoulder tightly – the way comrades in arms do when about to embark on a mission fraught with danger – and then placed a small silver key in Pierre's right hand.

On all fours, Loki sidled up to me. 'What's going on? What's he saying?'

'Not sure. I didn't understand it all.'

Marcel, Pierre and Xavier then left the warehouse together. It was six o'clock. Within minutes, others followed, leaving just the pair from Marseille. The two thugs sneered at us, and then sat down at a table and began playing cards.

'That man just now – he was telling his brother how, where and when to switch a key.' Sophie's voice was faint, barely stronger than a whisper.

Loki and I scrambled up close to her. 'Yes? Go on. What else did he say?'

'Something about sneaking backstage. To someone's dressing room. Does that make any sense?'

I pressed my head hard against the mesh of the cage and groaned in anguish. 'Hell, yes, it does. Pierre's wearing the sort of clothes an usher in a theatre would wear. He's going to sneak into Madura's dressing room and switch the key Madura needs to undo the locks holding the chains around him. Those bastards are going to make damn sure his illusion goes horribly wrong tonight.'

'Christ, Finn. So he'll be in the tank, holding his breath, and desperately trying to figure out why the key doesn't work. By the time it dawns on him that it's the wrong key, the bomb will probably have gone off.'

'Or else he'll drown.'

'Freya and Ross will be there too. We've got to get out. We've got to warn them.'

Sophie stirred. 'Bomb? Madura? Dad's going to perform again? Where? When? Why? What the hell is going on?'

We explained it all to an increasingly horrified Sophie.

'At least they'll be suspicious,' I said. 'They expected us at the theatre hours ago. They're bound to figure out that something's gone wrong.'

'Let's hope so, Finn.'

'He should have just let me die,' said Sophie, collapsing back down into a heap of misery in the corner of the cage. 'Now we're all going to die.' She sobbed loudly – not for herself but for others.

'*Taisez-vous!*' snarled one of our captors angrily, irritated by Sophie's wails.

Although she stank like a drain full of unmentionable stuff – she'd not been permitted to wash since her original arrest – I ignored it and placed an arm around her. 'Calm down. It's all right. It's not over yet. Like we said, we're British agents. We didn't spend weeks and months training for nothing.'

'Don't lie to me. I've heard enough lies to last me a lifetime. It's OK, you know. I'm not frightened of death. I know that today was my tribunal hearing. I know I was going to be found guilty and condemned to die. It'd be a release. I've come to terms with it. No more false hopes. Please. I'm ready to die.'

'Yeah, but we're not. Not yet, anyway,' Loki replied bullishly. 'Finn, I think it's high time we got out of here. There are just two of them now. Decent odds in my book. Unfortunately I think the lock on this cage door is beyond even your picking skills, so that means we switch to Plan B. *Out of sight, out of mind* is the one I'm thinking of. What do you reckon?'

'Sounds good to me. Do you want to attract their attention or shall I?'

'I'll have first crack at it, Finn. Tell me, Sophie — what's the French for *Oi, Fat-face — wasn't your mother born in a pigsty?*'

Having listened to Sophie translate, Loki hurled the abusive phrase at the two men from Marseille.

'Not bad for starters, Loki,' I remarked. 'Five out of ten, I'd say.'

At first Loki's taunts had little effect on the ugly brutes from Marseille. But he persisted, and I joined in with a choice phrase or two involving various parts of their anatomy, and even Sophie did her bit, calling them something that, for some reason, really riled them.

Eventually they'd had enough. One got up and stormed towards the van. He swore at us and slammed the metal outer door of the van shut, plunging us into darkness.

'Well, that was really good, you two. Any more bright ideas?' Sophie sighed despairingly.

'Actually, it's perfect,' I whispered. 'Now they can't see what we're doing. *Out of sight, out of mind.*'

Alan Munro had made a point of recommending the small but robustly made Special Ops Type Six, standard issue, heavy-duty wire-cutters. Maybe he knew that prison vans had inner wire cages and had considered the possibility that if Sophie was trapped, someone might have to cut her out. Loki and I had taped the cutters to our shins for concealment. They were perfect for the job. They had flared jaws so they could easily be engaged with the wires in the dark. Working side by side, we began cutting the mesh away from the cage door. Having completed the task, we readied ourselves.

'I reckon this escape would make your father proud, Sophie,' I said. 'It's all about misdirection. They think they've shut us up in here, but they didn't bother to lock the outer door. The key's still in the tunic pocket of the German uniform Marcel was wearing. He threw it on the pile with all the others.'

'So what now?' Sophie whispered.

'Crunch time,' Loki responded. 'Don't move until Finn and I have dealt with them. The guns are lying in the crate to our right, aren't they, Finn? About twenty feet away.'

'Yes. So the distraction should be to our left. We'll throw both charges at the same time.'

'Agreed.'

Also strapped to our shins were the small flash charges Alan Munro had devised. They were modifications of one of Special Ops' standard detonators, about the size and shape of a shotgun cartridge, and easy to conceal. All you needed to do was twist the cap a complete turn until it clicked. Precisely five seconds later it would detonate with a flash bright enough to blind someone for a few moments, and a bang loud enough to scare the crap out of the unsuspecting. How precise the timer was, we had no way of knowing. Many of our devices could not be relied on to be that accurate. But Alan Munro was a perfectionist. I reckoned if he said five seconds, he meant exactly that.

Easing forward, I grabbed hold of the handle to the van door. Gently I twisted it and opened it a fraction. Then a fraction more. I wanted to be sure we knew where the two men were. And they were sitting exactly as before. I relayed the information to Loki, who was poised at my shoulder. 'On the count of three we activate the flash charges, and then we count to two and throw. Ready?'

'Ready, Finn.'

'One . . . two . . . three.' We turned the caps. Simultaneously I kicked the door wide open. 'One . . . two . . . now!' We lobbed the charges to our left, tumbled out and started running.

The men from Marseille sprang to their feet and

turned. Blinding flashes and two loud bangs momentarily stunned, confused and mesmerized them. Huge plumes of dense smoke filled the warehouse. Loki and I arrived at the crate, seized two machine guns, slipped off the safety catches, turned and dropped onto one knee, and then we let rip.

A four-second stuttering blaze of bullets from our weapons finished the job. 'Check the door, Loki. Make sure no one's hanging around outside. I'll cover you.'

Outside, all was quiet. Not a soul to be seen.

Sophie had crawled to the van door and hauled herself painfully to her feet. I saw a tiny flicker of hope, of joy in her eyes, and then she collapsed, falling from the van like a rag doll that had lost its stuffing. She landed heavily. I ran over to her. 'Damn. That's all we need. Poor girl probably hasn't had a decent meal in weeks. Not enough energy left to even stand up.'

Loki leaned over me. 'Is she going to be OK, Finn?'

'God knows. She's in hell of a state. I mean, just look at her.'

'We can't leave her here, but we must get to the theatre and warn the others.'

'There's still plenty of time. I've got an idea.'

It was Sophie collapsing that triggered the scheme in my head. It made me think of the American Hospital. Dr Alexander would be able to provide Sophie with the best care available in the city, no questions asked. And then I remembered our first visit there, and our encounter with Chef and his black market piglets. They'd been delivered by Frenchmen dressed as

Germans. By men who had a car and petrol. A car and petrol that might just get us all out of Paris and heading towards Les Andelys. I outlined my plan to Loki.

'Absolutely brilliant, Finn. Just one tiny problem – how do the three of us get to the hospital in the first place? Surely not in that salad shaker.'

'Too risky. After this morning the authorities will be looking out for it. We'll use the bikes. Sophie can ride pillion. We'll strap her to me using some of the spare leather belts from the other uniforms. We'll dress her in uniform too. It's dark outside. With the blackout regulations no one will bat an eyelid.'

Chapter Twenty-one
The Mercy Dash

Together we swept through the streets of Paris, our motorcycles side by side, Sophie sitting astride the fuel tank and tightly strapped to me. Although half starved, she still proved a dead weight that upset the balance of my machine, especially round corners. I called out to her to lean with me, not to fight it. We ignored all the stop signs, and whenever anything or anybody got in our way, we gunned the throttles, dropped a gear or two, and accelerated past them. Foot patrols stopped and stared; one or two soldiers even tried to wave us down, suspicious of my passenger, probably thinking we were soldiers out on the town, messing around, and needed to be reprimanded. We ignored them and simply roared past.

With blackout regulations in force, the streets were in darkness, and the headlamps of our bikes had the usual covers on them, with narrow slits. This meant the beams were feeble and lit the way poorly. Added to which, we had only a vague idea of where we were going. The Eiffel Tower came to our rescue. Silhouetted against the night sky, it was so tall it could be seen for miles, head and shoulders above all the other buildings. We headed towards it, making left and right turns, cruising along boulevards, avenues and narrow streets, occasionally doubling back on ourselves when we realized we'd taken a wrong turn. As we reached the tower, my confidence grew. We knew where we were. The territory was familiar at last. Without stopping, we drove across the Seine. Loki waved to attract my attention and shouted, 'We'll make for the Arc de Triomphe, Finn, and from there to Neuilly. I know the route. And we can avoid the Avenue Foch.' I nodded. Loki accelerated away in front of me and led the way.

Just before eight o'clock we hit the Boulevard Victor Hugo, and finally swung through the entrance to the American Hospital. Hurtling up the ramp, we slammed on our brakes and skidded to a stop outside the main entrance. Loki leaped off his machine and ran over to give me a hand undoing the leather belts we'd used to keep Sophie tied to me. She was unconscious. Loki lifted her off my bike and carried her towards the door. I dismounted and followed, overtaking him and barging it open.

The nurse at the desk jumped to her feet and let out a shriek of horror on seeing our uniforms and weapons. 'Call Dr Alexander at once,' I ordered, lifting my goggles and tearing off my helmet. Stunned, the nurse simply froze. 'At once,' I shouted again. She fumbled for her telephone and nervously dialled his extension. She barely knew what to say and began stuttering. I snatched the phone from her. 'Dr Alexander, we have another patient for you. Come to the main entrance.'

He appeared in the hallway almost immediately. 'What the hell is going on?' he exclaimed. 'You two!

What the blazes . . .? And what . . .? Oh dear God . . .'
His gaze fell upon Sophie. The German uniform we'd
dressed her in was way too big for her and she reminded
me of a scarecrow you see in fields, just a bag of bones.
Loki was still holding her in his arms. Kneeling, Dr
Alexander gently grasped one of her ankles and
inspected the stained bindings to her foot.

'You've got to help her,' I said. 'And hide her too.
She's escaped from Fresnes. They'll be looking for her
everywhere.'

Anxiously Dr Alexander ran his fingers through his
thinning and receding hair. 'All right. Follow me.' He led
us down a corridor to a treatment room. 'Put her down
on that gurney.' He pulled open some cupboards and
hurriedly began gathering up a bottle of antiseptic, fresh
dressings, scissors and other paraphernalia. 'I'll do what I
can. But you've come at a bad time. The situation's
changing fast. I don't know how much longer we'll
be here.'

'Why? What's happened?'

'Haven't you heard?'

'Heard what?'

'The Japanese have attacked the American Pacific
fleet at Pearl Harbor.'

'The Japanese! Where's Pearl Harbor?' I asked.

'Hawaii,' Dr Alexander replied. 'America is bound to
declare war on Japan. And that means it's only a matter
of days before either Germany declares war on America
or vice versa.'

'Jesus!' said Loki, leaning back against the wall.

'What'll happen to you here? Do you have time to get away?'

Dr Alexander began cutting through the blood-stained material binding Sophie's feet. He paused and looked up. 'I have a hospital full of patients. I'm not going anywhere. I'll take my chances.'

Beneath Sophie's dressings were swollen feet, infected toes missing all their nails, and lots of yellowish pus and oozing blood. They smelled awful too. Loki looked away in disgust. The doctor began cleaning the wounds with antiseptic. 'I'll give her an injection of antibiotics and remove some of the dead skin. It's the best I can do. She's pretty undernourished and extremely weak.'

'Will she be all right?' I asked.

Dr Alexander nodded. 'The human body is a remark-able thing. It can withstand one heck of a lot. And she's young. Good diet and plenty of rest and she'll soon fatten up. As long as we prevent the infection spreading she'll probably live. Even her feet won't look quite so bad in a month or two. What's less certain is what psychological damage has been done. The real scars – the invisible wounds that never heal – will be inside her head. Her experiences will have changed her for ever. To what extent, only time will tell.'

'Is our pilot still here?'

'Yes. He's running a bit of a fever, but otherwise I think he's well on the way to recovery. Charles Thorpe hasn't come back to me yet regarding any arrangements for his escape. He'd better hurry up or else your pilot will be stuck here. I expect the American embassy is already in turmoil – they'll have to shut within days. Those who don't manage to get out in time will probably face arrest and internment.'

Sophie began to regain consciousness and, on opening her eyes, grew extremely distressed. She cried out and tried to get up. Dr Alexander held her down and reassured her with soothing words. Having put clean dressings on both feet, he lifted his stethoscope from round his neck, inserted the earpieces and began listening to her chest and heart. He then sat her up, removed the oversized army tunic, and lifted her filthy and torn blouse in order to place his stethoscope against her back. He baulked and took a sharp intake of breath. 'You poor thing,' he muttered. The scars and faded yellowish bruising told their own story of countless beatings and burns from a branding iron.

'We have one more favour to ask of you, sir,' I said, aware that the time was getting on.

'Go on.'

'We need a car with German plates and sufficient petrol to get us out of the city.'

He laughed sarcastically. 'We haven't got one of those, I'm afraid. Only an old ambulance that's converted to run on gazogène. And she's broken down.'

I explained about Chef and his 'friends'.

'I see. It might be possible, I suppose. When we're done here, I'll have a word with him. Make a call or two. They'll want something in return. They're black marketeers. They're in the business of making money. They won't care about your plight.'

I ground my teeth in frustration. We had nothing to offer. Most of our money was hidden in Trébuchet's apartment and there wasn't time to fetch it.

'Promise them anything you like. Whatever it takes,' said Loki. 'We'll deal with the problem of payment later.'

'Very well.'

'And one other thing,' said Loki. 'Please don't mention a word to Charles Thorpe about this. Not now, not tomorrow, not ever.'

This made Dr Alexander extremely suspicious. All of a sudden he saw us in a different light. He clearly trusted Charles Thorpe; we were unknown entities. I could see his brain working overtime as he judged his best course of action. I figured we had no choice. I had to explain everything.

'. . . So, you see, although Charles Thorpe is on our side, his orders effectively come from our superiors back in London and they've got it all wrong,' I concluded.

Dr Alexander heaved a sigh. 'I'm just a humble doctor. I help those I can with the limited resources I have. I can see from the state of this young lady that your efforts are all in a good cause and so I'm going to trust you. I shan't utter a word to Charles – at least not for a few days. Anyway, I suspect he's got his hands full packing up his stuff at the embassy and making his own arrangements to leave Paris.'

Sophie was slowly regaining her senses. She looked about the room. 'Where are we?'

'The American Hospital,' I said. 'You're in safe hands here.'

She peered down at the new dressings on her feet and smiled as if looking at a brand-new pair of shoes. 'Thank you.'

Loki continued, 'We're making arrangements to get us all out of Paris tonight. You, your father and Ross.'

'And Nils,' I said. 'If the shit's about to hit the fan with the Americans, then this place won't be safe for long, and it sounds like Thorpe's escape route will be closed down. Nils has to come too. It may be his only chance.'

Loki agreed. 'You go and have a word with Nils, Finn. I'll stay here with Sophie and help Dr Alexander persuade Chef's friends to lend us that car.'

'Bloody hell, Finn, why on earth are you dressed like that?'

Nils had been dozing, and he nearly jumped out of his skin on waking and seeing a German soldier standing at the door. His pyjamas were stained with sweat and his cheeks were flushed.

'It's a long story. Are you OK? Dr Alexander said you had a fever.'

'I think I'm over the worst, Finn.'

'Grand. Have you heard about the Japanese and Pearl Harbor?'

'Yes. Everyone in here's been talking about it. The nurses are quite frightened. They try to hide it from us, but I can see it in their eyes. Where are Loki and Freya?'

I summarized the situation.

'Christ! What a mess.'

'We need to find you some clothes,' I said, hurriedly checking the contents of a small wardrobe. It was empty. 'Damn!'

'There are some in a storeroom at the end of the corridor, Finn. I'll fetch them. So what's the plan?'

'We're getting out of Paris tonight.'

'You're the boss.' He tore back the bedcovers and sat up. A twinge in his guts made him wince.

'Are you OK to travel?'

'Fine. Don't you worry. What do you need me to do?'

'Loki and Dr Alexander are trying to arrange our transport. The girl downstairs is in a pretty bad way. I'd like you to stay with her while Loki and I go to the theatre and rescue Freya and the others. Be ready to leave the minute we get back.'

'Anything you say. What's her name?'

'Sophie Munro.'

'Right.'

'Oh, and by the way, just so you know, Charles Thorpe and his men in the OSS are out to kill us. Should he drop by while we're gone, say nothing.'

'Bloody hell, Finn. Listen, give me your revolver. Just in case.'

Chapter Twenty-two
Stage Fright

The treatment room was empty. Nils and I tried Dr Alexander's office. The others were gathered there and the doctor stood with his telephone receiver glued to his ear. '*Non! Ce soir. Ce soir! Maintenant. Voyons! Allons-y! . . . Oui, à l'hôpital . . . Bon! . . . Dix mille francs? . . . C'est de l'escroquerie . . .*' Placing his hand over the mouthpiece, he relayed to us, 'Jacques wants ten thousand francs. I told him it was daylight robbery, but I suppose we have no choice. He's got us over a barrel.'

'Take the offer. For God's sake just get them here as quickly as possible.'

'OK . . . *Oui, Jacques, dix mille francs . . . Oui . . . Bon! . . . Merci.*' He listened some more, and then gave us the gist. 'Jacques was wondering whether you'd like some SS uniforms. Those you're wearing are Wehrmacht, and given where you're going, I think that SS ones would make it easier.' He spun a prescription pad across the table and handed me a pen. 'Write down your measurements, including shoe size. Jacques, I understand, has most sizes in stock.' Having passed on our measurements and sealed the deal, he replaced the phone on its cradle. 'It's all agreed. He'll bring the car as quickly as he can. It's hidden some distance from here and there's the risk he'll be stopped at checkpoints. Jacques hopes to arrive sometime between ten and eleven.'

Loki puffed out his cheeks. 'That's cutting it fine.'

Dr Alexander opened a desk drawer and removed a key. Then he brushed past me and removed a painting from the wall of his office. Behind it lay a safe. He unlocked it and removed a thick wad of money and handed it to me. 'There's ten thousand there, give or take.'

I shook his hand tightly. 'Thank you.'

'Well, the way things are going, I shan't be needing it.' He slumped back down on his chair. 'Now, what else do you require? It strikes me that you've not had time to prepare properly. Neither your pilot nor this young girl has papers. What if you're stopped on your way out of the city?'

'We'll have to take our chances.'

'Perhaps. We keep all the patients' identity papers in the records room at the end of the corridor. With this place being full, I'm sure we can find some that at least bear some sort of passing resemblance. It's the best I can do. I'll also sort out some new clothes for the girl. And I'll get one of the nurses to bath her and wash her hair.'

'If we succeed in all this, much of it will have been down to your help and generosity,' I said. 'We can't ever thank you enough.'

Dr Alexander looked away. I think he was momentarily embarrassed.

'How are you going to get into the theatre?' asked Nils. 'There are so many senior Germans and officials attending the show, and security is bound to be tight.'

Loki reached for something on the table – a manila

envelope stamped with the eagle and swastika. 'Can we have this?'

'Yes,' the doctor replied. 'It only contained some routine information from the SS about new regulations they've imposed.'

'Thanks. We'll pretend we're delivering important messages to Major Kleb of the SD – messages from Berlin that can't be delayed. That plus our SS uniforms ought to at least get us inside.'

It was ten minutes after eleven when Jacques finally pulled into the driveway of the American Hospital. I'd almost bitten my nails to the quick. Money changed hands, and Jacques handed over the keys and opened the boot to reveal our uniforms. Five minutes later Loki and I had changed, combed our hair and smartened ourselves up. The SS were fastidious about their appearance. Everything had to be just so. We checked that our Luger pistols were loaded, and then Loki grabbed our MP40s and the envelope, which we'd stuffed with a wad of German edicts and regulations, so at least the pages were covered in official stamps and were in German. They looked pretty convincing unless you actually read them.

We shook hands with everyone and leaped into the car. We did not say goodbye, and Nils and the others did not wish us luck; no one wanted to tempt fate.

Loki drove and I gave him directions to the Theatre Royal. We arrived at twenty to twelve and parked right outside the front entrance, in full view of the sentries posted on either side of the doorway. Loki reached for the door handle and ground his teeth. 'Let's do it, Finn. Remember, we're SS. We're arrogant. We snap orders and look down on everyone else. Time to bury any nerves. Ready?'

Together we marched stiffly up the steps, the envelope tucked under my arm. The sentries snapped to attention and saluted. We returned the gesture as one of them pulled open the door for us.

The foyer was lit by sparkling chandeliers, and beneath our feet lay a rich crimson carpet. To my left was a sign to the lavatories and bar; to my right were the stairs to the upper circle; straight ahead was the ticket office, and to either side of it were sets of large double doors leading to the stalls. Sentries guarded both. We made for the left-hand one, and the soldier stood to attention and saluted.

'We have urgent telegrams from Berlin for Major Kleb of the SD,' I announced authoritatively and in perfect German, waving the envelope in the air. The sentry nodded and opened the door for us. He pointed and informed me that Major Kleb was sitting in the front row. I nodded curtly.

Inside, the theatre was dim and spotlights illuminated the stage. We paused at the back to get our bearings. There was a steady drum roll reverberating from the orchestra pit. Centre stage stood a huge tank of water, elevated on the box containing the explosives. Madura, bound in chains, stood motionless inside the tank, peering out towards the audience. Freya, wearing a sparkling gold dress and a fancy headpiece comprising a gold band and single white ostrich feather, quickly padlocked the tank's lid and then hurriedly draped a huge black cloth over the entire apparatus. Imagining the horror Madura would feel the second he realized his little silver key wouldn't work, I swallowed hard. With a flourish, Freya pretended to look at her watch, then pretended to look really scared and ran across the stage, shouting, 'Madura! Madura!' Everything she did was theatrical and exaggerated.

'How long do you think it'll take for Madura to realize he's been double-crossed?' I whispered as we hurried down one of the aisles towards the front, past a sea of uniforms and heads bearing caps of the Wehrmacht, SS, SD and just about every other German military organization.

'God knows, Finn. But did you see that tank? There's virtually no air pocket. Let's just hope Madura can hold his breath long enough. We've got to hurry.'

Reaching the front row of seats, we jinked to our left and located a set of steps that led backstage. We pushed through a heavy curtain and immediately saw quite a gathering of performers in the wings, all in glitzy costumes and plastered with heavy make-up, their attention fixed on the unfolding events on stage: the grand finale to an evening's star-studded show.

'What's going on? Monsieur Moreau should be getting them out of here by now. There's only fifteen minutes to go.' Discarding the envelope, I scanned the crowd and spotted Ross some distance away. We pushed and shoved our way towards him. In the gloom, others who had not yet spotted our uniforms swore at us. As soon as they saw the flashes of the SS on our shoulders, however, they cowered away, looking absolutely terrified. Loki reached Ross first, grabbing him by the shoulder and dragging him backwards, out of earshot of the others. Taken by surprise, Ross struggled until it dawned on him it was us.

'What happened to you?' he blurted. 'You were meant to be here hours ago.'

'Things got a little complicated,' I replied. 'There's a big problem. Marcel's men have switched the key Madura needs for undoing the locks. They want him dead. You do know there's a bomb underneath that tank, don't you? We've got to get him out before it's too late. It's set to detonate at midnight.'

Ross's eyes widened with alarm. 'I saw Marcel's brother, Pierre, here earlier this evening. He told Dad the escape had gone according to plan.'

'Well, Marcel's lot have double-crossed us – but don't worry, Sophie's safe. We rescued her and took her to the American Hospital. Now, we've got to stop this farce before we all die. How long can your dad hold his breath?'

Ross gulped. 'Over four minutes. Usually he gets out of there within fifty seconds. It's nowhere near as hard as it looks. He uses the key to undo the padlocks on his chains, and there are concealed catches on the inside of the lid that release it. Then he climbs down through a trap door in the floor just behind the tank, and emerges miraculously from the side of the stage. But if he can't free himself from the chains, there's no way he can release the lid! We'll have to do it. Or we can smash the glass using a sledgehammer. Several are always kept close to hand in case something goes wrong.'

'Hell. Go and grab one. Now! We'll find Monsieur Moreau and start getting everyone out of here. This place is about to go up in flames.'

'I am Henri Moreau, the stage manager.' A tall man with a ridiculously large moustache pressed through the throng with great urgency. 'I must ask everyone to leave now via the back entrance, as quietly and as calmly as possible,' he repeated over and over in French. 'Do not ask questions. Just do as I say.' Spotting our uniforms, he froze.

'My dad's trapped, Monsieur Moreau. We've been double-crossed by Marcel and his brother,' Ross shouted. 'Where are the sledgehammers?'

'Over there,' Moreau said, turning on his heels. He frowned. 'At least they were there earlier today. *Grands Dieux!* Someone's moved them!'

'That bastard, Pierre,' Loki hissed.

'How do we get Dad out?' Ross cried. 'The tank's lid is padlocked.'

Loki spun round, looking for inspiration. 'I'll think of something. Hurry! You've got about thirteen minutes before this place blows to kingdom come.'

A hideously loud scream came from the auditorium. *'Papa! Papa! Non!'*

The audience murmured in consternation. Heads turned and necks craned. All eyes peered towards the upper circle. A spotlight fell on the source of the outburst. A woman standing, screaming, '*Papa! Papa!*'

'Lou! What's she doing here?' Ross cried.

A man next to her stood up and tried to calm her. It was Wolfgang. I had to think fast. 'Change of plan. Loki, you and Freya help Ross get Madura out of that tank and off the stage. Head for the back entrance. I'll get Louise out of here and drive round and pick you up. Give me the car keys.'

I rushed off the stage and charged up the aisle between rows of seats in which men and women were now standing, muttering in consternation. Louise was still shrieking wildly and pointing to the stage. Wolfgang was unable to console her, but was trying to usher her to one of the aisles. It hadn't occurred to me that Wolfgang might be here or that he'd bring her along. As if the shock of realizing that he was performing wasn't enough, her worst nightmare was unfolding too: a repeat of the near tragedy Madura had suffered last time he'd tried Houdini's famous escape trick. Somehow I had to get them out of there – *fast*. Dressed as an SS officer, I could order them out, at gunpoint if necessary. But what if Wolfgang recognized me despite the dim lighting? I came to a decision. If I had to, I'd tell him the truth: that we were all sitting on a massive bomb that was about to explode. Surely that would get them moving. It would probably cause panic too. Panic was good – it would aid my getaway. I hammered up the stairs to the upper circle three steps at a time, kicked open the door and arrived just as Wolfgang reached the end of his row.

'Staffelkapitän Müller, sir, you must accompany me at once,' I said breathlessly.

He peered uncertainly at me a moment. My uniform scared him. No doubt he figured he'd be in trouble for ruining the evening because of his girlfriend's outburst. Then his expression changed. He recognized me. '*Sie! Aber . . .*' He reached for his pistol.

I grabbed his arm and drew close so I could whisper, 'Listen, Wolfgang, there is a bomb on that stage and it is set to go off at midnight. I strongly suggest that you get out of here immediately. *Sofort!*'

His eyes widened in disbelief.

'*Sofort, Herr Kapitän.*' I tightened my grip. 'And this was not our doing. Understand? Not our doing. I'm trying to save you, for Christ's sake. Just as you saved me from arrest.' I looked at Louise. 'You must get out of here *now*! I'll explain everything later.'

Realizing I was deadly serious, Wolfgang turned and shouted something to others close to where he'd been sitting, gesturing for them to follow. Half a dozen men and three girls headed towards us – the men all in Luftwaffe uniform: his men, his bomber crew and their girlfriends.

The drum roll from the orchestra pit ceased. Now the auditorium echoed with anxious, confused chatter. Moreau was ushering the musicians backstage. Loki yelled to Freya to give them a hand as he and Ross tried in vain to break the padlock holding the lid in place.

The audience's chatter turned to gasps, shrieks and screams. Madura was frantically squirming inside the tank, banging his head against the lid. His arms and hands were still tightly bound. Louise raised her hands to cover her face. She couldn't bear to look. Wolfgang grabbed hold of her, shook her and dragged her towards the exit.

Moreau hoisted himself onto the stage and ran to join Loki, Freya and Ross. Leaping onto the box containing the explosives, he helped as they desperately tried to undo the lid of the tank. It was a lost cause, and so Loki took to wildly kicking at the thick glass.

'Shoot it,' I yelled. 'Use your pistol. Shoot the glass.' They couldn't hear me amid the panic. 'For Christ's sake, shoot it!'

Out of the corner of my eye I noticed several senior German officers near the back of the auditorium peering up at me. Fearful that something terrible was unfolding, one reached for his pistol and shouted the order for guards to be summoned.

Ross jumped down from the box and ran to the side of the stage. Hurriedly he removed his catapult from his pocket. Retrieving a stone from his other pocket, he loaded his weapon, stretched it to his chin, aimed and fired. The stone struck the tank and the glass cracked but didn't shatter. Loki tried kicking it again and again.

Cupping my hands about my mouth, I called out again. 'Shoot a hole in the glass.' Still they couldn't hear me. I removed my pistol from its holster, undid the safety catch and took careful aim. The stage was a long way away. I reckoned I could hit the tank, but at that range I had an even chance of hitting Loki or Freya instead. I placed a finger on the trigger and began to squeeze it.

Inside the tank Madura had stopped thrashing about and was now motionless. It was no good. I didn't have a clear line of sight as Loki had moved round to the front of the tank. I heard someone shouting in German. I looked down and saw an SS officer pointing his pistol up at me. Hell, he must've heard me calling out in English. I lowered my weapon.

Ross wiped his sleeve across his face to clear the tears from his eyes. Removing the large lead bullet from his pocket, he quickly reloaded and stretched his catapult as far back as it would go. He fired. The bullet accelerated towards the tank. It fizzed through the air, smacked the glass, ricocheted and bounced across the stage. For a second nothing happened, and then a huge crack zigzagged across the glass and, without warning, the tank exploded. A vast surging wave of water crashed down, sweeping Freya, Loki and Moreau along with it. Together with the limp body of Madura, they slid across the floor of the stage, spinning.

Guards entered the auditorium and, amid the growing mêlée, filed down the aisles on both sides. Within seconds all exits would be blocked. I had to act quickly. I remembered Ross had mentioned a trap door on the stage, located right behind the water tank. As I watched Loki, Freya and Moreau trying to get a half-drowned, coughing and spluttering Madura to his feet, I realized it was our only hope. I hurried to the front of the upper circle, climbed onto the ledge and jumped down into the auditorium's centre aisle. The drop was a good twenty feet, but the SS officer who'd pointed his pistol at me broke my fall. I landed heavily on top of him. Up in a flash, I charged forward, leaped over the orchestra pit and scrambled up onto the stage. 'Freya,' I yelled. 'Catch.' I threw her my gun. 'Kill those spotlights.' Freya was by far the best shot among us. 'Do it *now*! . . . Loki, grab your other flash charge. Time for us to disappear!'

I reached down and tore the spare flash charge I had strapped to my shin. Freya raised her pistol, and two shots rang out in quick succession, each shattering a spotlight, plunging us into darkness. 'We'll get out via the trap door.'

'I know where it is,' Freya shouted. 'Follow me.'

Loki and Moreau dragged Madura behind the burst water tank, and Freya located the trap door, pressing a catch to release it. A light towards the back of the auditorium came on. Then another. I heard orders being shouted in German – orders to arrest everyone on stage. 'Quick, Loki, throw me your flash charge.'

About to climb down after Ross, Moreau and Madura, Loki lobbed his flash charge over to me. Catching it, I hurriedly twisted the caps on both. *One . . . two . . . three . . .* I flung them into the air. Two blinding flashes, two deafeningly loud blasts and, best of all, two billowing clouds of smoke. With my ears ringing and the stage cloaked in smoke, I dived towards the trap door and slithered through on Loki and Freya's heels. It was five minutes to twelve.

Chapter Twenty-three
The Unwilling Patient

Outside, I sprinted round to the front of the theatre and leaped into the car. I could hear church bells ringing in the distance. Fumbling to locate the ignition, I started the engine, slammed into first gear and sped off. People were streaming out of the theatre and running in all directions. Tyres squealing, I took a left turn, and then another, to reach the back entrance I'd emerged from seconds earlier. Screeching to a halt, I spotted Loki and Ross dragging Alan Munro down a short flight of steps. Freya was right behind them, clutching Loki's MP40 just in case they encountered any trouble.

The explosion rocked the car and blew the theatre's rear doors off their hinges. The blast threw all the others to the ground. Loki scrambled to his feet and helped the others up. Reaching into the back of the car, I grabbed the handle and flung open the rear door.

'He'll be OK. I think we were just in time,' Loki yelled as he bundled Munro onto the back seat. Freya and Ross tumbled in on top of him. Loki joined me up front. 'Step on it, Finn. They're bound to seal the whole area off in minutes.'

I hit the gas pedal, squealed round a corner, and accelerated up the road.

'Do you think Lou made it?' Ross asked. 'She wasn't meant to be there. What a disaster.'

'Let's hope so,' I replied. 'I think she and Wolfgang got out in time. Fingers crossed.'

'Where's Sophie? Is she safe? Please, tell me she's safe,' spluttered Alan Munro.

'She's fine. We're taking you to her now.'

'Thank the Lord. I don't understand what went wrong.'

Loki explained our escape with Sophie. 'Those wire-cutters came in really handy.'

'I should have known Marcel couldn't be trusted. But I was desperate and had no one else to turn to. But we've made it out of there alive. Mark my words, Marcel's days are numbered. His brother, Pierre, too. I'll see to it that they pay a high price for their treachery.'

'Well done, Ross. You just saved your father's life,' said Freya. She slid open the window and chucked out her headpiece with the ostrich feather. 'Horrid thing. I looked ridiculous.'

'I thought you looked rather nice,' Loki replied. He turned round in his seat and winked at her.

Freya gave him a friendly shove. 'Idiot.'

Arriving at the hospital, I pulled up next to another car. 'You all go inside. That car wasn't here earlier – I'm going to check it out. I'll be right behind you.'

As the others made their way in, I was struck by two things. Firstly, no one had come running out to greet them. Secondly, pacing around the other car, I saw that it bore official American embassy plates and badges. It could mean only one thing: Charles Thorpe was here. That had to be more than just coincidence given that it was after midnight. Somehow he must have known we'd be here. I peered through the car's windows to see if anything inside could tell me whether he'd turned up alone or with colleagues from the embassy, possibly fellow members of his OSS organization. There were documents on the passenger seat, and stuff strewn across the back seats. In all likelihood he'd come alone. I grabbed my MP40 from our car and hurried towards the main entrance.

Exercising extreme caution, I gently pulled the door open and slipped inside. No one was manning the front desk. I listened out for voices. Silence. Not a good sign.

I crept down the corridor towards Dr Alexander's office. At the end was the records room: the door was open and the light on. Nils's face appeared, and he held a finger to his lips. He pointed to Dr Alexander's office and held up one finger, and then showed me the gun I'd given him earlier. I nodded. He was telling me there was one man and he was armed and that everyone was in the doctor's office. Crouching, I eased myself along until I was next to the office door. Nils did likewise.

'Arrived about half an hour ago,' Nils whispered. 'I overheard him. Said he was in no hurry and that he'd wait for you to return.'

'How did he know?'

Nils shrugged. 'There was one hell of an argument in there.'

Suddenly I heard a raised voice. It was Alan Munro.

He was telling Thorpe in no uncertain terms for the umpteenth time that he wasn't a traitor. Then I heard Freya repeating that it was true. Then I heard Thorpe yell, 'Enough!'

I signalled to Nils that I wanted him to conceal his weapon, knock on the door and enter. It would give me a glimpse inside and then I'd barge in on his heels and deal with Thorpe. I'd shoot him if I had to, but my intention was simply to disable him. After all, he was OSS, supposedly on our side. It wasn't his fault that the orders he'd been given were crazy. Nils stood up, slipped his pistol into the back of his belt, and knocked briskly on the door. Muffled talk inside ceased. 'Come in,' a voice called out.

Nils grabbed the handle, took a deep breath, and opened the door.

'Oh, it's you,' hissed Thorpe. 'Where's that—?'

I leaped in, and before Thorpe could react, swung the butt of my MP40 and floored him. He was out for the count. 'What the hell is he doing here?'

'You're not going to believe this, Finn,' said Freya. 'HQ passed on to Thorpe the gist of our last message: that we were going to assist in some sort of prison escape. Thorpe heard about the break-out from Fresnes earlier today. He put two and two together, checked out Trébuchet's apartment, and realized we'd given him the slip. He figured that at some point we'd come to pick up Nils before getting out of Paris.'

'Well, he figured it all out pretty much right, didn't he? I'm just glad he came alone.'

In the corner of the room Alan Munro stood clutching Sophie and Ross tightly in his arms. So tightly, it was as if he never wanted to let go of them. Both Ross and Sophie held their father as if they were survivors from a terrible storm clinging to a life raft. Both had bloodshot eyes and cheeks wet with tears of joy and relief.

'I'm so sorry,' Ross sobbed. 'All this is my fault. It was my big mouth that led you to being arrested, Sophie. And look what they've done to you. You're all skin and bone. Please don't hate me for it. I was stupid, childish. I didn't realize the consequences. Please . . . *please* don't hate me. I couldn't bear it.'

'Of course I don't hate you,' she said softly. 'I forgave you a long, long time ago. I knew the risks I was taking when I agreed to work for the Resistance. And, anyway, if it wasn't for you, Father and Lou risking everything to save me, I'd be dead by now. You've been very brave. I figure you've earned forgiveness.'

Dr Alexander cleared his throat. 'Sorry to interrupt, but might I make a suggestion?' He leaned over Thorpe to inspect the damage I'd inflicted. 'Hmmm, still out cold. But your problems aren't over yet. To try and drive out of Paris at this hour will prove tricky, despite your uniforms. Best to wait until dawn. I could keep Charles here under sedation long enough to enable you to leave Paris. Shall we say twenty-four hours?'

'Why don't you just kill him?' said Ross hatefully.

'No,' said Freya. 'He gives me the creeps and has orders to kill us, but at the end of the day he's on our side. Killing him would simply be wrong. As long as we stay ahead of him, we'll be OK.'

'I should warn you,' Dr Alexander interrupted. 'I think he may know the location of your arrival in France, so I would advise against returning there.'

The others looked worried, but I had an idea. 'Yes, good advice. Thank you, Dr Alexander. We have no intention of returning there. But I don't suppose you could keep the unwilling patient here for forty-eight hours, could you?'

'Forty-eight hours it is then.'

'Thank you.'

Chapter Twenty-four
The Road to Les Andelys

We set off at dawn, having first removed the distributor cap from under the bonnet of Charles Thorpe's diplomatic car. I wanted to make sure we inconvenienced him as much as possible in case he had any crazy notions of pursuing us.

Loki and I rode our motorcycles up front, and Alan Munro drove the car, with Nils next to him and Freya, Ross and Sophie in the back. Alan was in uniform too. If we got stopped, our cover story was that the 'civilian' occupants of the car were wanted for questioning about black marketeering in Rouen, which just so happened to be in the direction we were heading. And we did get stopped. On the outskirts of Paris. A routine checkpoint. Our uniforms ensured that we got little more than a cursory glance before being waved on.

In fact, we were making for Les Andelys, but not for Laurent Laval's farm – at least, not in the first instance. My thinking was that the only safe place for everyone was the convent of the Order of St Anne's. I felt certain Mother Thérèse could be relied upon.

Late that morning we sped in convoy down the arrow-straight road bordered by tall poplars and drove through the convent's gates. Sister Maude was carrying a bucket across the courtyard when she spotted us.

Letting out a cry, she dropped it and fled inside, slamming the door shut.

'Stay here,' I said to Alan Munro, clambering off my motorcycle and removing my helmet and goggles. 'I'll talk to Mother Thérèse. Sophie, you come with me.' I helped her out of the car, and together we shuffled over to the main entrance. I yanked the bell pull and waited. I had the sense we were being watched, but simply stood, waited, and rang the bell again. Eventually I heard bolts being slid back and the door creaked open.

'Good morning, Mother Thérèse. I trust you are well.'

'You!' Mother Thérèse's eyes fell on the tiny, skinny figure of Sophie, and slowly down to her feet. 'Oh dear Lord,' she muttered. Then she frowned. 'Sophie Munro. Is it really you?'

Sophie nodded.

'You poor young woman. We've prayed for you day and night.'

'We need somewhere safe to stay for a while,' I said.

'We?'

'Sophie's father's here too. We helped him rescue her from Fresnes. And then there are the three of us, our pilot, and Ross. I'm sorry it's so many, but there were complications and it's too risky for us to stay at Monsieur Laval's farm. We didn't know who else to trust. And it's thanks largely to Dr Alexander that we've made it this far. You were right about him – he's a remarkable man.'

Hands on ample hips, Mother Thérèse considered

our plight. 'Very well, you can stay . . . temporarily. We have some rooms that are well hidden and can conceal you should the Germans search this place. But you must hide those motorcycles and that car.'

'We'll dump the bikes but the car's ours — I thought you might like it as a gift, and as a thank-you from us. Old Beelzebub has served you well, but once the war's over you'll want something better. Best if you change the number plates, though. Just in case.'

'Most kind — but Beelzebub suits our needs well enough, thank you. I'll call Sister Agnès. She'll drive it round the back for now. You can decide what to do with it later.'

'By the way,' I said, 'go easy on Ross. You're quite wrong about him, you know. He's helped us a great deal and last night he saved his father's life.'

Mother Thérèse diverted her gaze towards the back of the car and her face sharpened. 'That's as maybe, but that boy has a lot to answer for.'

'We know that it was his big mouth that got Sophie arrested. He admitted his foolishness to us.'

'Confessing his sins is a start, I suppose,' she responded grudgingly. 'But look at what this poor girl has had to endure, all because of his stupidity.'

'No, you don't understand. He was willing to lay down his life to save her, to make amends. I witnessed it with my own eyes.'

Sophie spoke. 'He's my brother. I forgave him a long time ago.'

'Then maybe I have misjudged him.' Mother Thérèse

looked at me and smiled. 'I guess it's true, young man.'

'What is?'

'Why, that our Lord works in mysterious ways, of course, and that wonders will never cease . . . and so on. Well, you'd better get everyone inside. And we'll find something for you to change into. Those uniforms make me nervous.'

Later we sat at a long wooden refectory table and gorged ourselves on bread, cheese and large slices of apple. Alan Munro's joy at having Sophie by his side was plain to see. 'We did it!' he kept saying, as if he couldn't really bring himself to believe it was true.

'So what's your plan of action?' asked Mother Thérèse. 'Tell me only what you feel able to, of course.'

'Our biggest problem is contacting HQ,' Freya replied. 'We left our wireless set in Paris. Batteries were dead, anyway. Somehow we have to make contact in order to arrange a pick-up. If that proves impossible, then we may have to head for the coast and try to steal a boat.'

'You said Monsieur Laval's farm was too dangerous for you. Does that mean he's in danger too?'

Loki shook his head. 'Not directly. It's just that there's someone who might think we've headed there, and come looking. You've met him – Charles Thorpe. He's actually on our side *officially*, not that you'd know it. He's part of an American organization that was supposed to help us find Mr Munro here. Unfortunately they have orders to kill him. Worse still, they seem intent on carrying them out.'

'Sounds a bit drastic.' Mother Thérèse shook her head as if bothered by an irritating fly. 'Surely no one would want to shoot Monsieur Munro.'

'Those were our orders too,' said Freya, wiping her mouth with a napkin, 'in the event we failed to get him to return to England with us.'

'I see,' said Mother Thérèse, although clearly she didn't.

'This mess is all my fault,' Alan Munro interrupted. 'And I have these brave young agents to thank that I'm still alive. I shall return to England and smooth things over.' He hugged Sophie. 'Everything will turn out fine.'

Loki rose from the table. 'We'd better get rid of those bikes. And then we'll pay Monsieur Laval a visit. He needs to know what's happening and to be on his guard. Come on, Simon, let's get out of these damn SS uniforms.'

A weary-looking Laurent Laval was ushering his cows into the milking parlour when Loki and I arrived at the gate to his farmyard. He abandoned his animals and took us into the house. We sat down and relayed everything that had happened, reassuring him that Sophie, Ross and Alan Munro were safe.

'We came here for two reasons,' I concluded. 'One, to warn you that a man called Charles Thorpe may turn up here sooner or later. Secondly, we were wondering whether you have any contacts that can lead us to a wireless operator. We need to get a message to HQ.'

The big man stroked his beard thoughtfully. Then he

rose to his feet and made for a cupboard under the staircase. He took out a shotgun, broke it, inserted two fresh cartridges, and then snapped it shut. 'This will scare off that Charles Thorpe,' he muttered, leaning the weapon up against the wall. 'As for a wireless operator, *non*. My group is isolated. We simply act on *messages personnels* from your BBC. However, there is something I'd like to show you.'

Laval led us to his barn. Inside it looked somehow different – smaller than I remembered. There was a huge stack of straw bales filling half of it. He knelt down and dragged out a single bale from the bottom of the stack. '*Suivre-moi*,' he said, disappearing through the hole on all fours.

We did as he asked and crawled after him. On the other side we got the surprise of our lives.

'She is nearly finished,' Laval declared proudly. 'Just a few more days' work, according to my brother, Paul.'

Before us stood the Lizzie. 'I thought you said you'd have to get rid of her. Break up what was left of her and burn or bury it.'

'*Oui*, but I showed my brother, and he insisted we had a go repairing her. He loves a challenge.'

We lit a couple of oil lamps in order to get a better look at her. As far as I could tell they'd managed to repair the gashes and damage to the fuselage near the tail. They'd also retrieved the rear wheel from the field and reattached it. Dents in the front cowling had been hammered out. She looked in pretty good shape – apart from having no propellers. I pointed this out.

'They shattered when you crashed. But my brother has a friend who knows someone whose father is a master carpenter and who worked for a small aviation company near Caen before the war. As you know, propellers have to be manufactured with great precision. My brother is going to collect the new set in a few days.'

Loki looked at me and grinned. 'Are you thinking what I'm thinking?'

'I expect so.'

For an hour we examined the Lizzie in greater detail, checking the repairs. Laval looked on with pride as we repeatedly congratulated him on doing a splendid job. Then it began to dawn on him what we were thinking. He waved his hands. '*Non!* Come down from there. This is my plane now. *Our* plane. *My brother's* plane. We mended it. You left us a wreck and we fixed it. That makes it ours.'

I jumped down. 'Why on earth did you show her to us if you weren't thinking we could use her to fly home?'

Agitated, he pointed to the cockpit. 'I thought you could use the plane's radio. Call your HQ. Ask them to send another plane.'

Loki whistled through his teeth. 'That radio hasn't got the range. The signal would be lost halfway across the Channel. Although it *would* get picked up by all the German coastal radio stations and, using triangulation, they'd pinpoint its position. I reckon soldiers would be here within about an hour of anyone trying to use it.'

Laval's shoulders slumped.

Loki pointed to the RAF roundels on the wings. 'See these? It means it belongs to the RAF. Not to you, or us, but the RAF.'

'Then I suppose you must use her to get back to England,' Laval eventually conceded.

'Yes,' I said. 'We must. But clearly all the hard work you and your brother have put in mustn't go un-rewarded. I'd like to offer you something in return. It's not exactly a fair swap, but it's the best we can do. We have a splendid car that's almost new – it cost us ten thousand francs. She can be yours in exchange, no questions asked.'

He frowned. 'Stolen from the Germans?'

'No. Purchased in Paris from a man called Jacques.'

'I'll talk it over with my brother. However, I don't suppose we have a choice, do we?'

'Not really, no! One thing your brother might want to fit a new set of number plates. It's better to be safe than sorry. As he owns a garage, I don't suppose that will pose a problem.'

Chapter Twenty-five
A Breed Apart

As we returned to the convent, Loki and I were on cloud nine: we couldn't wait to share the news with the others.

'When they arrive, we'll go and check that the propellers fit OK,' said Loki. 'You wait till you see her, Nils. She's as good as new. Well, almost.'

Nils was still feverish and looked incredibly tired. Nevertheless he still had his wits about him. 'That's good. But I'd rather Simon flies her in case I have a problem. I'm not sure I'm up to it. If this fever gets any worse, I might be delirious or fall unconscious. You'd have no way of gaining control of the plane – there's only room for one up front. Anyway, I'm sure Simon can manage. But there's one thing you seem to have forgotten. That plane can only carry three passengers. There's us four plus Alan. I doubt we can all fit in. Someone will have to stay behind. I'll volunteer if that helps. You can get them to send another plane for me, or I'll wait until the next agent is flown in and hitch a ride home then.'

Freya sensed I wasn't too keen on leaving Nils behind. Having him behind me in the plane doubled my confidence. Without him, well, the doubts started to creep in almost before he'd finished making the suggestion.

'I've got a proposal,' she announced. 'Mr Munro has given us his word that he's prepared to return to Britain and face the consequences, and I believe him. If he's willing to agree to return on the next flight out of here, then I think he should stay behind for now. It'll allow him to spend a little time with his family.' She looked at us in turn. 'Well?'

'That would be splendid,' Alan Munro said, but added, 'However, I'm aware that you've disobeyed orders to get this far, and that'll spell trouble for you on your return, especially if you arrive empty handed and I am still, you might say, *at large*. Your offer is greatly appreciated, but I really must accompany you. I have a lot of explaining to do and must face the music. I accept that without hesitation. This trouble has all been my doing. But I have achieved what I set out to do and, now that I know Sophie's safe, I am content. X can do what he likes with me. Is there really no way you can squeeze in an extra passenger?'

Hands on hips Loki blew hard and scratched his head. 'Well, we're not carrying any luggage. That ought to make a difference. Maybe, if we strip out one of the bench seats, we could all squash inside. It'll be hellishly uncomfortable but it's not a long flight.' He turned to Nils. 'Will the extra weight be a problem? She's a small plane.'

Nils shook his head. 'She can cope.'

Freya straightened up determinedly. 'That's settled then.'

★ ★ ★

That evening, along with the nuns, we huddled around a wireless set tuned to the BBC Overseas Service. The evening news confirmed what we all expected: both America and Britain had declared war on Japan. It was the eighth of December.

'It's only a matter of time,' said Alan Munro, sitting back in his chair.

'Question is, will Germany declare war on America or will it be the other way round?' said Ross.

'Does it make any difference?' I asked.

'Not a jot, young man,' Munro responded. 'It's the beginning of the end for dear old Adolf. He's already getting bogged down in the east in the fight with Russia. America has a good deal of muscle to support the Allies. A whole new front will be established. Mark my words, they'll work towards an Allied invasion of mainland Europe using Britain as a springboard.' He rubbed his hands together gleefully as if relishing the prospect. 'There's much work to be done.'

'We saw some of your earlier efforts,' said Loki. 'They showed us a fake airfield and demonstrated Starfish. Pretty impressive.'

Munro replied modestly, 'I was just part of a team. Still, I have a few more ideas that might help. When they build an invasion force, it will be crucial to mislead the enemy as to our chosen route for crossing the Channel.'

'Did Louise tell you what she learned from Wolfgang? About their new targeting system?'

'X-Verfahren, do you mean? Yes. Fits in with what we suspected. I suppose our lot might be able to jam it somehow. Let's hope so, anyway. I know enough to brief them when I get back.'

Freya had a question. 'Our superiors in Special Ops didn't know your true identity when you signed up, did they? So how did you manage to get transferred to the Ministry of Tricks if they didn't know you were a magician?'

'I included "magic" in my list of hobbies during interviews for Special Ops. Didn't think anything more of it until one day X was visiting F-Section at Handelbury Manor, and somehow the topic came up in conversation over lunch. I laid it on a bit thick about how good I was, and next thing I know I'm packing my bags and heading off to work for Sir Hugo.'

'Why the secrecy?' I asked. 'Why didn't you tell Special Ops who you really were right from the beginning?'

'Good question. I got to England during the Dunkirk evacuation. Despite the great success of the operation, I arrived to find Britain standing alone and virtually on her knees. Some were saying that it would all be over inside a year; that Britain would be invaded, defeated, and that would be that, Europe done for. I wanted to do what I could, and knew there must be some sort of organization like Special Ops. I also knew that if I got involved, and if Britain *was* defeated, any member of such an organization would be hunted down by the Nazis and executed. I figured a false identity would serve me well. They'd be looking for a Claude Chevalier and I could revert to my real identity and vanish off the radar; nothing in my personnel records would link me to the name Alan Munro, or Madura, the famous magician from Paris. It pays to think ahead, you know.'

For three days we twiddled our thumbs while life in the convent went on around us as normal. We slept in a tiny, cramped, windowless room hidden behind a bookcase in a library situated next door to the chapel. From the way the room was already furnished with beds and mattresses, we knew we weren't the first to have been given sanctuary. Mother Thérèse forbade us to wander about outside except in a small walled garden. Inclement weather meant we rarely ventured there. On our fourth day news reached us that Laurent Laval's brother, Paul, had returned with the new propellers. Loki and I set off across the fields, brimming with excitement and ignoring a persistent drizzle and mist rising from the nearby river. Nils, despite his poor health, insisted on tagging along. He wanted to check the Lizzie over with his own expert eye. We also needed to remove one of the Lizzie's seats in preparation for our departure. Having tried to remain on his best behaviour in the presence of the nuns, Ross reckoned he'd suffered enough, and so joined us too.

Paul Laval was the spitting image of his brother – huge and bearded – and spoke gruffly even when trying to be nice. Although not best pleased that we'd be flying his pride and joy into the sunset, he grudgingly accepted the inevitable, and his eyes lit up when he heard about our gift of the car.

Nils spent ages checking out all their repairs and, with reservations, declared the Lizzie airworthy once we'd sorted out the new propellers. Paul had transported them covered in old blankets in the back of a small cart drawn by a skinny grey pony. He carefully lifted them off the cart and carried them into the barn. Laying them down on some straw, he slowly unwound the blankets and we just all stared at them in amazement. They were works of art, beautifully smooth and planed with precision. The tricky bit was figuring out how to reattach them. The mountings had been damaged when the Lizzie pitched forward on crashing. Most of the afternoon was taken up with hammering and cursing, and arm-aching hours holding the propellers aloft while balanced atop rickety ladders, as Nils and Paul tried to figure out the repairs needed. Loki and I also tore out one of the bench seats, and by our reckoning we'd all just manage to squeeze in. By three o'clock I needed a break and ventured out of the barn in search of some fresh air.

I'd been standing outside for about five minutes when I heard a car driving along the lane bordering the farm. It drew to a stop some fifty yards from the entrance. Fearing it contained Germans, or maybe a furious Charles Thorpe intent on finishing his mission, I was about to dash and warn the others when Louise climbed out of the front passenger side. Wolfgang got out too, and for a couple of minutes they held each other in a tight embrace. Then, clutching a small suitcase, Louise began walking slowly along the lane towards the entrance to the farm. She didn't look back. Wolfgang just stood and gazed after her. He must've sensed he was being watched, because without warning he suddenly spun round and spotted me. I froze. With both of us taken by surprise, we stared at each other for a few seconds, and then he raised a hand and waved. I waved back. He gestured for me to join him. I figured I had no choice.

'I didn't expect to see you here, Simon,' he said with a mix of puzzlement and suspicion.

'It's a small world. We help out on the farm.'

'I see. Lou wanted to come home for a while. Said she'd had enough of Paris for now. She's spent the last couple of days trying to look for her father, to find out what happened to him. No luck. She hoped someone here might know. Do you know if he's alive?'

I shook my head. I don't think he believed me for one minute.

'As you can imagine, the SS are keen to find him, and his stage assistant – that pretty young girl in the gold dress.' He raised an eyebrow. 'They're also keen to locate two imposters dressed in SS uniforms and a black car seen parked outside the theatre.' He raised his other eyebrow.

'Were many killed?'

'A few. Most got out. It came as quite a shock to Lou, seeing her father on stage like that. She told me about the last time – how he'd promised never to perform again. She can't fathom why he did it. And then, well, for it to go wrong a second time. Her outburst at the theatre was understandable, I suppose.' He eyeballed me. 'Perhaps you can enlighten me as to what happened. Did your planned sabotage go horribly wrong?'

I shook my head. 'No. As I told you, it wasn't our doing. Nothing to do with any of us, including Louise's father. He was conned into performing one more time. The rumour on the street is that a group of communists organized it. They planted a bomb beneath the water tank. To cover their tracks they wanted to make sure Madura didn't survive. They swapped the key he needed to undo the chains. We only found out just in time.'

He pulled a face. 'Communists! Don't suppose you know who they were?'

I shrugged.

He frowned as if trying to figure it all out and failing to do so. 'Well, anyway, if what you've told me is true, then I'm glad you're here. It gives me the opportunity to thank you personally. When all is said and done, you saved Lou's life. Mine too. Thanks to you we made it away safely.'

We stood in an uneasy silence. 'So, what do you want? A boy or a girl?' I asked.

'*Ach*, so you know, then?' He beamed with delight. 'I don't care. As long as it's healthy. A small bundle of joy in this god-forsaken world of ours. To answer your question, though, what I *want* is what we all want – to be able to go home and live in peace.'

By now Lou had vanished from sight, but Wolfgang peered down the lane as if she was still there. 'Lou was having a hard time in Paris, Simon. I kept telling her she should leave. She could barely go out of her apartment without her neighbours calling her a whore and spitting at her in the street. She tried to rise above it, but I could see she was starting to get very afraid. I hope things will be better for her here. It seems quiet, peaceful, safe.'

I suddenly remembered the woman we'd met on the burning streets of London, and her small son, Sam. She'd asked Sergeant Walker what sort of world our children were being born into. It was a question that Louise was no doubt asking herself too. What had the future in store? That was the most important question of all, the only one that mattered. Right now, there was no answer.

'Her biggest worry might be that you lot could lose this war,' I said. 'What would happen to you then? And what would happen to her and the baby? They'd be reviled by most ordinary French people. They'd be outcasts in their own country. Would anywhere be safe for them?'

Swallowing uncomfortably, Wolfgang looked up at the sky and nodded. 'I fear you're right, Simon. You know, I was a humble teacher before the war. Life was so much simpler back then. Hopes and dreams seemed so much simpler too. Sometimes I find myself wondering how we ever ended up here.'

'You're not the only one.'

He laughed ironically. 'To tell you the truth, Simon, the only time I ever feel free is up there. It's a different world. To fly for hours surrounded by just a blue haze, the angry world beneath hidden by a thick layer of cloud. Sometimes I just want to keep on flying. Never come back down. *Ach ja, die Freiheit.*'

He observed me staring at him. 'What's the matter, Simon?'

'Oh, nothing. It's just that you remind me a bit of someone.'

'Really. Who?'

I hesitated. 'My father . . . He was a pilot too. And he used to say more or less the same thing. That he only felt truly free when he was ten thousand feet up in the sky.'

Wolfgang smiled. 'I remember you telling me you wanted to learn to fly. I suppose you want to follow in his footsteps. I hope you succeed. It is worth it.' Then the smile melted from his lips. 'You said he *was* a pilot?'

'He was shot down. Missing in action, presumed dead . . . But I've not given up all hope.'

Wolfgang studied me seriously for a moment and then nodded. 'I am sorry to hear that. I hope he is still alive and safe. I have lost countless fellow airmen, some good friends, others men I'd barely got to know before one day their luck ran out and they simply did not return. Their faces live on in my dreams, my nightmares.'

This was turning out to be one of the strangest experiences of my life. Here I was talking to the enemy, to someone who almost certainly knew I was fighting on the opposite side. I should have been scared. I should have been trying to figure out how I was going to silence him, to make sure he didn't leave this place knowing about us. I ought to have been thinking about how I was going to kill him. But I wasn't thinking that at all.

'What did he fly? Spitfire? Hurricane? Lancaster?'
'Spitfire.'

As I spoke the aircraft's name, I expected a fizz of nervous electricity to shoot through me. After all, I was gifting myself into the hands of the enemy. Was he about to reach for his pistol and arrest me? But I felt no sudden bolt of fear. For some reason I wasn't frightened. Not frightened at all.

'*Ach*, a beautiful aircraft. What I'd give to fly one of those. We have nothing to match it.' Wolfgang glanced at his watch. 'Please make sure Louise remains safe here. I don't know how often I'll be able to visit her, but I shall try to come when I'm next on leave. That's a month or two from now. God willing I'm still alive. Now, I'm afraid I must go. I'm late as it is. I'm heading to Caen to rejoin my crew.' He removed his cap and held out a hand for me to shake. 'It has been nice meeting you, Simon. And thank you once again for what you did the other day. I wish you a long and happy life.'

'You too, Wolfgang.' I hesitated then added, 'You won't say . . .'

'No. Don't worry, I won't tell anyone about you and your friends. Your secret's safe. You have my word.'

'Your word as a German officer or as an airman? My father always told me that airmen were different, special, a breed apart; that an airman's word could be counted on.'

He nodded. 'Both – but first and foremost as a fellow pilot, Simon. Your father was right. We are a breed apart. I think in this war we are unfortunately all just, erm, how do you say . . .'

'*Untergebene?*'

'Yes, we are all just unwilling servants in this night-mare.' Wolfgang turned and opened the car door. 'By the way, I doubt if you've heard the news yet. Our insane idiot of a Führer has gone and declared war on America today. I suspect it's the beginning of the end for us.' He laughed in a helpless way. 'Given those American papers of yours, take my advice and don't hang around. Get out of France if you can. Good luck, Simon. *Auf wiedersehen.*'

'You too, Wolfgang. *Auf wiedersehen.*'

As he pulled away, Loki appeared at my shoulder, breathless from running from the barn. 'Everything all right, Finn?'

'Yes.'

We watched Wolfgang drive off down the lane.

'What's he doing here?'

'Louise has come to stay.'

'Can we trust him to keep his mouth shut about us?'

'Yes, I do believe we can. Apparently Germany has declared war on America. Wolfgang suggested that we'd outstayed our welcome and I think he's right. How are we doing with those propellers?'

'All fixed.'

'Then I suggest we leave tonight. But first, we'd better go and say hello to Louise and tell her that everyone's safe.'

Chapter Twenty-six
Filles à Boches

Louise stood in the middle of the farmyard, shoulders back, chin up, her suitcase in her right hand. The constant fine drizzle settled on her hair, forming a crown of jewel-like droplets. Six paces in front of her was the imposing figure of Laurent Laval clutching his shotgun.

'Louise,' I called out. 'Your father's safe. Sophie and Ross as well.'

She shot me a glance, but there was only trepidation on her face.

I scrambled over the gate and Loki followed.

'*Fille à Boches*,' Laval hissed. He gathered phlegm in his mouth and then spat at Louise, the gob landing just feet in front of her. He gestured towards her belly with the barrel of his shotgun. '*L'enfant de Boche*.' He raised his free hand and pointed back towards the entrance to the farm.

'What's going on?' Loki shouted.

'He wants me to go,' Louise replied, her voice trembling. 'He meant what he said when he visited me in Paris. I am not to set foot on this farm again. If I do, he will shoot me.'

'Don't be ridiculous,' Loki replied, stepping confidently towards them.

Laval snatched his shotgun up to his shoulder and aimed it at Louise's head. 'Get this Nazi-loving whore out of my sight.'

'You've got it all wrong,' I said, fearing he was being deadly serious. 'Louise was just trying to get information from Wolfgang. Her father asked her to. It wasn't her fault that she fell in love.'

Laval peered at me as if I'd gone mad. 'That's as maybe, but while she was being wined and dined, laughing and dancing with the enemy, her little sister was being beaten and tortured, starved and humiliated. No, Simon Stevens, it will not do. Do you hear me? *It will not do.* This one here is no member of my family. Not any more. If I had a knife handy, I'd cut that devil's child out of her belly myself, here and now, and feed it to my pigs.'

'Lou, Lou, you're safe. I thought it was you walking up to the house,' shouted Ross as he charged up the track and vaulted the gate. He ran, flung his arms around her, and then almost instantly broke away. He'd registered that Laval had a gun pointed at her. 'What's going on?'

'Your whore of a sister has disgraced her country. She's carrying that Nazi's child,' Laval hissed. 'As far as I'm concerned she no longer exists.'

'No, Uncle Laurent, you've got it all wrong. Put the gun down. Tell him he's wrong, Lou. Tell him he's wrong . . . Lou . . . *Lou*?'

'It's true, Ross,' she said calmly. 'I'm sorry.'

The look of astonishment and disgust on Ross's face

was memorable. But it was fleeting. 'Even so, you can't shoot her, Uncle,' he said. 'You simply can't.'

'Move aside, Ross . . . Louise, I want you turn round and start walking. I'm going to count to ten. If you're not on your way by then, I will shoot you. Do you hear me? I will kill both of you.'

I was certain of one thing. Laval wasn't bluffing. I could see it in his face: the utter conviction, the narrow-minded loathing. He no longer saw his niece before him. She wasn't the pretty young magician's assistant and dancer he'd watched grow up, the daughter of his brother-in-law, Alan Munro, the sister of Ross and Sophie. He saw in her the enemy. Nothing more.

'*Un . . . deux . . . trois*—'

Panicking, Ross snatched Loki's revolver, which was wedged in his belt. Shaking, he held it in both hands and pointed it at his uncle. '*Non!* I won't let you do it, Uncle. You shoot her, and I will kill you.'

'*Quatre . . . cinq . . .*'

I stood in between them. 'Louise, turn and walk. We'll take you to your father and Sophie.'

'*Six . . . sept . . . huit . .*'

'Turn and walk,' I shouted.

Louise pressed her eyes tightly shut. Her eyelids squeezed out tears that hurried down her cheeks. She shook her head. I stepped forward, grabbed her arm, spun her round and marched her away, back towards the gate.

'*Neuf . . . dix!*'

I braced myself but the blast didn't come. I unbolted

the gate and dragged Louise through. I didn't look back. She resisted me, but I clung on tightly, and virtually dragged her down the track towards the lane. Having snatched back his revolver, Loki caught us up. 'He was going to do it. He was really going to shoot her.'

'I know. We'll take Louise to the convent. I'm sure Mother Thérèse will give her sanctuary.'

As we marched Louise along the lane, she threw her head back and, amid her tears of rejection, let out a cry. 'Dad told me I was a casualty of war. How right he was.'

Chapter Twenty-seven
Au Revoir

By ten o'clock that night our Lizzie had been dragged to Laval's field by his horses. He unhitched them and led them away. He had not spoken another word since the afternoon's debacle.

Paul Laval, on the other hand, had struck up quite a friendship with Nils, and they exchanged final goodbyes and promises to meet up after the war was over. Aware of his brother's intransigence, Paul promised us he would speak to Laurent about Louise, but reckoned it unlikely he could persuade him to look kindly on his niece ever again. 'We Lavals are a stubborn lot,' he said. 'Once our mind is made up, that's usually it.'

Ross came to see us off safely. He clutched a torch in readiness to mark the far end of our makeshift runway. Alan Munro had already bid an emotional farewell to Sophie and Louise at the convent – his tight hug had almost made Sophie faint. Now he turned to his son and placed a hand lovingly on his shoulder. 'I'm proud of you, Ross. You do know that, don't you? Without your help I'm not sure I'd have succeeded. Of course, I could stand here and tell you to stay out of trouble, to keep your head down and behave yourself until this war is over, but I realize that would be pointless, wouldn't it?'

Ross nodded.

'Hmmm, thought so.' Alan Munro smiled. 'Then listen to me. You're brave, courageous and spirited. But you must learn from your mistakes. Think before you speak, and be wary of anyone you would not trust with your life. Remember everything I've taught you, and if you must resist the Germans, then pick and choose your targets carefully. Have I made myself clear?'

Ross nodded and then threw his arms around his father and hugged him. 'Come back if you can. As soon as possible. I want to fight alongside you.'

Munro prised himself from his son's tight grip. 'We'll see.' He turned to Freya, Loki and me. 'I owe you three more than I can ever repay. I shall thank God every day that it was you they sent after me and not others who might have acted with haste and without thought. You disobeyed strict orders and were willing to give me a chance. It's more than I deserve. Thanks to you, Sophie is safe and will in time get well under Mother Thérèse's watchful eye. I have also reached an arrangement with Mother Thérèse concerning Lou. She will remain under her care until the baby's born. After that, well, who knows what the future will bring? I've given a letter written by Lou to Laurent Laval and instructed him to give it to Wolfgang Müller should he come to the farm again. It says that Lou has gone away until the baby is born and that she considers it best not to leave a forwarding address. She will contact him again after the birth. I have also instructed Laurent not to do anything stupid should he receive a visit from Charles Thorpe in the next day or so. He is simply to deny all knowledge of us. As Thorpe hasn't made a beeline here, he must be ignorant of the link between this farm and us. Still, it's better to be safe than sorry. Hopefully, once we've arrived back in Britain, Charles Thorpe and all the others sent after me will receive instructions to stand down.'

Ross wiped the tears from his eyes. Freya gave him a hug.

'You know, Ross, we've come across a lot of people during our missions, but we have never encountered anyone quite as talented as you,' said Loki. 'You've more courage than the whole of Brittany – not to mention those magic skills. Tell me, just how *did* you do that card trick?'

Ross managed to laugh. 'It's a secret, isn't it, Dad? I can't tell you, Johnny. We magicians have to swear an oath never to tell. If I was to let it slip, I'd have to kill you!'

We all laughed.

'And he's not even scared of heights,' Loki added. Then he stopped laughing. 'Take care, Ross, and your friend, Luc. Heed your father's advice. Don't go doing anything stupid – especially with that tin of carborundum we gave you.'

'I've got it all planned out. Luc and I can't fail. But Dad says we should wait until the right moment. He said he'll send a message to me when he wants us to strike. Isn't that right, Dad?'

Alan Munro nodded.

Aware that time was getting on, Nils tapped his

watch. 'Time to go. Are you ready for this, Simon? I'll fly if you're not up to it.'

'Are you kidding? This is what I was born to do.'

With our final goodbyes ringing in our ears, we climbed aboard, Nils, Freya, Loki and Alan Munro somehow managing to squeeze into the back. Their curses told of their discomfort. I eased myself into the pilot's seat and strapped myself in. My heart was already thumping.

Nils piped up, 'Finn, as we agreed, Loki and I will handle the navigation. You just concentrate on flying. Now, let's run through the final checks.'

I placed my hands on the spade grip on the control column and felt for the brake control. My feet searched for the rudder bar footplates. Nils was a lot taller than me so I had to adjust them. This was done via a knob on the instrument panel just to the right of the carburettor slow-running cut-out control. I adjusted the seat too, making it a little higher. 'Right,' I said. 'Setting the throttle a half-inch open, mixture control setting to normal, airscrew pitch set to coarse, fuel cock on, carburettor intake fully in for cold start.'

'Well done, Finn,' Nils called out. 'Now you've got to prime the carburettor. As she's cold, give the pump eight strokes, and then switch on the main ignition switches and the starting magneto. And call down to Paul and tell him to get away from those propellers before they slice him in two. We don't need him to turn them. We'll fire her up from here.'

I leaned out of the cockpit and called out to Paul. He

waved back, and then retreated well out of the way. I slid the cockpit canopy shut and locked it. We were ready.

'Everyone OK?' I asked. 'I'm about to hit the starter button. Once she fires up we'll wake up the neighbourhood, so we'll have no time to hang around.'

'Take a second to think, Finn. Are you ready?'

I looked up from the instrument panel and out through the cockpit window. For a second the darkness was so complete I wondered whether there was a world out there at all. Then I saw torchlight in the distance, Ross marking the end of my makeshift grass runway. I swallowed hard and reached for the starter button. 'I'm ready. Here goes.'

I pressed the button, and the engine began turning over. I held it down for five seconds but she didn't catch.

'Stop,' Nils shouted. 'Give her ten seconds and then try again.'

Second time lucky: the engine caught and fired up, the spinning propellers settling into a blur. I switched off the starter magneto and turned on the oil heating system.

'We can't wait for her to warm up, Finn. Final drill for take-off. Remember T – M – P: tail actuating gear setting, mixture control, and pitch setting to fine.'

'Done. Releasing brake . . . Opening throttle.'

The engine note soared and the Lizzie rattled. I opened the throttle some more. She began to roll forward.

'Keep her in line, Finn – watch the position of Ross's torch and give her all she's got.'

I shoved open the throttle fully. We gathered speed. She bumped and rocked and rolled over the uneven field. I glanced down and saw that our groundspeed was rising quickly: *thirty miles per hour . . . forty . . . fifty . . . sixty-five . . . seventy . . .* I looked up and saw we'd almost reached Ross's position: *eighty . . .* I gently pulled back the column spade.

Ever so gently we left the ground. The bumping undulations were suddenly gone.

'Watch your rate of ascent and keep your airspeed well above eighty,' Nils shouted. Then he added. 'You're doing just great, Finn.'

I kept the throttle open until my airspeed exceeded a hundred and ten miles per hour, and then kept us in a steady climb. Loki called out for my compass reading, and within seconds they replied with a new heading. I gently eased the column across and began a turn. Entering cloud, things got a bit bumpy, but within five minutes we were above it, our course set for the coast.

I remained vigilant, starting a routine of alternating my eyes from inspecting the controls to surveying the night sky, back and forth, back and forth. The Lizzie was flying smoothly, although she made quite a racket. Outside, above the clouds, a starlit sky stretched out before us. My father and Wolfgang were both right. This was a very special place. This was where only a select few got to go. We had the freedom of eagles up here.

'Keep your eyes peeled,' Nils reminded me. 'Their radar may have picked us up, but we'll be out over the coast pretty soon. Fingers crossed they won't bother sending anyone up to take a look.'

And they didn't.

By the time Nils and Loki instructed me to descend and we broke out from the base of the cloud, the glistening sheen of the Channel stretched out below us, and on the horizon was a smudge of something darker than either the sea or the sky – England.

Epilogue

Alan Munro never again took to the stage as Madura the Magnificent. On his return to Britain he was disciplined and fined three months wages. 'Not a bad deal,' he later remarked, 'given I'd cost the British government over two million French francs!'

Although he remained a member of Special Operations, his days of working behind enemy lines were over. The head of Special Ops, the enigmatic X, sent him to the Forgetting School in the remote Scottish Highlands, where he languished for a considerable time, forbidden to make contact with the outside world. Eventually, however, his skills simply couldn't be overlooked. Given the task of training new recruits in deception and disguise as D-Day approached, he also played his part in devising various schemes to confuse the enemy as to the site of the Allies' intended invasion of mainland Europe.

After the war Alan Munro returned to France and purchased a small hotel just south of Rouen. There was a great deal of speculation among the locals as to where he got the money from. It was rumoured he'd paid for it in gold. He rarely spoke about his past, although guests at his hotel often stopped to admire the photograph of him as a much younger man, standing beside the great escapologist, Harry Houdini. It took pride of place on the wall behind the hotel bar. Close by was a small, expensive-looking glass display case containing a strange object – a mangy old catapult forged from a piece of wood, bicycle tyre inner tubes, and what appeared to be the leather tongue from an old shoe. Every night, before retiring, Alan would carefully dust and polish the case. He never explained its significance, even to the most persistent and inquisitive hotel guest.

Sophie Munro remained hidden at the Order of St Anne's, under the watchful eye of Mother Thérèse, until the end of the war. Recovering from her injuries, she eventually returned to Paris to study medicine, married and had three children.

Louise Munro had her baby. She named him Christian. After the war she was reunited with Wolfgang Müller, and they were married in the summer of 1946. Initially they lived in Heidelberg but eventually went to America, where they set up home in Virginia. Right up until his death in 1974 Laurent Laval maintained that he never had a niece called Louise. They never spoke to each other again after that day in December 1941.

Ross Munro continued to do his bit to hasten the end of the war. Each night he and Luc went out on 'patrol', doing their best to inconvenience the local Germans. By early 1944 Ross found himself leader of the local partisan group south of Rouen. They called themselves the Catapult Club. As D-Day approached, Resistance networks like Ross's came to the fore, disrupting railway lines, sabotaging German communication networks and factories, all to pave the way for the forthcoming invasion. At last Ross got to use his stash of carborundum powder. One night in May 1944, however, his luck finally ran out. Captured by the Gestapo, he was hastily interrogated and, revealing nothing, was ordered to be executed. Accounts vary as to what happened next. Rumours quickly began circulating that he'd been taken to a courtyard, forced to stand up against a wall and unceremoniously shot. Others said that he was thrown into a cell, but by the next morning had vanished without trace. Several eyewitnesses confirmed this story, and noted they'd spotted nuns acting suspiciously in the vicinity of the Gestapo building.

Ross did indeed escape, aided and abetted by – as he later described it himself – 'divine intervention'. After the war, for outstanding courage, both he and Luc were awarded the *Croix de Guerre* (Military Cross).

Landing safely back at Tangmere, Finn, Loki and Freya were extensively debriefed before returning to their HQ at Mulberry House. They barely had a chance to catch their breath before our young heroes were sent into action once again . . .

Postscript

Harry Houdini (1874–1926) was the stage name of Erich Weiss, possibly the most famous conjuror and escapologist ever. As well as being skilled at freeing himself from any pair of handcuffs, Houdini created many death-defying escape tricks and illusions, including the Chinese Water Torture Cell – it's a version of this that Alan Munro, alias Madura the Magnificent, recreates in this book.

During the Second World War, astonishing efforts and ingenuity were expended in attempting to conceal and protect British airfields from the Luftwaffe's bombs. Many decoy airfields were constructed, some made visible during daytime, others only at night, using special lighting effects. As well as deploying un-serviceable aircraft, numerous dummy planes were built by the UK film industry's props departments to make the deception convincing. In addition, various ploys were used to conceal Britain's real airfields from attack. These included camouflage, hiding or storing aircraft some distance away, and even laying bands of black sand on the ground which, to someone examining air re-connaissance photographs, would look like hedgerows.

Most of Britain's towns and cities gained a degree of protection against night-time bombing raids using decoys too. 'Starfish' was probably the most advanced of these. Using controlled fires (burning various materials to give differing intensities and colours of flame), the aim was to simulate a town or city suffering an incendiary attack. The result confused enemy pilots as to the location of their targets. In hundreds of instances Starfish worked, and undoubtedly spared many civilian lives. Despite such successes, however, the Luftwaffe's radio-based targeting systems called *Knickebein* and later *X-Verfahren* ensured that many raids succeeded.

The clandestine organization Finn, Loki and Freya belong to is modelled on a real wartime department known as Churchill's Secret Army, or the Special Operations Executive (SOE). Thousands of men and women of more than fifteen different nationalities were recruited and trained as secret agents during the course of the war. Many were subsequently sent behind enemy lines to assist the Resistance and, as Churchill famously ordered, *to set Europe ablaze*. Recruits were often ordinary civilians who had useful skills, such as fluency in languages or a familiarity with a Nazi-occupied country. In the fight for freedom, many acted with astonishing courage and made tremendous sacrifices – sometimes the ultimate sacrifice.

During my research into the real SOE I came across a curious story about an agent entrusted with a large sum of money in old French banknotes. Sent into occupied France, he promptly disappeared (apparently he was last seen heading for the French Riviera). To disobey orders and go AWOL was a serious matter, and in working out the plot for *Dead or Alive* I supposed it might represent the act of a desperate man. And what more desperate than a race against time to save a member of your family from a firing squad!

Although it is a work of fiction, much of *Dead or Alive* is drawn from accounts of real clandestine operations. As in this story, agents were frequently dropped and picked up using Lysanders (*Lizzies*) of the Special Duties Squadron (*Moon Squadron*): the small aircraft was perfect for the task owing to her STOL (Short Take-Off and Landing) capabilities. Resistance fighters were often notified of agents' arrival by *messages personnels* broadcast on the BBC's Overseas French wireless programme after the evening news bulletin.

Agents were trained in ciphers and coding, and Morse transmission, and often had to carry their heavy suitcase wireless sets into enemy-occupied territory, knowing that should they be stopped and questioned by the authorities, their cover would be blown. They'd be arrested, interrogated, and most probably shot as enemy spies. Many were, their average life expectancy being measured in weeks.

Most of the action in *Dead or Alive* takes place in Paris. Finn and his friends reach the city using a vehicle converted to run on gazogène (coal or wood gas). Such vehicles were commonplace during the occupation, owing to Nazi restrictions on car ownership and extreme petrol shortages. Several variants existed, but all worked on the same principle of partial combustion of alternative fuel sources to generate the gases.

Surprisingly, engines were easily converted to run on gazogène, although the result was often mediocre power and excessive pollution.

After France fell to the Nazis in 1940 and the northern 'zone' was occupied, life for your average Parisian grew more and more difficult as restrictions to their freedoms and food rationing took their toll. The winters of 1940 and 1941 were also especially cold, which, with the fuel shortages and frequent power cuts, led to a great deal of suffering. While the black market thrived and the unscrupulous grew rich, most had to make do with what little they had. And they had very little.

Many of the locations in *Dead or Alive* are real – and not just the obvious landmarks such as the Eiffel Tower, the Arc de Triomphe and the Sacré-Coeur. For example, Fresnes prison, located to the south of the city centre, was taken over by the infamous SS, and many captured Resistance fighters and SOE agents spent time in its cells. The descriptions of the environs and conditions Sophie Munro endured are based on the accounts of real prisoners, including famous SOE agents such as Odette Hallowes (*George Cross*, and *Légion d'Honneur*), and members of the French Resistance like Agnès Humbert (*Croix de Guerre*). In truth, the situations and horrors they endured for real can only be hinted at in *Dead or Alive*.

Likewise, the Avenue Foch near the Arc de Triomphe was a focus for the offices of various parts of the Nazi intelligence services, number eighty-four being

SPECIAL OPERATIONS: DEAD OR ALIVE

occupied by the Nazi secret police, the SD or *Sicherheitsdienst*. It was in this building that many captured SOE agents, including Odette and another famous female agent, Noor Inayat Khan (GC, *Croix de Guerre*), underwent questioning. Neither of them broke under interrogation and torture.

Key parts of the story of *Dead or Alive* revolve around the American Hospital, located on the fashionable Boulevard Victor Hugo. The true story of the real doctors and nurses who ran this hospital during the war is remarkable. Dr Sumner Jackson and his wife Charlotte (pet name: Touquette) are worthy of special mention. Together with other members of staff, they managed to assist many wounded French and British soldiers and airmen, treating and hiding them. They helped many to escape to safety. Working for the Resistance, Dr Jackson also owned an apartment on the Avenue Foch (see above) which, despite its inherent dangers, was used as a mail drop for the Resistance network. His valiant efforts were to cost Dr Jackson his life.

Laurent Laval's angry reaction to learning of Louise's pregnancy was not uncommon. Inevitably there were many women who 'fraternized' with the occupying forces for all sorts of reasons – sometimes out of circumstance or necessity, sometimes simply because they wanted a 'good time'; a few in an attempt to extract useful information, or because they simply fell in love. Estimates vary as to the number of children born as a result of such liaisons. For France as whole, they range

340

from 50,000 to more recent data suggesting it was closer to 200,000. Sadly, these so-called *enfants de Boches* sometimes grew up being outcasts in their own society, disowned by grandparents and other relations, mocked and picked on by their classmates – occasionally even by their teachers. Others only discovered much later in life who their real fathers were.

The situation for their mothers was often equally bleak – and sometimes dangerous too, even for those like Louise who had, in secret, been working for the Resistance. As early as 1943, and even more frequently after France's liberation, many collaborators and women who fraternized with the enemy were subjected to brutal and humiliating acts at the hands of a population hungry for revenge. One of the most notorious of these was the so-called *tontes*, where women had their heads shaved before being paraded through the streets. Some were forced to leave their towns and villages; others were simply shunned and despised. In *Dead or Alive* Louise Munro's situation began as a straightforward willing act of Resistance to assist her father, which spiralled into something far more complicated as she came to love the man she was targeting for information. Undoubtedly such situations arose. Her predicament suggests that not everything in life can be seen as black and white, or right or wrong, especially during wartime.

MOST SECRET

NAME: Finn Gunnersen

AGE: 17

BACKGROUND: Born Trondheim,
Norway. Father RAF Spitfire pilot
(killed in action). Mother and
sister arrested by Gestapo.
Escaped from occupied Norway by
stealing Heinkel 115 float plane.

(File note dated June 1941
Addendum: father officially reclassified as 'missing,
presumed dead', based on advice received from
Air Ministry.
Signed — Brigadier Devlin, Commanding Officer,
Mulberry House — cross reference to file AirPMIA4)

ASSESSMENT: Basic training and assessment carried
out at Mulberry House under Brigadier Devlin. Key
observations: outwardly unremarkable. Taught to fly
by father and keen to obtain his official 'wings'.
Physically fit though not strong. Quick to learn
and resourceful. Responds well under pressure though
tendency to be rather reckless. Inseparable from Mr
Larson and Miss Haukelid. A decent, honest lad.
Brave but vulnerable. Far more courageous than he
realizes. Keen to follow in father's footsteps.
Survived Nazi interrogation in Holland.

COMPLETED MISSIONS:
Seen active service in France
and Holland.

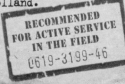

RECOMMENDED
FOR ACTIVE SERVICE
IN THE FIELD
0619-3199-46

Special Operations Personnel Files

MOST SECRET

NAME: Loki Larson

AGE: 17

BACKGROUND: Born Trondheim, Norway. Father commercial pilot and member of local Norwegian Resistance. Escaped from occupied Norway along with Mr Gunnersen.

ASSESSMENT: Basic training and assessment carried out at Mulberry House under Brigadier Devlin. Key observations: a large lad and as strong as an elk. Taught to fly by father. Good with his fists. Might be prone to shoot first and ask questions later. A loyal and courageous chap who can be relied on in a crisis. Lifelong friend of Mr Gunnersen and close to Miss Haukelid. All function well as a team.

COMPLETED MISSIONS:

Seen active service in France and Holland.

Special Operations Personnel Files

MOST SECRET

NAME: Freya Haukelid

AGE: 17

BACKGROUND: Born in remote part of Norway. Father arrested for actively resisting Nazi occupation (wounded at time of arrest). Mother deceased.

(File note dated January 1941
Addendum: Father officially reclassified as 'deceased', based on intelligence received from agents located in Norway. Did not survive wounds received during arrest.
Signed – Brigadier Devlin, Commanding Officer, Mulberry House)

ASSESSMENT: Basic training and assessment carried out at Mulberry House under Brigadier Devlin. Key observations: an intelligent girl with tremendous talents. Taught by her father, Freya is an outstanding marksman (rifle) – the best we've come across. Gifted at coding and Morse code, and learns languages quickly. Physically far tougher than her appearance suggests. Despite reservations about sending girls into the field, Freya has proved herself on missions. Survived interrogation by Gestapo during capture (rescued by Messrs Gunnersen and Larson).

COMPLETED MISSIONS:
Seen active service in France and Holland.

MOST SECRET

NAME: Claude Chevalier

AGE: 43

BACKGROUND: Nationality: French. Escaped France during Dunkirk evacuation. Identity papers mislaid. Claims to have worked at a number of menial jobs in Paris and knows the city streets extremely well. Speaks fluent English. Not married (no dependents). Has number of potentially useful hobbies, including conjuring.

CAUTION: Identity not proven. Routine checks via SIS (Security Intelligence Services) did not yield any alerts.

ASSESSMENT: Basic training carried out at Handelbury Manor (F-Section). Key observations: average skills in combat and survival training. Excellent performance in evasion and deception. Brilliant at disguise. Wireless and coding skills average.

COMPLETED MISSIONS: Performed reliably as courier to Rouen and Nantes Resistance circuits. March 1941 transferred to newly formed section in Sir Hugo Foster's Ministry for 'Special Projects'. November 1941 returned to active service with Special Operations to serve as courier to the Trébuchet circuit in Paris).

ALERT: November 1941 – Missing in the field.